# Belong to the Night

# Belong to the Night

SHELLY LAURENSTON
CYNTHIA EDEN
SHERRILL QUINN

**BRAVA**

KENSINGTON PUBLISHING CORP.

www.kensingtonbooks.com

BRAVA BOOKS are published by

Kensington Publishing Corp.
119 West 40th Street
New York, NY 10018

All Kensington titles, imprints, and distributed lines are available at
special quantity discounts for bulk purchases for sales promotion,
premiums, fund-raising, and educational or institutional use.

Special book excerpts or customized printings can also be created to
fit specific needs. For details, write or phone the office of the Kensington Special Sales Manager: Kensington Publishing Corp., 119 West
40th Street, New York, NY 10018; Attn. Special Sales Department.
Phone: 1-800-221-2647.

Brava and the B logo are Reg. U.S. Pat. & TM Off.

ISBN-13: 978-0-7582-3886-3
ISBN-10: 0-7582-3886-X

First Kensington Trade Paperback Printing: September 2009

10 9 8 7 6 5 4 3 2

Printed in the United States of America

# CONTENTS

# The Wolf, the Witch, and Her Lack of Wardrobe

SHELLY LAURENSTON

# Prologue

From the day the first one stumbled into the middle of town, beaten, tortured, and branded, witches had been a part of Smithville County. The first one had escaped her captors, religious fanatics determined to find out the names of the females in her coven. The elders of that town sent their strongest men to find her, tracking her right into Smithville. They found her, too . . . and the seven hundred pound tiger cautiously sniffing her. They'd started to back away, praying the beast wouldn't notice them. He didn't, since he was too focused on the pretty little thing passed out in the middle of the street. But the pride of lions noticed the men. So did the clan of hyenas. And then there were the wolves . . .

None of them liking strangers in their territory. Liking full-humans even less.

Although that witch was the first, she would not be the last that came to Smithville. When each coven grew too old or too weak to continue protecting the town from the evil outside its borders, another stepped in to take the old coven's place. Most came willingly, the powers they worshipped giving them the map to a place where they could feel free and protected. They'd show up one day, confused and lost, wondering how they got there and sensing that they'd never want to leave. They never did either. Most never bothered to try.

Each coven was unique, their particular strengths needed at that particular point in time. But they were also very similar.

Good, simple women who wanted a safe place to worship their gods and raise their children. They'd chant happily in the early evenings and dance naked under the full moon.

It was all simple, beautiful, and very "We are one world, love everyone, save Mother Earth." And for nearly four hundred years, none of that had changed.

Until now. Until the day the Coven of the Darkest Night came into town and changed absolutely everything.

# Chapter One

If there was one thing Tully Smith, Alpha Male of the Smithville County Smith Pack and mayor of Smithville Township, could say about Jamie Meacham, it was that he loved the way she made an entrance.

To think he used to find these elder meetings pretty dang boring. Mostly because there was a lot of talk, a lot of complaining, and lots of less-than-subtle threatening, but there was never any action. And then, ten months ago, a new coven had taken over from the old. The Coven of the Darkest Night was what they called themselves. All of them from up north or, as his stepbrother Kyle Treharne called it, "Yankee territory."

Jamie—dressed in her well-worn jeans, ten-year-old T-shirt, and five-year-old running shoes—came into the room the same way every time, slamming the double doors for the junior high's music room open and striding in. She seemed to stride everywhere. She was tall for a full-human. About five-eleven or so. But perfectly built with a strong body, a tight and exquisitely proportioned ass, and breasts that were definitely more than a handful, even for him. Even with all that to keep him entertained, he couldn't look away from those eyes. If he didn't know for a fact she was full-human, he'd swear she was one of them. It wouldn't matter what breed either. It was her eyes. She had the eyes of a predator and, he'd bet, the soul of one, too.

"Afternoon, everyone," she said cheerily, her grin wide. "How is everyone this beautiful day?"

Tully had to duck his head, rubbing his nose to stop the laughter. He could hear his stepdaddy, Jack Treharne, growling across from him, annoyed by Jamie's obnoxiously perky cheeriness.

Behind Jamie came the rest of her coven. As a functioning unit, they weren't half bad, although there seemed to be more infighting among five full-human females than there was among the nearly fifty-five members of the local Martoni Hyena Clan. But each coven member was so different, it amazed him the women had joined forces at all.

There was sweet Emma, whom Kyle had snagged as his own before the rest of them had even gotten a good look at her. Of course, she was such a cute and sweet little thing, Tully couldn't blame his brother. He definitely would have tried if it had been anyone but Kyle who'd been sniffing around her. Then there was the "always friendly, dang-near loved everybody, couldn't get enough of people, wanted everyone to be happy and show it!" Seneca. She'd somehow found her way among the bears, which only proved she was a sweetheart down to her toes because those easily startled, oversized bastards didn't like anybody but themselves and fresh salmon. The one he had the least interest in was Kendall, also known as Kenny. She was a real Yankee. Not remotely friendly, suspicious, paranoid, and almost defiantly plain. They rarely saw her during the day, and when she did come out after the sun had gone down she would usually head over to the edge of town where some wild dogs had opened up a comic book and gaming store.

The one Tully found much more interesting was the extremely statuesque Mackenzie. Mac was about his height, a cool six-three, and a former firefighter. It had taken her time to warm up to the locals but she'd found her way merely by not being her cousin. By not being Jamie Meacham.

As head of the Coven of the Darkest Night, Jamie was nothing but gorgeous trouble rolled in brown sugar and dusted in arsenic.

Yeah. Jamie was the one he found the most entertaining. Why? Because if he didn't know better, he'd swear that woman didn't give a damn about anybody. She strutted through life tempting fates and whatever powers she or anyone else worshipped. She brought out the worst in the predators around her, insisted on calling his baby sister "Snaggle" because of the state of Katie's fangs while in shifted form, and kept a sidearm on her at all times—last he checked it was a .380 auto—but was known to travel with a rifle at night. Both of which were illegal within Smithville County lines. Remind her of that, though, and she'd only laugh.

Bear McMahon, grizzly and sheriff of Smithville, had put it best one day when he said, "It's when that woman is quiet that I get worried."

Tully watched as she strode up to the big table they used for their meetings, walked around it to the small stage behind them, turned and lifted herself onto it. Once she settled in, she crossed her long legs and studied everyone. She smiled. And everyone but him leaned back from that smile.

She glanced over at Jack who'd ordered this meeting. He was second in charge next to Bear's momma, Gwen, and Jack's own momma had once been rumored to complain, "he came out of me snarling at the doctor who'd slapped him." And it was that snarling feline that Jamie turned away from when Jack opened his mouth to speak, focused those beautiful dark eyes Tully's way, and said, smooth as silk, "Tully Smith. You called?"

*Why do you insist on doing the things you do?*

It was the question her mother used to ask her constantly when they still spoke. But Jamie Meacham, former Nassau County Detective and High Priestess of the Coven of the Darkest Night, never had an answer to that question. All she knew was that she never colored within the lines, she didn't like boundaries, and she hated rules and regulations except the most basic kind. Anything or anyone that purposely set out to hurt others was wrong. Rapists, murderers, thieves, she'd hunt them all down and see them convicted without a moment's worry. That's what made being a cop so easy for her.

But when it came to more metaphysical matters, when it came to power and the obtaining of it . . . well, Jamie was a little more flexible on that score. And it seemed everyone in town had figured that out.

She knew she made them nervous. She knew they didn't like her. She knew that if a few of them had the chance to hunt her down and rip out her entrails, they'd do it in a heartbeat. For many people, this sort of realization of the danger they were in would worry them, but Jamie knew there were worse things in the universe than predators willing to feed on her. She'd been to hell and thrown back out again because, according to Satan himself, "You just don't know how to act, do you?" She'd faced off against some of the purest evil and once had a screaming match with Archangel Gabriel in the middle of a Billy Joel concert at Jones Beach until the winged whiny pot fled in tears.

So facing some hyenas, lions, and tigers who wanted her dead? Not a big deal to her.

Yet out of all of the residents of Smithville, all the predators, the townies, the whatevers, the one who never seemed to be bothered by her was the Mayor of Smithville, Tully Smith. When she'd first met him, she thought he was awfully young to be mayor of anything but a fraternity, especially with that stupid one gold earring he wore like he was still trapped in 1985. In fact, she'd figured the role of mayor was nothing more than a figure head for locals with ready cash. Because really, what could be involved in running some little nowhere town that most Americans didn't even know existed? It's not like the Mayor of Smithville could eventually move into higher political arenas. The last thing any of the locals wanted around here were cameras shooting hometown footage for a CNN special on a governor or senator candidate. These people took their privacy very seriously and she had no doubts they'd made it clear to anyone who took the mayor position that the government fast track stopped right there. So what could some extremely attractive, kind of charming, thirty-something wolf shifter want with being the mayor? Then, after a few months of watching Tully Smith amble his slow-moving—but extremely fine—ass around town, it suddenly hit her . . . he was *happy* with what he had.

Which, to be honest, Jamie found kind of fascinating. How could anyone be okay with what they had? How did he not want more from his life? Not even close to thirty-five and he was happy with living in a small town, wandering around all day on two legs and all night on four? She didn't get it, but then again, she didn't have to. His life was his own and Jamie didn't involve herself with other people's lives. She had enough trouble managing the one she had. And although she didn't really understand Tully Smith, she did find him entertaining.

Like now. Instead of bouncing this meeting over to his stepfather, Jack, Tully relaxed in his chair, one arm thrown over the back of it, smiled up at her and said, "Aww, beautiful. I call for you every night but you never show up."

"And I thought you were just serenading me."

They smiled at each other, Tully about to say something else, when Jack Treharne's hand slammed down against the table. Everyone else jumped, except Tully, who was most likely used to the drama after being raised by the man, and Jamie who had a very low startle response. She stayed still a moment, allowing the tension to ratchet up a bit before she moved only her gaze over to Treharne.

"Something wrong . . . Jack?"

His eye twitched, annoyed that Jamie insisted on calling him by his first name rather than "Mr. Treharne."

"Y'all are late . . . again."

"True. But we are running a hotel. Had a whole Pride to check out before we could head this way. But that's not why you demanded to see us."

"You were seen out in the woods again. At night."

"I didn't realize there was a curfew."

"There ain't. But you weren't out there wandering around. You were doing some ritual."

"I'm a witch. That's what I do."

"Without your coven?"

Jamie could feel her cousin's eyes on her, and knew she'd hear about this later from Mac. When Jamie had agreed to give up the life she had in New York and bring her coven down to Smithville, she hadn't really thought about the dynamics of small town life compared to suburban life. Since she'd had her first athame, a lovely ritual knife given to her by her first mentor, Jamie had been doing her own rituals and spells. And since she did these in the privacy of her basement or her backyard, and she'd never been friendly with her Long Island neighbors, her coven had never been the wiser. Something she'd appreciated since the work she did with her coven brought her much satisfaction, but there was something about the power she obtained on her own that drove her to find more and more of it.

In the end, though, it was no one's business what she did on her own. Unfortunately, those in Smithville didn't seem to feel the same way, no matter what she was doing. Every time she turned around they were in her business.

These people knew when she got packages from her father, when her allergies were acting up, when she and Mac were arguing. And not only did they know, but they butted in. Having locals walk up to her and hand her their favorite allergy medication was, to say the least, off-putting. To have them chuckle about "you and that cousin of yours" as if they knew her and Mac so damn well was pissing her off. And to find out that every time she went into the woods to handle a little personal business with the gods, they pointed it out to the Elders made her feel like she was living in a town not filled with predators but rats. Big, constantly-in-her-business, never-knew-when-to-shut-it rats!

"I was told when I came here that we'd be left alone to worship in the way we chose."

"It ain't what you worship that's the problem. It's you."

"You should have thought of that before you signed us up."

"And you should have some consideration for those who were born and raised in this town. You already poisoned one of our lakes."

"That was an accident and I cleaned it."

"I mean, how are we supposed to deal with pure evil in one of our lakes? Aren't you supposed to be keeping evil out?"

"I said I cleaned it. And you need to let it go."

"What about when you set the woods on fire?"

*Were they back here again?* "I put it out."

"What about the trees that were destroyed?"

"They'll grow back."

Treharne shook his head. "Do you care about anything but yourself?"

Done with this conversation, Jamie pushed off the stage and walked around the table. "You've all made it perfectly clear you don't like me and don't want me as part of your community. But even knowing this, my coven has been working its butt off to protect this town. If that's still not enough for you, then buy us out of the hotel and send us on our way. But don't think for a minute you can tell me how to live my life as a witch."

Jamie headed toward the doors, her coven in step behind her, when Treharne said, "You know, missy, it's real hard to be part of something that you think you're better than."

"I never said I was better than you," Jamie shot back as she opened the doors and walked out into the hallway. "But, then again, you haven't exactly proven that I'm not either."

Tully watched that sexy witch slam the doors open by doing nothing more than raising her forefinger. After she stormed out, her coven right behind her, Tully sighed and said, "I sure do like her."

That's when his stepdaddy threw his notebook at him, hitting him in the face. "You are the biggest idiot!"

Laughing, Tully placed the book back on the table. "What did *I* do?"

"It's what you're *not* doing, boy! You ain't taking care of what you should be."

"I'm mayor, not an Elder. And last I heard coven issues fall under Elder management."

"Well, ain't you smart."

"I ain't dumb."

"Then you'll watch her."

Tully blinked at his daddy before they both turned to Miss Gwen, who'd been the town's sheriff for more than twenty-five years before she became an Elder. "Pardon?" he asked, positive he must have heard her wrong.

"Don't 'pardon' me, Tully Ray Smith," the sow said calmly. "You wander around this town like you've got nothing but time on your hands."

"I'll have you know I'm working. You know I don't believe in sitting behind a dang desk all day signing papers. In order to find out what this town needs, I get out there and look."

"Exactly my point. So you're going to go *look* and find out what she's up to. And then you're going to put a stop to it."

"Me? What makes you think she'll listen to me anymore than she'll listen to y'all?"

"Because we all know you'll find a way to shut her down. That's what you're good at. And that's what you're going to do." Miss Gwen banged her gavel on the table. "Meeting adjourned."

No one said a word until they were on the quiet street of Cardinal Lane. That's when Mac grabbed Jamie's T-shirt and pulled her back.

"You're making them nervous."

"I make everybody nervous."

Mac released her T-shirt. "You don't have to look so proud about that."

Jamie stared up at her much taller cousin. Except for them both being black in a predominantly white town, there were very few indicators that Jamie and Mac were first cousins on their mothers' side.

"Not proud, sweetie. Just accepting. Nothing I do is going to make these people feel better about me."

"You could stop traipsing off to the woods in the middle of the night."

"I've got work to do."

"What work?"

Might as well tell them now. "I've been called to be a champion."

"For who?"

When Jamie only stared at her, Mac threw up her hands and paced away while the others simply looked worried.

"What is it with you and the Celtic gods anyway?" Kenny asked. "It's not like they're abundantly friendly."

"She called. I answered."

"She's always liked you," Sen said sweetly.

"Gods know why," Mac muttered.

"Mac, you know what's required for becoming a champion. So I'm not sure why the attitude about this."

"Because you're making them nervous."

"So what?"

Emma frowned, her arms crossed over her chest. "Don't you care about them at all?"

"I don't *not* care." They all stared and she added, "That's actually pretty good for me."

Mac stepped up to her. "One day you're going to go too far."

"I always go too far," Jamie said simply before turning and walking away. "You'd think you'd be used to it by now."

Tully sat on the boulder on top of Barrett Hill. He was still in human form since he'd headed this way straight from his last meeting. It amazed him how one simple, yearly event caused so much trouble. The Mayor's Spring Dance. The entire town was invited and usually came. Every year it was held in the Crystal Palace where most big parties for the wealthier residents took place. Tully would probably enjoy it more if he weren't in charge of it, but he was. Which meant lots of meetings with the Elders, the Mayor's Office Association, and the vendors. Bor-*ing*.

Normally, after a particularly long meeting—and Lord love him, but that last meeting was *long*—he'd head home. But this time, he found himself ambling over to this hill, which had a wonderful view of Jamie Meacham's cabin. She'd taken one of the cabins on the resort property. He didn't blame her, they were all nice, but she was also losing money by not renting it out. Then again, from what he'd learned over the last few months about Jamie was that money was not that big a concern to her. Not like it was to most people. No. She wanted something else. She wanted power. It worried him. Power corrupted the best people sometimes and Jamie was already starting from a faulty base. How much would really be needed to send her deep into the ravine?

He saw her pull up to the garage by the cabin and get out of her SUV. Carrying a small bag from Chandler's Grocery, she headed toward the building. But she stopped before she got to the first porch step, and spun around. Her eyes scanned the property and Tully wondered if she knew he was watching her. Yet she never looked in his direction.

She tossed her small backpack and grocery bag on her porch and lifted her hands, palms up. She raised them above her head, her eyes closing, her lips moving. He knew she chanted but he couldn't make out the words. As she stood there, with her hands raised, energy from the ground crawled up her legs, her torso, her chest. It swirled around her like a snake, finally sliding into her cupped hands. She closed her hands into tight fists, raised them higher and screamed something he didn't understand. The wind whipped up and she flung her arms down. Lightning shot from her palms and raced around the entire area of her house in one big circle, dissipating when it reached her again.

Tully didn't know what she'd done exactly or why, but he knew it had drained her. She rested against the porch rail for a long moment, her breath rapid. Then she slowly made her way up the stairs, picking up her bag and backpack. She opened her front door and before closing it, he heard her say, "Hey, baby. I'm home."

He didn't know why his eyes narrowed or why he wanted to go down there and demand to know who the hell was living in her house with her, but he wouldn't worry about why. He was more worried about what she was up to. If there was one thing he took seriously, it was protecting his town and his people. That's all he ever cared about.

Deciding to come back later after some hunting, Tully slipped off the boulder and headed on home. He was halfway there when his cell phone rang.

"Yep?"

"Boy."

He smiled. "Hey, Uncle Bub." Bubba Ray Smith of the Smithtown Pack in Tennessee. He loved his uncle—although they were actually cousins—and always would. "What's going on?"

When his uncle didn't answer him right away, Tully stopped walking. "What is it?"

"I got a call from your Uncle Darryl . . . Buck's heading to Smithville."

Tully's jaw tightened and his fangs eased out of his gums.

"All right," he said carefully. "I'll take care of it."

"You need me, you call. But don't do anything until you know you have to."

"You mean until you can argue I had a right to the rest of the family."

"Say what you want, Tully Ray, but this is how things are done. And the bottom line, Buck Smith is blood . . . and your daddy."

"No, Uncle Bub. The last thing that man is, is my daddy."

He disconnected the call and waited a moment before he speed dialed another number. When he heard the grumbling voice say, "It's Bear," Tully closed his eyes and answered, "Buck Smith's heading this way. Make sure everybody's ready."

# Chapter Two

Up half the night worrying about his father, Tully finally decided to deal with the one thing he could actually manage at the moment . . . Jamie.

Okay. Maybe he couldn't manage her, but she was definitely capable of keeping him distracted from what Buck Smith may be up to, and why he was coming back to the one town he'd been told never to return to. Although Tully didn't know any man alive who didn't have issues with his father, he knew his went deeper than most. After all these years the man still brought out Tully's rage and fear. Rage because the bastard plucked his last nerve and fear because Tully worried he'd one day have to kill his own blood. It was the last thing he ever wanted to do, but there was something in Buck that never stopped. He pushed and he pushed. And unless something had changed about his father, Tully doubted any of that would be different.

But he'd done what he could. Bear and his deputies were notified. Tully had given his daddy a heads-up so he could find the best way to tell Tully's momma, and the entire town was ready in case any attacks came. Other than sit around and uselessly worry, there was nothing more he could do.

Knowing that, he decided to track down Jamie. He found her, too. Having breakfast at the Smithville Diner. Considering the resort had a full breakfast menu, she'd be able to get her morning meal there for free. But he'd bet money she'd had another fight with her cousin. Rumor was the coven had stopped her over on Cardinal to talk after the Elder meeting. No one was sure what was said, but Jamie had left on her own.

If her own coven couldn't get through to her, then Tully had no idea what the rest of them thought he could do. She was definitely a woman who didn't let anyone get too close to her. Of course, the entire coven had been like that when they'd first arrived. Even Emma. But eventually, they'd begun finding their way, their own friends. Not Jamie, though. It was strange, too, because she was so friendly. She smiled, she chatted, but the walls were definitely there. She didn't want anyone getting too close to her and they all knew it.

So, doing something he'd never done before in the ten months she'd been here, Tully sat down at the table with Jamie. She glanced up from the book she was reading, blinked at him, and went back to reading. He had to fight hard not to smile. What could he say? He admired her restraint to not even *try* and figure out why he was sitting down with her.

"Mornin', Miss Jamie."

"Hey."

"How are you doing?"

Her eyes lifted from the book and focused on him. After a moment, she pushed the book away and relaxed back in her chair. "I'm doing fine. Would you like to join me for breakfast?"

"Why, that is mighty kind of you. I think I'll do just that." He motioned to the waitress and she came over. "Your morning special, darlin'. Easy on the grits, though."

"Coffee?"

"Please. And juice."

She smiled. "You've got it, Tully."

The waitress walked off and Tully focused back on Jamie. She was still watching him, smirking.

Resting his arms on the table, he asked, "So what are you reading? Fiction or nonfiction?"

"Non. History."

"About?"

Her smirk turned into a grin. "The Donner Party."

"Those are the people who . . ."

"Ate each other. Yeah."

"That's what you read while you're about to have breakfast?"

She shrugged. "I used to look at crime scene photos over a pastrami on rye at the diners back home. Doesn't bother me."

"All right then."

The waitress returned and placed a mug next to Tully and poured him a cup of coffee before leaving the carafe.

"What else do you do when you're not working?" he asked politely.

"Watch TV."

Tully sipped his coffee after blowing on it. "I don't even have a TV. Don't see the purpose." He placed his coffee down and for the first time since he'd met her, he saw a look of confusion and horror on her face.

"What's wrong?"

"You don't have a TV? How do you live without a TV?"

*How do I live?* "Easily. It's never been a necessity to me."

Jamie shook her head, her face conveying her disgust at his sentiment without her saying a word.

Tully laughed. "Of all the things that go on in this town, *that's* the one that bothers you?"

"Yeah. Yeah, it does. That's *crazy* talk."

The waitress placed a plate of food down in front of Jamie. She immediately reached for the hot sauce and completely saturated her fried eggs with it.

"You know, I can't help but notice you could be having this same breakfast at your hotel."

"Yeah, but then I'd end up fighting with Mac rather than eating, and I really want to eat."

"She's fittin' in nice," Tully remarked as the waitress placed his food down in front of him. The special came on a platter and could easily feed two or three full-humans. But he wasn't full-human and the elk he'd taken down last night had already worn off. "I see she's coaching the girls' softball league this season."

"Yep."

"While Seneca has become assistant coach for the junior and varsity cheerleading squads and Emma's teaching that tax and accounting class over at the senior center."

Jamie lifted her head, a piece of toast gripped in her hand. "Uh-huh."

"And even Kenny has volunteered her time over at the library to help upgrade the computer systems and help the kids learn basic computing."

"Your point?"

"I guess I was just noticing that you haven't really involved yourself with the town."

"Really?"

"Not that you have to, of course. Just sayin' that sometimes it does a body good to know you're helping others. And the more you help others, the more comfortable you'll feel here."

She raised her forefinger. "Hold that thought." Then she leaned back in her chair, her arm reaching toward the table of males behind her. As soon as she moved toward them, they jerked back from her. They were cheetahs, used to bolting from bored lions and startled bears, so they moved really fast. Especially now.

Jamie pointed her finger. "Mind if I borrow the ketchup?"

The older male, watching her close the entire time, grabbed the ketchup from the table and carefully handed it over to her. Once she had her hand around the bottle's neck, he snatched his hand back. They all waited until she'd turned back around before they settled back into their seats and went back to their conversation as if nothing had happened.

"So what were you saying about me feeling more comfortable around here?" she asked as she poured ketchup onto her hash browns.

Tully shook his head and went back to his meal. "Nothin'."

Jamie walked down Main Street, her book tucked under her arm, which was actually the latest Stephen King novel but she'd held the faint hope her lie would make Smith go away—he didn't.

*What, exactly, is that dog up to?*

For a good forty minutes, she'd watched him devour two platters of the diner's special and go on and on about . . . she didn't even know. People in the town. The town's history. She had no idea why he was telling her all that nor did she care. She enjoyed not knowing these people's business, shame they couldn't seem to be the same way. But she did hope to lead by example.

Was he trying to get her to feel something specific? What did he think that would change? Would she make them less nervous if she were like Mac, helping their brats with their curveballs and chatting with the moms after practice? The thought made Jamie shiver in disgust. She loathed children. She'd loathed them when she was a child, and that feeling hadn't changed in thirty-two years.

She was nearing her SUV when she walked right into someone. She immediately grabbed the person before they could hit the ground, but they lost control of their bags of groceries, apples rolling across the pavement.

"I'm sorry," Jamie immediately apologized. "I wasn't paying attention."

"It's just a little thing, sweetheart. Don't worry."

Jamie made sure the woman she had in her hands was not going to fall before she released her. "Are you sure you're all right?"

Millie MacClancy smiled at her. "I'm fine, dear. Just fine. You're such a little thing, I barely felt it."

Okay. *That* was something she loved about this weird little town. Around here, Seneca and Emma were practically hobbits, Kenny was called "the short one," Jamie was considered "petite," and Mac was just average. It was definitely the best feeling, especially for the cousins who'd been called "big boned" enough times by their country cousins to have them only allowed to attend family reunions if they followed certain rules. The biggest one being, "No hitting."

Millie started to crouch down to retrieve her bags and Jamie caught her arms again. "Don't you dare. I'll never hear the end of it from your son."

Just the mention of Tully had the older woman smiling. "That boy. What's he been up to now?"

"I wish I knew." Jamie gave a little laugh before crouching and picking up all the fruits and vegetables that had flown out of the bags.

"So how are things going with you, sweetheart?" Miss Millie asked.

"Fine." Jamie dropped the last of the apples and potatoes into the brown paper bag.

"Is the hotel doing well?"

"Yes. We've been really busy." Jamie stood, the bags in her arms. "We've had to hire some new staff."

"Good. I'm glad to hear that."

Millie reached for the bags but Jamie held on to them. "No. I'll take them to your car." Jamie frowned. "Miss Millie? Are you all right?" The older woman had some strain on her face that Jamie had never seen before. "Do you need a ride?"

"No, no. Just some things on my mind. Nothing to worry about. The shopping helped." She motioned down the street. "My car's right there.

"Are you sure there's nothing I can help you with?"

"No, sweetheart. But thank you for asking."

Together they headed down the street. "I don't understand, Miss Millie. Here you have this nice car and yet your son . . ."

Millie laughed. "What can I say? He likes to walk. Feels he finds out more about what's going on in the town when he's on two feet or four rather than when he's driving."

Jamie didn't know how much the man could learn from slowly ambling around the town but she wouldn't argue with Millie. There was something about the older woman that wasn't like the others. Something really sweet and just . . . innocent. Even though in her late fifties, Jamie could well imagine what had caught eternally cranky Jack's eye, but Jamie still couldn't believe that Tully Smith was her son. Slow-moving, not-always-the-brightest, studies-every-female-as-if-he-has-or-will-fuck-her Tully.

Talk about falling far from the tree. Then again, more than once she'd heard a family friend of her parents remark about Jamie, "She may look like you, Mary. But other than that . . ."

Jamie waited for Millie to unlock her trunk and then she placed the grocery bags inside. She slammed the trunk closed and, as she always did, shook her head at the car Tully's mother drove.

"Something wrong?"

"Not at all." Jamie sighed longingly. "I know people who'd kill for this car, though."

Millie's pretty brown eyes grew wide. "Really?" She leaned in and whispered, "I guess as a police officer you would know people like that."

"Former police officer, but yes." She gazed at the vehicle. "You just don't see a lot of '66 Camaros in this condition."

"Really?" Millie asked again, barely glancing at the car. "I try and take good care of it. To quote my daddy, 'You gotta be ready 'cause you never know when the Revenuers are gonna come.'"

Jamie nodded slowly. "I see . . . and the Revenuers are a big problem for you, Miss Millie?"

"Not anymore." She winked and walked around to her driver's side. She'd only just unlocked the door when Katie walked up to them, her gaze bouncing back and forth between Millie and Jamie underneath her annoyingly too-large Sheriff's Department cap. Jamie would think they could afford a cap that fit the poor girl's head. Gods knew, it wasn't like she had a small head.

"Everything all right, Momma?" Katie asked, eyes narrowing on Jamie in obvious accusation. Boy, you give a girl a little nickname and she was a total schmuck about it forever after.

"Of course," Millie said. "Why?"

"Just checking." Katie forced a smile. "Jamie."

"Snaggle." Jamie saw a flash of fang before she turned to smile and wave at Millie. "Bye, Miss Millie."

"Goodbye, dear."

Jamie headed back up the street but laughed when she heard Millie tell Katie, "Stop snarling, pup. I'm sure she meant Snaggle endearingly."

Tully was sitting in his parents' kitchen, eating the last of the key lime pie someone had buried far back in the pantry under a bunch of paper bags and behind several cases of Coors, when his daddy walked in.

"That was mine," the cat snarled before he'd even gotten past the doorway.

"Really?" Tully kept eating. "Don't think I saw your name on it."

Jack's hand swiped the back of Tully's head and Tully winced. "You know, the claws were unnecessary, Daddy."

Before Jack could attack him again, Millie walked in with Katie.

"What's going on?" his momma asked.

"Daddy started it."

The feline hissed before taking one of the bags Millie held. "Get off your ass and help, boy," he snarled.

"I'm eating."

Katie quickly grabbed the bag. "I've got it."

"He ate my pie," Jack accused before carrying the bag into the pantry.

"Why do you torture him so?" Millie whispered to Tully.

" 'Because I can' is just going to get me slapped in the head again, isn't it?"

"Yes." She wrapped her arms around his shoulders and kissed the top of his head. "How's your morning been so far?"

"Fine." He rubbed her arm. "And, Momma—"

"I don't want you to fret about your father, pup."

"I won't let him come here and start anything. I won't let him hurt you."

"Sssh, pup." She eased her palms across his shoulders. "It's just a little thing."

"Not really."

"Don't let Buck Smith do this to you. All you need to remember is that you're *my* son. Understand?"

"Yes'm."

"Good." She kissed him again before stepping away while he poured himself another glass of milk.

"So I saw that sweet Jamie Meacham in town just a little while ago."

"Sweet, my ass," Jack growled from the pantry.

"I don't know what you have against her, Jackie."

"She's the daughter of Satan. And when are we going to get a report back on her, Useless?"

Tully didn't answer until a roll of foil slammed into the back of his head. "*Ow!*"

"I asked you a question, boy."

"I'm working on it."

Millie leaned against her kitchen counter. "What report?"

"Daddy wants me spying on Jamie."

"Whatever for?"

"He thinks she's up to something."

"I'm sure she is," Millie easily agreed. "But that don't mean it's not in the best interest of the town."

"I doubt it," Jack grumbled back.

"I had breakfast with her this morning," Tully admitted. "She spent the whole time reading and ignoring my charm."

"She must have better taste than that," Millie said, winning a smile from her son.

"If I'm going to get any information on her, I guess I'll have to follow her."

"That's one option," Millie said. "Or you could try being friendly."

"Why would he do that?" Jack walked out of the pantry and stared at her. "Aren't you going to make me something to eat?"

"I just fed you."

"That was hours ago!"

Shaking her head, she ignored her husband and stood next to her son. "Well?" she pushed.

"I don't understand that word you used. Uh . . . frrrrrrrr . . ."

"Friendly," she said while tugging his hair and laughing. "Unlike the rest of you people, I've actually *talked* to her. She's ever so nice."

"She calls me Snaggle," Katie said.

Tully looked away from his sister and their daddy quickly went to the refrigerator to pull out the makings for a sandwich and hide his laughter all at the same time.

"She's only teasing you, Katie."

"Don't sound like teasing to me."

"Just try it, pup." Millie gave Tully another hug. "If you want to get through to her . . . just be nice."

Tully shrugged as he finished off the last of the milk. "I guess it's worth a shot."

Jamie's eyes watered and she held up her hand. "I'm sorry. If you'll just . . . I . . ." Shaking her head, she walked away from the front desk, through the dining room, and into the back kitchen where she found her coven.

"Someone needs to cover the front desk," she announced to the entire room.

Mac didn't even look up from her notes for that night's menu. She'd taken over the Smithville Arms restaurant without even discussing it with the rest of them. Not that it really bothered Jamie, but she didn't like when anyone was presumptuous. "I thought you were covering the front desk."

"Hippie alert."

Her cousin laughed. "What are they wearing? Rosewater or some obscure incense?"

"Patchouli oil."

"Ohhhh!" her coven sisters said in unison.

"Not the kiss of death," Kenny joked while she worked away on her extremely thin, extremely tiny laptop.

"You know I can't tolerate that smell. You just know she's into that whole earth mother crap with her hemp shoes and the too-long-for-her-age hair."

"You are in rare form today."

"I'm just saying. Ew." She gave a pleading smile to Seneca. "Please?"

"All right, all right." Seneca walked to the swinging door, took several deep breaths, then seemed to hold the last one. "I'm on it," she said before charging off.

"Is she really going to hold her breath?" Mac asked.

"Maybe I should have told her the hippie was checking in a whole pack of people."

"Don't bother her with those little details," Kenny suggested, probably hoping to find poor Sen passed out from lack of oxygen.

"Anyone we know?" Mac handed her menu over to her sous chef.

"Don't think so." Jamie walked to the back door. It was always open during the day, even in the winter because the kitchen would get so hot from the ovens. "Name she gave me was Wanda Pykes. After that I couldn't stand around to hear anymore. Too funky. Besides, what coven would risk coming here?"

Jamie stepped out on the back porch and stared off. It still always amazed her. The pure beauty of this place.

"We're going out tonight with Kyle and Emma. Wanna come?"

She shook her head at Mac's question. "Can't. Got a meeting."

"Something else to freak out the populace?" Mac sat on the railing, her legs straddling the wood. "What else is going on with you?"

"Nothing. Why?"

"To be honest, you look . . . tired."

"Thank you."

"You sure being called a champion is worth all this?"

"It's not. But it is worth the power it brings me."

Mac took a breath, let it out. She only did that when she was around Jamie and trying not to get upset. "I don't see why you need more than you have."

"I know. That's why having this conversation, yet again, is meaningless."

"Can't you just enjoy it here? I don't know what more you want."

"It's that feeling you get, when untapped power flows through you for the first time. When you know, in that moment, you can do *anything*."

"But how long before it's too much?"

"It's never too much."

"Bullshit. We both know what happens to the ones who step over the line, Jamie."

"That won't be me."

"What if you have no choice?"

"Nothing and no one can or will make me cross that line. Not now, not ever. And you should know that."

Mac slid off the banister and headed back to the kitchen. "Yeah, right," she tossed over her shoulder. "I should know that."

# Chapter Three

It was nearing eleven when she left her house. She wore a simple slip of a dress but no shoes or jacket, even though it was a bit chilly being as they were so close to the ocean. Her hair was wet, smelling like she'd just washed it and the already-curling locks stretched down her back. Most days she wore it in a ponytail but not tonight.

The only thing she carried with her was a very small bag, which he refused to hazard a guess at what might be in it, and a leather shoulder holster with her .380 that she didn't bother to put on properly but instead had hanging from her left shoulder like a purse.

Jamie trudged through the woods and Tully silently followed behind her. She made her way to the clearing she liked to use for this kind of thing after she'd "accidentally" burned down the last one. He stayed in the forest, moving up a small hill where he'd have an excellent view of what she was doing. She placed the holstered gun down on the ground. With the bag still clutched in her hand, she took several steps away from her weapon and kneeled in the grass. She unzipped the bag and pulled out a glass bottle that looked to be filled with water, and a knife with a jewel handle. She placed both items beside her and tossed the bag over by the gun.

Still resting on her knees, she closed her eyes and took in and let out several deep breaths. She did this at least five minutes before reaching down and grabbing the hem of her dress. She lifted the thin material up and off her body and Tully let out a soft growl. Dang, but she was gorgeous. Real curvy, bigger than what society ever approved of, but just his speed: Fast, mean, and a hell of a ride. At least that's what he was guessing.

He shook his head, forcing himself to focus on what she was up to, instead of wondering how good her pussy tasted. He didn't have time for that. Right?

*Right?*

She pulled the stop on the glass bottle and carefully poured out the contents around her in a large circle. While she did, she chanted softly. His wolf ears picked up her words but he didn't understand them. They weren't English or any of the other languages he knew. When she emptied the bottle, she placed it beside her and picked up the blade. It was a fancy looking thing and she used it anytime she worked alone. When she was working with her cousin, she had a different one.

Grasping the hilt of the blade in both hands, she raised her arms high over her head. Her chanting became louder, necessary with that wind suddenly whipping up all around her. He couldn't feel it near him, but it was definitely near her, her long hair blowing around her. And while the wind blew, flames burst up around where she'd poured out the liquid, surrounding her in a ring of fire. He worried about another forest fire situation but after the initial rise, the flames quickly lowered and then puffed out. Now he could clearly see she was in a circle from the burn marks surrounding her on the ground.

She was screaming the words out now, calling out to those she worshipped. She pulled her arms back a bit more before slamming the blade into the ground, and then . . .

*Lord.*

And then she was gone.

"I'm not getting in the middle of this," she said again in her soft Irish brogue. "I warned you not to anger him. You did. Now *you'll* need to deal with the consequences."

"I've tried everything."

"No." She shook her head. "Not everything."

Jamie briefly closed her eyes. "Are you telling me to—"

"There's no going back once you start down that path. Just remember that."

Jamie did remember that. "That's what he wants me to do, isn't it?"

"Of course. It amuses him to watch you twist in a noose of your own making."

Jamie threw up her hands. "Or you could help me."

"I'm not getting between you and him. You started it, you can finish it. Or . . . it can finish you."

"Thank you. That's very nice."

"I do try." She nudged Jamie with her shoulder. "You're up."

"Can't I do something other than this?"

"Do you want to earn the title of my champion or not?" Jamie *did* want that title—and the power that came with it—but these . . . these . . . *performances* were wearing on her last nerve.

"Fine." Jamie stood, staring ahead at the silver and black hall of the Dark Mothers, only the goddesses' chosen warriors and mages ever allowed through the gates. As soon as Jamie's feet had touched the marble floors, her naked body was wrapped in the garments of those she aligned herself with.

For tonight, it was the leather and chainmail battle gear of the Celtic gods. She'd been trained by Boudica, the Queen of Iceni, herself and wore two swords strapped to her back. She could use them like she used her .380—at least here she could, on this metaphysical plane of existence. At home, she tended to hit herself in the head with those long mailing tubes they had in the hotel's main office.

Jamie cracked her knuckles and watched as the opposing champion bowed before the goddesses. "Anything I should know about this one?" she asked the goddess beside her.

"He fights with fire."

Jamie faced her. "Huh?"

"He fights with fire." The Morrighan, the Celtic goddess of war, raised a brow. "That won't be a problem for you, will it?"

"Again with the fire," Jamie muttered to herself as she headed toward the battle pits. "I'm getting so tired of the fire."

Tully wondered how long he would have to sit here. He wasn't much for sitting when he'd rather keep moving. And although it had only been five minutes or so, he was already getting restless. Then, the earth beneath his feet moved, like a hard jerk, and the circle set into the middle of the clearing that was empty, now had Jamie Meacham in it once again. She was naked and on all fours, her body covered in bruises and cuts, and she was coughing up . . . uh . . . fire.

*You know . . . it's just not everyday ya get to see a woman cough up fire.*

Terrified he was watching her die, Tully tore down the hill he'd been on, heading right toward her. She must have sensed him, too, because she reached outside her circle, and picked up the .380 she had with her. She jerked it so the holster flew off, and aimed it right at him.

He slid to a stop, his eyes locked on that weapon. Any other human, he wouldn't be too worried. But her . . . ?

She was still coughing, but no longer big balls of fire, instead just puffs of black smoke. He slowly sat back on his haunches, letting her know that she had nothing to fear from him. At least, not at the moment. She waited a beat, then two, until she finally began to lower her arm. But a roar from the surrounding woods had her raising the gun again, but aiming it away from him. That's when they saw the first one. It came soaring at them, screaming in terror the entire way.

Jamie automatically fell back, the gun still raised, although he knew it wouldn't do her a damn bit of good. He shot up and dived at her, shifting from wolf to human with no more than a thought, and landed on top of her, rolling them both out of the way.

The first one slammed into the space Jamie had just been kneeling in before it bounced up and away. Then another followed, and another. Tully quickly rose up on his knees, and grabbed hold of Jamie's hand. But before he could pull her out of range, it came tearing out of the trees, running right at them on all fours. Rage making him froth at the mouth, fear making him completely irrational.

"Shit," Tully muttered before he yanked Jamie to her feet and tossed her over his shoulder in one move. She'd never be able to outrun it, so he didn't have much choice. He took off into the woods, knowing it was following right behind them. Desperate, he let out a short call and kept moving. It was gaining on him, getting closer. Taking a risk, he jumped up on the boulder and leaped onto the higher one next to it. He turned just as Bear McMahon tore out of the darkness and went after the outsider. Another grizzly. The bear roared, rising up on his rear legs as Bear did the same. They slammed into each other, their jaws opening wide, trying to get a grip on the other's head or neck.

That's when Tully's Pack charged in, going after the outsider—some Yankee businessman from Delaware, if he remembered correctly—and forced the bear back and away from Bear and, more importantly, Tully. The outsider caught a few of the wolves that came too close, batting them away, but there were a lot more of the wolves than of him and Bear wasn't backing off him either. He suddenly seemed to run out of fight, abruptly turning and charging back the way he'd come.

Tully's Pack and Bear followed after the bear, while one little hybrid wandered on up to him. She had the muzzle of her feline daddy and the ears of her canine momma . . . and she had that dang snaggletooth. She trotted over to the boulder Tully stood on and shifted into his beautiful baby sister—thankfully without that snaggletooth. Those braces had worked on her human form if not her shifted one.

Katie smiled up at him. "You all right, Tully?"

"I've been better." He let out a breath. "The hyenas must have startled that bear. He tossed them at me like hockey pucks."

"I'm glad we were nearby to hear your call, but uh . . ." She bit her lip, and he knew she was trying not to laugh.

"But uh what?"

"Well, that's a nice ass you've got there, big brother." Which seemed like a really strange thing for his baby sister to say to him when they were standing around naked. There were certain shifter protocols between siblings and blood kin to avoid awkward moments just like this one. But then she laughed and added, "You plannin' on keepin' it?"

"Am I plannin' on . . ." He cringed and glanced over at the ass resting on his shoulder. Something told him this wouldn't go well, but he had to admit his baby sister was right—this was a damn fine ass he had here.

"Why don't I leave you alone with your ass and we'll make

sure that tourist bear gets back on over to the bear side of the river so he can get some fresh salmon." She winked at him, shifted, and headed off, leaving Tully alone with one probably very irritated witch.

As a former cop, there were quite a few humiliations Jamie had been forced to endure. Losing control of a perp in front of other cops, having a crazed meth head sic his pit bull on her, and having a man she was dating arrested on embezzlement charges during a family dinner with her mother.

This, however, was a new kind of humiliation and one she wasn't particularly enjoying.

She didn't say anything until Tully placed her safely on her feet. He stared down at her for several long moments before finally asking, "You all right?"

That's when she grabbed him by that damn gold hoop earring he insisted on wearing, even when wolf, and twisted until he was nearly on his knees again. "When everyone talks about this"— *and gods know they will all talk about this*—"you just remember that I am as light as a feather and I'll remember that you are a very brave and well-hung wolf who protected me. That's the story, Marmaduke, and it better not change or by all that you hold dear, I will make your life one unholy nightmare after another. Understand me?"

Even with her dangerously close to ripping that earring right out of his head, the man still managed to grin at her. "I think I understand all that."

"Good." She released him and carefully made her way to the smaller boulder and then jumped off that to the ground.

"Are you going to finally tell me what you were doing up here?" Tully's voice asked from above her.

"Nope," Jamie easily replied as she turned and found the damn wolf right behind her. She instinctively raised her weapon that, she was proud to say, she still had a tight grip on, but he caught her hand and held it. She could feel the strength in that hand, knew he could break her fingers if he wanted to, but he didn't.

Instead he said, "Don't point that gun at me again, beautiful. I don't like it."

"Then you shouldn't have followed me."

"And if it hadn't been for me, you'd have been bombarded with all those hyenas."

Jamie paused a moment to think on that. "Those were flying hyenas I saw, weren't they?"

"With a little help from an out-of-town bear . . . yep."

"That's something you simply don't see every day," she murmured, then shook her head. "Whatever. I need to get home." She was tired, exhausted really, and running out of energy fast. She needed a carb-filled meal and she needed it in the next ten minutes.

But when she tried to pull her hand away from his grasp, Tully held on tight. Still not hurting her but not giving an inch either. After several tries, Jamie stopped and asked, "Why aren't you letting me go?"

"Because you need to realize that until people around here start trusting you, someone is always going to be watching you."

"That's not my problem, Tully. You people brought me here to provide a skill you were lacking. I never said I'd change who I was to keep everyone calm. That's not my business or my concern."

His thumb brushed against her hand. "You still don't see it, do you?"

"See what?"

"We're not 'you people,' we're *your* people."

Jamie didn't buy that for a second. "From what I understand from my Alabama cousins, if you're not born in the South, you're always an outsider and a Yankee. So let's not play that game."

"But something tells me, beautiful, that you don't think you belong anywhere."

"I'm going home," she said rather than replying to that surprisingly accurate statement.

"Why?" he asked softly. "Because you don't like where this conversation is going? Or because I look so dang good naked, you can't kept those beautiful brown eyes off me?"

"As entertaining as I find your little fantasy world, I need to go home because I'm about to—"

And that was the last thing she remembered.

\* \* \*

Jamie dropped like a sack of potatoes and Tully barely caught her in time, his arms wrapping around her and lifting her up before her head slammed into the ground.

"What did you do to her?"

Tully glared at Kyle over his shoulder, the scent of the overgrown alley cat warning him of his presence five minutes ago. "I didn't do anything. She just dropped."

Kyle stepped up beside him. "We can take Jamie to my place. Emma will take care of her."

"Nah. I'll take her home myself."

Kyle studied him for a long moment. "I'm not sure I'm okay with that."

"Why? What do you think I'll do to her?"

"It's not you I'm worried about, canine."

Tully couldn't help but smile. "Awww, Kyle. Does this mean you care about me?" Tully reared back with Jamie still in his arms. "Well, there's no call to hiss at me, feline!"

# Chapter Four

Jamie woke up on her couch, a quilt wrapped around her. All the lights on and a fire blazing away in her fireplace. An open bottle of water rested on the coffee table in front of her couch, along with a bowl filled with grapes she'd brought that afternoon from the farmers' market. Using what strength she had left, she pulled herself up until she had her back against the armrest. She grabbed the water first and swigged back half of it, her throat raw from the flames she'd been forced to eat before she figured out her opponent's weakness and won the tournament. After hydrating, she placed the bowl of grapes in her lap and proceeded to devour them. She was so glad she'd gone for the seedless when she made the purchase since she'd never been a big fan of spitting, unless she was in a fight with her cousin.

As she was nearing the last few grapes and wondering what else she had in her refrigerator or freezer to eat, she heard a loud bang somewhere in the back of the house followed by extensive cursing.

She started to get up when Rico flew into the room followed by Tully Smith trying to catch her.

"Come here, you little bastard!" He made a wild grab for the gyrfalcon and the bird went up into the rafters. One of the reasons Jamie had picked this cabin for her new home was because of the deliciously extravagant high ceilings.

"Don't think runnin' up there's gonna stop me," Tully growled.

He'd put on clothes—tragically—and she wondered how long

she'd been out for Tully to go to his place, change, and get back here without her knowing. Then, on the end table at the opposite end of her sectional couch, she noticed not only her gun but the dress and satchel she'd taken with her when she'd gone out to the clearing. *Christ, what time is it anyway?* Because if there was one thing she knew about the man, it was that he didn't have a vehicle to get around quickly in. Every time she saw him he was either walking on two feet or four, but he was always walking slowly. If he wasn't walking, someone else was driving. Yet she did have to admit . . . all that walking had done the man wonders. He had what could only be called an astounding body. The kind that the supermodels *appeared* to have in those giant billboards in Times Square but when Jamie had actually seen them in person—usually during drug busts—they were way too thin and narrow. But not Tully Smith. He was definitely a man who could handle her physically, which was a nice change of pace.

"What are you doing?" she finally asked when she saw the wolf bending at the knees so he could make a lateral jump to the bird. Although what the shifters could do—and withstand—physically did amaze Jamie, she also knew he'd never reach the bird. Then again, dogs could be kind of dumb sometimes.

Tully let out a breath before slowly turning to face her. "I'm trying to make you a fricassee."

Jamie snorted, wincing a little when it made her raw throat and nasal passages burn. "You may want to stick with easier birds to catch than falcons."

"Thought that was a hawk."

"Nope. A gyrfalcon."

"A what?"

"A jerr-falcon," she said slowly so he could understand the pronunciation. "A bird of prey. I looked it up."

"You got yourself a pet bird of prey?"

"I didn't get myself anything. One day I opened my front door and there she was. I call her Rico, after the Racketeer Influenced and Corrupt Organizations Act."

"Because Tweety was too obvious?" He walked toward her and Rico came down from the rafters and landed right on his head. The wolf stopped and let out a very long and very frustrated sigh. "It's on my head."

"Yes, she is on your head."

"Why is it on my head?"

"Maybe because you keep calling her 'it' when she's a 'she.'"

"Her talons are digging into my skull."

"She's just trying to protect me from the likes of you. She's my familiar, so that's her job."

"I thought you said she was a falcon."

Not in the mood to give a full explanation of the magickal connection between certain animals and witches, Jamie lifted her arm and Rico came to her immediately. She landed on her forearm, talons gently holding on to the skin. Jamie smiled at the majestic bird who'd chosen her. "Isn't she beautiful?"

"Oh, I don't know. I think I see much prettier things right here in this room."

Jamie looked up to find the wolf staring right at her chest, exposed because the quilt was down to her waist and she wore nothing else. Surprisingly embarrassed since, to quote Mac, "Jamie's all about being naked when she can manage it," she started to reach for the quilt when Rico spread out her wings, covering Jamie up.

Tully glared at the bird. "Spoilsport."

Tully heard the timer go off and went back in the kitchen to dump the pasta he'd made into the strainer. He didn't go for anything fancy tonight, more concerned with getting Jamie fed rather than dazzling her with his cooking skills. He dumped a healthy amount of spaghetti in a bowl and poured bottled sauce on top of that. Then he grabbed a fork, grated cheese from the refrigerator, and some paper towels. He took it out to the living room and found Jamie sitting up, the quilt wrapped around her from chest to feet. Too bad since he'd enjoyed staring at her beautiful body in all this light.

For a full-human her body was strong and riddled with scars. No fang marks, like most of the Smithville females received after they hit puberty, but knife cuts, bullet holes—at least two—and a scar across her upper chest that had probably needed more stitches than he was in the mood to count. And yet she didn't hide those scars from him or anyone else. Nor did she run around showing them off so that everyone could "ooh" and "aah" over her suffering. Like the beautiful brown color of her skin and those dimples in her cheeks, the scars were simply a part of her that she accepted and didn't question.

"Here." He placed the pasta in front of her. "Eat."

"Thank you." She dug into the meal and Tully went back to the kitchen to get her more water and some fresh bread she had lying on her counter. He took all that out to her and placed it on the coffee table.

"Anything else ya need?"

Busy eating, Jamie only managed to shake her head. So Tully dropped onto the other side of the big sectional, picked up the remote, and turned on the TV before putting his feet up on her coffee table and relaxing back. After five minutes of trying to find something decent to watch, he heard a delicate throat clear. He glanced over at Jamie and found her watching him.

"Comfortable?" she asked.

Tully grinned. "Mighty comfortable! Thank ya kindly."

How could he not be, with a beautiful woman wrapped only in a quilt within groping distance, a big-screen TV for his viewing pleasure—proving he didn't need his own TV when he had friends who already did—and a couch that his butt was taking quite a shine too? What more could he need?

Of course when that large splatter of bird shit hit him dead center of his head, he did realize that he could use a good rifle with a sight. Could this be the thing Jamie had been saying "Honey, I'm home" to the other day? Because Lord forbid the woman should do something normal.

Laughing so hard she fell back on the couch, Jamie couldn't manage more than, "Oh, my God! She *hates* you!"

Yeah, he was sensing that. And he'd be lying if he said that the feeling wasn't mutual.


Jamie watched Tully walk out of the bathroom with his hair freshly washed. He glared at the bird as he passed the bookcase she was perched on.

"I smell like damn honey," he complained about her shampoo and conditioner. "Every bear in three counties will be following me around town."

"I like all natural hair-care products. No sulfates or silicones for me." When he glared at her like he'd glared at Rico, Jamie could only laugh.

Tully roughly towel dried his hair before dropping on the couch and using her favorite comb to get the shiny brown locks off his face. The entire time he watched her.

"What?" she finally asked.

"I need you to tell me what's going on."

Not quite sure what Tully was asking, Jamie only replied, "Nothing. Why?"

Tossing her comb down, he rested his elbows on his knees, leaned forward, clasped his hands together, and said, "There's only a couple of ways we can do this, beautiful. You either tell me what happened tonight and you tell me right now. Or you get your shit and you go. You and your coven . . . including Emma."

The panic eased when she realized he was asking about a few hours ago rather than what had been slowly building for the last few weeks.

"Kyle's never letting that happen," she said confidently.

"You're right. He wouldn't. But Kyle don't run this town. For all the tigers, the lions, and the goddamn bears, only the Smith wolves have ever run Smithville County. And only Smith wolves ever will. That don't mean to say that Kyle won't go wherever little Emma goes. He will. But we both know that boy won't be happy anywhere else but here."

"But you're going to run us out anyway?"

"I'm going to protect my town. That's what I do. That's what I'll always do. And right now, beautiful, you are nothin' but trouble. So unless you start talking right now, and unless I believe every word coming out of your mouth, I want you gone by sunup." When she opened her mouth to respond, he added, "And stop trying to test me, it's only pissing me off and we both know I'll do what I say I will."

"We both know that, do we?"

"I'm a Smith, beautiful. There ain't nothin' I won't do."

Tired but no longer exhausted, Jamie leaned back into the couch and studied the man sitting across from her. "I'm on a search for power. Undiluted. Untapped."

"I thought you found that here."

"I did. But it's kind of like having a joint checking account. Every time I pull power from here, my coven knows."

"And they ask questions."

"Yep."

"So that's what tonight was? A search for more power?"

"Kind of. I'm trying to become the champion of one of my goddesses. It's hard, dirty work, and often requires me to fight Greek giants who like to use fire as a weapon."

"Sounds like a lot of risk for a Yankee from Staten Island."

She glared at him through slits as her eyes narrowed. "I'm from *Long* Island, Marmaduke. There's a difference."

"And it still sounds like a lot of risk."

"It is. But to become a god's champion is to enhance your power tenfold. So it's worth the risk."

"I don't understand you."

"What don't you understand?"

"You already have so much power. Everyone in town knows it, we can all feel it. But it's natural. Part of you like the wolf is part of me. I don't understand why you would want to enhance that."

Annoyed by his statement—although she wasn't sure why—Jamie lobbed back, "And I don't understand how you can be happy wandering around this town every day. Don't you get bored?"

"Nope. 'Round here there's always something interesting going on."

"I've been here ten months and I haven't seen anything all that interesting. It's a nice little town, don't get me wrong. But . . ."

"But what? Go on, say it."

"Don't you crave *more*?"

"No."

"So you're happy to settle?"

"I guess we have a different opinion of settling, beautiful."

She lifted her hands, palms up. She didn't want to fight since the man had saved her from flying hyenas. "Hey, you know what? To each his or her own. If you're happy here that's all that matters."

"Can you think of anything better than being happy where you are?"

"Yeah." Jamie smiled. "Power."

\* \* \*

*Lord. Like a dog with a bone.*

"There's nothing else you want? Nothing else that would make you happy?" *And, Lord willing, content.*

"I've tried the career thing. You know, moving up the Department's ladder but . . . eh. Money can only do so much, although it's always nice having it."

"What about a man?"

"The answer to all women's questions?"

He grinned. "For some."

"Tried marriage and that was extremely unfulfilling."

Tully felt his body go tight. "You were married?"

"You didn't know?"

"No."

"Yeah. Seven years of my life I'll never get back."

"What happened?"

"Nothing."

"It must have been something. Unless you're still married."

"Oh, no, no, no," she said quickly. "So *not* still married."

"Then what was it."

"Like I said. Nothing. That was the problem. When we'd argue, I felt nothing. When he yelled at me over something ridiculous, I felt nothing. When he threatened to out me to the Department as a witch and a kook, still nothing. And when I found him fucking a pseudo-friend of mine in my bed . . . more than nothing. In fact, I felt bad for him, because God knew he was doing it all for me. And I felt nothing."

"You never loved him."

"No," she said with a shake of her head. "I really never did."

"So why—"

"I went through this really weird phase where I wanted to be normal. Marriage is considered normal. My parents were happy. The people I pretended were my friends were happy. I was happy. Everyone was happy . . . but my coven. They were not happy."

"They knew it was wrong for you."

"Yeah. They did. And tried to tell me. Guess I should have listened."

Although curious why anyone would be with someone they didn't care about for seven long years, Tully decided to stick with their current topic of conversation.

"So, you get all that power," he said. "You scoop it up like my momma's key lime pie at the church social. Then what? What are you going to do with all that power once you have it?"

"Use it."

"To do what? Destroy the world? Become the almighty empress of the universe?"

"No," she said with an easy roll of her shoulders that told him she wasn't lying. "Don't want any of that."

"Well, that's the thing about power, beautiful. Once you have it, you've gotta do something with it."

She smiled, showing all those perfectly aligned, "my daddy is an orthodontist" teeth. "And I'm sure I will."

Jamie had no idea when she fell asleep, but she knew when Tully took her to bed. He easily lifted her off the couch and walked through the dark house to the back bedroom. He pulled off the quilt before covering her up with the sheet and comforter.

"You're leaving?" she heard herself ask.

"In a bit."

"Okay." She rolled over to her other side and tucked her hands under her cheek. Lips brushed against her forehead and then he was gone. He didn't make a sound, but she still knew he'd left the room and then the house from the amazing energy that went with him.

And with his energy gone, theirs returned. She could hear them scratching at the walls, the doors, the windows, trying to get in. Always trying to get in. It had been getting worse every night. At first, a simple spell could send them away, but now she had to use more than that. Even worse, it was getting to the point where she had to manage it constantly. One simple spell no longer covered her from moon to moon, or even day to day. Of course, they did have help, didn't they? They had the one who'd sent them.

She grabbed another pillow and put it over her head in the hopes of blocking out the sounds while Rico settled on her headboard, watching over her for the night.

Yet there was only so much her familiar could do. Once they broke through the barriers she'd created, Jamie doubted anyone would be able to protect her.

# Chapter Five

Jamie was mid-yawn when she heard the knock on her office door. Once Tully had left, she'd gotten no sleep and had spent the rest of the night watching bad television until dawn when she had to get to work and whip out some pastries for a Daughters of the Confederate Bears meeting. Even worse, her cousin had been an annoying heifer since she'd rolled into work later that morning. If Jamie didn't know better, she'd swear Mac was trying to pick a fight with her. Or maybe she was just being her usual nosey self. Whatever her damage was, Jamie had avoided her cousin by hiding in her office.

Hoping her cousin wasn't back to push her, Jamie wiped her tired eyes and said, "Come in."

Emma stuck her head in. "Hey."

"Hey. What's up?" When Emma hesitated Jamie motioned her in. "What's going on?"

Emma closed the door and sat down in the leather office chair across from her. "I was going to ask you that."

"Nothing."

"Jamie." Emma gave an exasperated laugh. "Look at you."

"Hey. I was spitting up fire last night. I deserve to look this tired."

"You don't think we feel it? Every night? Them coming for you? And I'm not talking about what you're doing to become Morrighan's champion."

Jamie relaxed back in her chair. Of course her coven felt it.

Soon they might be able to hear it too. The demands for entry getting louder, more angry, more desperate. "Let it go, Em."

"Let us help you."

"There's nothing to help."

"You're lying!"

Emma winced at the voice coming through the door. "Would you let me handle this?"

Mac pushed the door open. "You're not handling it right."

Exhausted, worn down, and just plain raw, Jamie warned her cousin, "You need to back off this, Mac, and you need to back off this now."

Her cousin snorted. "No."

Around early afternoon, Tully ambled on over to the Smithville Arms to check on Jamie. True, she wasn't his responsibility but he'd felt a kinship to her after talking for so long the night before. She was a sweet thing, if a bit misguided. Misguided because he couldn't understand how she didn't see the beauty of this place. Smithville wasn't just some town to him. He knew there was no place else in the world where he could go and be as happy and, more importantly, *content* as he was here. If she only bothered to open up her eyes and see what had been bestowed upon her, he knew she could find her place here. She could find something better than the hoarding of power.

And, as always, his mother had been right. Trying to force anything down Jamie's throat or even trying to smooth talk her would never work. She was way too smart for her to buy that move from him. So being her friend would have to be the way to go and he couldn't say that he minded. He liked her.

Hated her bird, though.

Tully ambled on up the great porch stairs of the hotel and opened the screen door, stopping right in the doorway. He watched Emma and Seneca, their arms wrapped around Jamie's waist, trying to pull her back. Across from them was poor Kenny, her arms around Mac's waist, trying to hold Mac back. The cousins had a healthy hold on each other's hair and didn't seem in the mood to let the other go while they yelled obscenities he was glad his momma wasn't around to hear because she'd have dealt with that right quick.

Deciding Jamie seemed basically fine and figuring he could talk to her later while she was cleaning up those bruises her cousin would give her, Tully turned back around, headed down the stairs, and got back onto the road. He needed to make peace between one of the Prides and one of the Clans again anyway.

He'd walked about a half-mile when he stopped and lifted his head, his nostrils flaring as he cast for a scent. When he finally latched on to it, when he finally remembered it, he spun around, and stared down at the wolf watching him.

Bracing himself, Tully said the first thing that came to mind. "And all this time I was really hoping you were dead."

Jamie finally had Mac on her back and was about to start spitting in her face when a strong hand grabbed hold of her arm and pulled her off.

She looked up expecting to see Kyle or Bear—they really hated when the witches fought—but instead she saw Tully.

"I need to talk to you," he growled out as he yanked her to her feet.

"Hey," Emma said, jumping forward and then scrambling right back again with the rest of the coven when Tully barked and snapped at them all. Besides being kind of disgusted at her easily startled coven, Jamie was also shocked at Tully. He never yelled at Emma. Or, as in this case, barked at her. He treated her like she was spun glass. "Sweet little Emma," he always called her which, until this moment, never bothered Jamie before.

Although why that was going through her mind now as he manhandled her right through the dining room, through the kitchen, and out the back porch, she had no idea.

"Why is Buck Smith here?" he demanded once they were on the lawn behind the hotel.

Jamie stared up at him. "Who?"

It was fascinating to watch the way his expression completely changed. She'd never seen him look like that. So angry. She didn't think she'd ever seen him miffed, much less homicidal. Even when she'd set the forest on fire and poisoned the lake, he'd never appeared this angry.

And, boy, did he look angry.

"You're supposed to protect this town," he bit out.

"Right. And I do . . . when I'm aware of a problem."

"How could you not be aware? *He's staying at your goddamn hotel!*"

Whoa. He was yelling at her. Normally, she'd bind his lips together with a Hoodoo spell she kept for just this type of situation, but this was Tully and this was not normal behavior for him. Something more than simply being a twat was in play here and, after last night, she felt she kind of owed it to him to find out what . . . *before* she bound his lips together.

"Tully, I don't know who Buck Smith is. I mean, I'm assuming he's family . . ."

For a split second, he looked like he might hit her. Or, in more canine terms, maul her. But instead he released her and began to pace.

"Momma's gonna lose her mind when she finds out he's actually *here*. We all thought he was just on his way, not *here*."

"I don't—"

"And Daddy . . . Lord."

"Tully?"

"I need to let the Pack know. I need to let everybody know. He's *here*."

Getting frustrated but not wanting to show it, Jamie gently placed her hand on Tully's shoulder, but he turned to face her so fast, she stumbled away from him, her feet catching, and she fell right on her ass.

Tully stared down at her with such horror that if she didn't know better, she'd have thought he'd slammed her to the ground himself. In fact, she knew that *he* believed he had.

"Oh, my God. Jamie." He reached for her. "I'm so sorry." She caught hold of his hand and instead of letting him pull her up, she tugged until he'd knelt in front of her. "Jamie, I'm so sorry." She went up on her knees and placed her hand against his cheek. Tully's eyes closed, his brows pulling down in a phenomenal frown of pain. Whoever Buck Smith was, he could get under Tully's skin as no one else could.

Jamie put her arms around Tully's big shoulders and pulled him in close until his head rested against her neck. She looked up to see her cousin standing on the porch watching her, her face filled with concern. Jamie tilted her head and, after a brief nod, Mac went back inside.

"Why don't we go for a walk?" Jamie softly suggested. "We'll figure it out from there."

Only his father could make him like this. Full of rage and uncontrollable fits of violence . . . *like father, like son.*

No. No. He was not like Buck Smith. He would *never* be like Buck Smith. Not if he could help it. And he would help it even if it took every ounce of willpower he possessed. Yet there was no denying that the one thing that could set him off, that could and would bring out the worst in Tully Smith was his father. Not his daddy. Jack Treharne with all his snarling and snapping and feline ways had earned that particular title, but he'd earned it and kept it with pride. Buck Smith hadn't earned anything from his son but Tully's distrust and paranoia.

"Buck Smith is my father," he explained to the woman walking beside him.

"I thought your real father was dead."

"No. I said I'd hoped he was dead."

"I see."

"He said he was staying at your hotel."

"I guess he is, but the reason it never occurred to me to say anything was that he didn't check in himself. If I'm thinking of the right Pack, a woman checked them in. Wanda something."

"Pykes. I'd heard he'd hooked up with a full-human a few months back. Can't believe he brought her here, though."

"Why?"

"He hasn't marked her as his own from what I've heard. We're more likely to trust a full-human bonded to one of us than one who has no ties. One good argument and she's running around, telling the world about shifters."

"I can handle that if she becomes a problem. Tell me about Buck."

Tully winced. He'd rather not, but after yelling at Jamie and knocking her on her ass for no other reason than him being a dang idiot, the least he could do was tell her everything.

"My direct kin come from Alabama. The MacClancys are my

momma's people and they're part of the Alabama Smiths. My father had been forced out of town when he was sixteen but he came back four years later when his granddaddy died. My momma was barely fifteen then and he latched on to her like a tic on a dog. Things got bad, again, between my father and his, and Buck was forced out . . . again. Only this time he took my momma with him because she was well pregnant with me. By the time she was about to pop, they'd made it to Smithville. I was born here about a week after they arrived. Then it started again. My father crossing his uncle and cousins, trying to take control of the Pack and, eventually, the town. They ran him off again but this time Momma didn't go with him."

"Why?"

"There were lots of reasons she'll give you. She had me. She wanted to give me something stable. She was tired of traveling all over the place. And there were lots of reasons everyone else in town had: That Buck fucked anything that moved even while she was pregnant with me; that after nearly two years of being together he had yet to mark her as his own; that he was cold to her, rude. And I'm sure all of that was true. Actually, I know it was. But what I figured out, what I *know* is the reason my momma stayed is that she never thought he'd leave. Not without us. She thought he loved her enough to simmer down and wait until he was really ready to take over. At the time, I don't think it ever crossed her mind that he would leave her. And then I don't think it crossed her mind that he wouldn't come back."

"I don't know which is worse," Jamie mused softly. "Being so confident in the power of love that you're willing to risk your heart, or knowing that love is just a cruel joke from the gods and never risking anything."

"I'd have to say that last one."

"Even after what your mom went through?"

"Yeah. I won't say it was easy on her. It wasn't. For six long years she waited for him. Waited while I grew into the most terrifying devil child this side of the Mason-Dixon."

Jamie laughed. "That bad, huh?"

"Yeah. That bad. So bad Miss Addie and her coven politely suggested that Buck was using astral projection to visit me at night in an attempt to turn me."

"It must have gotten better."

"I wouldn't say it got better but nothing lasts forever. And it was a cold, dark day when my momma had to come down to the school to meet with my second grade teacher because there was the *suggestion* I tried to drown another student in the boys' bathroom."

"A suggestion?"

"I didn't see any hard proof other than the little bastard's word and the fact that he was drenched from his head to his shoulders."

Jamie laughed, and Tully laughed with her. A shocking feeling since any mention of his father usually sent him into one of his rare funks for days at a time. But she was calming him down, easing him just by being herself, by being his friend. "I still say they misread the situation," he went on. "Anyway, my momma was called and she had to leave her job to come down to the school. And while she was waiting, she met Daddy."

"Love at first sight?"

"So they say. I still say the old bastard took advantage of her pure innocence."

Jamie snorted but she choked on it when Tully teasingly glared at her.

"Anyway," he went on, "Momma and Daddy met and, ignoring the grave indignities they were causing both me and Kyle, decided to get married. They didn't have to, this is a town of shifters, after all, and if there is one thing very few of us care about one way or the other is marriage. But I kind of understand why they did it, being different species and all. They wanted to show everybody how serious they were about each other, plus they wanted to make sure their children grew up feeling like they were family.

"But it got back to Buck what was going on and if there's one thing that man hates it's felines. So ignoring the fact he hadn't been back in more than six years, he sneaked into town with a Pack he'd created of forced-out Smiths and stray wolves he'd found along the way. The plan was simple: grab me, grab my momma. It might have worked, too, but Buck must have forgotten how loyal the Smiths are to their pups and the females who breed them. Although none of them were crazy about the idea of any wolf mating with, much less *marrying*, a cat, they still knew how much

Momma loved Daddy and, more importantly, how badly Buck had treated her. They also knew what a bastard he was. Most of the Smiths were already here for the wedding when my father came into the territory. He found me first. Told me I was his son and that he'd come to take me home with him." They stopped by a large boulder and Jamie leaned back against it, watching him closely.

"You know," Tully relaxed back against an oak tree, his arms crossed over his chest, "it's one of those things every eight-year-old kid is waiting for when he's grown up without a father. For his daddy to come back for him. You daydream about, wish on it, pray for it. And here it was, standing right in front of me. I knew he wasn't lying, I knew he was my father."

"What did you do?"

He shrugged, not sure even today he understood what he'd done that day. "I screamed for Jack. I screamed for my daddy and he came runnin'. Not seven years later, but right then. The Smith Pack with him. I'd never seen so much blood as I saw that day. Momma got hurt, too, fightin' by Daddy's side. When it was all over no one was dead but Buck's Pack had taken the worst of it, limpin' off back where they came from. But I knew that day, when Jack had carried me back into town and I saw ol' Buck watching us from the trees before he headed off for good that I was his enemy now. That I'd crossed a line with him that he would never forgive me for."

It sounded like some old tale her great-grandfather—whom the entire family referred to as "Big Daddy" although the man was no more than five-two—would have told her during one of the family reunions when her mother and aunt would drive for two days from Long Island to Alabama with two arguing brats in the backseat. The only difference was that the people in Big Daddy's stories were always full-human and Tully never ended every few sentences with, " 'Cause you know how those rednecks are."

It fascinated her even while her mind worked away at the problem.

"You think he's back here for revenge?" she asked but Tully only shook his head.

"Buck Smith is never that simple."

"He wants something."

"He wants this." He glanced around at the trees and up at the beautiful blue sky. "He wants this territory. Smithville is prime territory to our kind and the wolf who ran it before me was my Uncle Tyrus Ray." *Tyrus?* "Six-foot-seven and three-hundred-and-eighty-five pounds of dangerously unstable wolf, but he could be a big ol' teddy bear when the mood struck him. He died sudden about five years back and one of his sons, Johnny Ray, took over, but that didn't go well. He was pushy and testy and one day he just got on my nerves and I . . ."

"Beat the hell out of him?" she slipped in when he seemed to be searching for the right phrase.

"I prefer 'slapped some sense into him.' But whatever. Bottom line was when I woke up the next day I was Alpha Male and mayor."

"*That's* how you became mayor?"

"No. I was voted in as mayor of Smithville but Johnny Ray got on my nerves at my inauguration party."

*Fair enough.*

Gazing off, Tully murmured, "I gotta tell Daddy that Buck's back."

"Then what?"

"I don't know." His gaze moved over to her. "What happened when they checked in?"

"Nothing. Other than I had to walk away and let Sen handle the check-in."

"Why?"

"Wanda . . . she was wearing that"—Jamie shuddered—"patchouli oil."

"Lord, woman, what is your thing about that?"

"I hate it! It's my kryptonite. As are women like Wanda."

"Women like Wanda?"

"Yeah. Those hippie, dippy, New Age females I always want to stab in the face. The truth is if I hadn't met my coven in junior high, I would have been a solitary practitioner. So would Mac. I swear nothing gets on my nerves faster than those Artemis-worshipping, Patchouli-wearing, need-a-goddamn-haircut, shave-your-pits-once-in-a-while, still-driving-a-love-bus, insists-on-calling-me-sister, pains in the ass."

Tully stared at her. "But not like you have any strong opinions on the subject or anything."

"Maybe a little one. But it's because of those types that my coven is banned for life from the Green Man Festival."

"And I'm sure it had nothing to do with what you were probably up to at the time."

"Maybe a little," she shook her head, "but I still say they were being irrational. I mean they're all so busy *saying* they're drawing down the moon, but they get completely freaked out when someone actually does it."

Tully blinked. "You moved the moon out of orbit?"

She snorted. "Of course not."

"Oh."

"I just moved the earth a little closer to it."

Tully's arms dropped to his side. "You did *what*?"

"Don't get hysterical. I moved it back."

Tully didn't think it would be possible. Didn't think anyone was capable of doing it. But Jamie Meacham had managed the impossible. She'd gotten him to think about something *other* than his father.

"You're crazy," he accused, which was something he didn't toss around lightly considering his own family history.

"Not crazy. Just a bit of a show-off. I get so tired of them talking, talking, talking, but not *doing*. Don't *talk* about drawing down the moon. Fucking do it. If that doesn't work, move the earth closer. Not brain surgery, people."

"Did it ever occur to you that moving *any* planet out of its orbit could cause huge ramifications globally?"

"I was never really into science," she said dismissively.

"Oh. Well then . . ."

"Besides, I moved everything back and stopped most of the tsunamis, tornados, and spouting volcanoes before I lost consciousness."

Lord, now she had him laughing. Laughing so hard he couldn't even stand up straight. He didn't think it was possible. Not until his father was long gone and all was right in the town he loved. But somehow one full-human witch had managed to do the impossible yet again.

"Yeah, sure . . . laugh. But let me tell ya, all those hippie-dippy witches with their 'love solves all' platitudes and their 'make love not war' philosophies are at their very core—totally Stalin."

And ten minutes later, when the Elders had finally tracked them down, desperately concerned about what they'd heard through the town rumor mill and wanting some answers from Tully and Jamie on what they were planning—they seemed really concerned when they found Tully rolling around on his back laughing and Jamie snarling at him, "It's not funny. They were really *mean to me!*"

# Chapter Six

"Tell me again," Jamie murmured softly near his ear, her gaze examining the County Hall boardroom with its fine cherry-wood furniture and board table, "why the Elders insist on meeting at the junior high when you have boardrooms like this one?"

"Because if they use it too often, it won't still look so shiny and pretty," he whispered back. "Duh."

They both chuckled, their gazes briefly locking, and Tully couldn't explain what passed between them, but he'd felt it as surely as if she'd touched him with her hand.

"Are you two done?" Jack Treharne snarled. Of course, he snarled most things but until this was all settled, until his mate and the town he loved was safe from Buck Smith, the man would be damn intolerable. But Tully didn't mind because they both felt the same way about the town and about his momma. "Because that bastard wolf is a problem that needs to be dealt with."

"I understand that," Jamie told him calmly, "but I'm not sure what you expect us to do."

Jack pushed away from the wall he'd been leaning on and came up to Jamie. "Why the hell not? What's your purpose here if you can't do what we tell you to?"

"I don't *work* for you, Jack. I'm more like . . . free-range protection."

"Can't you set up those wards or whatever you call 'em?"

"We already have those in place," Mac cut in from her place across the room. "And we renew them each full moon, but it still doesn't help with your particular problem."

"Why not?"

"Because the boundaries we've created are to keep full-humans away and pure evil out." Jamie shrugged. "They won't keep out or harm animals and that pretty much includes you."

"We're still human. Mostly."

"True. But shifters are protected by the same gods who've empowered us to create those boundaries. That includes Buck Smith."

"So there's nothing you can do?"

"I didn't say that. We can do lots of things. Some of which will leave nothing but charred remains and fond memories. But if he hasn't done anything to warrant such an attack from me or my coven, I'm only putting our powers at risk." And Tully knew she'd never do that.

"Which is what I told you, Daddy," Tully reminded him.

"You want him here, don't you?" And if it sounded like Jack was accusing Tully . . . he was. "So you can *talk* through all your bullshit like you're in a goddarn therapy session."

"Old man, I can think of a thousand tortures I'd rather endure than dealing with Buck Smith, but it doesn't change the fact that we can't stop him from coming here with his Pack for a vacation." Which was what Wanda Pykes had told Seneca at check-in but Tully would never be stupid enough to believe it.

"And if they decide to stay?" Gwen McMahon asked.

"That I won't allow," Tully said simply.

"And how are you going to stop him?" Jack demanded.

And Tully answered his daddy the only way he knew how. "Any way I have to."

"I could talk to him," Jamie offered and it amazed her how quiet the entire room became. So quiet she could hear the crows and jaybirds outside the window get into a vicious fight over tree territory.

"Talk to him about what, exactly?" And what insulted Jamie was the question came from her own damn cousin. Where was the loyalty?

"Sweetie, I was a cop for years. I know how to do this. I'll go and check him out, talk to him, figure out what he's up to."

Mac stood beside her now, her arms folded over her nonexistent tits. "Or you can start shit."

Insulted, because her loyalty to Tully had grown leaps and bounds in less than twenty-four hours and she'd never put him at risk, Jamie snapped, "I will not start shit."

"You don't know how *not* to start shit."

Jamie turned so she stood toe-to-toe with her cousin. "And maybe you need to back up off me, cuz."

"And maybe you need to make me."

Jamie raised her hand. Not to hit her cousin but to toss her out of the room with one well-placed spell when Tully reached over and firmly gripped her fingers with his and pulled her in to his side. "I'd love for you to talk to Buck."

"Now, see," Jamie complained, "that sounds like sarcasm."

"It's not sarcasm," Jack said, watching his stepson. "The idiot actually wants you to do it."

"I value her opinion, Daddy."

"Like I said," the older man muttered, turning away. "Idiot."

Tully caught a ride with Kyle back to the hotel and Bear met them out front. The witches were climbing out of Jamie's SUV when Tully asked Bear, "Where are they?"

The grizzly, capable of catching a scent up to twenty miles away, lifted his head. He sniffed. Once. Twice. After the third, he nodded toward the west part of the resort. "Racquetball court."

Tully and Kyle stared at Bear. *Buck playing racquetball?*

"Seriously?" Kyle finally asked.

"Yeah. Seriously."

"Okay." Tully turned in time to see Jamie walking off in that direction. In several long strides he was beside her. "Are you sure about this?"

"I thought you trusted my judgment."

"I said I trusted your opinion. And we're not talking about either here."

"Well, you're going to have to trust me, Marmaduke."

"You make it impossible when you call me that."

She grinned up at him and winked as she trudged forward. Tully was keeping up with her when he felt someone grab him from behind and pull him back. He turned and came eye to eye with Mac. "Why do you want to hurt me?" she asked.

"I didn't know I was, darlin'."

"This can't go well."

"You don't know that."

"I know my cousin."

"Was she a good cop?"

"She was an excellent cop. One of the best."

"Then what's there to worry about?"

"This isn't about her helping strangers."

"It isn't?"

"Of course not. She's doing this for you guys, which can only spell disaster."

"Really? Because it doesn't seem like your cousin has warmed too much to everybody 'round here."

"Actually this is the friendliest I've ever seen her."

Tully blinked a few times before he asked again, "Really?"

"Yes. Really."

He shrugged. "All right then."

Letting out a rather overly dramatic sigh, Mac pushed past him. Tully followed and they quickly caught up to the rest seconds before they made it to the courts.

Buck was nowhere in sight but his sons were. Buck had at least three sons—that everyone was aware of—and not one of them worth a damn. Of course, they felt the same way about Tully.

Not surprisingly, they didn't find Buck's boys by the racquetball court, but the archery range right next to it. The thought of his idiot half-brother Luther playing with a bow and arrow did nothing but deeply concern Tully.

Jamie walked up to Luther, smiled. "Is Buck around?"

"Nope." Luther already had his bow loaded, the arrow nocked.

"Do you know when he'll be back?"

"Nope."

Tully rolled his eyes. Thank the Lord for his momma because

obviously his ability to think, reason, and communicate clearly came from her.

"Is there someone else I can talk to?" Jamie asked. "Because you're not fulfilling my needs."

Tully heard a chuckle and was shocked to realize it came from Bear. The man didn't laugh about much. It wasn't in his nature.

Luther studied Jamie close, then his big, dumb gaze examined the rest of them. There was only Luther and Tully's two other half-brothers, so maybe he wasn't in the mood to fight because he politely told her, "Daddy will be back in an hour. You can talk to him then."

"Great." Jamie turned to head back when Luther suddenly raised his bow. Not at her, or even at the target, but straight up. Tully heard that telling cry and quickly said, "Luther. Don't."

The dumb junkyard dog looked right at him—a smile on his face that looked so much like Buck's—and released the arrow.

Tully cringed when he heard the arrow hit its target, another cry echoing out as it fell to the ground.

Jamie stopped in her tracks and turned around, her eyes locking on the large bird no more than five feet from Luther.

When she only stood there, staring, Tully assumed she was in shock. Until she moved. No. She didn't go after Luther, although Tully would have loved to have seen that. Instead Jamie went after Seneca—who was going after Luther.

Jamie reached for her friend, but the little witch dashed around Jamie's arms and ran right up to Luther. She didn't say anything, but she did punch him. Right in the chin since she couldn't reach his face. Luther growled, his hand wrapping around Sen's throat, lifting her off the ground.

Mac, Kenny, and Emma moved to each other's side and Mac raised her hands, flames and lightning dancing at her fingertips. But before she could unleash anything, before she could wipe Luther out where he stood, Jamie made her move. Yet it wasn't the one Tully expected.

Because he really hadn't expected her to press her .380 to the back of Luther's head. The safety off, her finger firm on the trigger.

"We're all going to calm down now," she said softly, her gun to Luther's head but her eyes on her coven. "We're all going to take a deep breath and we're all going to calm down."

Mac's fingers curled into fists and the flames and lightning disappeared into her hands.

"You're going to put my friend down now," she said to Luther. And he did, releasing Seneca immediately. She stumbled a bit when her feet hit the ground, but she quickly turned toward Jamie's falcon, kneeling beside it.

Luther was a hell of a shot, Tully would give him that. The arrow had gone right through that bird.

Keeping his voice even and controlled, Tully said to Luther, "Targets are real specific in Smithville, Luther Ray. Arrows aren't supposed to be used on anything but the bull's-eyes down at the other end of this range. You wanna hunt, then you shift and do it proper."

"Just wanted to test my skill out, big brother," Luther said with more than a little bit of sneering to his words. "Nothin' personal about it."

"Good," a small, tear-filled voice said and Seneca looked over at Luther. "And this isn't personal either."

The petite woman drew her arms back then shoved them forward, a roar to rival any lioness bellowing out of her lungs, and Luther's body went airborn, flipping back and into the concrete wall of one of the storage units. The other two idiots made a move toward Seneca and Jamie aimed her weapon at the closest one. "Don't even . . ." she warned simply. They didn't, stopping in their tracks, their eyes on her gun.

Seneca, growling like the most adorable kitten, stood and advanced on Luther.

Without turning her gaze away from Tully's kin, Jamie barked, "Kenny."

"Got her." The dark-haired female grabbed hold of Seneca by wrapping her arms around the witch's waist and lifting her off her feet. Kenny carried her friend back to the hotel, Seneca cussing the whole way.

Jamie briefly glanced at Tully and motioned to the bird lying on the ground. "Tully?"

He knelt down and looked at it. He'd be the first to admit he didn't know anything about birds except which tasted good with barbeque sauce and which tasted better with lemon and butter, but he did know when something was alive and when it was dead.

"She's still breathing, but we need to get her to a vet."

Jamie nodded before glancing over at Bear.

"Y'all go," the grizzly said. "I'll take care of things here."

"You need my gun?"

And Tully didn't even have to look to know that Bear was smiling. "Darlin' . . . that's the last thing I need.

# Chapter Seven

"That didn't go as well as I'd hoped," Tully finally said to her after an hour of sitting in silence in the Colton City Veterinary Clinic waiting room, about forty-five minutes or so away from Smithville. He'd seemed surprised the bird had lasted the trip but Jamie wasn't.

"I'm sorry about that," she said.

"Sorry about what? Y'all didn't do anything wrong. It was them."

"It's not like they knew or could even comprehend the relationship I have with Rico. You can't really blame them. They thought they were just shootin' a bird."

"Exactly. That's the problem. We have a cooperative relationship with birds. Mostly crows but they're real loyal to their own. If we start shootin' them out of the sky, they will turn on us in a heartbeat."

"I didn't realize."

"Your bird shit on my head and lived to squawk about it. That wasn't a clue?"

"Now see? I thought you let that go because you liked me so much."

He leaned in until his shoulder pressed against hers. "She *shit* on my head."

Laughing for the first time in a while, Jamie nodded. "I got it. I'm clear."

"All right then."

The vet walked out of the back, smiling at them. "Well, much to my surprise, it looks as if your bird is going to make it."

Jamie widened her eyes and opened her mouth a little to give the impression this information really shocked her. "Are you sure?"

"I am!" the vet said. "Now, she is going to need a lot of care over the next few days."

"Of course."

"And I really should check, but do you have a falconers' license?"

Jamie didn't even know there was such a thing. "Well," she decided to go with at least a partial truth, "she showed up one day and didn't really leave. I didn't know I needed a license."

"Actually, one of you should have it. But I'm not going to make a big deal out of it. Just something to think about if you take her to another vet. They may ask a lot more questions."

"No problem."

"Okay." The vet smiled. "We'll have her ready for you in a bit and we'll give you the medications you'll need to care for her."

"That's great! Thank you!" Once the doctor walked out of the waiting room, Jamie let that painful fake smile drop. "I can't believe I have to pay all that money for crap that bird doesn't even need."

"And why doesn't she need it?"

"Seneca. She's our resident healer. As soon as that arrow hit Rico, she unleashed a spell to heal her. Which also explains why she went off on . . . what's his name?"

"Luther."

"Yeah. Luther. There are side effects when you use all that magick, that fast, with no prep. For her it's rage." Jamie shook her head. "I need a falconer's license. Are they kidding?"

Tully laughed but it died away as Jamie heard the tinkle sound of the bell at the front when the door opened and hit it. She looked up and watched the large, hulking man walk across the room toward them. He stopped in front of them and nodded at Tully before focusing on Jamie.

"Miss Jamie," he said, holding his hand out. "The name's Buck Smith, and I wanted to apologize about what happened earlier today."

\* \* \*

Tully didn't know what his father was doing there but as he watched Jamie slip her hand into his grip, all he wanted to do was break the old wolf's arm off at the shoulder.

"I'll be dealing with my boys when I get back but I wanted you to know right up front that what happened wasn't okay in my book."

*It wasn't? Since when?*

"I appreciate you coming here to tell me that yourself," Jamie said. "It makes me feel a whole lot better about everything."

*She can*not *be buying this.*

"And I appreciate you giving me my say. I also expect you to add whatever you pay here to my bill."

"That's not necessary."

"It is to me. You promise me that you'll do that."

"Okay."

"Thank you." He still held her hand, studying it before he released her, nodded at them both, and walked out.

Tully followed right behind him. As they neared the old coot's truck, Tully asked, "What the hell are you up to, old man?"

Buck stopped and faced him. "I'm not up to anything. And watch how you talk to me, boy. I ain't that feline you grew up with."

And there he was. There was Buck Smith.

"You ain't foolin' me for a second."

Buck smiled. "Don't know what you mean . . . son."

Tully growled while Buck walked around to the driver's side of his pickup. He got inside and slammed the door shut, his arm resting on the frame of the open window. "You know, I've been thinkin', maybe it's time we put the past behind us."

"Is that right?"

"It would make my Wanda real happy. She don't like all this discourse."

"Can you even spell discourse?"

"Funny. You were always real funny." Buck started up his truck. "All I'm asking for is a chance. A chance to make it all right. You think on it."

Tully stood in the parking lot for he didn't know how long after his father had driven away. Other patients came in, the dogs snarling and snapping at him or cowering on their leashes, the cats hissing at him from their crates. A stallion horse, brought in for treatment in the back where they took the farm animals, busted out of his trailer before his owner could even get out of her truck and took off running down the street, half the vet staff running after him. And the whole time Tully didn't move a muscle until Jamie came outside with a bandaged Rico in a makeshift crate and a bag of medicine hanging from her fist. She stopped beside him, studying him without saying a word.

"He says he wants to put the past behind us."

Jamie shrugged. "Well—"

"Don't tell me what you think I want to hear, Jamie," he cut in, desperate to hear truth. Absolute truth. "Tell me what you feel."

"What I feel?" She let out a breath. "I feel like I want a chocolate shake from the McDonald's down the street. I feel that Rico is going to really milk the sympathy as long as she can. And I feel if your father had half a chance, he'd cut your throat and leave you bleeding out by the lake I accidentally poisoned. But what's in your favor is that he wants something. And he's not going to make a move until he gets it. But if you push him out now, he'll only be back later. Maybe at a real bad time. I'm a big fan of waiting to see what people will do rather than simply reacting. Just make sure you're ready for him. Anyway . . . that's my opinion." She tugged on his T-shirt. "Come on. Let's get that shake." Then suddenly, she surprised him and, he was guessing, herself, by going on her toes and kissing his cheek. Her brown eyes blinked wide and then she tossed out, trying to sound casual, "That's for coming with me today. And for last night."

And for the first time since his father had driven off, Tully suddenly saw everything around him in crystal perfection. The blue sky above, the dusty dirt at his feet, the stallion charging back up the opposite side of the street, the vet techs and owner still trying to catch him, and the amazing ass hanging out from the back passenger side of the SUV as Jamie placed the crate with her bird inside the vehicle. After a few minutes of outright rude ogling by him, he heard Jamie let out an annoyed sigh and she turned to face him. "Mind giving me a hand, Tully?"

He refused to move because he didn't know what she wanted a hand with.

"She won't settle down back here. I think you may have to hold her."

*The bird. She's talking about the bird.* Which was a good thing, because if she was talking about something else, they wouldn't be leaving this parking lot for hours and Colton City was a family-friendly town. In the end it wouldn't be right. It would be fun . . . but not right.

At least not yet.

# Chapter Eight

Jamie parked her SUV and stepped out. She'd already taken Rico back home and left her walking on the furniture, pretending she was too weak to fly. Now Jamie was back at the hotel to check in with her coven. Especially Sen.

She walked up the porch stairs and was reaching for the door when she heard, "I talked to my boys. They're real sorry 'bout what happened."

She stopped and slowly faced Buck Smith. He sat in one of the rocking chairs that littered the wraparound porch. He watched her with eyes like his son's. But he was bulkier than Tully, dangerously large. The kind of guy she'd never want to be caught alone in an alley with.

"It was just a misunderstanding." She gave him the same smile she used to give perps she was sure had killed someone, but didn't have the proof yet to prove it.

"You ain't like the other covens."

She walked over to him but didn't get too close. There were just some people in the world she didn't get too close to. Buck Smith was definitely one of them. "You could say that."

"Y'all are definitely a lot prettier. Those Midwestern ones they had the last few years looked like they belonged behind a plow."

Jamie's laugh was real.

"So you and my boy together?"

That seemed an odd question coming from an uncaring father. "No. Just good friends."

"Something tells me you don't have a lot of friends."

"And something tells me you don't have any. But hey," she said before he could reply, "that's not why you're here. You're here to see your son. To mend that bridge. That's what you told Tully, right?"

"Yeah. Right."

He studied her and Jamie didn't flinch, nor did she look away. She didn't know what he was looking at or looking for but she'd be damned if she backed off of anyone. It was something she learned as a cop. Show any weakness and the scumbags would wipe you out before you took your next breath.

"There you are." Wanda waved from the path leading to the hotel. The woman hadn't even gotten ten feet when Jamie's eyes watered. *Does she bathe in that scent?*

Maybe Jamie wouldn't back off in a firefight or facing down Tully's sperm donor, but she'd be damned if she'd stay around for that smell. By the time Wanda made it to the porch, Jamie was walking inside the hotel, closing the door firmly behind her. She sneezed twice and Emma grinned at her from the front desk.

"Wanda?" she asked.

"We're totally going to have to fumigate her room when they leave."

Tully relaxed back in the half-circle booth at his favorite bar. It wasn't the fanciest one in town, but it was the most comfortable, had his favorite beer, and the best live reggae music anywhere on the East Coast.

As it turned out, soothing Caribbean sounds were just what he needed right now. He needed to be soothed. He needed to relax. Not easy when all he felt was uptight and stressed out because his father was up to something.

Tully sipped his beer, listened to the music, and let his mind turn until Kyle sat down on one side of him and Katie sat on the other.

"So how's that bird?" Kyle asked before taking the beer out of Tully's hand.

"Probably dive-bombing squirrels."

Katie rested her head on Tully's shoulder. "I think it's so sweet, you going with Jamie to take care of her bird."

"And, yep," Kyle muttered, "said out loud it does sound stupid."

Tully kissed the top of his baby sister's head. "It was the right thing to do."

"Why?" Kyle asked, placing the now-empty beer bottle back in Tully's hand. "It's not your fault. Seems to me if anyone went with her it should have been Luther."

"Luther Ray Smith in the same car with Jamie Meacham?"

"Why not? Set up a camera in the car for that trip and we could have sold that mess to pay-per-view."

The brothers laughed while Katie tugged on Tully's long-sleeved T-shirt. "What's going on with you and Jamie?"

"Nothing."

"Are you sure? 'Cause if you're going to get serious, she's going to have to stop calling me Snaggle."

"I'll talk to her about that," Tully said quickly and loudly to cover up Kyle's laugh.

Jamie walked in to the bar and immediately stopped. "A reggae bar in the middle of Nowhere, North Carolina," she said to her coven. "I find this a little frightening."

Sen pushed past her, once again all smiles and cheer. Her rage from that afternoon already forgotten. "You've missed some bands! I told you to come with me before, but no. You never listen!" She stepped farther into the bar and a table full of enormous men called out her name.

"See you guys later!" She ran off and launched herself at the biggest male there.

"Bears," Mac said next to Jamie.

"Polar, to be specific," Kenny added.

"Where was I when this happened?"

"We've been asking ourselves that a lot lately."

Jamie let out a breath, way too tired for this conversation. "Don't start, Mac."

"I wasn't. You asked a question, I answered it."

"Is it love?" Jamie asked.

"For now," Emma said, looking around the bar until she caught sight of Kyle and walked off.

"I hope it lasts until next winter," Kenny sighed out and both cousins turned to look at her.

"*You* want Sen to be happy and in love?" Jamie asked.

"Until winter time."

Mac shrugged. "Why?"

"Because . . . I wanna be there when she finds her polar-bear sweetheart splayed out on one of the frozen man-made saltwater lakes, patiently waiting for one of those baby seals we'll have flown in just for this reason to pop its head up so the polar can snatch it out of the ice cold water, tear it open, and devour it like a Girl Scout Thin Mint cookie."

"She really drives you crazy doesn't she?"

"Yes! Because no one should be that fucking perky and *mean it!*" She let out a breath, once again relaxed. "And on that note, I'm going home." When Jamie frowned, she added, "Gaming." As if that should explain everything and for Jamie and Mac . . . it did.

"You staying?" Jamie asked Mac.

"I could go for a drink."

"Yeah. Me, too." Jamie handed over the SUV keys to Kenny. "Take the car, we'll walk back."

"You sure?"

"Yep."

Together Mac and Jamie headed toward the bar but Emma was motioning them over. When they ignored her, she yelled out, "Hey!"

Jamie sighed as the pair changed course. "Remember when she was the painfully shy, insecure one?"

"Heady days."

"Now that she's getting regular cock, she's extremely pushy and demanding."

"Magick cat cock," her cousin whispered in her ear, which sounded so funny to Jamie she was still laughing when they arrived at the booth. And when Kyle said "Hey, y'all," the laughing only got worse.

"What's so funny?" Emma asked.

"Don't mind her," Mac said, pushing Jamie toward a chair.

"Wait," Katie said, sliding out of the booth. "I want that seat."

Mac stared at the chair. "Why?"

"Don't argue." Katie took Jamie's arm and shoved her into the booth. Jamie had finally stopped laughing until she looked at who she was sitting next to. Tully winked at her and gave her the biggest, cheesiest grin—which made her start laughing all over again, this time Tully laughing with her.

"*What?*" Emma demanded.

"I can't believe you actually ordered Long Island Iced Tea," Tully said to Jamie as she sipped her drink. "That's so cliché."

Jamie reached over and picked up his beer bottle. She held it up with the Coors label showing and Tully shrugged. "If it's good enough for NASCAR . . ."

"I don't even know what that sentence means."

"Yankee."

"Hillbilly."

Tully glared at her. "Do you know how wrong it is to call me that?"

"I didn't mean—"

"I don't even live in the hills."

Rolling her eyes, Jamie handed him his beer and relaxed back into the booth.

"You look tired," he told her.

"Gee, thanks."

He leaned back until their shoulders were touching. "I don't mean you look tired and old and it's time to put you in a nice old folks' home."

"Is this your idea of a pep talk?"

"I just mean you look worn out."

She sipped her drink. "Maybe I am. A little. Nothing to worry about."

But he wasn't sure he believed her.

"Are you getting enough sleep?"

"Are you seriously asking me about my sleep habits while we're listening to pretty good reggae, enjoying our favorite alcoholic beverages, and have so many people around us to make fun of?"

"Yes. I am. You know I like to take care of you. Wipe your nose when you've got the sniffles. Feed you when you're hungry . . . burp you when you're gassy."

"I don't even have a response for that."

His phone rang and while he pulled it out of his back pocket he said, "If you could excuse me a moment, beautiful. My adoring constituency is calling."

"It's your mother."

Without looking at the caller ID, Tully said into the phone, "Momma?"

"Hi, sweetheart. Do you have a minute?"

"Yeah, Momma. Hold on." He covered up the mouthpiece. "You freak me out."

"You and so many others."

Shaking his head, he went back to his call. "What's up, Momma?"

"I need to talk to you about something."

"It wasn't me," he responded automatically. Just like he'd been doing for the last twenty-five years. "It was Kyle. He's evil, you know? He's a cat."

"What are you going on about?"

"I'm pawning the blame off on my idiot brother. That's what I do." Tully grinned at the cat who was glaring at him while the cute little witch sat in his lap.

"You just leave your brother alone, Tully Smith," she laughed. "And nothing is wrong. But I did want to talk to you before I talk to your daddy."

"Talk to me about what?"

"The call I got a little while ago. From your father."

All the humor flooded out of him and he asked, "What did he want?"

"Now, pup, before you go gettin' all upset, let me say he was ever so nice." Tully knew it for fact. Knew his momma was the nicest woman on the planet. It was the Southern belle in her. The charming sweetness of her made more than one predatory female wonder how Millie MacClancy managed to live in a house with Tully, Kyle, and Jack without killing any of them. But that was her way and, on most, her innate kindness brought out the kindness in others. Even Jack Treharne. But Jack had proved himself to Tully a hundred times over. Buck had not. And Tully didn't want that old bastard hanging around his momma until he did.

"I'm sure he was, Momma, but I still want to know why he was calling you at all."

"He wants dinner." Tully didn't know he was snarling until he realized the witches at the table were all staring at him. Mac and Emma looked ready to bolt. Jamie just smirked. "Now calm down," his mother went on. "He wants dinner with all of us. You, me, Jack, Kyle, Katie, Buck's boys and Wanda."

"Momma, I've got a lot going on right now. The Mayor's Spring Dance is taking up a lot of my time and—"

"Tully, I know you don't want to do this. I know and understand that. Really I do. But . . . I just . . . I just want . . ."

Hearing her struggle for words, Tully felt his heart break a little. "You don't want it to seem like you tried to get between us."

She let out a grateful breath. "Yes. Exactly. I understand if you don't want to get too close to Buck. And in the end that's going to be your decision. But one dinner to make sure that's what you want . . . ?"

Anyone else he'd turn them down flat. Anyone else, he'd laugh at them and tell them to go chase their tail. But this wasn't just anyone. This was his momma. The woman who'd done everything to protect him. She loved him unconditionally and for that she deserved whatever she wanted. Especially when she rarely asked for anything except that high-powered vacuum for last Christmas and a half a pound of chocolates for Valentine's Day because, to quote her, "I can't eat a whole pound of chocolates! I have to watch my girlish figure."

Yeah. For Millie MacClancy Treharne, she deserved whatever she wanted, whenever she wanted it. "Of course, Momma. It's just a little thing," he said, using one of her favorite phrases. "I'll definitely go have dinner with Buck. And so will Kyle and Katie. They can't wait."

His siblings glared at him from across the table and he smiled and winked.

He heard his mother let out a soft, relieved sigh. "Thank you, pup."

"Anything for you, Momma. You know that."

"And I appreciate that. But now I gotta get your daddy to agree."

"You're on your own with that, darlin'."

"When it comes to Jack Treharne, I usually am."

They said their good-byes and Tully disconnected the call. He carefully returned his phone to his back pocket, moved his beer and the bowl of chips out of his way, and then slammed his head onto the table.

The pain helped but not as much as he wanted it to.

Jamie put her arm around Tully's shoulders as she wondered how the wood table had survived being attacked by such a remarkably hard head. "Buck up, little—" Tully turned his head so he could glare at her. "Okay. Wrong word to use. How about 'chin up'?"

"Or I can kill him while he sleeps and avoid this dinner all together."

"You should have told Momma no," Katie chastised.

"Can you tell Momma no?" Kyle asked.

She crossed her eyes and grudgingly admitted, "No."

"You should have the dinner at the hotel restaurant." Jamie suggested.

"Why?" Kyle asked.

"If you guys meet Buck at the hotel he's already staying at, you can leave whenever you want. If it's going well, you can stay and enjoy Mac's tolerable food."

"Tolerable?" Mac snapped.

"If it's going *really* well, you can enjoy my superb desserts."

"I hate you more and more every day," Mac muttered.

"But if it goes badly, you're not stranding Buck anywhere. He and his sons are already there. You don't have to worry about who's carpooling with who or who needs directions back to the highway, yada yada. You wanna go, you go."

Tully sat up, his pained expression gone. "You know . . . that's a really good idea."

She sipped her drink before admitting, "What can I say? I've had years of practice getting out of bad family dinners."

Tully walked Jamie and Mac home, swinging by Mac's place first and then heading into the woods toward the coast. Less than a mile from her house, Jamie stopped. When Tully faced her, she smiled and for some crazy reason, he thought she was about to kiss him. And he really wanted her to. He wanted her to kiss him so bad, he could actually taste her on his lips.

But instead she said, "Thanks for walking me."

"I can take you all the way home."

"That's okay."

He stepped in closer. "You afraid to take me to your house, Jamie? Afraid I won't leave until morning?"

"The way this town works?" she laughed. "I *know* you won't leave.

"Wow. You are *cocky*."

"Not cocky. I just know how it works in Shifterville, USA. One night leads into another and into another until one day I look up and all your shit will be in my house and you'll be wondering where your breakfast is."

"Oh, come on."

"I have seen this dance played out again and again for the last ten months I've been here, with couples who I wouldn't in a million years imagine together. Sorry, handsome, but that won't be me. I've done my time, paid my dues . . ." She patted his shoulder. "But thanks for thinking of me."

She stepped away from him and was several feet away when she stopped and looked over her shoulder at him. "And don't follow me to make sure I get home. That's just creepy."

He hated that she knew him so well.

Before walking the last stretch that led to her house, Jamie waited. She wanted to make sure Tully hadn't followed her. She knew he'd do it just to protect her and while she appreciated it, she simply didn't want to deal with the fallout from something like that. And the gods knew there'd be all sorts of fall out.

Confident the wolf had headed on home, Jamie took a breath and raised her hands. She held them palms up, her fingers spread out. She began to chant as she slowly moved the last bit to her home. By the time she was fifty or sixty feet away, they all turned toward her. The power she'd raised between her palms flashed hot and bright and she unleashed it. It flew from her and ripped around the perimeter of her house. When it was done, all was quiet but she knew they'd be back. Knew she'd get no rest tonight, as she'd gotten very little rest in the last few weeks.

Letting out an exhausted sigh, she walked into her house. Rico greeted her at the door, the gyrfalcon back to her old self.

"Hi, honey. I'm home."

The bird squawked at her and Jamie turned in time to see that the spell she'd used—one of her most powerful—had only worked long enough to get her from the road to her house. What she'd sent away had not only returned, but there were more of them now.

One ran at her, charging up the porch stairs. Jamie stepped inside and slammed the door, sealing it shut with a word. But they were banging at the walls now. At the doors and windows. They wanted in, and they wouldn't stop until they got in.

Swallowing down a bolt of panic, Jamie backed into her house and looked around. She was still safe inside although with all that racket, she'd never get any sleep. But if she couldn't sleep, she could research. She went to the bookshelf where she kept her Grimoire and spell books. She pulled off her jacket while her gaze moved through the titles. One book stuck out from the rest but she ignored it. She knew what it would tell her to do to stop the onslaught happening outside her house. It would work too. It would stop all this once and for all.

But she'd made a promise to her cousin. Hell, she'd made a promise to herself. She wouldn't break that promise now.

Still desperate, though, she grabbed other books, a handful of them and went into her living room. She turned her TV on loud and went to work, doing all she could to block out what was happening right outside her house.

# Chapter Nine

For the next two days, Tully spent a bit of time between his Momma's house and the hotel. He couldn't believe he was spending more time arranging this stupid dinner rather than the Mayor's Spring Dance that was coming up.

If nothing else, he got to spend a lot more time with Jamie. Unfortunately, it made him realize he'd been right. She was hiding something. And whatever she was hiding was exhausting her. That great sense of humor and natural sex appeal that drove him to distraction on most days was practically gone. Their discussions about the dinner were straightforward and businesslike, but nothing about Jamie was straightforward and businesslike. That's why they always got along—because he was the same way.

Even when he'd teasingly mentioned her being his date for the dance—whether he was joking or not, he still didn't know—Jamie didn't react in any of the ways he'd expected. Instead of completely blowing him off or, even better, teasing him right back, which was what she'd normally do, she—in a very businesslike way— politely said "No, thank you."

*No, thank you?* Who was this boring woman? Not the tart-tongue viper he'd found himself fantasizing about on more than one occasion, that was for sure. And he wanted his viper back. Now! He had enough going on with his father that the last thing he needed was Jamie acting like she'd been invaded by pod people.

He stopped in the middle of the dirt road that would lead him back to his house. Normally he'd go home, shift, and call his Pack to him for a hunt. But no. He needed to go see Jamie. He looked up at the sky. The sun was still up, so he'd wait until it was dark. No use in pissing her off unnecessarily since that was absolutely no fun.

Jamie used her own blood to reinforce the protections around her home. After that, she moved the furniture in her living room against the wall and set up a sacred space on the hardwood floor. Another reason she'd picked this house—the ginormous living room floor. Perfect for this sort of thing.

The circle made with sea salt took up most of the floor and a giant pentacle drawn inside that made up what she liked to call her "safe zone." She left a small window in the bathroom open so that Rico could get in and out if she wanted to or, if things went horribly wrong, really needed to. After building a fire in the fireplace, Jamie ate a protein-and-carb-rich meal, took a shower, and slipped her favorite NY Islanders hockey jersey on over her naked body. By the time she sat in the middle of the pentacle, the sun was going down.

Wiping her mind clean and focusing on the energy and power within her body, Jamie called on the forces that could protect her. She felt those forces coming toward her, moving from the land, sea, air, and fire in and of this place. She would not call to those powers that could not be contained.

But as those she called neared and the darkness settled in, powerful energies rushed her home, sending those protective forces dashing off and leaving Jamie to once again fight for herself.

The front door was thrown open and without moving from her place on the floor, Jamie slammed it shut again. She felt hands touching her and she swung her arms out, a short but powerful spell on her lips. The energy around her dissipated but the banging started again. Powerful, tortuous banging against the walls, windows, and doors. She covered her ears, trying to block the sounds out, and the front door was thrown open again. She swung it closed by swiping her middle and forefinger through the air.

Then the banging began again.

It had only just begun, but she was already wondering how much more she could take.

\* \* \*

Tully knew as soon as he arrived at Jamie's territory. Like any good predator, her markings were clear and concise, even if they were magickal rather than something excreted from her glands. But as soon as he stepped onto her property, he knew something was wrong. When he could see her house, he stopped for a moment and stared. Then he trotted closer. There was a long single line of them, mostly male, a few female. He moved in closer to the one at the very end. He sniffed him. He could smell the energy. A little like live electricity. The man looked down at him.

"Piss off," he snipped. "Shoo."

*Shoo?*

On a whim, Tully tried to bite him. His jaws went straight through the man's leg, the edges looking gauzy and luminous before closing up again. The man laughed. "Dumb dog."

Snarling at the insult, Tully walked straight through the line toward Jamie's house. As he did, the entities yelled at him and tried to swat him, and although he caused some discomfort from what he could tell, they couldn't touch him. Even though they tried. As he made it to the front of the line, he saw a man shove Jamie's front door open, ethereal muscles bulging as he cried out like he'd just done a dead lift of a thousand-pound weight. But as soon as the door swung open, it slammed closed again, sending the man flipping back until he hit a tree and vanished in a blast of sparks.

Yep. That was definitely an interesting sight. Kind of made the whole flying-hyenas thing a little less . . . shocking.

Another man headed up the stairs but Tully walked right through him—earning a snarled, "Flea-riddled bastard!"—and up to the porch. He pawed at the door a few times, nudged it with his nose, until he finally wrapped his mouth around the knob and turned while walking forward. The door wasn't locked and opened easily for him. He wandered inside and when he saw a female trying to run in behind him, he kicked the door closed with his back legs.

Once inside, Tully walked into the living room. There was a large circle on the floor and inside that a large star. He sat outside the circle and studied Jamie closely. She was sitting cross-legged in the middle of the star, her head down, her face drawn and tired. How long, exactly, was she expected to fight those outside? All night? He wasn't sure she'd last another five minutes, much less the rest of the night.

Lifting his paw, he carefully pressed at the energy surrounding Jamie. He couldn't see the energy, but he knew it was there. Could feel it. His paw, however, easily slipped in while causing no disruption to what she'd created. Satisfied, he walked toward her. He was only a foot or two from her when she looked up, her eyes blinking wide. He tilted his head to the side and she let out a shaky laugh. "That damn earring."

Tully moved in closer, nuzzled her cheek with his snout, and eased around her. By the time he settled in behind her, he'd shifted back to human.

Powerful legs bracketed her legs, and muscular arms rested against her raised knees. He'd entered her circle and shifted to human. She had no idea why.

He grabbed hold of the chalice she'd brought with her into the circle and held the cup to her lips. "Drink up, beautiful."

She did. She'd been so busy defending her territory she'd forgotten to keep hydrated.

"Better?"

She nodded. "You shouldn't be here," she told him.

"Why not?"

"Because when they get in here, there won't be anything you can do, and I don't want you to see what happens next."

"You so sure they'll get in here?"

"What is it? Ten o'clock? Maybe eleven? I can't last until sunrise at this rate."

He sighed. Big and heavy. "There has to be something you can do, because I'm not leaving."

"Why?"

"Because it's not even eight yet, darlin'. So we need to find you some way out of this."

If Jamie were a crier, she'd cry. With no shame she'd cry. *Not even eight? Shit.*

"What exactly is going on?" he asked against her ear. "And no more bullshit. Tell me straight."

Not seeing the point in denying him the entire truth, Jamie

thought for a moment, trying to find the best way to describe it to him. "Ever know a guy in high school who got shut down by some girl he liked? You know, he tried to ask her out and she turned him down flat."

"Yeah. Sure."

"And maybe that guy, because he was so pissed off and wanted to get even, wrote on the boy's bathroom wall, 'Jenny gives great head' and then put her number. And for a week, Jenny's getting a bunch of calls on her parents' phone asking for her to meet to have sex?"

Tully frowned. "Yeah."

"Well, that's kind of the situation I'm in."

"I'm not sure I understand. You turned someone down?"

"I didn't turn him down. I merely argued a point with him."

"With who?"

"Aengus. He's the Celtic god of love and youth."

"And you argued a point with a god?"

"Just a little one."

"Which was?"

"That love is nothing more than a psychotic reaction to really good sex."

"You argue just to argue, don't you?"

Jamie shrugged. "Sometimes."

"And those . . . people outside who are trying to get to you want to . . . uh . . ."

"Fuck me? Maybe some of them. But what they really want is my power." And what Aengus wanted from Jamie was to see her punished for daring to question him. He couldn't touch her himself. Not while The Morrighan protected her, so he'd merely given out information to every mage, witch, and shaman in a thirty-billion radius. Like placing a target on her back for every seeker of power to hone in on and come after. "Aengus wants to push me. To get me to cross a line that will destroy me."

"So what are you going to do?"

"To be honest, Tully . . . I have no fuckin' clue."

Seriously. Who else got into fights with love gods? Most women daydreamed about finding one, tried to turn their spouses and boyfriends into one, or wrote fictional accounts of meeting, seducing, and living happily ever after with one. But not Jamie Meacham. Nope. She started fights with them just . . . because.

And Tully didn't think he'd have her any other way. If nothing else, she was damn entertaining.

"So the short of it is . . . you're in a heap of trouble."

"Pretty much."

"Can't your coven help?"

"Not without Aengus coming after them next." Did she realize she'd relaxed back against him? Did she have any idea how good she felt? "Aengus wants me going through this all on my own. Without any help from them and without any help from you."

Tully shrugged, trying hard to look innocent. "But . . . he doesn't even know me."

How the man managed to annoy and soothe her all at the same time, she had no idea. She just knew she was glad he was here with her while at the same time she wished he would leave. She'd prefer he not be here when it all went to hell. She had enough of an audience, thanks.

"We both know I'm not leaving you to face those things alone, beautiful. Might as well face it."

"You can't stay, Tully."

"Why not?"

"Because once they get in . . ."

"It sounds like you've already given up."

"Maybe I have," she sighed.

"Well, don't. Come on, beautiful. That devious mind of yours must have something left. Something we can use."

"Yeah. Sure. Sacrifices," she spit out. "An offering to Aengus in blood from an innocent victim. Certain animals are good, humans are even better." She rubbed her eyes with her knuckles. "But I'm not doing that." Because she knew that's what Aengus wanted. She wouldn't give him that. She wouldn't hand him her soul just to protect her body.

"Well, I don't want you to do that either."

The banging started again and she covered her ears, not sure that Tully could hear anything. For all he knew she was just a psychotic having an "episode."

"But there has to be something, Jamie. Anything," he pushed, giving her a little shake, trying hard to help her, but she was so tired and the banging . . .

Jamie heard the distinctive cry of Rico and looked up to see her circling over their heads.

"What's that bird holding?"

Before Jamie could answer, she ducked as Rico released a thick book right onto Tully's head.

"Ow! *That damn bird!*"

She cringed even as she tried not to laugh. "I'm sorry." Rico really hated him, and Jamie had no idea why.

Rubbing where the book had hit him with one hand, Tully reached for the tome with the other. Jamie glanced at the book, saw the title and, feeling a sudden surge of energy, made a mad grab for it. Tully caught hold of her, his arm tight around her waist, and held the book out of her reach with that long arm.

"What's wrong?" he asked, eyeing her close.

"Nothing. Just give me the book."

"Why?"

"Because I'm telling you to *give me the book*."

Not surprisingly, he didn't. He had to be the most contrary canine she'd ever dealt with. He did not take orders well. Instead he flipped the book over and looked at the cover.

"*Sex Magick*," he read out loud. "Now, beautiful," and she didn't have to look at him to know the trifling bastard was grinning from ear to ear, "you know I'm willing to do whatever it takes to help you out. As many times as necessary."

Tully would admit that the stupid bird was starting to grow on him. And he wouldn't worry too much about whether it could read or not for the damn thing to grab *this* book from Jamie's extensive library.

He held up the book and asked Jamie straight out, "Can this work or not?"

"Yeah," she said on a sigh. "Yeah, it can work."

"Then why haven't you done it before now?"

"I need a partner."

"Well, I've got that covered. What else?"

"Tully—"

"What else?"

"The gods are natural voyeurs but they're not easy to please. We would need to be"—she cleared her throat—"entertaining."

"Nothing to worry about. I can make anyone entertaining."

She looked at him over her shoulder, one brow up. "I was worried about me making *you* entertaining."

"You don't have to throw down a gauntlet to get me to play along."

Jamie laughed but shook her head. "It's a very sweet offer, Tully, but I'm still going to say no."

"Why?"

"Because this is still magick, Tully. And you're a nice Christian . . . man-wolf thing."

"Gee. Thanks."

"I can't get you involved in this," she went on. "I *won't* get you involved in this."

"Seems you ain't got much choice since I'm not going to leave you here by yourself to deal with whatever is outside that door." He hated having to ask, but he did anyway. "If there's someone else in town you're more interested in and they're not mated, I can call 'em and see if they'll—owwww!"

Jamie jumped. "I didn't say anything yet!"

"Not you. It's that damn bird. Damn near pulled the hair from my head." He glared up at the winged bastard now glaring at him from the top of Jamie's bookcases. "What is her problem anyway?"

Jamie briefly closed her eyes, knowing exactly what was going on. When she spoke, it was to Rico. "Forget it."

The bird's feathers bristled and Tully said, "Maybe you shouldn't piss her off. I like my eyes to stay in my head, thank you very much. Besides," he added, leaning in close, "I like how her mind works. She knows this is the right thing to do. And so do you."

"Look, most sex magick rituals involve couples who've been together for a bit." Hell, was that the best argument she could come up with? And it would really help if he moved his lips away from the tip of her ear, the sensation made her want to squirm.

"Is that required?"

"No. But couples that aren't so well acquainted get . . . *tests* done. You know? To make sure that—"

"Yeah. I know. Well, are you adverse to condoms?"

"Not on a daily basis, but latex in my power circle? Why don't you bring in some acid rain too?"

Tully didn't answer and for a brief, surprisingly sad moment, she thought she'd won the fight. Until he said, "Look, do you trust your bird or not?"

Slowly, Jamie turned her head to look at Tully and asked, "Did you just ask me that out loud?"

"Yes. And I enjoyed it so much, I'm asking it again. Do you trust your bird?"

Jamie lifted her hands and let them drop. She'd completely run out of fight at this point. It had all gotten too weird—and her nipples were hard. "Yes, Tully. I . . . trust my bird."

"Do you think she'd do anything to hurt you? That she'd put you at risk?"

And, for one brief moment, she kind of hated the big, dumb hick. Because he'd found the perfect counterpoint to any argument she could come up with. Her connection to Rico was beyond owner and pet. The falcon had chosen Jamie, had guided her, aided her, and did what she could to protect her in all things magickal. Jamie knew, in her gut, that Rico would never harm her, never put her in a situation that would harm her.

And clearly, based on the way Rico's feathers kept bristling, this was what Rico wanted for Jamie. Knew that it was the safest choice she could make at the moment. Perhaps the only choice at the moment that would protect her soul and . . . well . . . the rest of her.

The front door swung open and, with a healthy snarl, Jamie slammed it closed again with a swipe of her fingers.

She looked back at him and he noticed that she no longer appeared as weak, much less drawn. If arguing with him was already helping, he could just imagine what a good fuck between them could do.

"Fine," she finally snapped, "let's just get this over—owwww!" Jamie covered the side of her neck with her fingers.

"Lord, are you all—*owwww!*"

Pain shot through his neck and Tully glared at that damn bird again! What the hell did she think she was doing anyway? He wiped the spot she'd nipped with her beak and his fingers came away with blood.

"Your bird has lost its damn mind!"

The falcon dropped in front of them, outside of the pentacle, but still inside the circle. She spit a glob of blood on the floor—their blood mixed together, Tully was guessing—and using her talons, Rico dragged a line of blood around the pentacle until she'd created another circle. When she was done, she looked up at them and gave what Tully could only call a nod.

"You know," Jamie said to the bird, "there was a much less painful way to do—"

The bird let out a high-pitched screech before its wings unfurled and it flew at them, talons first.

"Okay! Okay!" Jamie said when those talons moved a little too close to her eyes, her head buried against Tully's chest. "Don't yell at me!"

"It was more a squawk," Tully observed.

"Shut up."

"No call to get nasty."

The bird went back to its perch on the bookshelves and watched them.

"So is that it?" he asked.

"Except for the main event . . . pretty much. She created a circle of protection all on her own, so I don't have to bother. How kind," she sneered at Rico.

"Don't get that bird angry, woman. She's psychotic. And can she create birth control? You know, magickally?"

"What?"

"I like ya, Jamie, but . . ."

"I'm on the Pill, chief."

He reached around her and clapped his hands together. "Then let's get this thing started!"

"First off, feel free to curb your abundant enthusiasm. You're making me nervous."

"Sorry."

"And second, I don't want any regrets from you come morning."

"Regrets?"

"Whining. Complaining. Don't act like I took advantage of you and *do not* get attached. Understand?"

"Will I have horns?" he asked.

Jamie rubbed her temples with the tips of her fingers. "What?"

"When we're done . . . will I have horns?" A completely legitimate question in his estimation.

"No."

"Will I be alive to relive this in my fantasies? Or will my mind be wiped clean, so all that's left is an exquisite but useless shell of my former self? Wandering around town all day . . . drooling?"

"How's that different from what you do now?"

Grateful to hear the cruel teasing of Jamie Meacham, he grabbed her waist to tickle her, but she begged, "No tickling!"

"And," he went on, "will I still have all my important bits and pieces? Especially the one currently pressing into your back, since I am so fond of it."

"Yes, you'll have all your bits and pieces." And he knew she wanted to add, "You asshole."

"Then I think we're ready to roll."

"This isn't a road trip, Tully," and she sounded just like a chastising mother. "This is sex magick. That means all I need from you is a hard cock, a decent amount of stamina, and enough skill to get me off at least once." Well . . . that *last* part didn't sound too motherly.

"Hmm . . ." he said thoughtfully, trying hard not to laugh, "I *think* I can manage that."

Jamie focused across the room and blew out a breath. "Great."

# Chaper Ten

Jamie didn't know what was happening. How everything had gotten so out of control in such a short amount of time. And now it seemed as if there was only one way to get herself out of it. She glanced at the man sitting behind her.

*Well, things could definitely be worse.*

At least he was gorgeous and the steel pipe currently pressing into her back suggested he could handle the basics of the act. She'd have to run the show, of course, because entertaining gods was not an easy task for any mortal. After traversing the earth for millennia after millennia, they'd seen everything and seen it more than once. It wasn't that they always needed porn-quality entertainment. Long-term couples often received the gods' blessings because of the emotion behind the act, because of the love the partners held for each other. Since there was none of that here at the moment, Jamie and Tully would have to go with skill.

It had been at least a decade, maybe more, since Jamie had done this sort of thing but she had little choice at this point. Especially since even the bird was now in on it.

Already feeling a bit of her energy returning, Jamie decided to get this thing moving. She tried to sit up so she could face Tully, but the arm he had around her waist held her in place. His free arm came around and the tips of his fingers brushed along her cheek, her jaw. He gripped her chin and turned her face toward him. He studied her a long moment before his head lowered and his lips touched hers.

It was a sweet kiss, taking Jamie by surprise. But it also made her uncomfortable. She didn't want to confuse the issue. They had one goal here and she was determined to see it through as quickly and efficiently as possible. She dragged her tongue along his lips and when his mouth opened, she dived in, boldly stroking the inside of his mouth.

He groaned and Jamie again tried to pull herself up and away so she could push him to his back and take over, but the arm around her only tightened. He was fighting her and she didn't know why. She would have asked him, too, if their kiss hadn't turned from sweet to urgent, Tully's tongue pushing past hers and invading her mouth.

He began to move, going to his knees and bringing her up with him. His free hand slid down her chest, briefly stopping to stroke her breasts before continuing down past her stomach and sliding between her legs. Jamie let out a whimper as his fingers caressed her. She gripped his arm but didn't try to stop him. She didn't want to stop him. It felt really good.

If he was trying to get her wet, she was there, but again, he didn't seem to be in any rush. One of his fingers dipped inside her, followed by another. She groaned, her hips pushing down on his hand. He pulled his mouth away from her and the hand around her waist released her long enough to move up to her hair. He took firm hold and tugged her head back. He kissed her again, then said, "I am dying to see you come."

The grip at the nape of her neck tightened and his gaze traveled down the length of her body.

"Pull your shirt up a bit, beautiful. I wanna see everything."

Following his direction, she grabbed the hem of her jersey and pulled it up until it was under her breasts.

"You are damn luscious, Jamie Meacham." She might have had a response if she wasn't so busy panting, her body rolling with each thrust of his fingers. He tugged again on her hair and she bent farther back. "Pull your shirt up higher. Over your breasts."

Again, following his directions without wondering why, she did what he asked. "Thank you," he murmured before his warm mouth wrapped around her nipple and began to suck.

With her hands holding her shirt and her body bent back in such an awkward position, Jamie realized she couldn't do anything at the moment except feel what he was doing to her.

And, uh . . . what he was doing to her felt *really* good.

Even with his mouth on her breast, Tully couldn't look away from the sight of his hand stroking in and out of Jamie's pussy. He'd never felt anything so hot and wet before. So damn tight. The way she squeezed his fingers was making him absolutely insane. He wanted to make her come like this. He wanted to stand here and watch her writhe all over his hand. But it wasn't the right time yet. She needed more.

Before he pulled out of her, he used his thumb to slowly caress her clit until he felt her legs begin to shake. That's when he stopped.

She let out a strained moan and he felt her tense in his arms. Before she could pull away—something she'd been trying to do since they'd started down this road—he lifted her shirt up and off and chucked it outside the circle. He then spread her out on the floor before lifting up her legs and placing them on his shoulders. Rather than going down on her, he pulled her up until she rested on her shoulders. He nuzzled his nose against her clit, heard her whimper and knew she was still too close. He brought his mouth down and slid his tongue inside her. She gasped, her hands slapping down against the hardwood floor, her back arching as he fucked her pussy with his mouth and tongue. She wiggled her hips and he gripped her legs tight, not wanting her to move until he let her. He liked having her like this—trapped and wet and at his mercy.

He licked and nipped until she was clawing at the floor, then he sucked her clit into his mouth and nursed it between his lips until her body tightened again—and that's when he stopped.

Jamie slammed her fists down on the floor. The sound seemed magnified, rolling through the room and right out of the house. He thought he heard screams from outside, but he wasn't sure and he was too desperate to really care.

He knew when they started this they were doing it for some reason, but damn if he could remember what that was now. In fact, he couldn't think past the woman in his arms.

Tully placed her legs on the floor and leaned over her, his hand cupping her cheek. He gazed down at her and she shook her head. "Don't, Tully." But he couldn't stop himself. And he didn't really want to. He lowered himself down, stretching out. He didn't lay on top of her, but to the side, his right leg pressed between her thighs, his hand caressing her face.

"Damn, you're beautiful."

"This"—she swallowed, took a breath—"this isn't going to help anything."

"Help what?" Then he was kissing her, slow and easy like he had all the time in the world. She tried to turn away, but his hand against her cheek kept her right where she was and the knee pressing against her pussy, kept her right on edge. He kissed her until she kissed him back and that's when he felt confident enough to move his hand from her cheek and slide it down her body. He teased her nipples, stroked her belly while he continued to kiss her mouth. He languished in the beauty of her, reveling in everything about her.

When he knew he needed more, that he could no longer wait, she had her hands dug in his hair and her hips rocking back and forth, her pussy working on his knee. He had no idea how long they were like that, simply enjoying each other. But he knew when it was time to move, rolling her onto her stomach, sliding his arms under her, he lifted her up until she was on her knees. She braced herself with her hands but he wanted control of her pleasure so he caught hold of her hands and pulled her arms around until he had them at the small of her back. He gripped both wrists in one hand while he took his cock and led it to her pussy. Tully had never been inside a woman without a condom, not even as a teen popping his cherry for the first time, and the thought he was about to do it now and do it with Jamie had him so hard it was painful.

Placing the head of his cock against the mouth of her pussy, he pressed in far enough so he could move his hand away. Once done, he straightened up, his free hand siding across her back. Her pussy clenched hard and Tully's eyes crossed at the sensation. He took a breath, gave himself a moment, and then shoved his hips forward, his cock powering into her.

They both gasped out, Jamie whimpering after as Tully held himself for a long moment inside her. His head thrown back, his breath coming out hard, he had to admit, he didn't know if he would ever experience anything more astounding than being inside this woman. Then again, maybe that was just his cock talking, because it was so damn happy.

Jamie's fingers wiggled in his grasp and he understood she was more than ready. Tully tightened his grip on her wrists and gripped her right shoulder with his free hand, holding her steady for him. He pulled his hips back and then slammed them forward.

Jamie cried out. And she did it again each time he pushed into her, each time he took her. When it sounded like she was about to come, he stopped pushing and instead slowly ground his hips against her. After the third time, she panted out, "Tully, come on. Please!"

Unable to wait any longer, he released his grip on her shoulder and brought his hand down between her thighs. He brushed his fingers against her clit and Jamie's body immediately began to shake. He pounded into her while his fingers drew the orgasm from her.

When it came, it was as powerful as a hurricane, her entire body tightening before she exploded around him, her pussy clamping down on his cock like an industrial-strength vise. He let go a shout and, with his fingers keeping Jamie's orgasm going, he came hard inside her, his toes curling, his body shuddering over hers. When he was completely spent, he crashed on top of her and, assuming it was his mind playing tricks on him, as soon as their skin touched light exploded all around them, blasting from their joined bodies and bursting through the room and out of the house.

It was the last thing he remembered, too, before everything went black.

# Chapter Eleven

Jamie heard the banging at the door but she was relieved to realize it was merely a human being at her door rather than something . . . else.

A bit confused—for instance, why was she naked in her living room?—she glanced around but the brightness coming from outside the windows made it impossible for her morning gaze to take in any details. Although she did realize one thing—she wasn't alone.

She glanced over and saw Tully Smith sleeping next to her. He was turned away, his arms around him like he was cold. Then again . . . she was cold. Freezing cold. Maybe the AC kicked on during the night. She didn't know and she didn't really care at the moment because the banging started up again.

"Yeah, yeah. Hold on." She stood and was about to open the circle she'd created the night before . . . but it was gone. The blood, the salt, the raw power. All of it gone. That was strange. Most times the power of her circles lasted for twenty-four hours unless it was taken down by someone else. And the items she used to visually create the circle lasted until she cleaned them up. She examined the room and didn't see anything that suggested those who'd wanted in had gotten in. She even took a moment to go inside herself and she was pretty confident there was no one else in there.

She got to her feet and walked over to the couch, grabbing a blanket. She wrapped it around her naked body and walked to the front door. It was slow going, though, with her body feeling sore as if she'd run a marathon the day before.

Arriving at the door, Jamie cleared her throat and opened it. She looked at the huge expanse of chest taking up her doorway and raised her gaze up to what had to be nearly seven feet of cranky male.

"Hi, Sheriff."

"Miss Jamie," he said with that unbelievably low voice and with a tip of his head, his fingers touching the brim of his Sheriff's Department baseball cap. She had to admit, no matter how cranky the man ever got, he was always so damn polite. The perfect Southern gentleman.

She blew out a breath which tossed the hair covering her face out of the way. "What can I do for you?"

"Explain something to me."

"If I can."

"Why's there snow? And cold?"

Jamie frowned. "Sorry?"

"Snow, Miss Jamie. In the middle of May."

Jamie shrugged. "Freak storm?"

"I'd believe that except"—he moved his shoulder so she could see over it—"I don't think I've ever seen so many flowers blossom during a freak snow storm."

Jamie stepped into the doorway and looked at either end of her porch since Bear didn't seem to be in a mood to move out of her way more than he already had. She was wide awake now. Wide awake and shocked. Especially since she didn't have flowers in her garden. She hadn't been in the mood to try, so she hadn't bothered. Now she had a fucking garden covering the front and sides of her house, down the path and into the woods.

"It's all over town," the cranky male went on. "Flowers and snow damn near everywhere. I was hoping you could explain that to me."

"Uh . . ." *Oh, shit. Oh, shit. Oh, shit.*

"What's going on?" that voice said behind her and Jamie cringed, wondering why the damn wolf couldn't stay put until she'd gotten rid of McMahon.

The sheriff eyed Tully, then eyed Jamie. Then he eyed Tully

being naked except for one of her blankets around his hips. Then he eyed Jamie being naked except for the blanket she wore.

"I'm hoping this isn't some kind of trouble I need to worry about, Miss Jamie," Bear finally said.

"Uh, no. The snow will melt and, uh, the flowers can always be removed. Or kept, if someone wants to. Should bring them years of enjoyment."

He grunted—no, really, he *grunted*—and turned away from her. She watched him walk down her porch steps and, as he moved lower and lower, she saw what had been behind him the entire time . . . her coven.

Their gazes moved back and forth between her and Tully, even while their expressions remained frustratingly blank. They were all dressed in thick winter clothing and sipping Starbucks coffee from those paper cups except Kenny who had her own steel travel mug since she had what could only be called a serious addiction to overpriced coffee beans from foreign countries.

Bear, with a nod to the coven, walked around his inhumanly and not-very-PC SUV, got in, and drove away.

Tully stepped into the doorway beside her. "I guess it worked then, huh?"

"Seems so."

"Good. Will they be back?"

"Doubt it."

"All right."

They turned at the same time and faced each other.

"Jamie—" he began.

"Thanks," she said softly.

Then she shoved him out onto the porch, closed and locked her door, and headed off to the shower.

Tully slid to a stop on the front porch, a few splinters digging into the bottom of his left foot. The door slammed behind him and he spun around in time to hear locks turned. His mouth open, he stared at that closed door. She'd just thrown him out of her house. No breakfast, no morning fuckin', no nothing! He'd been treated better by she-lions the morning after too much tequila and barbeque at the Fourth of July Smithville Annual Picnic.

Not only that—but there was snow on the ground! She'd thrown him out in the snow!

Tully glared at the door again, debating whether he wanted to simply pick the locks or kick the dang door in. But before he could do either, Mac was beside him, pulling out her own keys and opening the door. She stepped inside, holding the door open as the rest of the coven walked in. They all looked at him as they walked by but no one, not even little Emma, said a word to him. And when Kenny, the last, finally made it inside, Mac stared at him for a long moment before she shook her head and quietly closed the door in his face.

He'd just been dismissed. By witches! Tossed out like yesterday's trash. And to be quite honest, he didn't like the feeling at all.

But it wasn't that simple, was it? It was Jamie that had him frowning, something he prided himself on not doing much of since most of the men in his family—blood and family by marriage—seemed to have been born frowning. It was the High Priestess who had him wanting to kick that door back open, toss those other witches out, before slamming Jamie up against the wall and fucking her blind. Making her come until she screamed his name so that everyone in town heard it and knew . . . knew . . .

*Lord.*

And knew who she belonged to.

The one thing she said she didn't want to happen. The one thing she said she had absolutely no interest in. She didn't want to be "attached," was her word. And she'd said the word the same way he said "taxes" in April.

Tully shook his head. Good Lord, what was he doing? It was one night. One time.

Deciding the last thing he needed to do was go back in that house, Tully raised his foot and pulled out the splinters before shifting to wolf and heading off the witch's territory.

Jamie stepped out of her shower. She'd scrubbed every bit of Tully Smith off her but she could still feel him everywhere. Inside and out. And she didn't like it. She didn't like it because once she was done, she was done. Even with her ex-husband, she didn't sit around *feeling* him after they'd gone a round or two. She'd forget him as soon as she turned over—and she liked things that way. She considered it a skill actually, and appreciated it as such. So where was her skill now?

Wrapping a towel around her, she walked into her bedroom and found her coven sprawled on her bed, floor, and witch's chest. Sen held up a cup of coffee for her and Jamie gratefully took it. They all watched her as she sipped her coffee and she watched them back.

She wasn't exactly sure how long that went on for but finally Jamie said, "Well?"

Mac, sitting on the old witch's chest that held all of Jamie's most-used witch items, raised her leg until the heel of her boot rested at the edge of the chest, her arm around her knee. "Well . . . I have to say we're damn proud of you right now."

Jamie didn't think anything could have surprised her more as that one sentence, especially coming from her cousin. But she hadn't counted on the sentence that followed.

"Because I had money on you sacrificing a human to get out of this thing with Aengus. It never occurred to me you'd go with sex magick."

"We're so relieved we didn't have to kill you first!" Sen said with a happy clap of her hands. And all Jamie could do as she looked into those beaming faces was stare.

Tully was stretched out on a large boulder when he saw his parents. They were both bundled up in their winter clothes and his mother clutched a bunch of flowers in one hand while she held his daddy's hand with the other. They were laughing and chatting, simply enjoying the day as was the rest of the town. As Tully had headed over here, he'd seen his neighbors building snowmen, having snowball fights, sledding down hills, and hunting down elk until snow in some of the prime hunting spots was drenched in blood. If anyone was concerned about the fact that there'd been a sudden snow storm combined with a burst of seasonal and unseasonal bloomings it didn't show at all.

His momma spotted him first, grinning and waving at him as Jack walked her over.

"Mornin', my pup." She kissed his forehead and scratched his neck until his back leg tore at the boulder he was on, leaving marks. "Wonderful day, isn't it?"

Tully barked in reply and she kissed him again. "I'm going over there to get some of those blue flowers. They're so pretty!"

"Careful now," Jack cautioned her before he leaned back against the boulder, his arms crossed over his chest. "This is all just weird. Your momma loves it, but the snow and the flowers . . . I think it's weird."

Tully laughed, the sound coming out as a soft bark.

"I've never liked any of this witch stuff. Doesn't seem natural, if you ask me."

*But shifting from human to a four-legged puma . . . completely natural.*

"But they have a purpose here, so I won't bother complaining."

*You complain when you breathe.*

"Anyway, when I saw all this when I woke up, I called up the other Elders and Miss Gwen had Bear look into it. Kind of surprised to hear you were at that woman's house. Naked."

*I've never been a fan of fucking while clothed.*

Jack stared down at him. "You going to answer me or you going to sit there looking like a big, dumb dog?"

Tully shifted. "Not sure what you want me to say."

"You had something to do with all this?"

"I was there to offer a helpful—"

"Cock?"

"I was going to say hand."

"I'm sure either word will do." Jack shook his head. "I don't know what you were thinking. Involving yourself with that woman."

"I'm not involved with anything, Daddy. She threw me out after Bear left."

"That surprises you?"

"A little."

"She's a cold girl, no matter how much she smiles. You're just lucky she didn't shoot you in the back of the head when she was done with you."

"She's not that bad."

"I'm bettin' you're the only one who thinks so."

"You've never liked her."

He shrugged. "Don't need to. It ain't my job to like anybody." Jack glanced at him. "And you're a fool if you think you'll be the one to break her."

"Who says I'm trying to break her?"

"It's the only way you'll hold on to someone like her. She's like a wild mustang who only lets you get right up to her so she can kick you in the head."

"Thanks. You've made me feel so much better."

"That ain't my job either."

"Come on, Jackie!" Millie called out, her cheeks bright red from the cold. "Let's go into town and get hot chocolate before it warms up again." She frowned at her son. "Lord, Tully! Put some clothes on before you catch your death!"

"Yes'm."

Jack stood straight, watching Tully's momma in a way that her son still wasn't comfortable with. The feline could at least hide that sort of thing from her only boy!

"You sure about that dinner with Buck?" Jack asked.

"No. But we'll all be there. I'll make sure Momma's safe."

"That man's here for a reason, but I don't think it's your momma. Not this time."

"He says he wants to mend bridges or some such horseshit."

"Do you believe him?"

"Let's just say I'm watching my back."

Jack nodded and followed after Tully's momma. "I'm glad you're doing *something*."

"Thanks for the support, Daddy."

"Whatever."

Jamie, bundled up in her jeans, NY Knicks sweatshirt, boots, and fur-lined parka, stomped through the snow-covered forest, her coven behind her.

"I didn't think you'd take this so personally," Mac called after her.

"You're right," she snapped back. "Why should I take it personally that those closest to me think I'm a murdering *sociopath*?"

"We don't think that," Emma said.

"It's not a big deal," Jamie lied. "It actually allows me to unleash my true homicidal tendencies. I think I'll wipe the town clean and then move on to the world!"

"Jamie!" Mac grabbed her jacket and swung her around. "Would you stop?"

"I don't wanna stop. I wanna walk."

"Can't we just talk?" Sen begged. "For a minute. Please?"

"What's there to say?"

Mac threw up her hands. "Look, I didn't mean to say—"

"That my own cousin thinks I'd kill those of innocent blood? 'Cause that's kind of what you said."

"I didn't mean it like—"

"And you knew!" she accused. "You knew what Aengus was doing. But you were so busy testing me—"

"I needed to know what you'd do. How far you'd go."

"Aaah!" Jamie yelled, startling the four women as her hands waved around as if to ward her coven off. "Get out of my face! All of you!"

"Jamie—"

"Rico!" The falcon dropped down between Jamie and her coven. "Don't let 'em follow me."

Rico lifted her talons and flew at the four women. Ignoring their screams of panic, and the sounds of running, Jamie spun on her heel and stormed off, her boots stomping through the snow.

She didn't know why she was so angry, but wow. Wow! How could she not see it? How could she not see that her coven thought so little of her? Well now she knew, didn't she? And she was glad she did. Because this opened up doorways for her, didn't it? She didn't have to worry about them anymore. She didn't have to worry she'd disappoint them or put them in danger or anything else. Now she knew she should have been a solitary all along. They'd been holding her back! Well, no more!

From now on she was going to be the witch they thought she was. She was going to be cruel and thoughtless and bloodthirsty and destroy any and everything in her way!

Nothing would stop her! Absolutely nothing!

And to prove it . . .

Jamie stopped walking, spotting a young deer quietly munching on tall grass shooting up through the snow. *A worthy blood sacrifice*. First she'd take its soul and then she'd take its blood.

She moved closer and the animal didn't scamper away. Good. It was a foolish animal to trust her, but so what? She'd been just as foolish to trust her coven. But she wouldn't be making that mistake again either.

Once Jamie stood over it, she raised her hands and silently called to the powers inside her. That was all she'd need to destroy it. The power inside her and the will to use it. And she had the will. She did. Just watch her.

Yep. She was going to do this.

Right now.

Any second.

Just watch her.

The deer stepped away from the grass and over to Jamie. It pushed up against her legs and waited.

Her shoulders slumped and Jamie reached down, brushing her hand over the deer's head. Stretching its neck up, it licked her hand before walking off.

"I'm so useless," she muttered, turning to watch it walk off but instead seeing it tackled from the side and slammed to the ground.

"No!" she screamed out. "*No, no, no!*"

The wolf stopped, its muzzle wrapped around the back of the deer's neck, its amber-colored eyes wide in surprise, and its simple gold earring hanging from the tip of its ear.

"Let it go," she said and Tully's wide eyes narrowed. "Please."

It was strange to hear a wolf sigh in clear annoyance and see it roll its eyes. No. It wasn't strange . . . it was *weird*.

Tully released the deer and it took off running, blood streaming down its neck.

When she knew the deer was gone, Jamie said, "Thanks," and started off again. But she only got a few feet when she stopped and stood there. She had no idea where she had been going earlier and no idea where she wanted to go now.

*Back to New York?*

Of course, she'd never be able to afford to buy back her condo or any real estate property in that overpriced state, and living with her parents or siblings, even temporarily, was equivalent to the short time she'd spent in hell. So where would she go? What would she do?

And then it hit her . . . that for the first time in Jamie's life she felt lonely. She'd always been alone, the nature of her personality and innate power making it almost a necessity, so she was quite used to it. But she'd never been lonely. Yet standing in the middle of a town with people she wasn't close to, a coven that thought the worst of her, and nothing to distract her, like books or TV, Jamie felt nothing but painfully lonely. And she hated it.

She blinked in surprise when she felt teeth—fangs really—grip her hand. She glanced down and was relieved to see that Tully wasn't about to rip her arm off. Instead he gave a tug, which she initially ignored. But Tully was like her and not easily dissuaded, so he tugged a few more times until she started walking.

"Is there a reason you won't shift back to human? Have you grown shy?" He snorted, finally releasing her hand when he seemed confident she would walk with him wherever he led.

She glanced around at the snow and couldn't help but smile a little. "Worried the cold will make you less of a man to me?"

He nipped at her leg and then pushed his large wolf body into her hip, making her laugh a little.

# Chapter Twelve

Jamie didn't know how long they walked but she knew she was getting tired, proving it was time to get back on the treadmill. Since leaving her job in law enforcement and spending the majority of her time on metaphysical planes where her mind had way more control than her body, she'd not kept up her physical strength training at all. And for the first time . . . she felt it.

Eventually, they made it to a dirt road. It was barely big enough for a vehicle and Jamie guessed it was the road Tully took everyday from his house to wherever he ambled to. After ten months, she realized she'd never seen where Tully lived. She imagined his place looked a lot like Kyle's, which was an extremely large wood cabin that Emma absolutely adored. It was rustic but with all the necessary equipment like working toilets and electricity. Then again, maybe Tully wanted something a little less permanent. There were two Packs of wild dogs that called Smithville home. One Pack lived in an enormous plantation-type place near the edge of town, but the other lived in RVs and trailers. Every nine months or so, they'd pack up and ship out . . . for about ten or twenty miles, then settle down again. It was weird but to be blunt . . . the wild dogs were always weird. Cute, but weird.

Of course, the way Tully seemed always to be roaming around town, she could easily imagine him having an RV as his . . .

Jamie stopped as they came around the last bend, her gaze moving up, her mouth hanging open.

Tully kept going, right to the front glass doors. He slapped at the stainless steel door handle with his paw. The door opened and he walked inside. But Jamie didn't move. She couldn't. Not with her gaze still fastened to what was in front of her. Three stories of glass, metal, and wood combined into what had to be the most amazing piece of modern architecture she'd ever seen.

After a few minutes, Tully stuck his head out the door. When he saw her still standing there, he trotted back outside and around her. His head pushed into her butt, making Jamie squeak in surprise before the continued pressure had her walking forward into the house. The door closed behind her and now-human Tully walked around her.

"Make yourself at home, beautiful. I'll be back in a few minutes."

He disappeared up a set of stairs and Jamie decided to follow Tully's example and amble around. All the floors were made of hardwood and there were big, glass windows in every room. The kitchen made her drool with all that hard, shiny chrome and marble counters while the first-floor half-bath was nothing short of exquisite.

Okay, she'd be the first to admit it . . . Tully's house was amazing. Not just nice or pretty or even fancy. It was beyond that. Yet, and this was what she found most shocking, it looked lived in. Her desire to stretch out on his shockingly oversized, light-colored couch nearly overwhelmed her and she instinctively knew he'd let her put her feet up on his tempered glass coffee table.

Done with the first floor, she went to the second. There were several elegant bedrooms, each with its own bath, and at the end of the hall was a really large office. It looked out over the ocean and Jamie could only let out a breath at the view. Shaking her head, she started out and then caught sight of the framed documents Tully had on his wall. She walked over and examined them closely before quickly heading out of the room and up to the third floor. There were only two rooms up here. One a bedroom and the other a bathroom. It was the bathroom she went to, walking in and all the way across the room to get to the shower. It was not a short trip.

She snatched the glass door open and stared at Tully.

Covered in soap and grinning, he asked, "Coming to join me, beautiful?"

"You went to *Dartmouth*? College?"

He blinked in surprise. "Only for undergrad."

She took a small step back. "And then Cornell?"

"To get my master's."

"In . . ."

"In architecture." His smile came back. "How'd you figure that out?"

Jamie sized up the wolf before her. "Are you T. R. Smith? Of the T.R. Smith Design Group?"

His smile became a little bashful and she wanted to punch his face in. "Yeah. I am."

Shocked and disgusted, Jamie slammed the shower door in his face and stormed off.

Tully had no idea what happened but he'd be damned if he'd let her storm off after all that.

She was already outside and stomping down his dirt road when he ran out in front of her. He'd shifted back, in no mood to deal with the cold. His fur was wet and he was damn unhappy about it all.

Jamie stopped when he skidded to a halt in front of her but tried to step around him. He snarled, bared his fangs. She snorted and rolled her eyes, which seemed a very Yankee kind of thing to do.

"Just move," she ordered and again tried to walk around him. He stayed in front of her and then shook out his wet fur. Jamie squealed, her hands covering her face. "Stop that!"

He did but took the moment to grab the back of her jacket and yank her to the ground. Then, with his grip tight, he dragged her back to his house.

She kicked and screamed and he knew she wanted to hex him or something but he also knew she wouldn't dare with him as wolf and since he hadn't drawn blood yet. See? That's what he tried to teach his daddy. It was always good to know a little something about "all that witch stuff" because you never knew when you'd need the information.

Once he had her back in the house, he decided there was only one way to keep her here until they were done talking. He had to get her naked. Which he did by shredding off her clothes with his paws and fangs. When he finished, her rude curses still ringing in his head, she sat on his floor with her knees raised and the palms of her hands flat on the floor. He liked how she didn't cover herself up, how she didn't try and hide her body from him. And yet . . .

*Lord, if looks could kill.*

He shifted once more and, on his hands and knees in front of her, asked, "Now isn't that better?"

Her hand shot out and she caught hold of his earring, twisting until she had him flat on his back. "I am ripping this thing off!" she snarled.

He caught hold of her around the waist, gripping her body to him and rolling them over. "Let go," he ordered now that he had her on her back.

"In hell!"

He knew if he loosened his hold to get a grip of her hands, she'd only follow through on her promise and rip the gold earring from his head. Desperate, he gripped the side of her breast with his mouth and unleashed his fangs until they rested just against her flesh.

Jamie gasped. "Don't even think it!"

He growled. A good, healthy wolf growl, making sure to show all those lovely fangs he flossed twice a day for good dental hygiene.

"Okay. Okay." She opened her hand, releasing his ear.

"Thank you," he said before he pressed his lips against the spot on her breast where he'd taken hold.

"I don't think so."

He smiled and moved his lips closer to her nipple. "You don't think so . . . what?"

"We're not doing this again."

Tully kissed the tip of her nipple. "You sure?" He swirled his tongue around it, enjoying how her breath caught. "I'm free until late this afternoon."

"I don't care if you're free until the end of—" Her back arched as he took her nipple into his mouth and gently sucked.

"There's no reason," she panted out, "for us to do this again."

"Who needs a reason"—he blew on the wet tip—"besides just wanting to?"

"I . . . I've had a bad morning."

"Mine hasn't been much better." He kissed his way across her chest to her other breast. "You tossed me out like a five-dollar hooker."

"So you've got something to prove?"

"No." Using his lips he tugged and pulled her nipple. "I've got something to get."

She needed to get out of here. She needed to get out of his arms and out of the immaculate architectural wet dream he called "his house" and get as far away from this man as she could manage without appearing as if she were running. She did have her dignity after all.

Reality was, Jamie had no delusions about who she was and what she wanted. Her coven may not know her, but she knew herself. Wielding the kind of power she held and not knowing your true self was simply a recipe for disaster. And in the end, what she understood about herself was that she couldn't get all tangled up with this man. She couldn't permanently attach herself to this town or this life, not when there was so much more out there for her. Waiting.

Yet even knowing all that, she still couldn't bring herself to pull away. Couldn't manage to drag her body out from under him and stomp off into the snow and out of this insane town for good. She could start over anywhere. She didn't have to go back to New York. Hell, she didn't have to stay in the States for that matter. There were power sources all over the world, waiting for her to pluck them up. The problem was, absorbed power never felt this good.

Tully moved down her body until he could take hold of her legs. He bent them back, her knees pressed into her chest, and then pushed them wide apart, his strong hands pinning her body to the ground. His mouth pressed against her, his tongue licking up the wetness he'd already caused from their scuffle while his fingers dug into her thighs.

Groaning, Jamie slammed her hands against his shoulders, trying to push him off, but he wouldn't budge. Instead he burrowed deeper with his tongue, stroking the inside of her pussy until she writhed from the pleasure of it. At that point she stopped trying to push him away and gripped the back of his head, the damp strands of his hair tight between her fingers as she pulled him closer.

Tully sucked Jamie's clit into his mouth and felt her body nearly shoot off the floor. Grinning, he nursed the tight bundle of nerves with his lips and let the sound of her rough screams sweep over him. By the time she begged him to stop, he was hard as steel and couldn't think past his need to be inside her.

He moved up her body, kissing her skin as he did until he pressed his mouth to hers and slipped his tongue between her lips while he pressed his cock inside her pussy. She let out a choked sob, her body shaking as he took her hard. Her hands came up and without thought, the wolf inside him instinctively grabbed hold of her wrists and pinned them to the floor beside her head. That one move had more warm wetness spreading over his cock, drenching it. Her reaction spurred his and he used the weight of his body to hold her down as he pounded into her, taking what she reluctantly offered and giving back whatever she may need.

His balls tightened, his back tensed, but he knew he could hold on longer. That is until Jamie came. Her head thrown back, she cried out, her arms still trying to struggle out of his grip, her legs tight around his waist, the heels digging into his ass. He had no hope then. No hope for control as he buried his head in the curve of her neck and snarled out his orgasm, his cock pouring his come inside her over and over until there was nothing left and he crashed on top of her. His entire body trembled the way it did after his first full shift, when he was only thirteen and had no idea what to do next.

Of course, he didn't know what to do next now either.

# Chapter Thirteen

She didn't know what she'd expected, but being pampered by anyone other than herself was definitely not it. And yet, here she was being carried up two flights of stairs to Tully's bathroom. As they moved, Jamie absorbed the light feeding into the house from outside. She'd never been anywhere that had so much brightness from natural light only. She never knew she'd like it so much. The power of it recharged her, made the drama from earlier with her coven seem so very long ago it didn't really matter.

Once in the bathroom—another blindingly bright room, especially with the white marble countertops, white Italian floor tile, and bright chrome fixtures—Tully took her to his shower and washed her. Two showers in one morning and she didn't really care. He wouldn't let her do anything and she didn't ask him why, instead she allowed herself to relax and enjoy. And although he stroked and fondled her body enough to make her reach for him again, he held her back.

"You made me give up my deer," he murmured against her neck while his soap-covered hands dragged down her back.

"I had to. She'd only been easy for you to pick off because of me."

"That's fine. But it doesn't change the fact that I'm hungry."

"You need more delivery places around here."

"Why?" His lips brushed against her jaw, her cheek. "I've got a chef standing right here."

"You've got a girl who learned to make great desserts from her grandmother. That doesn't make me a chef."

"If you feed me, I'll make it worth your while."

Because she liked the sound of that—and she was flippin' hungry, too—she agreed.

Thankfully the man had a lot of pasta. Combined with some steak, oil, garlic, and Romano cheese, they were eating before noon. They sat at the table tucked into the corner of his kitchen. If Jamie looked to her right, she looked at Tully. If she looked to her left, she could stare at his amazing view of the Atlantic Ocean. To be honest, she was having a hard time figuring out which she wanted to see more of.

"So," Tully said, his gaze on her face, his bare foot brushing against her leg under the table, "what's your problem with Dartmouth?"

"Nothing." She'd forgotten all about that, which was strange because she never forgot anything. "I just can't believe you went to Dartmouth."

"Just 'cause I'm from the South, beautiful, doesn't make me stupid."

"I know," she answered honestly. "You're stupid because you went to Dartmouth . . . but you still ended up trapped here."

Trapped? Tully wasn't trapped anywhere. It was the one thing he prided himself on.

"What makes you say that?"

"Come on." He shrugged and she said, "You went to Dartmouth, then Cornell. You have your master's in architecture. I know nothing about architecture but I know your company because my ex desperately wanted it to design and build his house— gotta impress the neighbors, you know—until he realized we couldn't afford it, which made me laugh and, according to my mother, completely explains why we're divorced now." She shook her head. "I guess I don't get why you'd give all that up to live here."

"I didn't give up anything. I cherry-pick the jobs I want, do them from here, and still get paid for jobs I never touch but that my company handles."

"Yeah, but . . ."

"Everything I want is here, Jamie." And he didn't realize how right he was until he looked into those brown eyes.

She stared at him as if he'd suddenly started speaking German. "You're serious?"

"Most of the time."

Jamie looked around and it suddenly dawned on him how anxious she suddenly was. As if the thought of staying in Smithville was the most horrifying idea she'd ever heard before.

"You know," he said carefully, pushing what was left of his delicious food around the bowl, "you've committed yourself to staying in Smithville as part of our deal. Is that about to change?"

"No. But would I have made the same choice if I had the kind of options you have? That I can't tell ya."

Tully released his fork and sat back in his chair. "I'd hate to think you were only here because you settled."

"I don't feel like I settled. But I have no idea what I would have done if I had other options."

"It's the 'ifs' that'll get ya, beautiful. *If* my parents were full-human, maybe I would be working myself into an early grave, pushing myself to accomplish all the things I was told I need to. But, thank the Lord, they're not and I'm not. So I do what makes me happy and don't worry about anything beyond that. And, not surprisingly, I have amazing blood pressure."

"I thought you came back here because your grandfather died."

"Not grandfather. Great-uncle. Everybody just called him Granddaddy. And I did come back because he passed. Wouldn't be right not to come to the funeral."

"And that's when you took over."

Tully laughed. "Lord, no. I just ended up staying 'cause I remembered what I loved about it."

"Which is?"

He looked out the kitchen windows to the beach not more than a few hundred feet away and shrugged. "Everything."

Jamie couldn't help but envy Tully a little. He didn't seem so ridiculously happy that she was convinced he was on some type of medication, and yet he didn't seem on the neverending quest for *more*. She was on that quest, although most outside her coven never knew it. To the world, even her ex, Jamie was the most laid back, uncaring female on the planet. She didn't need the latest and greatest and most expensive to be happy. At the time, it had been the biggest problem between her and her ex. His whole goal was to move up and out. He wanted the bigger house, the fancier car, the best of everything. Jamie, however, was more than happy with what she had when it came to material things. Jamie would buy a known reliable car and keep it anywhere from ten to fifteen years. Her ex would lease the hottest car out there and change it up every two to three years. Was it nice to ride around in new cars constantly? Sure, but for her the bottom line was getting from point A to point B as quickly and inexpensively as possible.

And, yet, while her ex was calling her "cheap" for not wanting more things in her life, Jamie was busy searching for more power. Because who needed a big screen TV when, with a little practice, one could levitate off the ground? Who needed the newest, hottest car when objects could be moved around, from the simple paperclip across the desk to moving the house of your enemies a hundred feet into a river?

Since she could remember, the only thing Jamie really craved was power.

Tully reached across the table and took her hand, laying her arm flat. He dragged his fingers across the inside of her forearm, moving slowly back and forth while his gaze stayed locked on her face.

The simplest of gestures and yet . . . and yet it felt like he was inside her again. He tugged her forward and she willingly went, her body in his lap, her arms around his neck, when his phone rang.

"Dang."

Keeping her in place with one arm, he reached over to the counter behind him and grabbed hold of the cordless phone. "Hello?"

She watched his expression change, felt the tightness of his body, and immediately knew something was wrong.

"Yep," he said. "We'll be right there. No. Jamie's with me. I'll bring her."

When he ended the call, she asked, "Why don't you just use a megaphone to announce to the universe we're fucking."

"It's a small town. They already know." He lifted her off his lap and placed her on her feet. He patted her ass and stood. "There's a problem."

"I figured."

"We need to get to—"

"That won't be easy," she cut in. "Since you tore up my clothes."

He had the decency to grimace and even blush a little. "I did, didn't I?"

Jamie nodded.

He took her hand and headed back to the bedroom. "We'll come up with something."

Although the Elders were kept fully informed of what was going on, for something like this they weren't brought in. Being able to move and react quickly without worrying about permission was so important. And so far, it was sounding like this was a "situation."

Kyle, his arms folded over his chest and his legs braced apart, quietly explained what he'd seen. "There were about thirty, maybe forty more vehicles. Mostly RVs."

"How far out of town?" Bear asked.

"No more than forty miles. But so close to Everettville, none of us would have stumbled across it."

"Why?" Jamie asked. She was bundled up in one of Tully's black seaman sweaters, his sweatpants that were embarrassingly too long, and one of his leather jackets. The boots were hers and she looked so fuckable in those oversized clothes, he was having a hard time concentrating on a very serious situation.

"Because we don't go to Everettville," Bear said.

"Why?"

"It's not a good idea," Kyle told her.

"Why?"

Bear snarled a little, but Jamie only shrugged her shoulders and stated, "If you'd answer my question, I'd stop asking 'why.'"

Tully snorted and now he was being glared at by a cat and a bear.

"What'cha all glarin' at me for?"

"Can't you control her?" Kyle snapped.

Tully and Jamie looked at each other and then they burst out laughing, leaning into each other until Tully abruptly stopped and said, "No." Which only made Jamie laugh harder.

Kyle's eyes narrowed and Jamie cleared her throat, brushed off her clothes, and wiped the tears of laughter from her eyes. Then she said, "So why don't you go to Everettville?"

"It's horse country," Kyle snapped. "Okay?"

"Ohhhh. You mean like centaurs!"

Tully was bent over at the waist he was laughing so hard as his brother's rage exploded around them. "*No! I don't mean like centaurs!*"

"What the hell's a centaur?" Bear grumbled, which only made Tully laugh even harder.

"They're half man, half horse," Jamie explained sweetly, so sweetly Tully knew she was fucking with Kyle something awful.

"Which half?" Bear asked.

"*Would you shut up?*" Kyle yelled, but when the grizzly slowly turned his head to glare at him from under the brim of his Sheriff's Department baseball cap, the cat cleared his throat and added, "Boss."

Wiping the tears from his eyes, Tully explained, "Nearly everyone in Everettville either owns a horse farm or they work on one. You'll probably find more horses there than you'll find cars. One of us gets too close to town limits and all hell breaks loose. So we stopped going over there."

"But wouldn't the same thing happen if—"

"If Buck Smith's Pack was holed up over there? Absolutely." And based on what Kyle had told them, that's exactly what was happening. Buck's entire Pack wasn't having vacation at Smithville Arms, it turned out. Instead, a majority of them were hanging out on unused territory near Everettville. Anyone else, the Smithville locals would just keep an eye on them. But when it came to Buck Smith . . . nothing was ever as it seemed. "The difference is, that old bastard don't care what happens with those horses."

Kyle relaxed back against a tree. "Chances are they've snuck on to farms and chased a few of the horses down for food."

"Or because they were bored," Bear added.

"Which will only be more trouble for us," Tully said. "Because those people love their horses more than they like each other, and most of them have the money necessary to get the government involved to look into it."

"And the last thing we need is the government involved." Kyle took off his cap and scratched his head. "It always gets a little messy when that happens."

"Right now, they're probably going to blame the red wolves that got introduced back into the population a while back, but the reds are definitely smaller than we are. About eighty pounds soaking wet while even my momma is a good one-fifty when she shifts."

"Does Buck know all this about Everettville?"

Tully could only chuckle. "Trust me . . . he knows. That man don't do nothin' without knowing exactly what he's getting into. He stationed his Pack there for a reason."

"An attack."

"He takes out Tully and a few of his stronger cousins and Buck will get control of this town." Kyle pulled his cap back on his head. "And trust me when I say that the other Smiths aren't going to stand for that. Not for a second."

"And that would mean civil war among the Smiths. Knowing my father, he's hoping to get it all sorted before the other Packs move in, but I think he's being unrealistic in his old age."

"Why?"

"It wouldn't be the first time there's been some infighting among the Smiths, beautiful. One time it got so bad that the Van Holtz Pack moved in—"

"And that's when it got out of control."

Tully nodded at Kyle's words. "We lost half our members, including pups. Same with the Van Holtz."

"They ain't brawny, but they're wily."

"Yep. But when the pups start ending up as collateral damage . . ." Tully let out a breath. "They knew the war had to end or we risked losing Smith and Van Holtz territories on the East and West coasts to the Magnus Pack who were slavering to get in once the smoke had cleared. So a decision was made."

"What decision?"

"That there would be a truce between the two Packs, no territories given up, no retaliation for the lost Packmates. All we had to do was take out our Alphas at the time. And that's exactly what my ancestors did."

It reminded Jamie of the New York mob wars that happened before she was born. One "family" against another, with lots of bodies around when everything finally settled down. She'd prefer not going through that. The few mob hits she'd seen over the years had meant little to her because she didn't personally know the scumbags who'd bought it. If anything, she knew their business dealings, which usually involved drugs, gambling, and human trafficking, which was a very nice way of saying "slavery."

But none of the people she'd met so far were like that. The worst she'd seen was an insane fight between the Smith Pack and the Sahara Pride over a rotting elk carcass. It had happened not far from her house and Jamie kept having to turn the sound up on her TV in an attempt to shut out the noise. The next day when she went into town . . . it was like it never happened. Why? Because at their core they were hungry predators looking for food, not lowlifes looking for a quick buck.

Still, no matter how much she wanted to help, there was only so much she could do given the confines of her coven.

"My coven can't get in the middle of this as long as you guys are covered in fur when you go at it."

"We know that." Tully smiled at her and . . . wow. How unfair was *that* to her? "But my father's set himself in the middle of his enemies for a reason. He's playing this game for a reason. I need to know what."

"The dinner with you, your parents, and Buck is tonight, right?" Tully nodded. "Good. The coven will be there anyway to make sure it all runs smoothly. I'll have Sen spend some time with him."

"Sen?"

"It's a gift she has. She can talk to nearly anybody and get a good idea of what they're up to. That's one of the reasons she loves it here. You guys are rarely up to much of anything outside of sleeping, feeding, mating, and more sleeping."

"Are you trying to say we're lazy, beautiful?"

Jamie snorted. "I'm not *trying* to say anything. I'm just sayin' it."

# Chapter Fourteen

It was Seneca, dressed in a tight, floor-length dress, who met them at the door of the hotel and led them to the large table in the middle of the dining room. It kind of fascinated Tully how Seneca had such a sweet, almost angelic face, with that sexy, smokin' hot body. It didn't seem right, actually. Sort of misleading.

The party wasn't large. Just Tully, Kyle, Katie, Momma, Daddy, Buck, Wanda, and Buck's three sons. Okay, the party wasn't large for a Southerner.

Seneca sat them all down, gave them menus, and introduced them to the two waiters who would be taking care of them for the night. The entire time she stood by Buck's chair, her hand resting on the back of it until she moved it to his shoulder, the other hand on her hip. She smiled and laughed the entire time and, when she finally walked away, she had the largest smile on her face.

To say it confused him was kind of an understatement. Maybe they had nothing to worry about with Buck after all . . .

Jamie looked up from the dark chocolate ganache she was mixing as Sen pushed through the kitchen double doors.

"They're all set," she said cheerily before slipping onto a stool by the main workstation and nibbling on a plate of cheese and crackers Mac had set out for her.

"And?" Emma asked, when Sen said nothing else.

"Patchouli alert on Buck's date. I know how you get, Jamie, and didn't want you to start World War III when you smell that stuff."

"Hippies and their damn patchouli oil," Jamie jokingly snarled.

"What about Buck?" Emma snarled with none of the joking.

"Oh." Sen studied the ceiling and nibbled on a cracker, carefully thinking over her answer. "Well, based on what I saw he's a real asshole and he'd kill each and every one of us if it got him what he wanted." She was silent for a moment, smiled and nodded her head, and said, "Yep! That's what I saw when I looked inside him."

"Could you look . . . perkier?" Kenny asked.

"There's no use in getting upset. Besides, Jamie will handle it."

"Yeah," Jamie tossed back casually, "I already have a young virgin male trussed up and ready to be sacrificed, so we're ready to go."

"Oh, my God!" Mac burst out. "Would you let that go already?"

"No! I won't let that go, heifer!"

Cooking utensils in hand, the cousins moved toward each other but Emma jumped between them. "Stop it! Both of you!" Emma motioned Mac back to her workstation and then Jamie. "We don't have time for this."

"Personally," Jamie said as she began mixing again, "I don't think Buck will make a move during one of Mac's overwrought courses."

"*Overwrought?*"

Ignoring her cousin's screech, "I think he'll wait until early morning, around dawn, when he knows that almost everyone in town is asleep."

"You know this because . . . ?"

"You keep using that tone with me, cousin, and I'll show you exactly what I know."

Tully, Jack, and Kyle stood when Bear walked into the restaurant with his momma. Unfortunately, Buck only eyed her, smirked and said, "Well, hey there, Gwenie. Still lookin' damn good."

If Miss Gwen had a reply, they'd never find out what it was

as she had to quickly grab her son's arm, insisting she needed his help to the table the hostess, not Seneca, was trying to lead them to.

Snarling and keeping a firm hold on his momma's arm, Bear followed after the hostess, but stopped when Mac was tossed out of the kitchen. The tall female landing at his feet.

Kyle leaned over to Tully and whispered, "How long ya think he's been waiting on that?"

"His whole life?"

"Miss Mackenzie?" Bear said softly.

"Hi, Sheriff." She ignored the hand he held out to her and got to her feet. "If you'll excuse me." She stormed back into the kitchen and came flying back out three seconds later, this time right into Bear's arms.

By now, the rest of them had returned to their seats and were fully entertained by the activity going on in and around the kitchen.

"That bitch," Mac snarled under her breath. She pulled away from Bear, cracked her neck and her knuckles, before marching back toward the swinging door. She was only a few inches away when the door swung out, slamming right into her face, shoving her right back at Bear.

At that point, Bear looked back at Tully and Kyle as if they could somehow tell him what to do.

Mac was busy trying to staunch the flow of blood from her nose when Jamie walked out. Unlike her cousin, she wasn't decked out like a chef. No chef coat or hat. She did have her mass of brown hair in a loose ponytail and a bandana tied around her head, but nothing else that suggested she was part of the staff. Just loose blue jeans and a black v-neck sweater that was doing wonders for that beautiful chest of hers.

"Oh, honey," she said sweetly to her cousin. "Was that *you* on the other side of the door? I'm so sorry! Here. Let me help you." She grabbed Mac from Bear and moved her forward, slamming her into the wall by the door.

"Ooopsie! My bad." Jamie yanked her back by the neck and shoved her forward again. This time she aimed correctly and got her into the swinging door but she did it so hard that Tully knew

Mac would be feeling the pain for days. Poor full-humans. How they handled the pain from those minor wounds lasting days—sometimes a full week!—he'd never know.

After the cousins disappeared into the kitchen, there was some screaming, slamming, and what sounded like the throwing of metal utensils coming from behind the swinging door but only Bear seemed deeply concerned about it. He was still standing there, looking as confused as only a grizzly could sometimes, when Seneca walked out. She gave him that big, blinding grin, and said, "Sheriff! What are you doing standing here?"

The grizzly pointed at the door and Seneca gave a little laugh as she took his arm and led him to the table where his mother was already sitting. "Don't worry about that blood on the wall and door. Our staff will clean that up in no time."

"But—"

"You just enjoy your meal and night out with your mother. Hi, Miss Gwen."

"Hello, Seneca."

"I recommend the salmon!" she said happily before rousing her staff to clean off the wall and doors.

Kyle grabbed a piece of bread from one of three platters in the middle of the table. "Did she just recommend salmon to bears?"

The dinner was going better than Tully thought it would. He wouldn't say anyone was friendly but everyone was at least polite. Then again, conversational lines were pretty safe. Jack was chatting with Millie; Kyle, Katie, and Tully were chatting with each other; Wanda was chatting and Buck was grunting in response; and Buck's sons were staring at Katie, which meant they were about to get their asses kicked if they didn't quit it.

Yep. It could be worse.

Tully was almost finished with his steak when, laughing at something Kyle had muttered, he heard the bickering between Buck and Wanda. He did his best to ignore it—Lord knew it was none of his business what his father and his unmarked woman were up to—but couldn't once his father leaned back in his chair and said, "I'm moving my Pack back here. It's a good place for us to get settled."

Tully continued to chew the piece of steak he had in his

mouth, staring at his father while he did. He knew everyone was waiting for his response, waiting to see what he'd do. Especially Buck.

Wanda gave the most forced smile Tully had seen in a long time. "Now, Buck, I thought we talked about waiting—"

"Quiet."

He didn't yell at her, he didn't need to. But the way Millie flinched, Tully knew what that tone was leading up to if Wanda didn't back off. She did, but it was a struggle, her hands curling into fists where they lay on the table.

Tully swallowed his food and simply said, "No."

His father smiled, probably hoping for that. "You think you can stop me?"

"I know he can," Jack growled from across the table.

"I haven't seen anything that tells me that. My Pack is stronger and—"

"Right outside town." Tully used a slice of French bread to sop up what was left of the amazing sauce Mac made to go with the steak. "At least they *were*. The fine law enforcement officials of Everettville were kind enough to send them on their way. They didn't like a band of rovers being that close to their precious horses." Tully popped the piece of bread in his mouth and winked at his father. "The rest of your Pack has been shuffled out of town too. I swear, the bears love making wolves leave. It gives them almost a perverse joy."

"You always play it so nice, don't ya, boy?"

"I haven't had to get nasty. And if you leave after this wonderful, thrilling dinner, I won't have to. But that's up to you. At the very least do it for your woman."

"She can handle anything. She may be full-human, but she ain't weak." And Buck's eyes slid over to Millie. "I never could find a use for a weak female in my life or my bed."

Katie slammed her fist down on the table, cutting off anything Tully, Jack, or Kyle were about to say. "You watch your mouth, old man."

Seneca suddenly appeared, sliding to a stop by their table and clapping her hands together, her smile way too wide and bright. "How are we doing? Are we ready for dessert?"

\* \* \*

Jamie would never admit it out loud but her cousin had a hell of a right cross.

And although trying to plate the desserts for Tully and his family would be easier with both eyes open, she was going to show her inner tenacity and ignore the swelling of her left eye.

Once she finished, Jamie grabbed two plates, Mac grabbed two, and the waiters took care of the rest. They slipped out the swinging door and over to the large table in the middle of the room. From what she could tell, all seemed to be going well—until she actually saw everyone. They looked . . . tense. Dangerously tense. It looked as if things had moved along a lot faster than she'd thought they would.

*Time to get this over with.*

Moving around the table to stay downwind of the patchouli funk Wanda had brought in with her—Christ! She hated that smell!—she carefully placed her specially prepared dessert in front of Jack and Kyle while the waiters and Mac took care of everyone else.

"Nice eye," Tully mouthed at her and she gave him a little sneer that made him laugh.

Sen, always the one with the charm, clapped her hands together and said, "This is Jamie's Dark Chocolate Path of Destruction cake"—which made Tully chuckle, Buck Smith glaring at him from across the table—"but we all call it Chocolate Overload for short. We hope you all enjoy it and that you enjoyed your meal and we wanted to thank you for coming tonight."

"It was lovely, sweetheart," Millie said as she gave them all a brave, if rather desperate smile.

Jamie grinned and gave her a wink. "The dessert's killer, Miss Millie, but I think you'll love it." Then Jamie slapped her hands down on Buck's shoulders. "You, too, Buck. You'll just *love* it." She walked off behind her coven.

But Jamie slowed to a stop, her head swimming. *It must be that goddamn patchouli crap!* Then pain tore through her brain and everything around her spun out of control . . .

Tully was moments from having an orgasm over Jamie's cake— *had she put anything else in here but chocolate and some nuts? Heroin, maybe? Crack? Damn!*—when he saw Jamie suddenly stumble to a stop. She rubbed her forehead with one hand and slowly turned toward the table.

"Jamie?"

She shook her head before slowly walking forward. Her coven, about to push through the swinging door and head back into the kitchen, stopped and watched her closely. Even little Seneca seemed concerned.

"Is everything all right, sweetheart?" his momma asked. "You need a glass of water or somethin'?"

Jamie shook her head again and said, "No, ma'am. I just..." She blinked hard as if trying to focus her eyes. "I just..."

She stood by the table now and, after a moment, looked at Tully.

"Beautiful?" he asked. "What's wrong?"

"I'm sorry," she said. "I'm so, so sorry."

And before he could ask her what she might be sorry for, she grabbed Wanda by the back of the head, a handful of her hair wrapped around her fingers, and flung the woman out of the chair and across the room. Bear pulled his momma out of the way and over to Tully's table where they were all now standing, watching as Jamie swiped up a steak knife from one of the tables and stalked over to Wanda. But her coven cut her off, Mac catching her around the waist.

"Jamie, don't."

"She doesn't smell that bad!" Seneca argued. But it was Emma that had Tully's attention. She was watching Wanda close as the woman slowly got to her feet. He wasn't sure what she saw, what clued her in, but Emma got out a squeaked, "Jamie!"

Jamie shoved her cousin aside, raising her hand and blocking the power suddenly flowing from Wanda in a huge wave.

"Get out!" Jamie yelled at them over the roar of sound, but they didn't move fast enough and Tully watched as Jamie was forced several feet back.

Growling, Jamie pushed and the power lashed back at Wanda. The other woman stumbled, snarled, and flew at Jamie. And he meant that literally. She *flew*.

Wanda slammed into Jamie, hands tight around her throat, and that funky scent clogging up Jamie's delicate senses. She wouldn't stand for it! But she didn't have a chance to do anything as Wanda's strength and power shoved Jamie back into the kitchen, through the kitchen, and out the back door, with Wanda still holding on tight.

Once outside, Wanda flew them up until Jamie's back collided with a tree. The air surrounding them kept the pair aloft, and Jamie knew that Wanda's goddess had imbued the witch with serious power although Jamie wondered what Wanda had to give up to get it.

The witch chanted at her and Jamie could only smile. "You'll have to do better than that, hippie," she taunted, releasing her desperate grip on the hands Wanda had around her throat and digging her thumbs into Wanda's eyes, forcing her back.

Once she had Wanda completely arched over, the hippie screaming from the pain in her eyes, Jamie ripped the power out of Wanda, and made it her own. Then she slammed Wanda's stinky ass into the ground.

They all ran out the back door in time to see Jamie and Wanda fly into the top of one of the older trees. There was rustling and then screaming but, to be honest, Tully was too confused to know who was screaming or why.

Leave it to Buck. He'd come here to test the new coven. To see if they were as strong as the ones before them. If not, he planned to try and push his oldest son out. As if Tully would ever let that happen. He may be different from the rest of his Smith kin, he was definitely nicer than most of them, but that didn't make him weak. No matter what Buck Smith thought.

Tully heard a roar come from the tree Jamie and Wanda had crashed into, dark light exploding around the leaves. He knew that "dark light" didn't actually make sense, but there was no other way for him to describe it. But if he could harness it and turn it into one of his home designs . . . he was pretty sure that only someone with a really dark sense of humor could live there.

A body flew out of the tree and crashed into the land beneath, dirt and earth exploding out as it settled into a crevice.

Tully stepped forward, needing to know if it was Jamie, but Jack caught his arm, held him back.

"Don't get in the middle of this, son."

And before he could argue, before he could tell his daddy he couldn't leave her alone, Jamie landed beside the now-moving body. She landed with the sure-footedness of a cat, cracking her neck and shoulders like a boxer. He briefly wondered why, until she grabbed Wanda by the front of her sweater with one hand, lifting her up, and punched her in the face with the other. She did it three times. Short, powerful rabbit punches.

"You're gonna tell me where your coven is, hippie." And her voice was so calm, Tully could only think of death. "Because we both know you didn't come here alone. You didn't hide who you are alone. Not from me."

As she spoke, Jamie's own coven moved in behind and around her. Mac standing the closest. Their faces were hard, their eyes cold. Even sweet Seneca and little Emma. It seemed all of them were as territorial as any predator he knew.

Jamie drew her fist back again. "You're gonna tell me. When I'm done, you'll tell me everything."

But she didn't have a chance to follow through on that as Buck's gravely voice cut in and said, "Let her go."

They all looked up at the same moment, and if Bear hadn't grabbed Tully and Kyle hadn't grabbed their daddy, all hell would have broken loose in that moment.

Buck had Millie by the throat. They were both still human but his claws were right against her jugular. And there was nothing in those eyes that said he'd have a moment's hesitation about killing her while they all watched. Behind him stood his sons, ready to back him up like always. Ready to enjoy whatever their father would do to Tully's momma.

Jamie, still crouching, spun Wanda around until her back was to Jamie's front and Jamie's arm was around the woman's neck. She locked eyes with Buck, and Tully wondered what the old bastard saw because he was watching her real strange.

"You're going to let Miss Millie go," Jamie said, softly. "You're gonna let her go now."

Buck didn't say anything, just kept watching Jamie. Waiting.

"You don't think I'll kill her?" Jamie asked. "You're kinda right. I may not kill her because I don't have to."

She raised her arm and her cousin brushed her hand across Jamie's palm. An essence, like pure crystals, passed between them and Jamie flexed her fingers before placing her hand against Wanda's stomach.

"So the question you need to ask yourself, Buck . . . is what *will* I do?" That's when Jamie plunged her hand inside the woman, her fingers moving past cotton and skin and flesh until she was in up to her wrist. Wanda screamed. As he'd never heard another living being scream before. " 'Cause you see," Jamie went on, "I can spend all day hurtin' her." She moved her hand around inside Wanda. "I can hurt her again and again and I won't care." The hand inside Wanda moved up while Jamie's other arm held the other witch in place. "And once I reach her heart, I'll squeeze it"— Jamie jerked her hand up again—"and squeeze until it bursts in my hand like a ripe tomato. Wanda knows I'll do it. Wanda knows my reputation. She knows I'll crush her heart, and I'll take her soul as mine. I'll keep it on a leash . . . like a puppy. Now you maybe thinking, 'so?' And that's completely valid. I mean, how you tolerated the funk for this long, I have no idea." She moved her arm back and forth and Wanda's scream echoed through the trees and night-filled sky. "But then everyone will know, won't they? They'll know that you were too weak to protect your woman. That you let another full-human torture and kill her and there was nothing you could do. So let Millie go. Let her go before I get really angry."

Tully watched Buck close, watched what he'd do next. If the old bastard did anything to his momma, it would be the last thing he ever did.

Jamie was still staring into Buck's eyes, her gaze never moving from his. When he didn't release Millie, Jamie jerked her arm up one more time, Wanda's scream as painful as her first, and like that, Buck pushed Millie away.

Tully's momma jerked away from him, her hand rubbing her throat. Then she spun on her heel and slapped at Buck's jaw, knocking his face to one side. When he turned back, her claw marks ran down his cheek and blood down his neck.

Seneca stepped forward and held her hand out. Millie took it, letting the witch lead her back to Jack, gripping him tight when his arms wrapped around her.

Buck stepped forward and Jamie said, "Now, now. We ain't done. She still needs to answer my question. Don't you, Wanda?"

Wanda nodded desperately even while her eyes begged Buck to do something—*anything*—to help her. "Where is your coven? Tell me or your pain is just beginning."

"Out . . . outside of town about ten miles," she gasped. "On Perkins Road."

"Emma. Kenny. Go. Kyle, Katie, go with 'em."

Pulling her arm slowly out of Wanda's gut, smiling at Buck as Wanda panted and writhed and tried not to scream in excruciating pain, Jamie stood, taking Wanda with her. The others were gone by the time she got to her full height. But she didn't release Wanda right away.

"Are we done, cousin?" she asked Mac.

"No. We're not."

Jamie held out her hand and Mac reached under her chef's coat, pulling out an eight-inch cooking knife from where she'd tucked it between the thick black leather belt she had around her jeans. She laid it into Jamie's palm, her eyes never leaving Buck's as she did. The cousins may fight like two pitbulls chained together in a junkyard, but once there was a common enemy in front of them . . .

Jamie's hand closed around the knife handle and she flipped it around until she held it blade down. That was when she dragged it across Wanda's collar bone. Wanda screamed again, her arms reaching out for Buck.

"Now I've got your blood," Jamie told Wanda even while she continued to stare at Buck. And with her hand still holding Wanda's hair, she lifted her leg and kicked the woman toward him. Wanda landed in Buck's arms and Jamie held up her fist, a handful of strands wrapped tight around her fingers. "And your hair." Her head tilted to the side. "We both know what I can do with this, hippie. If you lied to me, or you try anything . . ."

She let the threat hang out there as she grinned and turned away from Buck and the others, Mac walking backward for a bit before she followed after Jamie, Seneca falling into step beside them.

"Thank you so much for your patronage at Smithville Arms," Jamie said while she walked up the steps, sounding more like an airline ad than the deadly witch that she was. "I do hope you had a lovely time and that you'll remember us the next time you're planning a business trip, a family vacation, or just a quick week-end getaway with friends."

Then she was back inside the kitchen, the busted screen door awkwardly slamming closed behind her.

Tully looked back at his father but the old man, his sons, and his tricky mate were already gone.

"He'll be back," his momma said from the safety of his daddy's arms. "You know he'll be back, pup."

"I know, Momma." He smiled at her and kissed her forehead before locking eyes with his daddy. "But it's just a little thing."

# Chapter Fifteen

Jamie sat on her couch with her feet up on the coffee table, Rico asleep on the bookcase with all her reference books, a good episode of *Law & Order: Special Victims Unit* on her TV, and a nice, large bowl of pasta to help her mood.

If nothing else, it was a quiet night. There'd been nothing waiting for her when she got home. No screams, bangs, or door slamming. And that was all because of Tully.

Tully. She wondered how far and fast that wolf would run, now that he'd seen how far she'd go. She should feel guilt. She should feel *something*. But other than mild annoyance that she had to shower, wash her hair, and do a load of laundry to get that damn patchouli funk out, she didn't. That was why she was in a mood, because she didn't feel any remorse about what she'd done and she knew she should.

Shouldn't she?

But she'd worry about all that tomorrow. Not tonight. Tonight she was going to eat her delicious pasta, watch one of her favorite shows, and relax all by her—

Jamie sat up when she heard her front door open and close. Her *locked* front door. After a few moments, the wolf walked in to her living room. She knew it was Tully from the earring, but she had the feeling that she'd know it was Tully without it, too. He wandered into the living room, his bushy tail twitching behind him, and came right up and onto the couch. He moved in close to her, pushing up against her side. And that's when he shifted.

She didn't know why he was here. While she was standing in the hotel kitchen, bagging the blood and hair from Wanda for future use—only if necessary, of course—their shifter guests had walked in and right back out through the swinging door without saying a word to her or Mac. She and her cousin had passed quick glances, both of them thinking the same thing, *How long before they ask us to leave?* but neither had said it. Why bother?

But here Tully was, eyeing her pasta in a most territorial way. "Can I help you with something?" she asked.

"I smelled food." He leaned over her bowl of sautéed pasta. "Dang that smells good."

"Sorry. I only made enough for one bowl."

"No problem." He took her fork out of her hand and the bowl out of her lap. "We can share." And then he began to eat.

"Shouldn't you be outside with your Pack . . . killing something?"

"They can hunt on their own," he said around his food. "Or just go to McDonald's. We don't need fresh deer every night."

"I see."

After what should have taken a lot longer, the fork he held scraped the bottom of the bowl, and those strange-colored eyes peered up at her through long lashes. "I finished your pasta."

"Yeah, ya did."

"Sure there's no more?"

"Are you asking for you or me?"

"Both. I'm still hungry."

"Too bad for you. That was it."

He placed the bowl on the coffee table and settled in next to Jamie. "Buck's gone."

"For now. He'll be back."

She saw him smile from the corner of her eye. "We know."

"He'll be back for you." She wanted him to understand how bad this was. She *needed* him to understand it. The thought of something happening to him . . .

"And you," he said casually. "I reckon he hates both of us now."

She took in a breath, let it out slowly. "Should I have done things differently?"

He shook his head. "No. We needed to find out how far he'd go. Now we know."

"And you know how far I'll go."

"Is it supposed to bother me?"

"Does it?"

"You protected my momma, this town, and your coven. That's all I want."

He suddenly moved away from her and stood. He didn't walk out, though. He held his hand out. "I'm tired, beautiful. Let's get some sleep. We can discuss the moral ins and outs of gut molesting tomorrow. Not tonight."

Jamie took his hand and let him lead her to her bedroom. He crawled under the covers and tugged her in with him, wrapping his arms around her, tucking his bent leg between her thighs, and resting her head against his chest. She fell asleep moments later, understanding that everything had changed . . . for her.

Tully slipped out of bed before Jamie woke up, went home, showered, and then headed to his parents' house. His momma was out, having gone shopping bright and early but his daddy was there.

"What's wrong with you?" Jack asked.

"I love her."

Jack sighed, rolled his eyes. "I knew it. As soon as she stuck her arm in that woman and twisted her organs around like she was squeezing melons to see if they were ripe, I knew you'd be keeping her. 'Cause God forbid you should get a nice gal, like your momma."

"Momma likes her."

" 'Cause your momma's nice. She'd find a reason to like anybody."

"Jamie says she doesn't want to be attached. That she doesn't want to go through that again."

He saw Jack smile. "Your momma gave me the same speech the night I asked her out."

"And you got her, despite my earnest attempts to ensure that you didn't."

"You were such a little bastard, too," Jack muttered, shaking his head, but Tully knew it was a compliment.

"So tell me what to do, Daddy. Tell me how I can get Jamie and keep her?"

"Well . . . Lord knows you don't have my charm."

"Or your disturbing cat-stare."

His daddy gave a little snarl and flashed a fang before he finished with, "But I'll help ya. 'Cause any woman crazy enough and strong enough to stand up against Buck Smith and live to tell about it is definitely a keeper."

# Chapter Sixteen

She was grabbed off the street and dragged in to the local salon that she never used because she knew they could never handle her or her cousin's hair. And there, waiting for her, were her coven, Katie, Miss Millie, and the sow who'd grabbed her, Miss Gwen.

"Could you really be that stupid?" Miss Gwen snapped at her. A lovely woman unless you startled her or made annoying sounds.

"It's possible since I don't know what you're talking about."

That's when Katie suddenly lunged for her and Miss Millie had to snatch her back. "Sweet girl," Millie said to Jamie, "we understand you're a little . . . confused."

"I am?"

"It's all right. Gwenie and I have been there. Emma's been there. Now it's your turn."

Needing help, she looked to her coven—who were so busy snickering at her, they turned out to be no help at all.

"Maybe you could tell me clearly what you're talking about."

"If we tell you," Miss Millie explained, exasperated, "then it's like we're telling you what to do. We won't know if it's what you want."

Taking a breath, Jamie said, "But if I'm not clear on what you're asking me about—"

"What is wrong with you?" Katie demanded from behind Millie.

Jamie stared at Tully's sister for a moment and then said, "Snaggle."

"Oh!" Katie stormed around her mother. "Let me just slap her around a little, Momma. Then she'll get it!"

Miss Gwen caught Katie by her ponytail and yanked her back. "Beatin' her up is not gonna help if she's this dumb."

Then they all stared at her, waiting. And she still didn't know what they were talking about. Jamie would be the first to admit it. She didn't *get* women talk. Movies with a bunch of broads sitting around, talking about life and men, never made sense to her and she ended up rolling her eyes or sleeping until the credits rolled. So sure, some other female may know what they were all going on about, but Jamie wasn't some other female.

She was about to simply walk out when she saw Bear walking by the wide store window. She opened the door, grabbed his humongous forearm, and pulled him in.

Okay. She was lying about that part. She actually *tried* to pull him in to the store. What she ended up doing was leaning so far back, it looked like she was in the middle of a hurricane. Bear only stared at her, too. That permanent frown etched into his face somehow growing more frown-y.

"What are you doing?"

"Need your help. In here." So he started walking inside and then grabbed her before she could hit the floor.

Once he got her back on her feet, she pushed the hair off her face and said, "They're yelling at me and I don't know why. They won't tell me. I don't know why. I'm beginning to panic . . . but I know it's because of them."

Bear glanced around the salon, his eyes briefly lingering on Mac for two seconds longer than he gave to anyone else before he returned to Jamie and said, "Probably 'bout Tully."

"What about him?" she asked with all sincerity and Katie lunged at her again. This time Bear stopped the psychotic hybrid, the palm of his hand pressing against her forehead as she swung at Jamie wildly. If Jamie weren't the focus of the insane stray's attacks, she'd find the whole thing pretty damn humorous. "*What did I say now?*"

Bear sighed. "Y'all make this so complicated," he muttered to everyone before saying to Jamie, "How do you feel about Tully?"

"Tully?"

"Yeah. Tully. The canine who's been sleeping at your house every night the past week."

"All up in my business," Jamie sneered.

"Unless you want me to let this one off leash"—he gestured to Katie with a tilt of his big grizzly head—"you'll answer my question."

"Fine. I love him. Okay?" And then she felt bad when Miss Millie and Miss Gwen looked so happy, that she quickly added, "But I don't think he feels the same way about me."

This time Bear had to catch Katie around the waist and take her over to the other side of the room.

"Lord, you are *dumb!*" Katie snarled. "The dumbest Yankee this side of the Mason-Dixon!"

"Katie, please!" Miss Millie snapped before she focused back on Jamie. "Now, sweetheart, what makes you think Tully's not interested?"

Was Jamie really supposed to tell the man's mother that he hadn't fucked her in more than a week? That he'd treated her like a good friend since the face-off with Buck? She'd thought maybe seeing her torture a woman had turned off any sexual feelings Tully'd had for her, but saving his mother had made him feel a sense of loyalty. She figured he was easing his way out of her life and since she'd insisted on no attachments, she didn't think it was right to argue. Yet Jamie was pretty sure that saying any of that to Tully's *mother* would be considered inappropriate.

And to solidify that feeling, Kenny leaned forward and said, "Awkward moment, Scene one, Take one. Action!" Jamie glared at the geek and watched as she jumped behind Mac.

After clearing her throat, "Look, Miss Millie, I appreciate—"

Miss Gwen patted Millie's arm. "I bet he stopped fucking her."

Bear jerked tall, his head nearly colliding with the salon ceiling. "*Momma!*"

"Hush now, Bear," Gwen chided. "Is that it, sweetie? Has he been giving you 'space'?" And she used air quotes.

Horrified where this conversation had led them, Jamie said, "I didn't really ask—"

"Bet he got that from Jack," Miss Gwen singsonged to Millie.

Millie rolled her eyes. "Lord, tell me that boy isn't taking love advice from that man. Don't get me wrong," she said to Jamie, "I love Jack more than I knew was possible but I wasn't ready to have another male in my life after I'd finally gotten Buck out of it."

"Which Jack thankfully had enough brains to figure out on his own."

"Tricky felines," Millie joked and the two women giggled like schoolgirls. "Now, dearest girl, this is what you're going to do. You're going to go to Tully's place and you're going to make him dinner. Something hearty that'll stick to his ribs. Pretend like you need to talk about something, and he'll think this is his moment to get it all out in the open, which trust me, you don't wanna do. Too much talking just ruins a relationship."

"Ain't that the truth," Gwen muttered, sounding a lot like her son.

"And then, when he's all relaxed and comfortable from the food, you're gonna pounce! And you're gonna fuck the living hell out of that boy!"

"*Momma!*" Katie barked, her hands covering her mouth, the fight no longer in her. Bear took off his cap, running his hands through his hair, and his big brown eyes scanning the room for emergency exits. And Jamie's coven laughed. Clearly they were having the best time *ever*.

"Hush now, Katie." Miss Millie took Jamie's right arm and Miss Gwen took her left, they dragged her to the front door, the bell over it ringing when they pulled it open. "You go on and get what you need and be at his place around six. That's usually when he gets home from work. And you do as I tell ya now. You *work* him."

"Work him," Miss Gwen added, "like you ain't never worked a man before. Hard. *Real* hard."

"Uh . . ."

"Go on now. Don't keep my boy waitin'. Life's too short."

Then they closed the door in her face.

Tully had given her a lot of space the past few days. Well, as much space as he was willing to allow.

Every morning Tully ambled on over to the hotel to have breakfast with Jamie and her coven. Mac usually made the hot food and Jamie usually made the pastries. Kyle and Katie were usually there, too, and that helped to keep Tully from grabbing Jamie and walking off with her. After breakfast Tully would go off and get some work done or amble around town to see if there was anything that needed doing. When the sun went down, he'd get a little hunting in with his Pack and maybe Kyle, before he'd head on over to Jamie's for a late night supper. He stayed every night but they never had sex. Not yet. Not until she faced the truth about them. Not until she realized she'd fallen in love with him as much as he'd fallen in love with her.

He knew it was driving her crazy, and to be honest, his cock *hated* him at the moment. Not that he blamed it. His need to be inside Jamie was tearing at him from the inside out. But Tully resisted because he knew he had to and because his daddy told him, "If you wanna keep her, you're going to have to give her up a little." And Tully understood the logic. He knew if he'd taken her that night after they'd run Buck off, she'd dismiss everything as "the heat of the moment." It wasn't. What happened between Jamie and his father may have opened Tully's eyes, but that was it.

Still, Jamie was as stubborn as Tully. She refused to accept the fact that she was crazy in love with him and he refused to give in to their needs because she was refusing to accept the fact she was crazy in love with him.

Did she even comprehend how different everything was now? Not only between them but between Jamie and the town? And it was different for one simple reason. Because she'd gone toe-to-toe with Buck Smith to protect Millie. That was something his neighbors would never forget.

It was funny, the day he'd met Jamie he knew her only concern at the time was protecting herself and her coven. Ten months later, though, the entire town of Smithville had done what only true Southerners managed to do when they were of a mind . . . they'd burrowed their way into Jamie's cold witch's heart and made it home. Now she would protect everyone in Smithville the way she would protect her coven.

Did she even realize she was already "attached" and not just to him? Probably not. For a smart girl, she could be kind of dumb sometimes when things were real obvious. Her coven had caught it, though. The way the men tipped their hats at them or smiled while opening a door. The way the ladies started gossiping with them at the coffeehouse or explaining their "Pride's secret recipe" for chitlins. They knew something big had changed, but Jamie was still in the dark. So pretty but dumb as a six-legged piranha when it came to her own feelings. But Tully was determined to get her to understand. Not hard for him, when he'd already made up his mind about her. When he already knew he loved her.

But Lord . . . a few more days of this and something was going to snap. He simply wasn't strong enough to resist her soul-devouring little charms anymore.

He'd talk to her tonight. He had to. Before his cock found a way to strangle him.

In sight of his house, Tully stopped when his phone rang.

"This is Tully," he answered.

"Boy."

Tully smiled. "Hey, Uncle Bub. What'cha need?"

"I don't need nothin', but you need to keep your eyes open. Word is Buck's heading back to Smithville with his Pack."

"It's a dumb move. The town's ready for him."

"Good." Bubba took in a breath, then said, "And I'm gonna make this real clear for ya, boy. So there's no misunderstandings later. If he does come back there, if he steps on Smith territory . . . you feel free to end it, if it comes to that. You understand me?"

Tully closed his eyes, but answered, "Yes, sir."

"No more games, and no guilt. The rest of the family has already agreed to this, and understands. It ain't like he left you much choice and sometimes it's just gotta be done. Understand?"

"Yes, sir."

The call ended as abruptly as it started and Tully walked to his house. As soon as he stepped inside, he knew she was there. He went straight to the kitchen—since he could smell the food cooking—and found her sitting on his kitchen table, reading a magazine and eating cut-up pieces of apple.

He stood in the doorway a moment, wondering how much longer he'd have to wait before he could come home to this sight every day, and said, "That smells good."

She grinned without looking up from her magazine. "Beef stew. *Much* better than Mac's, although she's still in denial on that topic."

"You two . . . like cats in a bag."

"Some say." She placed the magazine down and lifted her gaze to his. "You out hunting tonight?"

"No set plans. Why?"

"I thought maybe we should . . . talk."

And that's when his phone rang again. "Dang it!" He answered. "Yeah?"

"It's Kyle . . . Buck's back."

Just by the look on Tully's face, Jamie knew it was Buck. Knew he was coming back here to confront his son. She didn't understand it and wouldn't try. Fathers and sons had their own language and she was not one of those women who felt the need to understand or analyze it. Seriously, didn't she have enough to do?

"Yep." Tully disconnected the call and looked at her.

"It's all right," she said. If there was one thing she'd always understood was the need to handle an emergency. You couldn't be in law enforcement or any kind of crisis-type position and not understand it. "Food's not done yet anyway. Stew takes a while, so it'll be ready when you get back."

"I wanna talk."

"We'll talk." She owed him that. "When you get back."

Tully nodded and stripped off his clothes. "You'll be all right here by yourself?" he asked.

She grinned. "Would you go already?"

He turned to leave but then, just as quickly, turned back. His hand slid behind the back of her neck and he gripped it tight. The kiss was not friendly. Far from it. But it made what his mother told her seem all the more real.

Jamie kissed him back, making sure that her mouth and tongue made it clear that when he got back tonight, all the bullshit would be over. She didn't know how long they kissed, but when he finally pulled back, they were both panting and she knew she'd be counting the seconds until he returned.

He licked his lips. "Apple."

Jamie smiled, watching as he shifted from human to wolf almost faster than her eye could catch. He licked her bare foot and headed toward his front door.

\* \* \*

"Tully."

Tully stopped at the front door, looking over his shoulder as Jamie came around the corner.

She knelt down in front of him and rubbed her hands together for nearly a minute. When she stopped, she ran her hands from his muzzle, across his head, and down his back. She dragged her hands over his entire body until he was pushing into her, pressing his big wolf body against hers. He felt the energy she'd smoothed against his fur. It felt good, but meant more because it was from her. From his Jamie.

"For luck . . . and protection," she said when she stopped. "My gods will watch over you this night." She kissed his forehead and stood while Tully pressed up against her hip, lifted his head and nuzzled her breast, before he headed out the door and went off to face his father for the last time.

# Chapter Seventeen

M ost of the town had turned out for this. The ones who hadn't were mostly the bear sows—including grizzlies, polars, and blacks—because they stayed to protect the pups, cubs, and the elderly shifters. Even if the town failed on this ridge, there was no doubt that the sows would never let anything happen to the town's children. Their strength and power would be missed in the fight, but to have the sows protect everyone's offspring would always be worth the loss.

Kyle stood on one side of Tully, Jack on the other. Katie next to Jack, and Bear right behind them. The grizzly stood on his hind legs, sniffed the air, then came down with a *Wham!*, the ground shaking beneath their feet. He'd seen them. Tully knew because Bear pushed past them and lumbered down the ridge toward the clearing. Halfway down he broke into a run, the rest of the town right behind him. He'd just made it into the clearing when Buck's Pack exploded from the trees.

Baring his fangs, already tasting the kill, Tully charged forward and set to work.

Jamie shut off the heat under the stew and secured the lid. Tully had been gone a while and she was trying really hard not to worry about him. She kept telling herself she couldn't risk her soul and her power to go running to his rescue. Especially when she didn't know if he needed to be rescued.

So this was it, huh? What it felt like to be in love? Panic, nausea, and the slightest sense of doom. Nice. She'd be better off a beat cop in the South Bronx.

She heard the side door open and let out a breath she'd been unaware she'd been holding.

"Perfect timing," she said, not ready to show him yet how scared she'd been for him. "I just finished cooking the stew." She turned from the stove and only had a second to register the fur leaping at her. What had to be about two hundred and fifty pounds of canine, slammed into her, ramming her back into the counter, her head colliding with the stainless steel.

Tully tore off somebody's leg and chucked it over to Dale Sahara, M.D., who chewed on it before he went after somebody else.

Something wasn't right. Tully stopped, shook the blood from his eyes and studied the battlefield before him. Kyle pushed into him and they stared at each other. His brother felt it, too. Something wasn't right.

Tully watched one of his half-brothers get slapped across the clearing with one swipe of Bear's claw—and that's when it hit him. *Where's Buck?*

Jamie knew she blacked out because one second she'd been looking down at the stove and now she was lying on the floor looking up at it. Her head was throbbing, her mind confused. A face appeared before her, staring down at her.

"There you are," the face said. "Had me worried I'd hit ya too hard. Didn't mean to do that."

The face looked her over. "You'll be fine. I'll get you a pillow for your head. That flouncy boy of mine probably has lots of pillows."

He stepped over her and walked out of the kitchen. Not sure what she was doing, only knowing she couldn't lay there, Jamie dragged herself to her feet. It wasn't easy. Everything around her was turning and she couldn't focus.

If only it hadn't been her head. Any other damage she could handle. A broken arm, cracked ribs, knife wound to the back, gunshot to the neck. She would have been grateful for any of that, as long as it hadn't killed her outright, because it would have allowed her mind to do what it did best. Call upon the power she held and use it to control the situation. She'd bet that making her dazed and confused wasn't the face's idea, but that bitch, uh . . . his girlfriend . . . W-something. She probably told him to do that. Now all Jamie could manage was to stumble out of the house and away from that face. *What's his name?*

She had no idea where she was going—*although that tree over there looks kind of familiar*—she just knew she had to get away. But she wanted to sleep. She wanted to sleep so badly.

Luther hit him from behind and Tully shrugged him off. He didn't have the time or patience to fight one of Buck's sons. He wanted Buck.

Luther got back to his feet and charged him again. Tully batted him across the muzzle, sending him flying and took another look around.

*Something isn't right.*

Had Buck ever missed a fight in his life? Especially one that he made sure happened?

Tully heard a yip and looked down at his baby sister. She was watching him close, her dark gold eyes concerned. He tipped his head and motioned to Luther, who was charging his way back over to Tully. Katie's gaze followed, then she examined the area, cat eyes narrowing. Tully barked and motioned with his head. She nodded and took off running. If Buck was in town, Katie would find him. She was the best tracker they had.

He watched his sister sprint across the clearing until she made it into the trees on the other side. And that's when he was slammed from behind, all three of his half-brothers on him.

She stumbled through the trees, her eyes trying to clear. Everything was fuzzy. Everything out of focus. But she kept moving anyway. She kept going, pushing. She couldn't stop. Yet even that one, overpowering thought couldn't stop her from knowing when he was right behind her. She turned as he launched at her, her body instinctively dodging out of the way so he sailed past her. He turned from animal to human and spun to face her.

"Now look," he told her, moving toward her, "I'm trying to make this good for you. But if you keep runnin', if you fight me,

I'll just take what's mine anyway. And trust me, little girl—I'll make sure you don't enjoy it."

She had no idea what he was talking about. Her head hurt. She was sleepy. And the birds were too loud. *Were they always this loud?* He was right in front of her now. "Give me what I want, little girl, and I'll give you anything you need. Together we'll take over the Packs, then we'll take over *everything*."

An offer. An offer of power. His hand reached for her, to cup her cheek. She took hold of his fingers in hers and twisted his arm, off and away, while she brought her foot down on his instep. He cried out and she turned so her back was against his chest. She brought her left elbow up and back, impacting directly with his throat. He staggered back and she turned, slammed her fist into his face.

He dropped to his knees and she walked off. She glanced down at her hands. They were bloody. *When did that happen? Am I bleeding? Should I be at a hospital?* She kept moving. Part of her felt like she should run but she didn't know why. So she kept walking but quickly, pushing past hanging tree limbs and going around giant oaks and pines.

It sure would be nice to know where she was going.

Tully and Kyle fought off Buck's sons, pushing them back until a few more of Buck's Pack ran in to help. It didn't seem strange to Tully that he was fighting off fellow wolves—blood kin—with a cat by his side. Kyle had always been more brother to him than any of Buck's boys. They may argue, especially over the last piece of their momma's pecan pie at every Thanksgiving dinner, but he trusted the feline. Kyle was family. He'd always be family.

He threw Luther off—yeah, again—but stopped from going after him, instead stepping back and gazing up. The crows sure were complaining about the fight. They were making all sorts of racket.

Kyle shifted, looked up. "What the hell's going on?"

Tully wished he knew.

Jamie stopped, the odd-looking feline staring at her. Her fangs were odd. She was odd. Or maybe it was her head. Everything around her was pulsating and her headache was getting worse.

Yet even with all that going on, she couldn't stop herself from trying to get the cat or whatever to run. She knew it was in danger.

"Shoo," she told it. "Shoo. Go." She waved her hands at it. "Go. He'll kill you. Go!"

Something large and powerful slammed into her from behind, forcing her to the ground. Jamie landed, her hands bracing her fall. But he was on her now, flipping her over.

"We can do this any way you want, little girl. Even this way."

She swung her fist, connected with his jaw. His eyes flashed, shifting from one species to another. Then he punched her back. She felt something snap inside her face, her teeth suddenly not fitting together. The pain had her screaming but she was unable to open her mouth.

"Much better," he muttered. He sat back on his haunches, staring down at her. "That'll keep you quiet until we're done. Until I've fucked ya and marked ya as mine." He moved his own jaw around, gave her a little smile. "No way that boy of mine could handle a female like you." He smiled. "But I can."

That's when that strange black cat attacked, slamming into him, wrapping her paws around his head and neck. Snarling, he batted the feline off. She flipped head over tail, slamming into a tree. But she got back to her feet and she shifted to human. "Jamie, run!"

Jamie forced herself to roll over and crawl off. He watched her. She could actually feel him smiling as she made her slow painful way.

"Now where are you going, darlin'? Because we both know an ass like yours needs somebody in it."

Tully didn't wait until his sister's return. He took off but the closer he got to town, the louder those damn birds became. He stopped and turned, quickly realizing he had Kyle, Bear, Daddy, and half the town with him. He glanced back at the way he'd been headed but there were crows there now. They spun like a tornado, clearly blocking his way. They blocked the south and west as well, leaving only the east, which led deeper into the forest and toward the ocean.

Having no choice but to trust them, he headed that way and hoped for the best.

\* \* \*

She could hear the fight going on between the feline and that wolf. Could hear that the feline was getting her ass kicked. She was smaller than the wolf and although faster, he had years of fighting on his side.

Jamie reached what she wanted, her hands wrapping around the large limb that was laying there. She closed her eyes and then got to her feet. The pain from her jaw nearly made her black out again, but she fought it hard. She wanted to shake her head but the thought had tears sliding down her cheeks and falling into the leaves around her.

She turned and walked back to the feline and the wolf. She waited until the wolf had the feline on her back, then Jamie raised the tree limb over her head. She was swinging it down, aimed for the wolf's head but halfway to its destination it stopped. She yanked but it wouldn't move, then it was snatched out of her hand.

She spun around and there were three more of them. Three more like the one who'd grabbed her.

The one who took the tree limb caught hold of her by the back of the neck and held her.

"Daddy," he said, "we better get a move on. A bunch of 'em suddenly went rabbit and took off."

"No." He held the now human feline down while she tried desperately to get loose. "I finish this here. Once she's marked, there ain't nothin' they can do about it."

He gripped the feline by her neck and got to his feet. "I took some of the fight out of her," he said, tossing the feline to the one who had Jamie. "Use her as you want while I deal with this one."

He took Jamie by the hair and shoved her forward. "Let's get this done, darlin'. Lord knows, I've been waiting a long time for you."

"Daddy?"

Growling, Buck stopped and faced the other male. The two with him where moving back, their eyes wide, and he'd dropped the feline. She hissed, her back arching.

"What the hell's wrong?"

"Daddy?" he said again. And then he started screaming. Screaming as flames engulfed him. He dropped to the ground, rolling his body, trying to put the flames out.

The four women who'd been standing behind the one in flames watched but said nothing. Then their gazes moved to Jamie. As soon as she saw them, the headache ended, her mind cleared. She knew where she was, what she was, and what Buck had been trying to do to her.

She looked up at Buck and the wolf released her, stepping away from her. But it was too late for that. Too late to just walk away.

Jamie raised her hand, flicked her fingers, and Buck went soaring.

Tully had just made it past the trees, entering the clearing where he'd saved Jamie from flying hyenas, when something shot out from the other side.

He slid to a stop, his eyes wide as Buck Smith came tumbling to a stop. Two of Buck's sons came out after him, running like the devil himself was behind them. They stopped beside Buck, staring at Tully and the others.

From Tully's right and left, came the rest of Buck's Pack. It was a strange standstill. No one moving forward, no one backing off. He felt like they were all waiting for something, but he didn't know what.

Tully saw Jamie being helped into the clearing by her cousin. Her arm was around Mac's neck, she was covered in dirt and bruises. But even from across the clearing he could see she was in terrible pain, and her face looked strange. Swollen . . . broken.

Tully felt cold, then hot. His body began to shake and everything turned kind of red. Then his sister ran out of the trees, her human body covered in fresh claw and fang marks. She pointed at Buck and yelled out, "It was him, Tully! Buck did this to Jamie. It was Buck!"

His father got to his wolf feet and watched his firstborn. He snarled, daring him. But he didn't need to bother. It was all over now.

Tully charged across that clearing toward Buck, his family and neighbors behind him, and he knew nothing would stop him from killing that old bastard.

Jamie and her coven moved through the battle going on in the clearing. No one came near them, and no one tried to stop them. She rested against her cousin, Mac's arm strong around her waist. They reached the circle she'd created several days before when everything had been so simple and Mac helped her kneel in the middle of it.

Sen kneeled down in front of Jamie, her eyes filled with tears. "Oh, my God, Jamie. What did he do to you?"

Jamie took Sen's shaking hands and placed them on her swollen face, fighting the urge to flinch from the pain of that simple, soft touch.

"It'll hurt," Sen warned her between what had quickly turned into sobs. "It's going to hurt really badly. More than it hurts now."

Jamie kept Sen's hands on her with her own and begged her with her eyes. She didn't care about more pain. There were worse things than pain. But the pain was distracting her from doing what she needed to do. She needed it to stop.

Nodding, Sen agreed. "Just hold on. Okay, Jamie?" She glanced at the rest of the coven. "I'll need you guys, too. Give me what you can but not all of it. Understand?"

They nodded and moved around the pair, their hands clasped together. And outside the circle the fighting brutally continued. It felt like they were behind glass. Protected. And they were, in a way. Their goddesses were protecting them, the Dark Mothers, allowing them to do their work.

Sen closed her eyes and focused all her energy on Jamie, the others doing the same. While they worked on her, Jamie looked over at the battle going on all around them.

She watched as Tully and his father fought, tearing into each other. Two males charged Tully, taking him down to the ground, trying to take pieces out of him with their fangs and claws.

And Buck focused on her. She tensed, but not from the pain tearing through her from what Sen was doing. But because she couldn't stop Sen so that they could fight Buck. If she stopped the healing now, it could fuck up her face forever. A long time to go with your jaw unable to open or close.

Buck knew it, too. He could see it in her eyes, understood it because she didn't move away from Sen. She could tell he was grinning, even though he was still wolf. He lowered his body and charged straight at her.

Jamie waited, her body tensing, the pain getting worse as Sen had warned.

He was almost on them, only a few feet away, when a sudden flurry of feathers startled her and Buck.

Rico's talons extended and tore at Buck's face, trying for his eyes. Tully pulled away from the two wolves holding him back, slamming them to the ground before charging over to Buck, and brutally dragging his father down. Kyle joined him, focusing on the old wolf's hip and tail.

Jamie was grateful for that, grateful she didn't have to stop her coven from what they were doing. Grateful even as the pain grew horribly, horribly worse.

Nothing would stop him now. Nothing would stop him from killing the one wolf who deserved it.

If Buck had merely tried to kill Tully, had merely tried to become Alpha Male of the Smithville Pack, Tully would be able to let this go. He'd be able to walk away and let his father limp off to lick his wounds and try again another day. Like Buck had been doing for his entire life.

But Buck Smith had crossed the one line no self-respecting shifter would ever cross. Forced matings were one thing. A few decades ago, they happened all the time. But that wasn't what his father had been doing. He knew that because he knew Buck. Knew what the old man would do to make the witch his. He'd allow his Pack to fight to the death in his name while he used the battle to keep his firstborn busy so he could rape and mark Tully's woman.

Knowing the pain Jamie had suffered, knowing the fear she must have felt . . .

For that alone, the old man would die, and Tully would be the one to kill him.

He'd just gotten his jaw wrapped around Buck's throat, was moments from tearing out flesh and fur and a nice, thick artery, when he heard, "Tully. Don't."

Keeping his grip, Tully looked up and saw Jamie standing in front of him. Her face was no longer swollen, her bruises and cuts nearly gone. "Don't," she said again.

Growling, he dug his fangs in deeper, bit down harder, tasted blood. How could she want him to stop? How could she want to let Buck Smith off for what he'd done and what he'd been trying to do?

"Remember, Tully. There's some lines you can't cross. Once you do, there's no going back. Take this step and you become him. I love you too much to let that happen."

He stared at her. Hard. He saw the truth of her words in the way she gazed down at him, the way she gave him a soft smile. "Please, Tully."

It was strange, the way the fighting sort of tapered off. Everyone pulling back and watching . . . waiting.

With a nod to Kyle, Tully and his brother stepped back from Buck. And, like everyone else, they waited.

Jamie went to her knees beside Buck's wounded body. She petted his fur and Kyle glanced at Tully, probably thinking the same thing he was, *What is she doing?*

Jamie placed one hand on Buck's side and one hand on the ground, fingers digging into the dirt. She closed her eyes, her brow drawn down in deep concentration. Her coven stood behind her, Seneca now being held up by Mac. The poor thing looked moments from passing out.

Light came up through the ground, swirling around Jamie, covering her from toes to head. She gasped, she panted. She threw her head back as she often did when she was in the middle of an orgasm. The air crackled around them and lightning shot threw the sky.

She tore away from Buck, her body shaking. Kenny and Emma caught hold of her, held her up while Tully glanced at his father. He was still lying there, unconscious, except that he'd shifted back to human.

Still shaking as if she were freezing cold, Jamie said through chattering teeth, "Better this way, baby. Worse than death. Promise."

Without another word, the coven turned and walked away, each of them leaning on the other for strength and support.

All of them, local and interloper, watched the full-humans walk away. Then, once they were gone, they all focused on Buck.

He didn't look different. He didn't have horns and a pointed tail. He was still breathing, although covered in fresh wounds.

Knowing that everyone was waiting for him, Tully carefully walked forward. He leaned down, trying to catch a glimpse of something . . . *anything* that might be different about the old bastard. That would prove Jamie had done something to the old wolf who'd assaulted her.

But the more he looked, the less he saw. Until his eyes watered and Tully jumped back, sneezing and sneezing, trying to get that scent out of his nostrils.

"What?" Kyle asked, shifting back to human and watching him. "What's wrong?"

Tully shifted, as did almost everyone else, and he watched as Buck began to wake up, his head slowly lifting off the ground.

Unable to help himself, Tully laughed. Just a little. "Worse than death," he repeated.

Kyle shook his head. "What are you talking about?"

Tully pointed at Buck. "She made him . . . she made him full-human."

Jack came around Kyle, staring down at Buck with something akin to pure horror. "That's impossible."

"Not for her," Tully said. "Not here."

Buck glared up at him, talon marks covering his face from Rico. "Wrong. You're wrong."

"I know what I smell, old man. And I smell a full-human. She made you full-human." And Jamie was right. To them, to shifters, no matter the breed, being full-human was worse than death. It *was* death. But especially for someone like Buck. For someone whose whole being was wrapped up in the strength and force he wielded from the wolf inside him.

Buck closed his eyes and they watched him struggle to do what had always come so easy to them as soon as they'd hit puberty. To shift to wolf.

But nothing happened.

"Won't last," Buck said desperately.

"It *smells* like it'll last," Jack sneered.

"She got you, Buck," Tully said, backing away from him as did everyone else, even his sons. Buck had raised them so that their loyalty would always be to the strongest of their Pack. A full-human would never be the strongest. Unless it was someone like Jamie . . . and Jamie was his.

"She got you," Tully said again, and this time he laughed. So did his Pack, his family, his neighbors. They all laughed. And he knew this was so much worse than death to Buck.

Tully turned his back on Buck, something he would never have done even ten minutes ago, and walked off.

"Don't you walk away from me, boy!"

But Tully did, and he laughed as he did. Never once looking back.

# Chapter Eighteen

Emma met Kyle and Tully outside Tully's house. As soon as she saw them, she said, "I can't believe this is your house!"

Kyle shifted and glared at her. "Could you focus?"

"It's amazing! Why haven't you had a party here?"

Grinning, Tully kissed her cheek. "Thank you, darlin'." He glanced at the house and back at Emma. "How is she?"

"Sleeping. What she did . . . took a lot out of her."

"Will she be all right?"

Emma smiled. "Absolutely. She just needs sleep."

Mac and Kenny walked out, Seneca in Mac's arms, snoring against her shoulder. "So does this one."

"He broke Jamie's jaw," Kenny explained, her hand resting on Tully's shoulder when he cringed at her words. He'd already known it, but it still hurt to hear. Still hurt to know how much Jamie had suffered. It simply never occurred to him that his father would go that far. But now he knew.

"It's healed," Kenny went on. "Sen did an amazing job." She winked at him and whispered, "But don't tell her I said so. I'll never hear the end of it."

"Make sure she eats when she gets up," Mac explained as Kyle took Seneca out of her arms.

"I will."

"I found your cell and programmed my number in it. Any problems, you call. Okay?"

"I sure will. Thank you all."

Mac lightly punched his shoulder before saying to Kyle, "Can you take us back out to the woods?"

"What for?"

"We need to clean up some . . . uh"—she glanced at Tully—"burnt remains. Nothing to worry about it."

They headed toward Emma's bright red Jeep and Kyle looked back at Tully before following after them, Seneca still in his arms. "What burnt remains?" Kyle asked Mac. "What does that even mean?"

"You going to be all right?" Emma asked Tully.

"I'll be fine. He wanted Jamie all along, didn't he, Em?"

"I don't think so. I'm of the mind"—she grinned at him—"I got that line from Kyle." She chuckled, before finishing. "I'm of the mind he thought Wanda and her coven, the Lightest Dawn"—she rolled her eyes in disgust at that name—"would be able to fight us. I mean, they weren't bad. They blocked their presence and who Wanda was a lot longer than most could. Using the patchouli was really smart. Jamie hates that crap so much, she was always busy trying to get away from Wanda rather than focusing on her energy. But when Wanda wasn't strong enough to fight Jamie one-on-one, I think Buck's interests—moved."

"That sounds about right. He always liked strong females but they always ended up trying to kill him while he slept."

Emma giggled and patted his shoulder. "Look, don't worry about Jamie. She'll be fine. Just make sure she sleeps and eats, in whatever order she wants to."

"Okay."

"And Tully"—she took a breath—"what she did to Buck . . . it's not something you guys have to worry about. She can't go around ripping everyone's DNA apart."

"You don't have to explain it to me, darlin'."

"I guess I don't want everybody afraid of her, thinking that if she gets pissed over someone giving her the wrong change or bumping into her, she'll do *that*."

"No worries, darlin'. I'll make sure everybody understands."

"Okay."

"Now you take that pretty face home and let Kyle whine about his pathetic excuse for wounds."

"You two are so hopeless," she teased, going up on her tiptoes and kissing his cheek.

He watched her go down the stairs and get in the front passenger seat. Once the Jeep was heading down the road, Tully opened the door and walked into his house.

Jamie was in his bed, right where she belonged, and out cold. He thought about taking a shower first, but he needed to touch her, to hold her, to make sure she was okay.

He slipped in beside her and she made small mewling sounds in her sleep. He shushed her and brushed his hands against her hair and body as he settled in behind her, spooning his body around hers. She grabbed his hand and held it between hers, sighed once, and slept peacefully again.

Tully kissed her forehead, thanked any stronger power than himself that might have helped him in the last few hours, and dropped off.

Tully woke up when he finally couldn't ignore the sun beating against his face. His momma had been right. He needed some damn blinds. *Ruin the aesthetic, my ass.*

Jamie was comfortably wrapped around him but still sleeping hard. Making sure to not wake her, he eased out from under her, his body grumbling at the loss of her warmth. But he didn't want her to wake up to a dirty, blood-covered male. She deserved more than that. So he silently headed to the bathroom for a quick shower with additional plans on making her some breakfast before they had a nice little discussion about their future together.

Tully was in the middle of washing his hair and debating on pancakes or waffles or both, when the shower door opened, slamming against the wall beside it. The sound had him spinning around, ready for a fight until he saw Jamie standing there . . . staring at him.

"Jamie?"

Her gaze swept down to his feet, then slowly back up until she gazed into his face. Tully instinctively took a step back. "Jamie?"

She licked her lips and stepped in to the shower. Water poured down on her and she used both hands to swipe her hair off her face.

"Are you all right?"

"Uh-huh." She openly stared at his cock, the damn thing rising without direct orders from him. "I feel great."

"Are . . . are you sure. Because you don't seem yourself."

She stepped closer and Tully realized he was now backed up to the shower wall—and his shower was not small.

"When you"—she licked her lips again, blew out a long, desperate breath—"use as much power as I did last night, there are . . . side effects. Remember? We talked about side effects."

"Right. Sen gets angry and you get—"

"Horny."

"Horny?"

She pressed her hands against the shower wall behind him and leaned in, taking a long sniff before she let out a groan. "Yeah. I usually take care of it myself with an hour or six with my vibrator."

He swallowed. "Six?"

"But it's back at the house and you, oh, God, you smell so good."

"But—" he stopped, cleared his throat because it was cracking, and tried again. "But we're supposed to talk."

"Talk?" She glared at him. "I don't wanna talk. I wanna fuck." She reached out, wrapping her hand around his cock.

Tully felt his knees weaken, much more and he'd drop completely.

With soft fingers, Jamie slowly stroked him. "Don't you want to fuck me, Tully?"

Tully nodded. "Uh-huh."

"A lot?"

"Uh-huh." He swallowed again, his eyes crossing as he desperately tried to focus. "But we need to talk."

"About?"

Panting, he said, "About . . . uh . . . us."

"What about us?"

"I don't remember."

She smiled, the sweetest smile he'd ever seen. "Then we'll talk when you do remember."

"But," he said quickly, his mind trying to work past what her insistent hand was doing to him, "you went through a lot last night. I should be taking care of you, pampering you, showing you I'm sensitive or whatever." *Oh, my God! What is that twisty thing she's doing with her hand?*

"Tully," she purred, "I want you to take care of me and pamper me and show me you're sensitive and all that other bullshit people need. And, yeah, I sometimes need it too. But right now all I need is a good, solid, *hard*"—she pressed her lips against his chest—"fuck. Think you can help me with that?"

"You're—Lord, that feels good—sure?"

Her tongue swirled around his nipple while her thumb swirled around the head of his cock. "I'm sure." She looked up at him with those dark brown eyes. "I am so fucking sure."

He shrugged. "Well . . . all right then."

She'd been pushing him hard, demanding what she wanted and needed from him. She needed to know now if he could handle this side of her. It happened anytime she called on that level of power, used that amount of energy. Because of what she'd done the day before, the need for sleep came first. Other times her first need was food. And sometimes all she needed was to fuck. This time she needed all three, but her body told her in what order. Sleep first, fuck second, food third.

But Jamie knew it wasn't that easy. Her ravenous needs after casting had scared off more than one man. All men said they wanted a sex machine . . . until they actually got one. Then suddenly they were overwhelmed, she was too needy, and how could anyone expect them to live this way? If Tully couldn't handle it, she needed to know. Would she end it? No way. She loved him. But she'd have to arrange her schedule differently, make sure the freezer was always full with lots of easy-to-make meals, and that she maintained her monthly delivery of batteries for all her vibrators. She wouldn't make the same mistakes she'd made with her ex. Not with the way she felt about Tully. She loved him so much it hurt. And she wouldn't risk losing that because maybe he couldn't handle—

Tully lifted her up, turned, and pushed her into the wall. With one hard thrust he was inside her, Jamie crying out as he drove into her, nailing her against the wall with the strength of his body and the power of his cock. And he was relentless, his mouth finding hers, his tongue stroking, his hands gripping her flesh hard.

It was too much. It wasn't enough.

Jamie's legs tightened around Tully's waist, her heels digging into his ass, her arms holding onto his shoulders as the orgasm ripped up her spine, exploding through her. Tully followed close behind, his body shaking as he released inside her, his mouth pressed against the side of her neck. They stood there, for how long she didn't know, holding onto each other.

Finally, Tully reached over and shut off the water. Still holding her, still buried deep inside her, he walked out of the shower and back into the bedroom. With each step he took, the amazing sensation of his cock inside her radiated through her, and she knew she wasn't done. Knew she needed more. The beauty of it? She didn't have to say a word. Tully stopped by the bed and then he was taking her down to the mattress. By the time she felt the comforter against her bare ass, Tully was hard again and driving into her.

Worries about finding workarounds to manage the immediate hours after spellcasting flew out of her head as it suddenly occurred to her she wouldn't be needing any of that. Not with her horny wolf. He was as insatiable as her, as demanding. And he gave as good as he got. She couldn't have asked for more, hoped for more.

She couldn't help but smile either at the realization and Tully, not missing a thrust, said, "Look at that smile. Tell me what I need to do, beautiful, to keep you smiling like that every day."

Jamie laughed, hugging Tully tight against her. "Well, um . . . this works."

They slept most of the afternoon, both exhausted to their bones. But when Tully woke up, he was alone and didn't like it. He went down to the first floor and when he heard the ocean, he headed to his kitchen. His sliding door was open, which explained the ocean sounds he heard, but he barely glanced at it with all that food covering his kitchen table.

"I came down here," Jamie said, "and found it like this."

"Of course you did." He grabbed one of the large paper plates someone thoughtfully put out and began spooning someone's mac and cheese onto it. "We take care of our own around here. And everyone knew you'd be too plumb tired to cook for me."

Jamie leaned against the sliding glass door frame. She had only a sheet wrapped around her and Lord knew she didn't need anything else. "I'm cooking for you now?"

"If you love me . . ."

He left it out there hanging, expecting her immediate response. When he didn't get it, he dropped his food on the table and stalked over to her. "You do love me. You already said so."

She looked off and Tully gave her his best "basset hound" expression. "Don't you love me?"

"That is a pitiful face."

He stuck his bottom lip out as far as possible and Jamie laughed hard, pressing her body into his.

"Tell me you love me, beautiful."

"Of course I love you."

He kissed her smiling mouth and pulled her to the kitchen table. He sat down and sat her on his lap, reaching around her to get his plate of food.

"There's no way we can eat all this food," she said.

"Speak for yourself, Yankee."

"Do I have to do anything now?"

Fork poised in front of his mouth, "Sorry?"

"I mean . . . all this food. Should I send them cash or something? Mow their lawn? Babysit their kids?"

Tully put his food back down on the table, sure he wouldn't get his meal anytime soon.

He ran his hands down her arms. "Look, the only thing you'll have to do is maybe make a pie when someone's momma passes on. Or bake a cake for someone's birthday. And you'll do it 'cause it's a nice thing to do and because you know that when you need something, there'll always be someone there to help. That's just the way it is around here. You'll get used to it."

"Will I have to start being less sarcastic? And mocking?"

"No one's expecting more than you can give, beautiful. Stick with the pies and the cakes, don't make fun of the dead at their funerals, stop shooting at the hyenas on your territory—because we all know you have been—and you'll be just fine."

She nodded, then said, "But if the hyenas are *illegally* on my property—"

"Jamie."

"All right fine."

"Thank you." He kissed her shoulder and reached for his plate but she caught his wrist.

"Oh, no, you don't."

"Woman, I'm hungry!"

"You're not getting a bit of this damn food until you say it."

"Fine. You're light as a feather."

Jamie slammed her elbow into his chest.

"Ow!"

"Say it."

He laughed even as he rubbed where she'd hit him with that chicken wing of hers. "I love you."

"And?"

*And?* He smiled. "And you're as light as a feather."

She grinned. "Thank you." She put her arms around his neck. "So now what?" When he frowned, she added, "*After* you eat."

"Sleep some more? Or maybe play another game of gropey hands?"

"I meant where do we go from here?"

"Oh that's easy. When you're at work, I'll start moving your stuff in. You won't notice at first, and by the time you do, it'll all be here. Every night you'll make noises about going back to your place, but you won't. And then one day you'll wake up with me sleeping beside you, and you'll realize it's thirty years later and wonder how you ever got so lucky as to have me in your life all that time."

"So I was right? One night and we're now irrevocably attached."

"Yeah. But you were lucky enough to get *me*."

"True. And you were lucky enough to get me." Her grin grew. "And Rico." That's when the bird flew in through the open door and landed on his shoulder, predator-talons digging into Tully's flesh, her little beaked head turning toward him.

"Great," he lied. "Because I do so love your bird."

Jamie lifted up his plate of food and held it out so her mooching little fricassee could eat his mac and cheese. "And I can so see that love too," she laughed.

# Epilogue

Tully pulled his cell phone out of his jacket pocket, moving away from the small group he was speaking to and into a small hallway.

"Hello?"

"Boy."

And Tully had to smile, but he was glad Bubba Ray couldn't see it. "Hi, Uncle Bub."

"You all right?"

"Are you checking up on me?"

"Asked you a question, boy."

Tully stifled a laugh. "I'm fine, sir."

"Your, uh, Aunt Janie was worried about you is all."

Tully had to admit it warmed his hard heart to realize how much his kin cared. It had been more than three weeks since Buck Smith's body had been found. The rumor was that his two sons—Luther having disappeared—had turned on him. They'd even been bragging about it, trying to keep their Pack of strays from bailing. Maybe hoping to work their way into one of the other Smith Packs. But Tully knew the truth, had heard it from Kyle who'd heard it from some tree-dwelling feline kin of his out of Alabama.

It had been the females who'd ended it for Buck Smith. Some Reeds, a few Lewises, and lots of Smiths. All of them She-wolves. When they'd heard what Buck had tried to do to Jamie, they'd descended on him like the wrath of God. It was the one thing female shifters wouldn't put up with from the males and if the She-wolves hadn't taken care of it themselves, the other breeds would have. Which would have led to mocking . . . and She-wolves hated being mocked.

He probably should feel something about the man's death, and he felt kind of guilty that he didn't, but Buck Smith had reaped what he sowed. In the end, all that mattered to Tully was that his momma would never have that man's hand around her throat again, and Jamie would never worry that he'd be coming back for her. Then again, he got the feeling Jamie was a little disappointed Buck wouldn't be. She'd had all sorts of "stuff" waiting for him.

"Well you tell Aunt Janie I'm fine."

"All right. Good. You need anything, you call."

"I will. Have a nice night."

"Yep." Then the call ended as abruptly as it had started.

After sliding his phone back into his jacket pocket, Tully adjusted his bow tie and headed back into the Mayor's Spring Dance. It was a success, but he was painfully bored. Happy, but bored. He stared out the big glass doors and he saw a sleek swath of red silk slip by.

"Hi, Tully."

A long arm wrapped around his shoulder and he grinned. "Hey, Mac."

"You need us to distract the crowd so you can get out of here?"

"Nah. I made my speech, made sure the food and liquor are ample, and that everyone will have a good time."

"Then go on. She's waiting for you outside."

"Thanks, darlin'." He studied Mac a moment. "That's a beautiful dress on you."

"Thanks."

"I think Bear likes it, too."

Mac blinked, looking slightly panicked. "Um . . . huh?"

"He's been eyeing it all night. Maybe he wants to borrow it."

She let out a mighty relieved laugh before she pushed him away. "Go. Or I'm rattin' you out to ya mother."

"Traitor."

Tully moved through the crowd and out the door, waving at his momma before he stepped out. Her smile was wide as she waved back and winked, her arm around his daddy's waist, looking happier than she ever had before. Knowing Millie was in good hands—even if they were feline hands—Tully slipped outside.

He saw Jamie leaning against a tree, completely unconcerned with the strapless five-thousand-dollar designer dress he'd had made for her. Like him, she'd rather be in jeans and a T-shirt. Heh. Like him, she'd rather be naked. He headed toward her but stopped by one of the large bushes that surrounded the Crystal Room.

"What'cha doin'?"

His brother stepped out from behind the bushes. "Nothin'."

"Is that right, Emma? Is nothin' going on back there?"

"Go away," Emma's voice ordered from behind those bushes.

"You sure you don't need some help?"

"*Tully!*" she squeaked.

Kyle shook his head. "You are such a bastard."

"Not since my momma married your daddy."

He approached Jamie, marveling at how beautiful she looked in the moonlight. He kissed her cheek, his finger tracing the black Celtic Knot on her upper bicep that they'd woken up one morning to find marked into her skin. Proof she'd become a powerful goddess's champion. It didn't mean much to him, but Jamie had been really happy about it. And pretty damn cocky about it, too—much to her cousin's intense annoyance.

"You were great tonight," he told her. "Who knew you were a natural politician's wife?"

"Bite your tongue."

"I'd rather *you* bite my tongue."

"You say that but then you bite back." She pouted. "And I'm so delicate."

"Heh."

The valet pulled Tully's car up and Jamie shook her head. She'd done the same when he'd pulled up in front of the house in it.

"I still can't believe you have a car."

" 'Course I have a car. We're not savages."

"But you never use it."

He shrugged. "I ain't runnin' from nothin'. And everything I want is in walking distance." He winked at her. "Even you."

"But it's a . . . a Lamborghini . . ."

"You don't like it?"

"Are you kidding?" They stood staring at the car until Jamie asked, "You'd rather walk home, wouldn't you?"

He couldn't lie to her, so he said, "Yeah."

She rolled her eyes and Tully looked at the grizzly cub he'd hired to take care of the parking for him. A nice, reliable kid. And Bear's son.

"When you're done here tonight, Luke, think you can run the car back to my house?"

Luke stared up at him with wide eyes. Like his father, he was probably going to be a late bloomer. Nearly seventeen but barely five-foot-seven. It made him a target with the other cubs and pups, but he took it well and held his own. If he was anything like his father, he'd wake up one day and be twice the size and much less tolerant.

"Are . . . are you sure, Uncle Tully?"

"Yep. And don't let Kyle try and talk you out of it. I don't let him drive it at all."

"Okay."

"And no dents or evidence girls have been back there." He leaned in and whispered, "No *evidence*. You know what I mean."

"Oh, my God," Jamie snapped. "Can we please go?"

"See how she is, Luke? Busy trying to get me alone."

Jamie started walking away from him, but he caught her hand. "Not yet." He crouched in front of her and pulled off her high heels. "You won't make it a mile before you're whining about your feet."

"I hate these shoes."

Tully held the shoes by their straps in his left hand and grabbed hold of Jamie's hand with his right. They headed home, taking their time and enjoying the night. She complained about it an awful lot, but Tully had noticed that Jamie had taken to ambling more and more these days. It was good for her, too. Made her appreciate what she already had rather than always being busy trying to get what she didn't. And the more comfortable she grew with everything around her, the less she felt that driving need to search out more and more power. Somehow, without saying much about it, Jamie had found that balance. That balance between what she had and what she wanted. And the funny thing was . . . it was by finding this balance that allowed more power to blossom within her, naturally.

He wasn't even sure if she'd realized it yet—she could be kind of dumb about the obvious. Beautiful, charming, and lethal—but dumb.

But he loved her anyway.

Jamie made his days bright and his nights . . . unbelievable.

"Doing any casting soon, beautiful?"

Head thrown back, Jamie laugh. "You ask me that every night."

"I'm just trying to be helpful."

"Oh. Okay."

"Tomorrow's Sunday," he needlessly reminded her. "I'm assuming we're sleeping in."

"You assume a lot. I figure we should get up at six, face the day bright and early."

Tully stopped, forcing Jamie to stop with him.

"Tell me you're joking."

"I didn't say we had to actually get out of bed or put on clothes in order to face the day bright and early." Her hand still gripping his, she stepped into him, pressed that perfect, curvy body against his. "I'd prefer we stay right where we are."

"Now that sounds more like my speed, beautiful." He kissed her chin, nuzzled his nose against hers. "Not too slow, not too fast."

"Just amble the morning away?" she sighed.

"Can you think of anything better?"

She cupped his cheek with tender fingers and softly replied, "For once . . . no. I can't think of anything better."

# In the Dark

Cynthia Eden

# Chapter One

Her dead lover stood on the other side of the bar, rubbing his hand against the back of some long-legged redhead and looking very much *alive*.

Sadie James drew in a deep breath. Caught the scent of smoke. Expensive perfume. Sweat.

*I went to that jerk's funeral. Cried over his grave.*

A grave he didn't seem to be occupying.

She'd even taken flowers to the graveside.

The redhead laughed. Tossed back her head. The man turned, braced his hand against the wall behind her head and leaned in even closer to her.

Rage had Sadie's back teeth grinding together.

She stalked across the bar, elbowing dancing men and women out of her way. Her fingers curled, and a hard fury tightened her body.

*Two years.* For two damn years she'd thought he was dead. While he was out there screwing redheads. Redheads who wore really trashy pink dresses.

He was bent over the woman, his mouth poised over her throat.

Sadie was going to rip the bastard apart.

The redhead laughed. A high, tipsy giggle.

Sadie growled.

Even though she was still at least ten feet away, and the music blaring from the band jumping on stage was earsplitting, Liam

Sullivan stiffened. His dark head snapped up. He spun around, scanning the crowd.

His eyes, too damn blue and bright for a dead man, locked on her. She saw his stare widen and his lips began to curve into a smile—

A smile she was going to knock off his still too-handsome face. "*Liam.*" A snarl.

The ghost of a smile vanished.

The redhead shifted beside him. "Uh, honey . . ."

Oh, no, she did *not* just call him . . .

He glanced back at the redhead. Touched her cheek. "Give me a minute, Sharon." The Irish whispered beneath the words, softening the vowels, hardening the consonants. Cagey bastard. Usually, he could all but make the soft rolls of his native Ireland disappear from his speech. The Irish was strong, though, when he was angered or aroused. His fingers curved under the redhead's chin. "Why don't you go dance?"

And the chick nodded her head. Walked away without another word.

*What the hell? Had the woman never heard of a backbone before?*

Sadie stalked toward him. Jabbed one finger into his chest. "Hey, asshole. Long time no see."

He grunted.

"Tell me, shouldn't you be . . . I don't know, in a *grave* somewhere?" She'd put him in one, she'd—

"You shouldn't be here." Weaker accent now, but the vowels were still soft. His gaze swept behind her. "You need to leave, love."

Love. Her heart took the hit and her entire body trembled. "I'm not going anywhere." Not without one hell of an explanation. She'd *cried* over the bastard. "If you wanted to break up with me, Sullivan, all you had to do was say so."

The sex had been great between them. Better than great. Wild. And she was the kind of woman who really, really needed wild.

They'd been teamed up on an FBI assignment. He'd been a liaison from Ireland, working secretly with them on a hunt for a global killer. She'd never slept with another agent—she didn't like mixing her business and her play.

But with Liam . . . she'd broken all the rules.

Their first date they'd never even made it out of her place. She'd had him naked in less than five minutes. He'd taken her against the wall in her den and had her coming in one.

That had just been the beginning.

He'd been the first human to match her stamina, because matching someone with her *unique* characteristics was damn hard.

His nostrils flared as he stared down at her. "Sadie, you don't—" He broke off, and his eyes widened in surprise. "Your scent . . ."

"Oh, great, you've been playing dead for two years and now you want to talk about the way I *smell?*" Her claws were out now. The fury was too strong. Rage, betrayal.

Dammit, she'd trusted him. The night she'd learned of his death . . . hell, they'd been planning to meet after his last op. She'd planned to tell him the truth about herself.

She'd never told a human lover the truth before.

But Liam, he'd been different—or so she'd thought.

The lighting in the bar was dim, but she'd never really needed much light to see. His face was just as she'd remembered. Strong, square jaw. Dimple in his chin. Eyes like the skies over his Ireland—so damn blue. Sexy lips, high brow, chiseled cheeks. A nose that had been broken a few times because her Liam hadn't grown up easy. He'd lived on the streets of Dublin from the time he was eleven until he'd reached seventeen.

His skin looked a bit paler than before. His hair was a little longer. The black locks skimmed his broad shoulders. He wore a battered black, leather coat, a dark shirt, and loose jeans.

The guy was big—way over six feet. She had to tilt her head back a bit to stare up at him. No, to *glare* up at him.

"I was told *everyone* on your team died on that last operation." She should have been on that team. But someone, somewhere, had passed on the word about her relationship with Sullivan and she'd been yanked at the last minute. Reassigned to some bullshit security detail.

When she'd gotten the news about the slaughter—Sadie couldn't stop the shudder that worked over her body. God, but she could still see those photos—*it had been a bloody massacre.* One look at those photos, and she'd almost fainted. *Because Liam was one of the victims.* Or so she'd thought.

Normally, Sadie wasn't the fainting type. More the kick-ass, make-'em-sorry type, and that was just what she was about to do. Make the Irish devil very sorry that he'd ever been born.

He grabbed her. His hands locked around her shoulders, and he lifted her up onto her tiptoes. "I missed you."

*What?* Lying jerk—

Then he kissed her. His lips were firm against hers, slightly cool, and—*oh, hell.*

Her mouth opened. She gave a little moan when she felt the strong thrust of his tongue. The guy had always been one hell of a kisser. He knew just how to move his lips against hers. Knew just how to use his tongue. Sliding it against hers. Teasing her mouth. Tasting. Sampling. Taking.

A ball of heat in her belly had her rubbing against him. Pushing to get closer. She didn't want soft and easy, she'd never wanted that.

Hard. Wild—that was the only way she'd take a man.

And Liam, damn his black soul, knew it.

His hands smoothed down her body. Locked on her ass. Squeezed. His erection pushed against her belly. Long and hard. Thick. Oh, she remembered it well.

She remembered too much.

That was the problem.

She tried to pull back, but Liam's hold didn't weaken.

Sadie twisted, putting some of her enhanced strength into play. *Oh, damn, but the man's tongue . . .*

His hold tightened.

*Too strong.* What the hell?

His mouth lifted, just an inch. "Fuckin' missed you," he rasped, then captured her lips again.

Ice blasted through her veins. *Fuckin' missed you.* He hadn't looked like he was missing her when he'd been all over the redhead.

Bastard.

Sadie purred, a low, rumbling sound.

And bit him.

The coppery taste of blood flooded her mouth.

Liam's head jerked up. He stared down at her, and his eyes, the beautiful eyes she'd seen in her dreams for so long, flickered sickeningly from blue to black.

Shit.

Not playing anymore, she shoved against him and managed to break free of his hold. Stumbling back, she lifted her hand to her mouth and shook her head, struggling to deny the truth that was staring her right in the face.

*No, not Liam.*

He licked away the drops of blood on his lips. "*A ghrá*, you do know what I like." *A ghrá*. One of his Irish endearments—one that used to make her heart leap, but now had her tensing.

Liam smiled at her, but it wasn't the boyish smile of the man she'd known.

It was a hard grin. One that showed the sharp points of his too long canines.

Her nostrils flared. Scents assaulted her. The same smoke she'd smelled before. The alcohol.

Liam. The crisp scent of an ocean. The sweet fragrance of clovers.

Ireland.

He didn't smell like decay or death.

Impossible.

But his eyes were black and his teeth, they were *too* long.

Sadness filled her. She knew his type. Knew what drove them. So much darkness.

Liam *was* lost to her. His kind lived for terror and fear.

True monsters.

She'd never thought she'd have to do it, but it looked like she might have to kill her ex-lover.

Hell. *Could* she do it? A tremble shook her body, and, for an instant, she didn't see his face.

No, she saw the pale face and shining eyes of Jasmine. Her friend smiled, and blood trickled down her neck.

Sadie blinked, and Jasmine was gone, but Liam, a new Liam, still stood before her.

"Somethin' you should know, Sadie." His brogue thickened, deliberately, she knew. "I didnae exactly survive that ambush . . ."

Her hand lifted. Traced the line of his cheek. "I know." Soft. "And I hope you understand . . ."

A line appeared between his brows. "Understand?"

She knew her smile was broken. Her hand dropped. *Do it.*

*Don't think.* She reached for a nearby chair. Lifted it and shattered the wood in a blink.

"Sadie—"

Her kind moved fast, always had. Her right hand locked around the broken chair leg. She raised her hand, preparing to plunge her makeshift weapon into his heart. "I'm not killing you—I'm killing what you've become."

His black eyes widened.

*Vampire.*

Sadie drove her stake straight toward his heart.

*I'm sorry, Liam.*

He reacted too slowly. Liam swore, trying to twist back, but he was trapped against the wall.

The wood drove into his chest. He grabbed her wrist, holding tight, fingers clenching around the delicate bones.

*Sadie James was a hell of lot stronger than she looked.* Her golden eyes were determined, but her mouth, that sweet, beautiful red mouth quivered.

He could feel his blood rushing out. Soaking his shirt front. There were screams around them. Folks had turned at the sound of the shattering chair.

The wood was in his chest, about an inch and a half deep. But it wasn't in his heart. He'd managed to turn just enough—

*"She's killing him! Oh, my God, that crazy bitch is killing him!"*

He knew the voice. Susie. Sharon. He couldn't exactly remember the redhead's name. She was the one screaming, but she didn't seem to realize that the bar she was in . . . well, it wasn't exactly normal.

Folks there weren't going to lose any sleep over another vampire getting staked. Hell, he could see the faces of the other vamps in the bar. Smiling bastards. They were afraid to take him on, but they were sure happy to let someone else take a stab at him. Or a stake, to him.

"Love, I don't want to hurt you." Truer words he'd never spoken. But Liam had already died once, found the whole experience to be a damn nightmare, and he didn't plan on passing over again.

He could break her wrist. Snap it easily. And if he had to, he would.

The trembling lips rose into a grimace. "Hurt. That's all vampires do. They hurt, they torture, and they kill."

Pretty accurate—for *most* vampires. "I'm not like that." The stake was digging deeper into his flesh. Not a killing wound, but it still burned—and his kind didn't do so well with blood loss.

He could see the doubt in her eyes.

Fine. His teeth clenched. So be it.

Liam snarled—and attacked.

He lunged forward, and the stake drove deeper into his chest.

Sadie stumbled back and her hand finally, *finally*, fell away from the stake when she tripped over the remains of the chair and tumbled onto the floor.

He stared down at her. Beautiful Sadie.

Soft locks of blond hair fell around her heart-shaped face. Her mysterious eyes glared up at him.

His hand lifted. He grabbed the end of the stake. Yanked it out. Felt the rough splash of blood.

A choked cry. For an instant, his eyes lifted and met the redhead's shocked stare. She looked like she was going to pass out. Instead, she turned and ran, as fast as she could.

The band kept playing.

He tossed the stake onto the table. "That hurt, Sadie."

She barred her teeth at him. Teeth that were too sharp for a human's. Why hadn't he noticed that before? "It was supposed to."

His head cocked. *Sadie*. He'd wanted her from the first minute he saw her. Petite, curvy, with that come-hither smile and those fuck-me heels she liked to wear.

Most of the men in his unit had fantasized about her. There was just something about Sadie James.

Something stirring. Something untamed.

A fire, a passion that he'd never seen before—or since.

His gaze slid over her. She hadn't changed much. Her hair was a little shorter. Maybe she was a bit thinner. He didn't like that. His eyes narrowed as he studied her. She still had great breasts—full and high. But her hips weren't as curved, dammit. He'd sure liked her lush hips.

His stare skated back to her face. Such a lovely face. Wide eyes. So golden. A straight, sharp little nose. High cheeks.

A beauty, no denying it.

One that had nearly taken his heart. Then, and now.

"Ah, love . . ." Because she had been. He shook his head and felt real regret as he stared down at her. "You made me lose my meal." And his fuck, but they'd get to that, later.

Her brows rose. "Tough shit, vampire." In a flash, she'd bounded to her feet.

Fast. *Too fast.*

Just as her teeth were a bit too sharp.

His nostrils flared. Her scent surrounded him. The wild scent of a forest. The rich scent of woman.

Odd. Humans usually smelled like food to him. Blood and sex.

But Sadie—there was a heavy fragrance that clung to her. A deep scent. Heady.

His cock tightened.

He'd wanted her like mad when he was a human, and, being a vampire hadn't made the desire lessen.

It had just made the hunger more dangerous.

"I cried for you." The words seemed ripped from her. Her hands were clenched. Her small body taut.

The heart many humans foolishly believed didn't beat inside of him began to thunder against his chest. His hand lifted. The back of his fingers brushed over her cheek.

Soft. So fucking soft.

"Sadie, soon you'll bleed for me." A promise.

Sadie wasn't getting away from him.

Besides, the woman had tried to kill him. She owed him. Blood, sex, *everything.*

She blinked. Shook her head. Blond strands of hair bounced against her shoulder. "I'm not your prey, vamp."

*Vamp.* "Liam." He said his name deliberately. Just how much did Sadie know about his kind? She knew how to kill them, obviously. When he'd known her before, he'd thought she was a human, just like him.

One who didn't know about the true darkness waiting just behind the closed doors of the world.

She caught his wrist. Jerked his hand away from her face. "Don't touch me. You lost that privilege a long time ago."

The anger inside began to boil. "You're playin' with fire." The last warning he'd give her.

Liam figured he'd been a pretty good sport so far. He'd let her attack him. Nearly stake him. He'd even let the sexy blond eat his head off with her insults.

But enough, well, was enough. The wound in his chest was slowly closing, but his shirt was soaked with blood. He needed to drink soon, and he hadn't been kidding when he said Sadie would be giving him her blood.

In the next two minutes, he planned to have her pinned against the wall, her soft body pressed to his, his teeth piercing her pale throat.

He could hardly wait to taste her blood on his tongue.

"I'm not afraid of fire, asshole." That chin of hers lifted. Stubborn. She'd always been stubborn—and there hadn't been much that Sadie had feared.

But, that had been before . . .

She cast a disgusted glance over his body. "And I sure as hell am not afraid of you." She spun around, took a step away from him. "See you later, vamp—"

Liam grabbed her. Jerked her back and shoved her against the wall of the bar. He leaned over her. Pushed his weight against her and trapped her against the wall—just as he'd planned. Her breath panted out. She twisted, snarled, but she didn't break his hold.

Sadie was strong, but *he* was stronger. "I told you, already, you made me lose my prey." His head lowered. His mouth hovered over her throat. His teeth were burning, stretching. The already sharp canines elongated in preparation for that sweet bite. "Now, I'm going to have to take *you*." His mouth opened. His tongue swiped over her flesh.

Fucking delicious. Tangy.

His cock was rock hard. His teeth were ready.

Time to take a bite.

She shook against him. A small tremble. His lips widened. Teeth pressed right over her pounding pulse.

And her claws—*damn claws*—dug into the bloody mess that was his chest. "Not so fast, vampire."

His head lifted. He gazed into her eyes. Eyes that were shining, no, *glowing*, with some kind of bright light.

His breath heaved out. "Well, well . . ." Looked like he wasn't the only one who'd taken a walk in the *Other* world.

Sadie James, the best lover of his life, the beautiful dream he'd held in the darkness of his heart, wasn't human.

She bared her fangs and growled.

He smiled.

Then Liam ignored the fiery pain of those wicked claws. He moved fast, ducking his head and sinking his teeth into the side of her throat.

# Chapter Two

It wasn't supposed to feel good. A vampire's bite was a degradation. An unforgivable crime against her kind. Blood was sacred. Blood was power.

No, a vampire's bite wasn't supposed to feel good, and his didn't feel good—*it felt damn amazing.*

Sadie gasped as a hot pulse of lust and hunger shot through her. Her breasts ached. Her sex tightened.

And, humbling as all hell, she found herself arching her throat and *offering herself to him.*

If her brother had seen her, he would have roared his fury.

Thankfully, Jacob wasn't around—and Liam was.

She didn't remember taking her claws out of his chest, but her hands were now curled around the strong width of his shoulders. Holding him tight, pulling him closer.

Sadie could feel his tongue. The press of his lips. The hard bulge of his cock.

Voices buzzed around her. Music. Scents. She ignored them, closing her eyes to the sight of the bar.

She'd been a fighter all her life. It was all she'd known.

But for once, she was tempted to just be . . . taken.

*Taken.*

The word echoed in her mind and had her lashes snapping open.

*Taken*—the name for the vampires who were converted. No,

no, what was she doing? She wasn't some drugged vamp slut. She was a shifter—the strongest of the *Other*.

"No!" Husky. Not nearly loud enough. *Get a grip, girl. You know vamps don't stop with a sweet "please."*

She clenched her teeth. This was gonna hurt.

Sadie shoved him back a good two feet. His teeth raked over her throat, leaving a trail of fire.

"*What the hell?*" He swiped his hand over his mouth, wiping away her blood, and she almost slugged the jerk.

Drinking without permission. Vamps always thought the world was their damn drive-in restaurant.

She put her hand to her throat. *Shit, it hurt.* Another sin for Sullivan. "What do I look like?" she demanded. "A buffet?"

His eyes, still the soulless black of a vampire in hunting mode, swept down her body. "Love, you know how I like to eat—"

She caught the scent then. The wild fragrance of the animal. Fur. Fury.

Sadie shoved around Liam. Her eyes scanned the bar.

*Business.* Hell, she'd almost forgotten why she'd come into this little shithole of a vampire feeding room, er, bar in the first place.

She had a case to solve. One of her kind had gone rogue. Two bodies had turned up in Miami within the last month. Nearly ripped to freaking shreds.

Her boss in the Bureau had thought that a vamp was behind the slaughter, but one look at the claw marks and Sadie had known that she was after a leopard.

After someone just like her.

Someone who was in the bar right then.

Her kind could always smell other shifters. Her too-sensitive nose was the perfect homing device.

Her gaze tracked to the left. Followed the scent. Saw the man. Tall, sleekly muscled. Long, blond hair. He caught her stare, lifted a brow, and smiled.

A smile that chilled the blood in her veins.

A vampire lover and a shifter gone bad. Her luck so sucked.

The jerk across the bar lifted his hand and crooked his finger.

Her muscles quivered. Time to give that jerk an ass kicking.

"Who the fuck is he?" The rumbling demand came from Liam.

The Irish was heavy in his voice again, blending perfectly with the rage.

She didn't glance his way. The shifter had caught sight of Liam, not a very hard task. The blond's eyes were narrowed, his head cocked.

"The new lover?"

Not likely. Her nose twitched, catching the heavy odor of blood. There was so much blood in the bar now. It was a scent her kind enjoyed too much.

A scent that she'd known would draw the killer.

"Stay out of my way, vampire." Her turn to give the warning. "I'm going to—"

Too late. The shifter spun around, pushing his way back toward the door.

*Not that easy.*

Sadie raced after him. Three weeks worth of tracking wasn't about to go down the drain just because she'd gotten a brief case of lust-induced insanity.

Lust . . . for a damned vampire!

When Sadie bolted away as if level ten demons were after her—level tens being the absolute strongest and baddest of the demon assholes who strolled the earth—Liam followed right on her heels.

He could still taste her blood on his tongue. Sweet but tangy. Absolutely delicious.

Different from a human's. He'd known that fact from the first sip. He'd gotten a staggering rush of power and a hit of stark hunger from the precious liquid.

So the rumors were true.

The blood of a shifter was much, much stronger than a human's. And his Sadie, he'd bet his undead life she was a shifter.

The glowing eyes. The claws. The teeth.

That sweet little purr she'd made when he'd had her against the wall and her body had gone all soft against his.

Damn, but he'd wanted to fuck her.

Now, she was chasing after someone else. Another man. One who smelled like some kind of wet animal.

His teeth snapped together. *Not the way the night was going to end for Sadie.*

She was fast. Leaping and running so quickly that he struggled to keep up with her. In and out of the shadows. Around the corners of buildings. Over cars. Out of alleys.

Make that *damn* fast.

Shifter.

How had he missed that? What other secrets had Sadie kept from him?

Just then, she zipped between two parked cars and headed into the darkness of an abandoned lot.

Good thing her blood was pumping through him. He leapt over the cars. Charged into the woods at the back—

And found Sadie facing off against a crouching leopard. A right ugly beast—matted fur, yellow, spotted, and with a mouth full of razor sharp teeth.

*Fuck me.*

"Get back, Liam! The bastard's shifted—"

Yeah, he could see that for himself. But no damn way was he about to back off. Liam Sullivan had never run from anything before.

Well, except from *her.*

The leopard sprang forward, launching an attack right at Sadie. They crashed onto the ground. The beast's broad head and snapping teeth went for her throat.

Sadie screamed and managed to hold him off, just barely. His teeth were inches away from her delicate neck.

A neck Liam particularly liked. He shot forward. Grabbed the shifter around the middle, and jerked back with all of his considerable vampire-enhanced strength.

The leopard let out a roar of fury and twisted, swiping his claws at Liam.

Luckily, the big cat missed.

A very near thing.

Liam stepped in front of Sadie. "You want to play, do you? Well, come on . . ."

Instead of springing forward, the leopard padded back. The animal paused, its body close to the ground. The broad head tilted up, and glittering eyes measured Liam as a long, pink tongue flickered out.

"Not . . . your . . . fight . . ." Sadie's voice was strangled.

He grunted. Like he would have walked away and left her alone.

"Don't . . . watch . . ." The last of her words ended in a growl. *What?*

Don't watch what? He jerked his gaze away from the leopard, for just a second, and glanced back at Sadie. She'd stripped off her shirt, giving him a truly splendid view of her lacy black bra and those gorgeous breasts that he'd never been able to forget. She was on her knees. Head tossed back, arms up, and—

Her bones began to snap.

Oh, for the love of—

A train hit him, knocking Liam off his feet. No, not a train. A stinking, snarling, teeth-snapping one hundred thirty pound jungle cat.

The beast's breath choked him. A foul stench. Saliva dripped onto his face, but Liam held the cat back, using a white-knuckled grip around the animal's throat.

"I'm not . . . easy prey . . ."

Liam gathered his strength, then hurled the beast toward the line of trees.

But the damn cat twisted in midair and landed agilely on his feet.

Piss.

Liam rose to his feet, brushing off his hands. Okay, time for another round.

He stepped forward, just as a blur of gold and black fur streaked past him.

Snarls.

Growls.

Claws and teeth.

His mouth dropped open. Two leopards were before him. Muscled bodies moving. Tumbling across the earth. The second cat was smaller, its fur a rich gold dotted with dark circles—rosettes. The cat's long tail swished behind it—

No, not *it*. Her.

The second leopard was Sadie.

And she was fighting for her life.

Like he was just going to stand on the sidelines.

He dove into the fray, grappling with the larger leopard, pounding him with his fists, avoiding those dangerous claws as best he could.

They'd take the beast down, together, just like they'd taken down so many other bastards.

His Sadie was a fighter.

And, apparently, a large, spotted cat.

The wail of sirens cut through the air.

The larger leopard's head rammed into Liam's chest, knocking him back. Then the cat leapt away from Sadie, shaking his body and swishing his tail.

The sirens screamed. Tires squealed as patrol cars came to a shuddering halt nearby.

The bastard leopard disappeared into the woods. And Sadie tried to go after him.

"Sadie!" The demand was fierce.

Humans were around. Even now Liam could hear people rushing toward them. She couldn't be seen as a leopard. She had a job. A career with the FBI.

She couldn't afford to be careless.

She glanced back at him, whiskers twitching.

"Change." An order.

The leopard bared her teeth, but her ears were up, and he knew that she heard the approaching footsteps, too.

His gaze locked on her as the change began. In seconds, the fur melted away. Bones reshaped. Supple female limbs reappeared. Soon he was staring not at an animal, but at the nude form of a woman.

A woman who had been his for all too short a time.

A woman who was about to be discovered naked by half of the Miami PD.

Liam shrugged out of his jacket and reached for her. "Sadie . . ." He kissed her. A hard, fast kiss. Lips open, tongues ready. Mouths stayed locked as he wrapped the jacket around her.

"Freeze!" The yell came from less than ten feet away. "Put your hands up and step away from the woman."

Liam's mouth lifted. His gaze met hers.

A bullet wouldn't kill him, but it would make his night suck even more.

Slowly, he raised his hands, but he didn't step away from Sadie.

"I'm with the FBI," she said, her voice clear and cool. Her hands fumbled with the jacket, managed to zip up the front. She was such a tiny thing, the heavy leather fell all the way to midthigh. "Agent Sadie James. I've been tracking a suspected killer in the city and—"

"Christ, James, save the explanations." A darker voice, one tinged with a Chicago street accent. "I told them who you were."

Liam stiffened. No, no bloody way.

Talk about sucking.

He turned slowly, hands still up, but fury boiling his blood. Special Agent Anthony Miller blinked when he saw him. "What? *Sullivan.*" Surprise, disgust. "Dammit, you were supposed to stay on the other side of the ocean, you bas—"

"*You knew!*" Sadie stormed past Liam. A few of the cops gasped when they caught full sight of her, clad only in his jacket. Liam couldn't help it, his gaze dropped to the perfect lines of her legs.

Oh, to take a bite.

"Sadie, you don't understand!"

She punched the special agent right in the face. He stumbled back, swearing. The uniforms around him lifted their guns and pointed them right at Sadie.

Hell, no. Not an option. "Stand down!" The order was Liam's. Shouted. "Miller, tell 'em to drop their weapons." A bullet in the heart or head would kill a shifter. A scenario not about to happen in front of him.

"D-down . . ." Blood dripped from Miller's nose. The agent stumbled to his feet and only looked at Sadie's exposed legs *three* times.

Liam felt his teeth begin to burn—from the lure of the blood and from his growing fury. He'd wanted to rip out Miller's throat for a long time.

Ever since the thick bastard had turned his back on Liam and left him struggling with his new life alone, and with the guilt of ten dead men and three dead women on his soul.

Screw the hands-up crap. If they wanted to fire at him, he didn't care. Right then, he wanted to know just what the hell kind of case Sadie was on and why she'd been tracking that other shifter.

"You let me cry for him—and you *knew?* You *knew?*" Her claws were out, and if Miller didn't watch it, he might be losing some flesh.

His muddy brown eyes swept the circle of armed men and women. "We can't talk about this here, Agent James. *You* know better."

A growl was her answer.

Miller swallowed. "Wh . . . where's the suspect?"

She jerked her thumb back toward the waiting darkness. "Long gone. The sirens alerted him, gave him a chance to run."

His stare narrowed. "The perp got away from *both* of you?"

"Wasn't your typical perp," Liam said blandly. "Something else I don't think you want us discussin' here." Oh, but the smug bastard was due for a serious set down.

Soon.

Miller swore. "Spread out," he yelled to the cops. Obviously, they thought the wanker was in charge. Fools. "Search the woods. We're looking for—"

Oh, yeah, this should be good.

"A man in his late twenties," Sadie interrupted. "Blond hair. Blue eyes. Six-foot-four, two hundred pounds." A pause. "He's quite prossibly naked, too."

*Definitely* naked. The guy's torn clothes were less than a foot away. Of course, the shifter could have stashed spare jeans or a shirt somewhere close by. Shifters usually had a backup clothing plan.

"He should be considered armed and very dangerous," she continued. "Approach with extreme caution."

"Shoot first." From Miller. "Not a kill shot, but take the bastard down."

The cops scrambled to obey. Sadie didn't move. The wind tossed her hair.

Damn but she was sexy. Soul as hard as nails. Skin as soft as satin.

"You've got some explaining to do." Her hands were on her hips. "You should have told me, you should have—"

"I didn't know *what* you were, Agent James, until about five months ago." His upper lip curled. "You didn't exactly go around advertising your true self, now, did you?"

Liam didn't like the tone the guy was—

"If you hadn't bugged my house, you would have never known."

Ah, so that was how the Bureau had discovered Sadie's not-so-little secret. Interesting.

Liam had long known that the Bureau had a special division, a group of agents with particular . . . gifts. But he hadn't realized exactly how most of the agents for that unit were recruited.

He should have known the agency would be screwing over its own people.

Big Brother liked to know everything, and use everyone.

"So I didn't tell you that your ex-lover had turned bloodsucker."

Liam's teeth snapped together. "You're pushin', Miller." It wouldn't take much more to send him over the edge.

"I figured you'd be grateful, after what happened to your friend Jasmine—"

Sadie swayed. Stumbled. "Bastard!" The snarl was directed straight at Miller. "Don't talk about her, *ever*. I agreed to stay on with this unit to help—"

Instantly, Miller went from attack mode to kind friend. "You *are* helping, Sadie," he murmured, brows lowered. *Fake bastard.* "Only someone with your talents could work this case. You're going to catch another killer, keep the streets safe—"

"I didn't catch anyone tonight." She shook her head. Looked fragile, as she'd never looked before. "Just let the jerk get away—and tipped him off to the fact that another shifter is hunting him." Her hand rose and raked back the fall of her hair. "I'm going home. The guy's long gone tonight. Tomorrow, tomorrow—I'll start tracking him again."

She turned away, never once looking at Liam. She headed in the direction of the bar. Her steps were slow, steady.

He watched in silence, willing her to glance back, just once, and look at him.

But soon she disappeared into the shadows and left him with the bastard who'd sent him off to die two years ago.

Miller began to edge back. Cautiously, moving like a snake and—

Liam's hands flashed out. He grabbed Miller, effectively halting his exit. "Goin' somewhere?"

His Adam's apple bobbed as the special agent gave a frantic shake of his head.

"I didn't think so." Liam stared into those lying eyes. "Who's Jasmine?"

Miller's lips thinned.

"Who. Is. Jasmine." He let the power of the vampire sweep through him. Knew that his voice had deepened. That his eyes had darkened to black.

But it apparently took more than a few theatrics to rattle the special agent. Miller inhaled on a rasp. "You weren't put on the extermination list, Sullivan. That's the only favor you'll be getting from me."

*The extermination list.* The list the Bureau kept of the *Other* who'd gone bad and needed to be eliminated. A harsh laugh broke from his lips. "Let me clue you in, Miller. In the last two years, I've learned that famous list of yours? It's not worth a shit." The handful of names. The list of paranormals who'd blatantly killed.

Barely scratched the surface of the evil out there.

He leaned in close to the special agent. "And even if you'd sent your men . . ." His teeth came together on a snap. "They wouldn't have stopped me." Less than three months after turning, he'd killed the bastard who'd transformed him and slaughtered his team. A few humans would hardly have slowed him down.

He let his gaze drop to the man's throat. "I'll ask once more, and then I'll stop playin' so nice." He smiled. "Who is Jasmine?"

Miller began to shake. Liam knew the truth about the bastard. He wasn't human, either. Not really. A charmer. A being gifted with the ability to talk to animals.

Liam didn't know precisely what animal linked with Miller, but he was betting it was a rat.

His hands tightened around the bastard, the enhanced strength easily bruising the flesh, and, if he just applied a dash more pressure, he could break—

"V-vampire killed her. When she was sixteen." The words rushed out, nearly tumbling over each other. "Jasmine—she was Sadie's best friend. She died in her arms."

Well, fuck.

Liam shoved the special agent away from him.

That explained a few things.

Like the way Sadie had come at him with a stake.

What a damn tangled mess. Sadie wouldn't want to be around him, not knowing what he was. She'd never agree to be with him, unless—

His lips curved.

Miller flinched.

"Tell me about the man Sadie is huntin' for you." Not a man, though, he knew that. "Tell me why she's after him."

"Th-that's confidential. Only FBI—"

Liam laughed again. He couldn't help it. "Right. Save the bullshit for someone else." Someone who didn't know the real score.

Miller's brows raised. "Only if . . . you agree to help on this one." More confident. But then, maybe the fear had been a show. Cagey, that was Miller.

Sly jerkoff. "Talk, then we'll deal." The way of the world, living and undead.

The agent began to talk—about blood and death, bodies found in trees, and the claw marks of a monster.

And Liam began to plan.

He followed the woman back to her house. He'd transformed, picked up the clothes he'd hidden, and blended in so easily with the humans milling on the streets.

He'd passed right by two uniformed cops and they'd never given him so much as a second glance.

Humans. Not even worth his time most days, but *she* was different.

*A female shifter. A leopard.* Someone with his strength. His cunning.

He'd never thought to find a female like her.

So perfect.

He used the wind, knowing exactly how to manipulate the breeze to hide his scent.

And he hunted.

He watched her through the windows of her house. Watched her silhouette. The supple curves. The veil of hair.

He'd been settling for humans, enjoying the prey's screams, when he could have had . . . her.

She opened the balcony doors. Let her gaze sweep over the block. Stared right past him.

Leopards were so good at blending in with their surroundings. *She* should know that.

Her head tilted back as she glanced toward the sky, exposing the slender column of her throat.

A sign of submission for his kind, from one lover to another.

He purred.

# Chapter Three

She'd left her balcony doors open. The better to let in the gentle breeze of the night.

And him.

Her back was to the doors when she sensed him. She caught the whiff of the ocean. Heard the faintest rustle of sound.

Sadie had known that he would follow her.

Just as she'd known that she wouldn't be able to kill him at that bar. She'd missed his heart, not because he'd turned, but because she'd weakened.

*Liam.*

She hadn't seen the monster when she'd looked at him, just the man.

And her aim had wavered.

Her head lifted and she moved, very slowly, to face him. "Into scaling buildings these days, are you, vampire?"

He strode forward, looking so sexy and strong that an ache lodged above her heart and heat bloomed between her thighs.

His lips curved into a smile that had her breath catching. "Ah, love, the trellis made it too easy for me."

*Love.*

Her gaze dropped to his chest. To the dried blood. "I'm sorry, Liam. I-I shouldn't have—" *tried to kill you* "attacked you back at the bar. You just—um, caught me by surprise." *When I saw your teeth, I remembered that other bastard and the way he'd laughed.*

Fury, instinct—she'd moved too fast. The stake had been over his heart when she'd glanced into his eyes and seen the stare of her lover.

And she hadn't been able to kill him.

She was too weak where he was concerned. Always had been.

Liam stepped toward her in a long, smooth glide. "Not the first time an old friend has tried to murder me."

She blinked. "But I—"

His fingers pressed against her lips. "I'm not the monster you think."

*Vampires are evil. Predators. They live to kill. Live by draining their victims dry and stealing their screams. Even the devil won't let those bastards in to hell.* Her brother's words, when he'd learned of Jasmine's death.

"I didn't choose this life. Didn't go searching for the exchange."

Others had. Others had bartered more than souls for the blood-soaked promise of immortality.

His fingers slipped down to cup her cheek. "I spent the day with you, tasting heaven, then when I went on my assignment that night, I found hell."

She shivered. From his touch. His words. Sadie didn't know. Didn't care. "Liam . . ."

His hand stroked lower, curving over her neck. The wound had already healed. Her kind healed fast—some faster than others, depending on the beasts they carried—and the shift had only sped up the restoration. "We were ambushed," he told her, voice rasping. "A fuckin' den of vampires were waitin' on us. It wasn't some kind of cult who'd been kidnappin' and killin'—it was vampires. My team wasn't ready to face them—there were too damn many."

Pain was in his words and in the memories she saw in his eyes.

"The leader, I swear, he looked like some twenty-year-old kid."

Because he'd been the Blood. Jacob had made certain she had a very through vampire education after Jasmine's death. The Blood were born vampires. They stopped aging in their late teens or twenties and developed a ravenous hunger for blood.

They were the most powerful. Both psychically and physically.

"He sank his teeth into me, but I fought him. Clawing. Shooting. Punching." He drew in a breath. Because, yeah, vampires still breathed. Their hearts still beat. The *Taken,* vampires who'd been made, not born, only died for an instant, then their bodies awoke with a flood of power.

And with a desperate hunger for blood.

She wanted to touch him. To hold him. But he wasn't her Liam anymore, if he'd ever been *hers.*

The hand against her throat seemed slightly cool, but so strong.

"How did you . . ." She stopped, cleared her throat and tasted the breeze from the balcony on her tongue. "How did you change?"

His hand fell away. "Wasn't supposed to. Bastards left me for dead, like they did the rest of my team. All I can figure, I must've got some of his blood, the one who attacked me. I shot him to hell. Blood was everywhere."

Becoming a vampire didn't really take three exchanges like the movies said. Just one. The victim had to be nearly drained for the transformation to work, but he didn't need to take much blood from the vampire. A few drops had been known to do the trick.

Vampire blood was powerful. *Tainted,* Jacob had said.

"Why didn't you tell me?" Hell, why the whole charade? The funeral? The closed casket? She'd thought the casket had been sealed because the damage to Liam had been so severe. Sadie had heard about the ravaged conditions of the agents' bodies.

But, no, the casket had been closed because Liam hadn't been inside at all.

"At first, the Bureau took the choice out of my hands." Anger simmering. "They're the ones who found me and threw me in a cell for five days while they tried to decide if I was going to live or die."

*The extermination list.*

His smile was grim. "They decided I got to keep livin', provided I agreed to do the old U.S. government a few favors."

She didn't want to ask about those favors, not then, because she knew just what sort of deeds Miller would give to a vampire.

"When I was stable, I did my part." The faint lines around his eyes tightened. "Then I settled some scores of my own. After that . . ." A shrug. "Well, let's just say for a time it was better for me to go back to my Ireland." *And to leave her behind.*

"Why are you back now?"

"Because I want to be."

Okay, not exactly the *oh, my God, I missed you and couldn't spend another day without you* response she'd been hoping to get. But, then again, the guy sure as hell hadn't bothered to look her up the moment he'd come back to town.

An image of the redhead flashed before her. No, he'd been a bit occupied.

She stepped away. "I don't need this crap now. I've got a case—"

"*We've* got a case."

Hell. That sinking—it was her heart. *No way.* Her eyes closed for a moment. "Come again?"

The floor squeaked as he crept forward. "Miller thinks you could use some backup on this case."

So he was gonna send the big, bad vamp to cover her ass. "I don't need help. I could've taken the guy down tonight—"

"But you didn't." A calm statement. "And he almost got you, instead."

Her nostrils flared. "I haven't worked with a partner since Miller dug into my life and blackmailed me into this unit. I don't need a—"

"You've got a partner now." His eyes were expressionless. "We worked well together before. Remember, love?"

Forgetting was the problem.

"You need someone to watch your back. Miller told me about the bastard out there. Hunting on your own isn't the way to handle this."

But her kind usually hunted alone.

Damn Miller.

And damn Liam—for making her *feel* so much again.

He offered his hand. "Partners, Sadie?"

Oh, it grated. But she stuck out her hand. *He's not like the others.* Her fingers wrapped around his. "Partners." She met his stare. "For now."

His hold tightened and Liam pulled her forward. "Sealed with a kiss?" he asked.

She shouldn't. Damn, but she knew it was a mistake.

And she also knew that she wanted him. Vampire. Man. Didn't matter. She'd wanted Liam for years.

No other had ever made her feel the way he did. No other had ever come close to satisfying the woman or the beast that lived within her.

So she was the one to lean into him. The one to open her mouth, to have her lips and tongue ready.

Mixing business and pleasure—they'd done it before.

They'd do it again.

His mouth locked onto hers.

*The bitch.*

He shifted in the darkness, aware of the crunch of leaves beneath his feet.

She was letting that vampire bastard touch her. Kiss her.

A snarl rumbled in his throat.

She'd pay for that. Pay for allowing one of the damned to touch her.

Leopard shifters—they were blessed. Superior.

Not to be touched by fucking bloodsuckers.

She'd pay, but first, he'd get the vampire. He'd killed his share of the undead before. It wouldn't be too hard.

Then the woman would be his.

The thrill of the hunt flooded his veins.

Sadie was back in his arms, and this time, she wasn't staking him.

Oh, yeah, this was what he wanted.

His hands were around her waist, fingers pressing just over the sweet curve of her arse. Her breasts were crushed against his chest. Liam could feel the soft stab of her nipples.

Pretty pink nipples. Nipples that tasted like candy.

He'd taste them again.

His mouth fed on hers. Took. Savored. It'd been too long.

She'd been in his dreams for years, and part of him was afraid *this* was a dream. That he'd awaken without Sadie, as he'd done so many times.

*Couldn't go back to her as a monster. Couldn't watch the terror on her face.*

But Sadie, his Sadie had been hiding secrets.

*Not the fearful human he'd expected.*

A warrior queen, a shifter.

More than a match for the undead.

His hands rose—he'd come back to that arse later. His fingers caught the edge of the T-shirt she wore. He tore his mouth from hers as he jerked up the shirt.

"Liam . . ."

The husky whisper of his name had him stilling. *No, she couldn't turn him away.*

Her eyes were so damn gold. Deep, and filled with secrets.

Why hadn't he noticed the secrets before?

He swallowed back the desperation that rose in his throat. He wouldn't beg her. If she didn't want his touch, he'd pull away, he'd—

She yanked up his shirt. The garment hit the floor with a faint rustle of sound.

Then she smiled.

And he was lost.

"This time . . . don't be easy with me." Pure seduction dripped from her words. "You know what I am—I don't need soft touches and candlelight."

His body was tense. His cock so hard he ached. "What do you need?"

Her hands were on his chest. Smoothing over the muscles and sending a spike of fire to his groin. "You." She licked her lips. "Fast. Hard. Deep."

She was going to bring him to his knees.

Her fingers traced over his nipples. "Make me forget," she whispered the order. "Make me forget everything."

Forget that he was a vampire?

The stark thought ran through his mind, but he didn't step away from her. Hell, nothing would have made him leave then.

His gaze dropped to her breasts. No bra. Round. Firm. Tight little nipples. His mouth watered and he just had to get a taste.

His arms wrapped around her. He lifted her, lowering his head and lashing his tongue over her left nipple. Swirling over the areola. Nipping lightly with his teeth.

Her moan filled his ears.

Liam's mouth widened as he began to suckle.

*Even better than I remembered.*

Soft flesh. Wild woman. Rich scent of creamy arousal.

After one more hungry swipe of his tongue, Liam managed to lift his head. His teeth were burning. The bloodlust rising with his need.

"Get on the bed." Guttural.

She wanted fast and hard—oh, but he'd give it to her.

One golden brow rose, but she didn't move toward the bed. Instead, she looped her fingers in the waist of her shorts—faded, loose shorts that skimmed the tops of her silken thighs—and with a little push, she sent the material dropping to the floor.

Her feet were bare. She lifted one foot, then the other as she stepped out of the shorts. Clad now only in a pair of black bikini panties, she stared at him, hunger gleaming in her eyes.

The bed was five feet away. But if she didn't move soon, he'd take her where they stood.

"Sadie . . ." A warning.

One she ignored.

Her hands were on his chest. Soft fingertips smoothing over him. Her scent flooded his nostrils and pushed him to the edge of his control.

Her head lowered. Her breath fanned over his flesh, and her mouth closed over his right nipple.

*Oh, fuck.*

He shuddered and tried to ignore the bloodlust that burned ever hotter within him. He knew his eyes would be turning, darkening into the black of a hunting vamp.

For prey or for passion . . . that was when the eyes changed. It had been the first lesson he'd learned.

Her fingers were on his belt. Unhooking the buckle, easing open the snap of his jeans.

Liam had never been the underwear type—not living and not undead. So when Sadie pushed open his jeans, his cock sprang out, ready, standing up, the thick head straining toward her.

She took him, wrapping her hands around him, squeezing tight and—

He grabbed her. Lifted her high, kissed the lips parted in surprise. Drank from her mouth. Fed. And let the hunger rage.

A red haze seemed to cover his eyes. It had been far too long since he'd taken his Sadie. Dreams weren't enough. Memories were too weak.

He needed the woman, and he needed her *now*.

They fell onto the bed together. Mouths locked, tongues taking. With one hand, he pinned her wrists to the bed, locking them over her head.

His right hand snaked down her body. Pushed between her thrashing legs and stroked the wet silk of her panties.

She moaned and arched toward him. The drumming sound of her heartbeat filled his ears.

He ripped the silk away from her flesh. Drove two fingers into her sex and felt the tight, strong clasp of her inner muscles around him.

*Can't wait.*

He freed her hands. Caught the head of his arousal and guided his cock toward her creamy warmth.

His mouth tore from hers. Liam gazed at her, at the wild tangle of hair, the glowing eyes, the red lips.

*Fucking beautiful.*

He thrust deep into her, as deep as he could go, and felt the lash of pleasure resonate through him.

Tight. Wet. Hot.

Perfect.

Her legs locked around him and she met him thrust for thrust. Harder. Wilder.

"More!" The demand was from her, echoed by him.

The bed squeaked beneath them. Slid an inch, two, and rammed into the wall.

He took her breasts, bending low over her, licking, kissing, biting.

Her fingers fisted in his hair. "Liam!" A demand.

His head rose. Her breath was ragged, so was his.

His hips drove down, again and again. Her sex clenched around him with a telltale ripple of her sweet muscles.

Her climax was close, bearing down on her.

Faster, faster, he thrust into her. She smiled, then she moaned, and her claws—ah, damn but he could feel the sting of her claws as she pressed him ever closer to her—dug into his hips.

She'd mark him.

He'd mark her.

Her body stiffened. Her face flushed with pleasure. He felt the contractions along his aroused length, the silken caresses as Sadie came beneath him.

Her head tilted back and her lips parted on a hard sigh.

Her throat, long, vulnerable, was bared to him.

His mouth was on her before he even thought. Lips caressing. Tongue stroking.

Release neared for him. The promise of a fiery pleasure. A pleasure to end the cold that had haunted his days and nights for so very long.

His teeth raked over her pulse. He'd tasted her before. The wild honey of her blood.

Liam wanted to taste her again. Just a quick bite, a soft sip—

Sadie rolled him, pushing with her arms and hips so they moved in a tangle of limbs.

Blinking, he looked up. She rose above him, a goddess with eyes of gold. His cock was lodged fully inside her snug depths, her thighs on either side of his hips.

And her throat so far away from his mouth.

"No blood." She whispered the words as her hips lifted, fell. Lifted. "No . . . bite. L-like before. Just like—"

His hands clamped around her hips and he surged once more, his climax rocking through him as he seemed to explode inside of her.

And she was with him. Tensing, squeezing, breathing his name as her second release shuddered through her.

His teeth snapped together. He closed his eyes as the ecstasy poured through his body.

Sex with Sadie . . . fucking amazing.

He emptied into her, satisfaction weighting his limbs.

She was still the best lover he'd ever had.

And the one who could hurt him the most.

She hated what he was, he knew it.

But she needed him, just as he'd always needed her.

Her body curled around his, and she stretched—like a cat. The rumble in her throat could have been a purr.

*Why didn't I see it before? Why?*

Maybe if he'd seen, maybe if she'd trusted him enough to tell him her secrets, their lives would have been different.

"This doesn't change anything." She whispered the words even as she wrapped her arms around him.

He pressed a kiss to her head. "I know." But he would find a way to change things between them.

One way or the other he wasn't going to lose her again.

He planned to keep Sadie with him, forever.


It was the cry that woke her. A rough, choking snarl.

The cry of a leopard. Sadie's eyes flashed open. A weight was over her chest. Strong, familiar.

*Liam.*

A roar echoed.

Christ, the leopard, he was close—*too* close.

"*Sonofabitch.*" From Liam. He jumped from the bed. Jerked on his jeans. "Bastard followed us."

Us . . . no, he'd followed *her.*

Sadie moved as fast as she could. Pulled on her shirt, yanked up her shorts. "Liam, stay here, let me handle—"

He spun on her, his eyes dark pools. "Do not finish that."

She swallowed as she eyed his sharp canines. *Not a man anymore.* No matter how much she'd like to pretend otherwise.

They ran to the balcony together. Jumped to the ground below. A short drop, barely fifteen feet.

Her knees didn't buckle, neither did his. Her heart raced as adrenaline pumped through her.

The male shifter's scent was strong there. Her eyes narrowed and she saw the deep claw marks cutting into the side of her house.

*Bastard.*

She glanced toward the darkened trees alongside her house. Close enough to watch.

Shit.

The light of dawn trickled across the sky. Fighting shadows, and, she knew, weakening Liam.

Vampires could walk in the sunlight—Stoker had gotten that part right in his book—but they didn't like to be out during the day. They were weaker, almost . . . human then.

Vulnerable.

Maybe that was exactly the way the leopard wanted Liam.

Her throat dried. *Go after the weak.* It was the way of her kind.

She stepped in front of Liam. He might be a vampire, but he was still *Liam.* The leopard wasn't going to get him.

Not without one hell of a fight.

# Chapter Four

They hadn't found the bastard. He'd clawed up her house. Left his stench all over the place, but the shifter had gotten away.

For two days, Sadie had tried to track the killer.

No luck.

But, at least she hadn't found any more of the freak's sick kills in the city.

Those poor women. Clawed. Bitten. Their bodies hanging from the trees.

"How long are you going to keep pretendin'?"

Sadie's gaze stayed locked on the darkness just beyond her small FBI office. She didn't jump or gasp when she heard Liam's voice. She'd known he was behind her.

His scent. The faintest whisper of his steps.

She swallowed. "Any sign of the leopard?" Liam had gone out with a team earlier that night, scouting the swamps in the southwest.

"Hell, no, the bastard's good at hiding."

True.

"You didn't answer me, Sadie love." A rustle of fabric. He was coming closer.

Her shoulders straightened. He hadn't been back to her apartment, *to her bed*, since they'd discovered they had an unwanted guest watching them. It was good that he hadn't come back to her. Sleeping with him had been a serious mistake.

A mistake that had felt too good.

"Look at me." A gruff order.

Drawing in a deep breath, she took a moment before she turned to face him. She had to be careful with Liam. He'd always seen so much.

He caught her shoulders, pulled her around to meet his blue stare. "Are you done tryin' to freeze me out?"

One blond brow raised. "Is that what I've been doing?"

His lips tightened. "Don't fuckin' play with me, Sadie. Two nights ago you were growling my name."

And he was whispering hers.

"Now you tense up every time I get within five feet of you."

True. *Why did the guy have to look so sexy?* That tousled hair. Those deep, look-into-me eyes. He made her want to forget.

But she couldn't do that. Not again. Because being with him was too much of a temptation. "I have a case to work, Sullivan. I don't have time to screw around—"

"Love, you've always had time to screw around with me." Sensual memories filled his eyes.

Her breasts tightened. Ah, damn. "It was a mistake, okay? A weak as hell moment for me. Seeing you, after I'd thought . . ." Why was she even trying to explain? She didn't really understand herself. "I was weak." Better. "But we've got a case to work and we should keep things . . . professional."

Silence. His nostrils flared. Then . . . "Bullshit."

She blinked.

"You think I don't know how you feel about me?" The hands on her shoulders tightened. Yanked her up against his chest. "I can *smell* the fear on you."

Her hands rose and lodged against his chest. "I'm *not* afraid of you." She wasn't afraid of anything. *She* was a shifter, one of the strongest paranormals out there. The baddest of the bad. The creature who could transform and kill and—

"Bullshit," he said again. "I know about your friend, you know. All about her and the night you learned to fear vampires."

Her entire body went stone hard. Miller—that *jerk*. He should know to keep his mouth shut about her business. Her face was burning and she knew her cheeks had to be flushing dark red. "You don't know—"

"Little Jasmine . . . killed by a vampire."

Her claws dug into his chest as she remembered.

*Long hair matted with red. A wound that wouldn't close.*

*Tears on her tongue.*

*Screams—desperate pleas.*

*And Jasmine, her lips moving as she tried to talk.*

*But her throat had been ripped open.*

*She was dying. The light in her eyes fading, fading.*

*His laughter. Mocking. Close.*

*"You're next."*

Liam shook her hard, sending her head snapping back. "Sadie!"

The past vanished. No, no the past was right in front of her. She could see the fangs, glinting.

Vampire.

"Sadie." Softer now, almost a caress. "It's all right, love. I understand."

She shook her head. "You don't know—"

His lips twisted. "I took your blood. You have to know what that means."

Her brow furrowed. He'd only taken a few sips. Hardly enough to—

"We're linked, Sadie."

The blood link. *Hell.*

Her brother would freak.

*She* was about to. "No, that's not possible. You didn't take enough—"

His hands smoothed down her arms, his fingertips brushing ever so briefly around the outside of her breasts. "I *feel* you. Your anger. The fear inside. The pain. I can feel it all."

She wanted to close her eyes and block him out, but she knew there was no escape.

If Sullivan was telling her the truth and a blood link connected them, there would never be any escape for her. He'd be able to track her anywhere, anytime.

The blood link was one of the most powerful tools a vampire possessed. By drinking, the vampire became linked with prey. Sometimes the link became so strong that it was rumored the vampires could eavesdrop on thoughts and even completely control humans.

Now she was one of the linked?

Shit.

Sadie broke free of his hold. They were sharing this office—*thanks, Miller, I sure owe you*—so she couldn't tell him to get lost.

But she could get the hell out of Dodge. Her hands were clenched as she headed for the door.

"Sadie."

She didn't look back.

"I know what you see when you look at me."

Her steps slowed, just a bit.

"I didn't want this."

He'd said the words before, but, this time, she believed him, and she looked back. "What did you want?"

A sad smile twisted his lips. "You."

And she'd wanted him so much. That hunger and need, always there. She'd given in to her feelings the other night, and she knew, if she didn't stay on her guard, that she would again.

She'd survived losing him once. It had hurt like a bitch, but she'd made it.

No way was she going through that hell again.

There was no future for her with Liam.

"You had me." Harsh and so hard to say. She spun around, stormed for the door, and heard the faint whisper of his words follow her.

"And I'll have you again."

The great Sadie James was running scared.

Liam probably should have been amused by that fact. There was something that could scare the superwoman, er . . . shifter, after all.

But he wasn't amused. He was pissed off.

She had no fucking right to fear him. Sadie should *know* better. He wasn't some psychotic who would start slaughtering the innocent.

He had fangs.

He drank blood.

So what? Everybody had flaws.

Liam prowled through the city streets, hearing the flow of

music and laughter echo around him. After Sadie's glorious exit—he'd gotten a fine view of her hips swaying—he'd decided to hunt. Solo.

It was night, he was at full power, and he was more than in the mood for a fight.

Or a fuck. But since Sadie wasn't particularly acting like *she* was in that mood, he'd settle for knocking the shit out of some deserving bastard.

Because he wasn't fucking anyone else. He'd had lovers since his Sadie. The blood hunger mixed with physical lust drove him nearly mad, so he'd had no choice but to take others. But since he'd tasted Sadie again—knew the pleasure he could find with her—he didn't want to lay with another.

Two women and a swaying man hurried out of his way when he stalked toward another club's entrance. *Fire*. What the hell kind of name was that? The last joint he'd searched had been *Taboo*. Screwy names. He'd keep . . .

The scent of blood teased his nostrils.

Liam stilled. The women whispered and he felt their gazes sweep over him.

His canines pressed against his lips.

*The scent's too strong.*

There was no feeding room in this part of town. He shouldn't be smelling this sweet scent here, not with the blood seeming to weigh down the very air around him.

His head jerked to the left. His ears, sharper than a human's, but not close to being on par with a shifter like Sadie, strained to hear.

The music drummed. High laughter.

There were too many people out. So much noise.

A whimper. His eyes narrowed. Could have been a word. Could have been—

*Help.*

Piss. Liam snarled and took off running.

He knew exactly where the scent of blood would take him and he was more than ready for this fight.

"Why the hell are you telling Liam my personal business?" Sadie's fisted hands came down hard on Miller's desk. "I work for you, but you *don't* have any right to tell my secrets."

"Not even to your lover?" His voice was expressionless.

"Ex-lover," she gritted. Not that it was any of his business. Boundaries. Miller needed them, desperately.

"Hmmm . . . weren't you together at your place on Saturday?"

She sucked in a breath. "If you've got me bugged again, Miller, I swear you'll—"

"Relax, James." He smiled at her, an almost . . . warm smile. Weird, seeing it on a snake. "That was pure guess."

Bastard.

Fear was in the air. A harsh smell, one that blended with the rich scent of fresh blood.

A fact of life: Most vampires liked fear. Their bodies responded instinctively to it.

Many vamps that Liam knew got off on the fear. They loved power and they loved making prey tremble.

Liam, well, the fear just didn't do it for him. Whenever he caught that acidic odor, he remembered his last night as a human.

*Fear.* It had been the last thing he'd smelled as a human. His own wild, overwhelming fear. And it had been the first odor he'd caught on waking. Two of his men had still been alive. Barely. Seconds from death. Their fear had burned him, even as the blood around him triggered new instincts.

*No.* He wouldn't remember that night.

He had another monster to catch.

Buildings loomed around him. Tall and dark, with windows of thick glass that looked black in the night.

His heart raced, his eyes narrowed, and his nose twitched.

*Where are you?*

The question was not for the victim, but for the—

"*Help!*" Not a murmur this time. A woman's scream.

Up ahead.

A building with a FOR SALE sign. No lights. About seven stories. A chain across the front entrance.

His legs burned as he ran, traveling faster than a mortal could. He saw the window on the second floor. The broken glass.

Broken deliberately? The better to smell—

Animal. Savage. The scent hit him even harder than the blood. *Shifter.*

*"Oh, God, help me, somebody—"*

No one else was going to help her.

Liam let his own claws spring out from his fingertips. "Get ready, bastard, here I come."

"I can't keep working with him, I—" Sadie broke off, frowning. The hair on her nape was rising and a knot had twisted her stomach.

"Sadie?" Miller frowned.

Her lips parted. "Where is Liam?" She'd left him in the office, but . . .

She spun around, dashing for the door.

"Wait, James! I've got—"

Scaling the building wasn't hard. He was at the second story window in less than thirty seconds. The stench of the shifter was stronger, and so was the sweet smell of blood. He hurtled through the window, shattering the remnants of the broken pane and feeling the sharp sting of jagged glass cut into his arms and side.

Liam rolled, rising in a crouch with his arms up and his teeth bared.

He saw her first. Curled in a fetal position in the corner, the woman was whimpering. Blood covered her bare limbs. Dripped onto the floor around her.

The shifter had done one hell of a number on her.

A growl rumbled. "Like the look of all that blood, do you, vampire?" A man stepped from the shadows near the door. His claws were up, stained red. "Thought it might tempt you."

Liam lunged, jumping the span of the room in an instant and grabbing the shifter by his neck. "Fuckin' bastard."

The shifter slashed with claws, cutting into Liam's chest and breaking his hold with a fast twist.

He sucked in a sharp breath at the pain.

"Came alone, did you?" The shifter shook his head and his green eyes glinted. "Mistake, vampire. Serious mistake."

The woman scooted even closer to the wall. Liam was aware of her furtive movements, but he didn't dare glance her way.

He wasn't about to give the shifter even a moment's advantage.

"You really think you're gonna take me in?" The shifter shook his head. "I'm not made for a cell. My kind don't take so well to captivity."

A chatty prick. "Who said anything about taking you in?" Miller had told him from the beginning that this was a death case. *This one's too dangerous. He likes the kill too much. Containment isn't an option.*

The leopard had made the extermination list.

Blood dripped from the cuts on Liam's body and splattered onto the floor around his feet. "Ready to die, shifter?"

The blond man snarled. His bones began to snap and crack as the transformation swept over him.

*Better the man than the beast.*

Liam attacked with teeth and claws.

"You've got a tail on him?" Miller's words had stopped her at the door. Sadie shook her head. "Why the hell would you put a tail on your own man—" She broke off, huffing out a breath. *Never mind.* Sneaking and double-crossing his own agents was the way Miller worked.

"I don't trust him yet, not one hundred percent." He leveled a stare at her as he cradled his cell phone to his ear. "Thought it'd be best to keep an eye on him."

"Liam would have made any man on him." The guy was good. And why, *why* was her stomach in knots? Why did she keep thinking about him?

Thinking that the Irishman needed her—and that she had to get to him, fast.

"He wouldn't have spotted Lance."

Lance. Hell. The fox shifter.

No one ever spotted that tricky agent.

"Where is he?" The demand was barked into the phone. "What? Shit, hell, *yeah, go.*"

Sadie rocked forward on to the balls of her feet. The leopard was snarling. The woman was shaking. "Miller . . ."

He was already on his feet. "Building at the corner of Burns and Montay. Lance said he heard screams and then Liam scaled the wall."

Her heart slammed into her chest. "The other leopard?"

"Looks like. Lance is running in for backup, but Liam is gonna need you—"

She left him in her dust.

The woman wouldn't stop screaming. The leopard wouldn't stop attacking, and Liam couldn't seem to stop bleeding.

Piss.

The leopard's teeth had clamped on to him too many times. The beast's claws had raked and pierced his flesh.

The blood loss would soon slow him down, even as his hunger for fresh blood—*the injured woman smelled so sweet*—pushed at his control.

The leopard slammed into him. Liam managed to wrap his arms around the shifter and roll. He gathered his strength and tossed the animal against the wall. Sheetrock littered the floor.

The door flew open. Liam turned, ready to face a new threat. A small man stood in the entranceway, his brown hair slicked back and his black eyes darting around the room.

Who the—

The leopard's teeth sank into his shoulder.

"*Ah!*" He swiveled, drove his fist at the creature. The leopard fell back, dazed.

Vampire strength. Not something to sneer at.

"I'm here to help you, Sullivan!" The shout came from the man in the doorway.

Liam crouched, fully facing the crouching leopard. "Get the woman out!" The guy sure as hell wouldn't be any help in a fight. One punch would knock him out.

But if he could get the woman to safety and remove the distraction of her flowing blood—

He heard the scuffle of footsteps. A woman's moan. She was bad off. She needed to get to a hospital, right away.

And the leopard needed a swift trip to hell.

Time to send him there. "No more games," he growled, knowing the man within the beast would understand him. "I'm going to—"

The leopard streaked past him and shot through the window, a blur of yellow and black.

"No!" Liam bounded after him, ready to hunt the bastard down and *finish this*.

But his right leg gave way beneath him and he hit the floor, hard.

Shifters had a well deserved reputation in the *Other* world. They were tough as nails and it took more than a few lucky swipes to kill them. It took one *hell* of lot to bring a shifter down.

"No, n-no, l-let m-me go!" The woman. Screaming. Sobbing. Fighting the weasel-looking guy.

She was using up strength she couldn't afford to lose.

Casting one last look out the window—the leopard had already vanished—Liam promised, "I'll find you again." And they'd finish the battle they'd started.

Shaking, biting back vicious hunger and pain, he rose to his feet. The right leg was still weak, the shifter had torn into his calf with his teeth, but it would hold. For now.

Blood followed his footsteps.

The woman was fighting wildly, her dark eyes huge, her black hair flying around her. "No, d-don't h-hurt—" She caught sight of him. A piercing shriek burst from her. "Devil!"

Maybe. "I'm the devil who saved you, lady."

Her eyes rolled back. Liam caught her when she fell. "Hospital," he ordered as his hands curled around her. "Now!"

He fought to stay upright. He couldn't fall again. The woman came first. It was always about the victim. He'd learned that on the streets of Dublin.

As a kid, he'd seen violence first hand. The bombings. The murders. The survivors left standing with haunted eyes.

*The victims came first.*

Vampire or human, the rule was still the same for him.

But, damn, he sure could have used Sadie right then.

*Sadie . . .*

Flowers. Woman. A racing heart.

"Liam!"

Her voice. His gaze rose. She ran through the doorway, other armed agents following on her heels.

The *real* backup.

He could have kissed her.

Two agents dressed in op black took the woman from him.

Sadie's eyes were wide as she stared at him. "Liam." A breath of sound. Her gaze raked his body. *"Liam."*

He stiffened. He didn't want to be weak in front of her and the others. His arms snaked out. Caught Sadie and pulled her close.

His kiss was wild, and more than a little desperate.

He could hear the drumming of her heart, the soft flow of her blood.

He needed to drink.

But, even more, he needed her.

Pity he couldn't have her.

His arms dropped. "He . . . got away." His tongue felt thick. His teeth too sharp.

Sadie reached for his hand. Her soft fingertips brushed across his skin. "Are you . . . Liam, dammit, you're bleeding out. Let me help you, let me—"

"Other guy . . . worse than me." True, that. The shifter had retreated because he'd been badly wounded. Maybe they'd all get lucky and find his carcass with the coming of dawn.

The agents were spreading out, some searching the room behind them, some carrying the woman out into the hall and toward the stairs.

"You need help." Worry in her voice. Fear in her eyes. "What can I do?"

His gaze lazered in on Sadie's sweet throat. "Let me drink." A stark demand.

She knew about vampires. Knew that he couldn't afford this level of loss. If he didn't feed, soon, he'd weaken too much.

Blood loss—one surefire way to kill a vampire.

If he didn't feed, he'd fall at her feet.

*"Let me drink."*

Her breath whispered out, and she nodded.

# Chapter Five

Liam was in trouble, and Sadie was afraid. So afraid that her knees shook and her hands were sweating and she felt like her heart was going to burst from her chest.

*I can't lose him again.*

He had so many wounds. His chest. His arms. His shoulders. Even his legs. The shifter had savaged him.

"Don't die on me." She gave the order as she kicked in the door to her left. They were far away from the rest of the team. They'd managed to sneak up to a higher floor while the other agents fanned out below. Liam needed safety, but she didn't have time to get him back to her place. He needed to feed.

Now.

"Too late, love." A ghost of a smile feathered his lips and the ache in his tone made her hands clench. "I died two years ago."

Her jaw locked. "Do it, Liam. Go ahead, just—"

*Drink from me.*

He couldn't afford to be so weak. Liam had his share of enemies, she knew that. All vampires had enemies—there were too many folks, both human and *Other*, running around out there with a Van Helsing complex.

She'd been one of them.

No longer. She didn't care that he was a vamp. He was hers, and she hated to see him like this.

Sadie was going to kill that shifter.

She wrapped her arms around Liam and felt the wet touch of his blood.

*His wounds weren't closing.*

There wasn't any time to spare.

"Sadie . . ." Hunger. Fear?

She shut her eyes. She'd been taught vampire feeding was a degradation. The worst insult to her kind.

The hunter, becoming prey.

Screw that.

Liam needed her. Pride could take a hike.

Tilting back her head, she bared her throat and waited.

She expected the hot flash of pain that came from his teeth. At the bar, the sting of his bite had been brief. Then there had been such unexpected pleasure.

Yeah, she expected the sharp press of his teeth.

Instead, she felt the soft brush of his lips and the wet slide of his tongue on her flesh.

Her mouth parted on a sigh. Her breasts tightened against him, and heat bloomed between her thighs.

Sadie's hands rose and tunneled into the thick strands of his hair. "Liam."

Her Liam.

His teeth pierced her flesh. A split second of sharp pain and then—

The pleasure. The fast, hard rush of sensual energy heated her blood. Her thighs shifted as she strained to get closer to him.

His mouth moved on her. Lips. Tongue. Teeth. And it felt so *good*. As if she'd climax, with just the press of those teeth.

Her hands tightened in his hair, forcing him closer.

Her panties were getting wet.

She wanted him inside of her, thrusting and drinking.

No one had ever told her that a vampire's bite could be so amazing. Pain. Fear. That's all the whispers said.

But what about the rush of pleasure? The wild heat of hunger and lust? She rubbed against him, her breasts aching, her sex yearning.

More.

She wanted—

Liam.

His hands slipped between them. Caught her breasts, stroked and teased through the thin blouse she wore. His thumbs raked over her nipples and a growl burst from her lips.

And still he drank from her.

Every nerve in her body seemed electrified. Her skin too sensitive, her lust too fierce.

The beast snarled inside, demanding release. A release the woman wanted just as badly.

But part of her was afraid. Liam was hurt so badly, she didn't want to injure him, didn't want to make it worse.

So she bit back her hunger. And let him take.

Mouth.

Tongue.

Teeth.

And his hands—cradling her flesh. Tugging her nipples. Feeding the sensual need. Those long, strong fingers knew just how to touch her.

The scent of her arousal filled the air. Whimpers slipped from her lips. Hungry growls.

Her hands dropped to his shoulders. Curled tight. Held on for the ride.

Still he drank.

An explosion of lights appeared behind her closed lids. Her sex throbbed. Her knees shook.

Sadie licked her lips and swore that she tasted him. He hadn't kissed her, but he was all around her.

She could feel him. Inside.

Heart.

Spirit.

Everywhere.

*The blood link*. She knew it was getting stronger. The more he took, the deeper the bond.

Forever.

His teeth withdrew. A wet swipe of his tongue.

Her eyes opened.

A tender kiss on her neck. Right over the mark he'd left.

Soon, she'd be marking *him*.

Liam's head lifted, and when his eyes met hers, there was no blue in his gaze.

Only darkness.

Those black eyes narrowed. "You know . . . what happens now."

No, she really didn't have a damn clue. She wanted him. Naked. But the guy was injured and, even with her blood, it would take hours for him to heal completely.

Already, though, his voice was stronger. And the wounds were starting to close—she could tell by the smaller scratches on his face. They were shrinking before her eyes.

The relief sweeping through her body made Sadie almost dizzy.

Losing him again—not an option.

Shit.

Realization had her eyes widening.

She still loved the Irish bastard.

"We need . . . to get out of here."

A nod.

"Your blood—it's damn strong, but I'm goin' to crash soon. To heal, I'll have to sleep."

Another nod. Her blood would give him the strength to get past the other officers and to make it back to her place.

Then she'd keep him safe while he slept.

His fingers caught her chin. "When I wake, I'm goin' to have you."

A dark promise.

She smiled. "No, Liam, when you wake . . ." She paused, just long enough to have his brows lowering, "I'll have *you*."

Vampires dreamed. Some folks thought they didn't, but, then again, some folks also thought his kind didn't have souls.

Vamps had souls, some were just blacker than the night they loved so much. Evil was a choice, not a punishment for his kind.

Free will.

Everyone—every*thing* had it.

Just as creatures like him, well, they had dreams.

But sometimes, those dreams weren't fantasies. They were memories. The vampire's. His prey.

Shared visions given by the blood.

When Liam slept, the visions came to him. He saw a girl, smiling, long black hair around her shoulders. She was laughing, pointing.

Beside her, he saw his Sadie. Younger. With eyes not so hard and with a curving mouth.

Innocence.

Youth.

A beautiful dream. Happy.

At first.

Then the woods around the girls grew darker. Laughter reached his ears. Cold. Insidious.

And he wanted to wake up.

But he couldn't. The sleep was too deep.

*The vampire attacked the dark-haired girl. Jasmine.*

*"Change, Sadie, change! Help me!"*

*The snap of bones. The rolling cry of the leopard.*

*The vampire had a tight lock on little Jasmine. Blood dripped down her neck and her cries grew weaker.*

*Sadie attacked. Biting. Clawing. Fighting as fiercely as she could.*

*But her leopard wasn't fully grown. The leopard aged as the girl did. Still young. Still weak.*

*The vampire dropped Jasmine onto the ground. Her eyes were wide open, terrified.*

*The vampire was going after Sadie.*

*"You'll taste so good."*

*Another roar filled the forest. Shook the earth.*

*Not from Sadie. From another. Coming closer.*

*The vampire glanced over his shoulder.*

*Too late.*

*Blood covered the ground.*

*And Jasmine—her eyes closed.*

Liam's body stiffened against her. Sadie frowned, stroking her hands over his chest. He'd been out for almost twelve hours. The sun was setting.

His night was coming.

The wounds on his body had healed. Not even a scratch marred his flesh.

She leaned over him, her gaze on the shadows cast by his lashes. He was almost beautiful in sleep. Damn too-good looks of his. No man should be so sexy.

Her hand lifted. Traced the curve of his lips.

He woke instantly, his eyelids flying open. Liam's right hand snapped around her wrist in a steely grip.

"Who was the other leopard?" Gruff.

Sadie blinked. "What?" Was he talking about the asshole who'd attacked him? Unfortunately, the team still hadn't tracked him, but she knew they would, it was only a matter of time, especially once she and Liam went hunting.

"In the woods that day . . ."

Chill bumps rose on her flesh.

"Who killed the vampire?"

Her gaze held his as her breath rushed out. "The link's that strong, huh?" The blood link was one of the few real mysteries still in existence. Just how strong, how deep, it really depended on the vampire and his victim.

She swallowed. "My brother, Jacob." Thank God he'd decided to come looking for her and Jasmine. If he hadn't—

She would have died that night, too. Because their attacker . . . "He'd been watching us. For days." Hiding his scent—the tricky bastard. "Waiting for that one moment when we were vulnerable." They'd been having so much fun. Running. Laughing. Enjoying the wild woods.

His lips tightened. "How can . . ." He stopped, jaw clenching.

"Liam?"

His gaze was stark and his brogue thick as he asked, "How can you let me touch you, knowin' what he did?"

"Because you *aren't* him." Liam had fought like hell to save the woman in that building. He wouldn't attack innocents.

Not his style.

Never had been.

Never would be.

She was an idiot for ever thinking otherwise.

"Let go of my hand," she told him quietly.

The body beneath hers—*delicious naked flesh*—tautened even more.

But he let her go.

"I shouldn't have—" He shook his head. "That first night, I-I needed the blood, but I should never have taken—"

She snorted. Probably not her sexiest moment. "Please, vampire. If I'd wanted free of your hold, it would have been too easy."

Not a youth anymore, her beast was fully grown and more than a match for a vampire.

The stark truth: She'd wanted to be in his arms again. If she hadn't wanted to feel him, flesh to flesh, she could have put up one hell of a fight.

Her fingers brushed down his cheek. "I'm touching you," she told him clearly, "because I want to."

Liam's nostrils flared.

"Because I have to." Softer.

She kissed him. An open-mouthed, I'm-starving-for-you kiss. Lips. Tongues. Heat.

Sadie felt the surprise ripple through him.

Crazy vamp. Didn't he remember what she'd told him?

It was her turn to have *him*.

She nipped his lower lip. Vampires weren't the only ones who liked to bite. Liam should have remembered that about her.

She smiled at him, then caught the bottom of her T-shirt and jerked it over her head. It hit the floor after she threw it, but Sadie didn't care.

No bra. She'd stripped down to shirt and panties after she'd gotten him in bed.

And she'd stripped him completely.

His eyes were on her breasts. The blue began to darken.

She caught his hands. Brought them to her flesh. Enjoyed the strong weight of his hands over her. He knew just how to stroke her nipples. Just how to play and torment.

But then, so did she.

Sadie's fingers trailed down his chest. Over the nubs of his nipples. Liam was so sensitive. Always had been. And when she put her tongue on him—

Leaning forward, her tongue swiped over his left nipple.

Liam hissed out a breath and nearly came off the bed.

"Ah, not the way we play tonight." She pushed him back, deliberately injecting extra strength into the move. "Tonight, it's my game."

And she intended to enjoy herself fully.

Rising onto her knees, she shoved the sheets out of her way. Liam was aroused. The hard flesh of his sex rose toward her, long and thick.

The cat inside purred.

Time to get wild.

Her lover had healed, no need to go easy on him.

Her nails scored the flesh of his stomach. Not deep enough to cut the skin, certainly not enough to hurt.

Just enough to have him sucking in a sharp breath and to have those blue eyes turning completely black.

Fear didn't shoot through her at the sight of his eyes and his sharpening fangs.

*This was Liam.*

"No pretendin' this time?" He grated the words.

Her fingers wrapped around his aroused flesh. Felt the jerk of his sex.

She knew what he meant, and part of her felt a flash of shame. "No pretending," she agreed, her voice a whisper. The present was all that mattered.

Not the past—no way to go back.

And not the future—because, really, what future could they have? She'd age, slip away one day, while he stayed forever young.

No past, no future.

But they could sure enjoy the present.

Her fingers tightened.

Liam's teeth snapped together.

Then she lowered her head.

"Sadie!"

Her lips feathered over his aroused length. Soft as silk, but so hard and strong. Her tongue snaked out, licked the head of his shaft and tasted the tang of his flesh.

She took him in her mouth.

"Fuck! *Sadie!*"

She knew what he liked, oh, yeah, she knew. Licking. Sucking. Swirling her tongue over his aching flesh.

His hands clamped over her hips. She felt him rip away her panties. Then he touched her. Slid those long fingers between her thighs and pressed against her sex.

Pushed against her sensitive core, found her wet and ready.

He knew what she liked, too. He'd levered his upper body up to touch her better.

One finger drove inside of her.

*Yes.*

She looked up at him, into those dark eyes.

A second finger.

Her sex tightened.

Not wild enough, not yet.

Sadie gave him one long, last lick, from root to tip. She kissed away the moisture on the head of his cock. Wanted more.

"In . . . side." A grated demand. "Put me . . ."

His fingers felt fantastic in her sex, but she wanted his cock in her—just as badly as he wanted to be there.

Liam's thumb stroked her clit, making her cream even more for him.

His fingers withdrew, thrust, withdrew—

Sadie moaned, then moved, fast. She pinned his hands to the mattress. Shifted her hips so that his shaft brushed against her open core.

Her cream coated the head of his cock. Damn, but he was beautiful.

Sadie arched her hips, then drove down onto him, taking that wonderful, thick flesh deep inside.

They both gasped.

*So full.* Her sex felt stretched, tight.

Her knees dug into the mattress as she flexed. "Ready?" she whispered.

His hungry snarl was her answer.

Sadie started moving. Rising, falling. Faster and faster. Her breath left her in hard pants, her heart drummed against her ribs and sweat slickened her flesh.

And she kept riding him. His thighs were like steel beneath her. His cock her perfect fantasy.

Again, again, *again.*

His lips were parted, those teeth gleaming.

His gaze was on her throat.

Sadie rose, fell. She tightened her grip on his wrists.

Release bore down on her. Just a few seconds away—

Her cry filled the room. Her sex clenched around him and ripples of pleasure rolled through her body.

But she didn't stop moving. Rising, falling. No, she didn't stop—

Because Sadie was just getting started.

She was so fucking beautiful. Liam stared up at Sadie, at her glowing eyes and red lips, and his cock swelled even more within her slick depths.

Oh, damn, but her climax was milking him. Squeezing him so tightly in her warm, wet sex.

But he didn't want to come yet. Not yet.

She let go of his hands. Smiled at him, the smile that always made his mouth go dry and his cock twitch.

"I want a bite," she said, her voice husky. Pure damn temptation.

He almost came. His heels dug into her sheets. He wasn't going to last much longer. She was so hot and snug.

Sadie bent over him, and her nipples pressed into his chest. Beautiful nipples. Red like cherries, with tight tips. He loved her breasts. Loved having them in his mouth. Sucking them until her face flushed and the scent of her arousal filled his nostrils.

His hands caught her hips, urging her closer. His fingers locked on the round curves of her arse.

*Beautiful arse.* Now he'd like to bite—

Her lips brushed the curve of his neck. She kissed him, mouth open.

Then his Sadie bit him and Liam's control vanished with a roar.

He came, exploding deep within her body. The release was savage. So strong his whole body shook and so good—oh, *fuck,* so good.

*Sadie.*

She kept riding him as he came. Kept lifting her hips, sweeping her sex over his sensitive flesh.

The release wiped him out, hollowed him, and made him crave more.

He shuddered and wanted her blood.

Wanted *his* bite.

*How did I walk away from this? From her?* The questions flashed through his mind.

How the hell had he been strong enough to leave her before?

She raised her head. Licked her plump lips and—he kissed her. And started thrusting again.

Her sex was swollen and still so wonderfully wet. He moved slowly at first, as his cock began to grow within her.

Then the thrusts became stronger. The kiss harder.

She broke free from him. Pushed up on her knees. Sadie looked down, and he followed her gaze. The head of his cock was inside of her, shielded by the light covering of her blond curls.

She took all of him inside.

Liam pressed his lips together. *A bite, just one—*

She was too far away from him. Fully on her knees. He pushed up, managing to shove even deeper into her.

The pleasure on her face made him crazy.

Bloodlust rose, so hot and powerful that he started to turn away from her.

"No!"

Her nails—no, too sharp for mere nails—dug into his shoulders. His gaze shot back to her face.

He watched, stunned, as she tipped her head back and bared her throat. "Your turn."

His arms clamped around her. Liam's right hand pulled back her hair, as his left stroked her throat.

And his cock was still deep in her sheath.

Her knees were on either side of his hips. Face to face now, they stared at each other. Black eyes to gold.

Her sex rippled around him, a silken glide that had him groaning. Her pulse raced, he could hear the drumming, the soft whoosh of her blood.

He would take it, as he took her.

Liam pierced her flesh. Tasted the wild flavor of her blood.

Her inner muscles clamped around, squeezing, tightening.

He drank.

They climaxed. An explosion of sensation that rocked between them both. Waves of fiery pleasure, consuming.

Liam could feel Sadie, inside, out, her mind, spirit . . .

*All of her.*

In that one, blinding instant, when the world disappeared in a veil of red, she was completely his.

And he was hers.

His teeth withdrew.

Liam pressed a kiss to her throat.

*His.*

Now they were both marked. Beyond flesh.

*How the hell did I let her go?* The question rose again, and he knew, there would be no escape for Sadie this time.

*Beyond flesh.*

# Chapter Six

Staying in bed, having pillow talk—well, that really wasn't an option for them.

Sex with Liam had been necessary, as vital as breathing for Sadie. She'd had to feel his flesh within her.

To make absolutely certain that Liam was all right—*alive,* or, at least still undead.

But they had a killer to catch. As much as she would have liked to stay in that bed with him all night, a job waited.

Sadie's life wasn't an easy one. Not a lot of down time for a leopard shifter who spent her nights tracking killers.

There was fresh blood on the streets. She had to hunt, no, *they* had to hunt.

So less than an hour later, she and Liam were scouring the streets of Miami. Her nostrils twitched as she fought to catch the scent of the other leopard. But she didn't detect the deep, musky odor. Just caught the smell of cigarettes, car exhaust, whiskey, and too expensive perfume.

"Anything?" Liam asked.

Sadie shook her head. "Not yet." But she'd find him. Her gut told her that the leopard hadn't turned tail and fled the city. Not his style.

He'd needed to heal, just as Liam had, and when his strength was back—*could already be back*—he'd hunt again.

She wasn't in the mood to find any more savaged human

women. Women whose bodies had been tossed into trees and left for their blood to drip onto the ground.

In the wild, leopards often stashed their prey in trees to keep other predators, like lions, from taking their precious food. The better to savor the meal.

This was Miami, not the wild, and the leopard was leaving his kills in the trees for one reason: to make the humans afraid. To leave them a message.

*There's something in the night you need to fear.*

Yet despite his taunting warning, the streets were packed this night.

More prey, just waiting.

"They don't believe what they see," Sadie whispered, feeling Liam come to a stop behind her. "They won't know what's coming for them until it's too late." A human would be no match for a full grown male leopard shifter. The leopards were so strong.

"We're going to find him." Liam sounded certain. "The bastard can't hide forever."

But he could kill again, before they found him. He could—

The cell phone on her hip vibrated. Sadie had the phone out, open, and at her ear in two seconds time. "Miller?" He'd be the only one to contact her now.

"Brently and Moore Street." The special agent's voice was thick with excitement. "Abandoned house. Got a phone tip— some guy swears he saw a jungle cat crawling into the house."

No, it couldn't be this easy . . . could it?

"He wants animal control," Miller continued, "he's getting us."

Sadie turned, her gaze meeting Liam's. "On our way."

The FBI team wouldn't go in without her. Miller understood what he was facing.

She ended the call. Raised her brows. "Our hunt just got a hell of a lot easier." *Maybe.* The leopard should have been too skilled at camouflage to be seen, but perhaps he'd been so badly hurt that he couldn't properly cover himself.

Perhaps.

"Keep your guard up," she told him.

Leopards loved to lure their prey in close—close enough to kill.

\* \* \*

"Lance says the leopard's smell is all over the damn house."
Miller stood behind an unmarked police car, his brown eyes glaring at the small house across the street. Boarded windows. Slumping roof. Overgrown yard.

Sadie's nostrils flared. "He's right." Her hands clenched into
fists. The scent of the leopard was everywhere. So heavy.

Too heavy?

She could just make out claw marks along the top of the old
porch. Embedded deep into the faded white wood that clung to
the front of the house.

"I'm going in—"

"*We* are," Liam corrected softly.

She gave a grim nod. "Keep everyone else back. Let's make
sure there aren't any surprises waiting for us."

"James." Miller lifted his hand, palm up, and motioned toward the waiting house. "This show's yours."

Because a charmer knew better than to tangle with the killer
that waited.

Sadie and Liam went in fast. Guns up and ready. She didn't
shift, couldn't, with so many people around. So, this time, she
was going to use cold bullets. The right aim, and the leopard
would be out, permanently.

They sidled up to the house. Swept to the left, keeping cover in
the overgrown grass as much as possible. Sadie had her eyes on
the second window on the left side, the one criss-crossed by two
boards. One yank should have those down, then they'd be inside.

"So much blood . . ." Liam's voice was a breath of sound behind her.

Her head moved in the slightest of nods. The coppery odor
was even stronger now. And the blood smelled very, very fresh.

What if he had another victim in there? She could smell the
traces of a human's presence. The faded whisp of perfume. A
woman. *Was another victim inside?*

Or was that just the scent memory of one of those poor
women he'd killed?

No time to waste.

Sadie reached the window first. But Liam's hands lifted before her. He had the boards down, ripped away without so much as a sound.

Then it was her turn.

Sadie dove through the window, landing in a crouch, gun ready, eyes searching the darkness to find—

A large gold and black spotted leopard. On the ground. Covered in blood. Barely moving, gasping for breath.

*Thud. Thud . . .*

A weakening drum—his heart struggling to beat.

"Search the rest of the house!" Her order was given instantly.

*Never let down your guard.*

She'd learned that lesson long ago.

Liam moved like a shadow, drifting soundlessly through the small rooms.

"Clear." His gaze swept back to the leopard. "Looks like the bastard won't be a problem much longer." He unhooked the radio on his hip and called out to Miller.

The rest of the cavalry would be inside the place in moments.

Sadie couldn't take her gaze off the leopard. Golden fur matted red. She stepped forward. "We're with the FBI . . ." Why was she bothering with the whole spiel? Miller would order him dead the minute he walked into the house.

Not that it looked like the leopard would live much longer anyway.

A whimper rolled from his throat. A stark cry of pain and fear.

Her nose twitched. The scent of the leopard—it wasn't *quite* right.

Not as musky as before.

But maybe the blood was just too strong.

*Maybe.*

"Fuck, the bastard's still alive." Miller's voice. He'd stepped into what amounted to the den in the house. Sadie turned her head and found him glaring at the trembling leopard. He'd come in alone, for the time being. As she watched, Miller pushed back his jacket and reached for his gun. "This one's not going in—"

"No!" The cry burst from her lips, instinct kicking into high gear.

Miller's eyes widened and an *are-you-insane* look covered his face.

The scent should have been the same. "Don't—don't kill him yet." Because dammit, something was *off* here.

His eyebrows shot up. "James, you *know* what we have to do. That jerkoff's been slicing women to bits. Rehabilitation is not gonna work for him."

Yeah, right, as if there were a monster rehabilitation program. The powers that be would just rather see her kind dead.

"Why is he still in leopard form?" The fight between him and Liam had happened over fourteen hours before. The shift itself helped to speed healing for her kind. He should have transformed—

Not crawled into the house to lick his wounds and die.

"Maybe he couldn't," Miller groused. "Maybe he was hurt too bad from tangling with Sullivan."

Maybe.

But shifting after injuries like this—it was second nature. No, more than that—survival instinct.

"Sadie . . ." Liam's voice now. Liam's eyes met hers with worry lurking in his stare. "Don't think because he's one of yours that he can be saved."

*One of yours.* "*Mine,*" she gritted. "No, he's not mine." Her kind—her family—didn't savage innocents. "Something feels *wrong.*" She shook her head, wishing she could put into words just why the scene made her feel so uneasy.

The leopard she'd faced before had been so vicious. She'd almost smelled the evil and decay of the soul dripping from him.

*This leopard was different.*

*Same overlying scent. Earth. Wild animal. But . . . not decay.*

She stepped in front of Miller's gun. "Put it down."

His jaw dropped. "James, you're stepping over the line—"

"Put. It. Down." He wasn't killing the leopard, not until she figured out what was happening.

Lines bracketed Miller's mouth, but he slowly lowered his weapon. "You've got two minutes, then I'm putting a bullet in his head. No more women are dying on my watch."

*Two minutes.* Giving a quick nod, she spun around. She had to get closer to the shifter. The leopard's head was turned away from her. She needed to look into his eyes.

She stepped in his blood. No way to avoid it. Blood had pooled on the floor.

*He wouldn't live much longer.*

She kept her gun out and her body ready. If this was a ploy, he wouldn't catch her off guard.

"Stop." Liam's voice. Vibrating with leashed control. "That's close enough."

Less than two feet away. Her tongue licked desert dry lips. "Look at me." She knew the leopard had heard every word spoken in that house. He'd heard, but hadn't reacted.

As he didn't react now.

Too far gone from pain?

Or part of his plan?

"If you don't look at me now," she raised her voice, injected steel, "then you're going to die. Miller can fire that bullet into the back of your skull and—"

The leopard's head whipped toward her. His mouth opened in a snarl. His teeth glistened.

But his eyes were too bright. Brighter than any shifter's she'd ever seen. It almost hurt her to look into them. *Chips of emerald ice.*

"Get the hell back!" Liam's snarl as he grabbed her arm.

She didn't move. Just stared into those eyes and realized that the leopard wasn't seeing her.

*Eyes as blank as glass.*

He wasn't seeing anything.

*Blind.*

She shook Liam off and dove to her knees. Her hands went to the wounds, so many, and she tried to staunch the blood.

"Don't touch him! Sadie, what are you—"

Her head snapped toward Liam. "Help me." She'd never asked for his help before, but she needed him now. "This isn't the same leopard."

"*What?*" Miller bellowed.

"The eyes." She swallowed. "They're green—but his are different." The leopard wasn't attacking her, damn lucky that, but his body had stiffened. *Hold on.* "His stare's too bright. Liam, he's blind." A blind shifter. He would have been born with the vision loss, because if the problem had developed later in life, the beast within would have been able to heal him. "He's *not* the one who's been killing those women." But if they couldn't help him soon, he would be the one to die that night.

Liam fell to his knees beside her. Buried his hands in the matted fur. "Fuck. What happened to him?'

She had a good look at his wounds. At the marks that could only have been made by claws. "The same thing—the same shifter—that happened to you last night."

"Christ." Miller exhaled heavily. "How many damn shifters are running around this city?"

Sadie didn't answer because she didn't think Miller really wanted the truth.

She looked back into the beast's blazing eyes. "Stay with me, okay? We're gonna help you." He had to shift to survive. "Miller, get him an ambulance—he's gonna have to be sewn up at the hospital, because when he transforms, he's not—"

Fur began to melt away. Muscled, golden flesh appeared as bones snapped and reshaped.

"*Sonofabitch.*" Miller's breathless voice.

Guess the guy had never seen a shift before.

Good thing the rest of his team members, the humans, were still outside.

The shifter lifted his head, no—*tried* to lift his head. Blond hair. Strong chin. High cheeks.

Liam tensed beside her. "Sadie . . . are you *sure?*"

She understood his doubt, because the man she saw now was an exact copy of the shifter she'd seen in the bar that first night.

Same shaggy blond hair. Same strong chin. Cheeks. Nose.

An exact copy.

Exact for the eyes.

If the leopard had been dead when they arrived, and those too bright eyes were closed, wouldn't she have thought that she'd found her killer?

*Sneaky bastard.*

"Get the EMTs in here!" Her voice snapped like a whip. "He needs blood, stitches, and a hell of a lot of morphine!"

Miller swore and hurried outside. She heard him shouting orders.

The blond's lips trembled. Cracked, caked with blood.

No, his injuries were far too severe to heal with one transformation.

Maybe they were too severe to heal at all.

"In . . . no . . . cent . . ." So weak, but she heard him. Then his bright eyes closed.

"No!"

"It's the same man." Miller paced the hospital hallway. "He fits the description. He's a leopard shifter—*he's the same damn man.*"

Sadie glanced up at him. The special agent was almost vibrating with tension.

"Lance says the smell's the same. Same scent, same man. We've got doctors in there trying to save a sadistic killer when—"

"He's innocent." From Liam.

Sadie turned to him in surprise.

He gave her a rueful smile. "Hey, a guy doesn't forget the man who tried to kill him." He looked back at Miller. "It was a setup. We were supposed to find a dead body to satisfy us."

She nodded, not the least bit surprised that Liam had come to the same conclusion she had. They'd always been in sync on their cases. One of the reasons she'd been so drawn to him.

Their minds worked alike.

And their bodies were pure fire together.

"Should have been a perfect setup," Liam continued. "But the bastard didn't contend with that guy—" he jerked his thumb toward the operating room "—fighting so hard to live."

"I figure them for twins," Sadie said. Only thing that made sense. A sigh as her shoulders fell. "I'm guessing the prick who left him for dead didn't count on him being strong enough to survive." A hard smile, one that she knew showed her sharp teeth. "He was wrong."

Miller ran a shaking hand down his face. "So the killer's still out there? Hunting on Miami streets?"

Unfortunately.

"*Christ.*" He reached for his phone. Pressed speed dial. "Jennings, get the men back on the streets."

Sadie watched him pace away.

"You saved his life, you know." Liam reached for her hand.

Her lips twisted. "Maybe, maybe not." Attacked like that, by his own brother. *What kind of life had he led?*

Hell. Jacob would sooner bite off his own hand than ever hurt her.

*Blind.* She'd never met a leopard shifter who couldn't see. The senses were so much a part of the beast.

And so necessary for hunting.

"You gave him a chance, then." He nodded. "Better than letting him take a bullet—which would have happened without you."

Her hand turned in his grasp so that her fingers locked with his. "Thanks for backing me up."

Liam's head inclined toward her. "Don't you know yet, love, I'll always back you?"

Yeah, she knew. No, she'd *thought* she knew that he'd have her back. Until he'd left her all alone in a house that smelled of him. He'd been with her so much in her home and in her bed, that his scent had marked everything.

As he'd marked her.

Every day—every damn day—she'd smelled him and thought that he was lost to her.

"Why, Liam?"

His brows pulled low. "I don't know what makes a man cross the line and start killin'—"

"No." Sadie wet her lips, rose to stand right in front of him. She had to find out, because she *hurt*. In her heart, the one he'd touched. Then and now. "Why did you leave me?"

Understanding flashed in his eyes even as his lips tightened. "I didn't exactly have a choice."

She wasn't going to let him off that easily. Her shoulders stiffened. "There are always choices. You could have come to me—told me what happened—"

"And what?" His voice was harder, the Irish he could hide when he wanted rolling under the words now. "Have you turn from me? Call me a monster? You tried to kill me when you realized I was a vampire!"

"If I'd wanted you dead, the stake would have been in your heart." Hell, she felt like the one who'd taken a weapon to the heart. Damaged. Broken. She'd been like that for two years. "Didn't you ever *think* about me?" Sadie couldn't believe she was even asking him the question. Where was her pride?

But she had to know. She'd thought about him—

"Every night. You were the last thing I thought of before sleepin' and the first thing on wakin'.."

The hole in her heart closed a bit and her breath seemed to come easier at the absolute truth she saw on his face. "But you never came back to me." Because, as he'd said before, he thought she was a human and wouldn't be able to handle him? No, it just didn't ring true, there had to be something more.

He caught her hands. Held tight to her. "Sadie, I'm not the man you remember."

No.

"After I got out of containment, I-I did things . . . things I never thought I'd do."

Her hands were still in his grasp, but her heart pounded too fast and she knew, with his enhanced vampire hearing, that he heard the hard beats. "Tell me." The darkness was within him. She'd seen it from the beginning. Maybe, if he'd stayed just a man, the shadows in his soul would have eventually disappeared. But he wasn't just a man.

"You know the stories about the Born Masters . . ." No Irish, just cold, dark words.

The vampires who'd been born, not made. The ones who had the strongest psychic powers and the deadliest desires. Sadie nodded.

"Well, those tales don't even scratch the surface." An orderly walked down the hall and Liam paused, waiting until the man vanished. "The Borns can touch the minds of all they make—but it's not just through the blood link. They can *control*, sneak inside, and steal every damn thought you have."

Goose bumps rose on her flesh. She'd never encountered one of the Born Masters. Few had, and lived to spread the story.

"Ozur—"

*Ozur.* Oh, shit. Her claws sprang at the mention of his name. She'd heard of that ancient Viking killer. Insane, bloodthirsty, and sadistic. He'd left a trail of bodies around the globe.

"He's the one who turned me that night and, later, he tried to control me."

Her heart stilled, then raced in a triple-time beat. "What did you do?" Not her Liam, he wouldn't hurt—

"I incinerated the bastard."

Her breath left her in a startled rush. "What? How?" As far as she knew, only level ten demons were strong enough to control fire to the degree needed to—

He laughed, but it was a harsh, cold rumble of sound. "I let the bastard think he had me. I drank from the prey he gave me, I hunted his enemies, and I got close. And when he rested, I fuckin' torched him."

Silence.

Then the intercom crackled to life as a Dr. Tom Brown was paged to ICU.

Liam dropped her hands. "Don't look at me like that."

What? She shook her head. "No, Liam, I—"

"I did what I *had* to do in order to survive. I didn't kill the prey he gave me. I let them live, Sadie, and when that prick was dead, I freed them. Yeah, I killed other vampires, I killed demons, but not innocents. *Not—*"

She rose onto her toes and kissed him, shutting off the tumble of his words and offering him the only comfort she could.

*I fuckin' torched him.* She'd heard the agony in his voice. Knew that he'd lived through hell.

His arms swept around her, nearly crushing her with his too strong grip. His mouth was frantic on hers. Kissing. Taking. Tongue driving between her lips.

She met him back with full passion and hunger. To know the torment he'd lived broke her heart.

*Liam.*

He ripped his mouth from hers. Breath ragged, eyes wide, he stared down at her. "You still want me?" Stunned disbelief.

*What had he expected?* "I'll always want you, Liam." Utter, stark truth.

His gaze, darkening, held hers. "I watched you." An admission that seemed torn from him. His fingers tightened around her, holding her in a grip that would have probably been painful for a human.

For her, it felt just right.

"October twelfth, last year, I came to you. Watched you—you were walking in the rain, just before dawn. Going to your house."

She remembered. She'd smelled him. Caught the faintest trace of his scent on the wind and ached for an hour because she'd missed him so much. She'd thought the scent was just a trick of her mind.

"I'd just killed Ozur. His blood was on my hands. I wanted you so badly *but I couldn't go back to you.* I was a killer, *am* a killer, and I couldn't ask you to accept me."

Her hands pressed against his chest. Such a strong chest. Sculpted muscles. Beneath the flesh and bone, she could feel his heart. Pounding out a frantic rhythm that matched hers. "You don't have to ask, Liam. I want you, *all* of you."

She'd given him her blood and her body. She wasn't turning from him now.

The doors of the OR swished open behind him. Liam turned at the sound, and Sadie saw a tall, golden-skinned doctor storm toward them.

His face was all angles and harsh planes, his eyes a dark silver. He pointed at them, one long finger raised. "You." His coat flapped behind him.

Oh, no. This couldn't be good news. Hell, if that shifter hadn't made it, then—

"Why the hell did you bring a shifter to my OR?" The doctor, whose name tag read Dr. Jonas Micco, glared at Liam.

Sadie stepped forward. She wanted to jump Liam and let the wild sex settle things between them, but now wasn't the time, and with the furious doc glaring at them, certainly not the place. "*I* brought him here." Her nostrils twitched. This guy didn't smell like a vampire or a shifter. A human?

She studied him again, noticing the closely cropped black hair and high cheekbones. Native American. The *Other* had always heavily populated their ranks.

"To a human hospital?" He shook his head. "What, you want him to be on the six o'clock news as a freak show?"

He was about to piss her off. A growl rumbled in her throat. His eyes widened and the doctor backed up a step. *Good move.* "We didn't have a choice," she told him, voice cool. "He was dying on us." It had been the human hospital or nothing.

"Well . . ." He exhaled and seemed to become a bit calmer. "You're damn lucky I was on rotation tonight."

"Is the guy still alive?" Liam asked.

"Yeah, alive and healing at an in-freaking-credible rate." He shifted from one foot to the other. "You've got to get him out of here before folks start asking questions."

She caught Miller's cheap cologne scent behind her. "Will do." Her head cocked as she studied the doctor. "You know, we could use someone like you . . ."

Another hasty step back. "I'm not a shifter."

"No." But he knew the score, and someone like him—a guy with medical training who wouldn't start screaming if he cut open a body and saw two hearts inside—he'd be a serious asset. "But you're someone who knows all about the *real* world, aren't you?"

She didn't need his grim nod for confirmation.

"I know about it, and want to stay the hell away from it." His jaw was clenched when he gritted, "I've seen just how much hell the *Other* can wreak." He jerked his thumb toward the ER. "He wants to see you, and I want you to get him *out* of my hospital before I have to convince any more nurses that they imagined skin sealing back up on its own." Shifter flesh could mend itself. Not a perfect repair—the flesh would be lined with a faint red scar at the wound site, but it was still a damn amazing trick.

A genetic trait she'd always loved.

He spun away from them just as Miller arrived. "Hey," he began, eyes on the doctor's retreating back, "is that the doctor who—"

"Shifter's ready to talk," Sadie cut through his words, deciding, for now, not to mention the full details of her conversation with the doctor. She knew a scared man when she saw one, and if she told Miller about the doctor right then, well, Micco's choices would be ripped away.

Like hers and Liam's had been.

He whistled. "Damn, that was fast. Thought the cat was dead."

She was already marching toward the swinging doors, with Liam at her side. "Well, you know the old saying, cats have nine lives." More than that, really.

"Yeah," Miller muttered behind her, "but I think that shifter used up about twelve."

True.

Liam's hand shoved open the green door.

They stepped inside.

And found the shifter on his feet, clothed in a loose hospital gown, with fangs bared and claws up.

*Oh, hell.*

No wonder the doctor was freaking out.

# Chapter Seven

Liam's first instinct was to fight. To go in punching and slashing with his own claws, but Sadie stepped in front of him, chilling the blood in his veins and making him realize that his lady walked on the wild side *way* too much.

"It's all right." Her voice was pitched low. "We're not here to hurt you."

The shifter's eyes, bright, glassy green, locked right on her. "I *smell* you," he spat. "I know what you are." That stare shot to Liam. "And what *you* are."

"We didn't do this to you." Still low, soothing. Sadie crept toward him. They were lucky, all of the nurses and doctors had cleared out, probably courtesy of Dr. Micco. "*We* didn't—"

"I know who the hell did this to me!" Fury. Pain. "The bastard who's spent thirty years trying to kill me. Thirty damn years." His blond mane shook. "He didn't succeed before, and he *won't.*"

Liam kept his attention fully on the shifter. Sadie might feel pity for the man, after the hell he'd been through, but Liam knew a wounded beast was one seriously *dangerous* beast. One most likely to bite off the hand that wanted to help him.

No one would be biting Sadie but him.

If he had to throw the shifter across the room to protect her, he was more than ready for the job.

*She still wants me.* She'd looked at him with honest desire in her eyes. She knew the truth about him, and she still wanted him.

Hell, no, he wasn't about to let anyone hurt so much as a single hair on her gorgeous head.

"Ease up, shifter," he ordered, aware of Miller stumbling to a stop behind him. "We pulled your body out of that dump and saved your hide."

"Hell. Knew we should have killed him." Miller's quiet mutter.

The shifter's head snapped up. "What?" His nostrils flared. "*You.* The trigger happy moron."

Uh-oh. Looked like the shifter hadn't been quite as out of it as they'd thought.

Silence.

Then Miller brushed past Liam. Liam lifted his brows but made no move to stop the man. If Miller wanted a beating, fine by him.

"That's *Special Agent Miller*, cat. And, yeah, I'm the one who almost put a bullet in your head." His right hand brushed back his jacket, revealing his weapon.

Didn't the guy understand that if the shifter decided to attack, he'd never have time to so much as draw his weapon?

Apparently not because Miller continued, "When I got dead women in the city, *butchered* women, I don't play nice. The last vic is alive, thank Christ, but—"

The shifter was on him in an instant. "Su is alive?" Hope had his face lighting up like some kind of candle.

Ah. Sadie glanced back, met Liam's gaze. No denying the connection there.

He gave a slight nod.

"Liam saved her," Sadie said. "She's in this hospital, recovering and—"

"What the hell?" Miller shook off the shifter's hold. "Why are you telling him?"

"Because now, he's going to tell us some information." Her left eyebrow raised. "Aren't you, shifter? Tit for tat. You wanna know about the vic, you tell us about the bastard who tried to slice you open."

*Tried?* The guy *had been* sliced open.

The shifter's shoulders fell. He turned around, paced a few steps away, and gave Liam an unfortunate view of his arse, courtesy of the gaping gown.

Liam glanced up, found Sadie getting the same view. He snarled.

The shifter spun back around. "He—he's my brother. Michael Munroe." He gestured to his face. "Twin brother, but I guess you already knew that, huh?"

Liam stared into the face that was the perfect reflection of a killer's. "He set you up—*you* know that, right? He wanted us to find your body and think that you were the killer."

A nod.

"Where is he?" A demand from Sadie.

"I don't know, I—"

"He has to have a safe house around here. Friends. Hunting grounds." She pushed relentlessly. "Tell us. We can't let another woman die!"

"Dammit, I know that!" His hands shot into the air. "Don't you think I fucking hate him? He took Su!"

"Just who is this Su to you?" Miller asked. "A lover—"

"She could have been." His shoulders fell. "She could have been . . . everything."

Almost helplessly, Liam's gaze rose to Sadie.

*Everything.*

Poor bastard. He knew just how the guy felt.

"Now, she'll never be mine." Desolation washed across his face. "Because of that sick asshole!"

"Where is he?" Sadie asked the question again.

"I don't know." His lips pressed together for a moment, then, "Hiding. Waiting. Getting ready to watch the news and see the story about the dead body that was found—*my* body."

A story he wouldn't see and he'd become enraged.

"You're coming with us," Miller said, crossing his arms over his chest. "Until this bastard's caught and I know for absolute certain that you weren't involved."

"Involved? I'm not a killer!"

"Sure you are." Miller glanced from his face to the claws that were still out. "Everyone is, human and *Other,* deep inside. All that matters is how much of a push it takes to get the killer out."

Liam knew that, for once, Miller spoke the truth.

"You stay under guard," Miller continued. "Until your brother's body is at my feet."

They took the shifter to a safe house, one surrounded by guards who were *Other.*

Sadie tossed a suitcase onto the floor near the guy, Kyle. Kyle Munroe. Miller had sent an agent out to get clothes for him. "You should have everything you need."

Liam waited for her, just outside the room. She hesitated. She knew she should go but—

"You don't have to pity me." The man's shoulders were stiff, his back to her. Clad now in green scrubs—courtesy of Dr. Micco—he wasn't flashing golden skin any longer.

His words had her flushing. "I-I don't." Okay, she did. The guy's brother was a psychotic who'd tried to kill him. She had a brother who faced devils to protect her.

"I might not be able to see, but it doesn't mean I'm weak." Harsh.

Her lips parted in surprise. "No, it's not because of—"

He turned toward her and his eyes zeroed instantly on to her face. "You're five-foot-two, one hundred fifteen pounds. You've got blond hair, you use rose-scented shampoo, and you've been fucking the vampire who is pacing outside the door."

Her brows rose.

"I can't see, but I can hear, smell, taste, and feel everything."

Yeah, shifters had incredible senses, she sure knew that. Hers were far, far superior to any human's.

"My remaining senses are stronger than other shifters'." Said simply. "Like they kicked into high gear to make up for my eyes."

She'd heard about something like that happening with humans.

"I don't need sight—no, forget that." He drew in a deep breath and stalked forward, stopping inches away. "I was lying earlier, I *can* see, I just don't use my broken eyes to do it."

"*Sadie.*" Liam's voice. He stood in the doorway, face tense and black eyes on Kyle.

She held up her hand. "It's okay, Liam." Time for truth. "And I was lying, too, Munroe."

His lips parted. "I *knew*—"

"I pity you because you had the shit-screwed luck to be born with that asshole as your brother and that he hurt you." Probably more than the guy would ever reveal. "But I don't pity you for any other reason." She'd be a fool if she did. She could *feel* the man's power. "Got it?"

Maybe someone else would think that a shifter without vision was weak, but she knew her kind too well.

No shifter was weak. Ever. They were the most dangerous hunters in the world.

And she pitied anyone who thought otherwise.

He inhaled. "Got it."

"Good." She stepped back. "If you think of anything else to tell us, Moody's outside." The giant demon with the snake tattoos was a damn fine guard. "Let him know and he'll get word to Liam or me."

Liam wasn't looking real happy right then. He stood in the doorway, filling the space, and his burning glare focused on Kyle.

"Do you . . . know how she is?" Sounded like the words had been ripped from the shifter.

Sadie didn't have to ask who "she" was. "Su hasn't woken up yet." Su Kent, the victim Liam had managed to rescue.

Su Kent, age thirty-two. Art director at the Miami Museum. Her mother had immigrated from Thailand and married Jonathan Kent, an ex-Marine.

"Is she gonna make it?"

"I think so." She hoped so. From all accounts, Su Kent was a genuinely good person, a pretty rare thing. She donated food to the needy, taught an after-school art program for disadvantaged kids, and even had a recycling bin at her house. Yeah, Miller had checked her out thoroughly.

A nice lady. One who sure hadn't deserved the horror she'd suffered.

Sadie walked to Liam.

Just like *he* hadn't deserved the horror that had happened to him and his team.

Sometimes, life really sucked.

"I-I'll help you." Kyle's rushed words had her glancing back at him. "I want Michael stopped. My whole life my parents hated me because of the way I was. Said I was weak."

The pain on his face was gut-wrenching.

"Michael made my life *hell*. You don't know what he did all those years—" He broke off, shaking his head. "Doesn't matter."

But she thought it did.

"*I* survived," he continued. "But he's not going to, not this time."

"We'll stop him," Sadie told him, meaning the words. "He's not going to hurt anyone else."

Yeah, they'd stop the bastard—once they *found* him.

The shifter whore was with the vampire again. Walking with him, his arm around her shoulders, flesh pressed to flesh.

She was with the parasite, all but purring up at him.

*She knew better.*

He snarled and lowered his binoculars.

Binoculars—human invention, one that was coming in handy. He couldn't risk getting close enough for the female to smell him—or close enough for his freak of a brother to catch his scent with that hyped-up nose of his.

*Should have cut off Kyle's nose years ago. Should have killed him years ago.*

'Course, he'd tried—and nearly succeeded more times than he could count.

Lucky bastard. That luck wouldn't last forever. He'd make sure of it.

But *she'd* been the one to save his brother this time. Sadie James. Tough agent. Sexy bitch.

Soon-to-be dead woman.

The vampire bent and pressed a kiss to her temple.

The binoculars seemed to explode in his hand. Glass, metal, and blood fell from his fingers.

Blood.

Sadie had given her blood to the vampire. Freely given blood and body. She wasn't a worthy adversary. Not a shifter of skill to fight and challenge.

She was garbage. A whore who'd spread her legs too quickly for the undead.

She'd pay for that. Pay for desecrating their kind.

It was time for the hunt to come to an end.

Time for Sadie James to die.

He wouldn't lose her.

Liam held Sadie close, his arms tight around her as they hurried up the steps to her house.

The desolation on the shifter's face when he'd asked about his Su—

No, that *wasn't* the end Liam would have with Sadie. He wasn't giving her up. Wasn't going to live his life, hell, such as it was, without her.

The instant the door shut behind them, his mouth was on hers. The need and the blinding lust had his body shaking. His cock was rock hard, fully erect, and ready to thrust into her tight sex.

Her lips and tongue met his with the same feverish intensity. He could taste the hunger on her tongue. Wild fever.

Fuck, yes.

She clawed at his shirt, shredding the material so that her hands could get to his flesh. Her fingers curled over his muscles, hot hands that sent sparks dancing over his body.

A purr rumbled in her throat and his cock jerked in hungry anticipation.

Her fingers went to the buckle of his belt.

Liam ripped his mouth from hers. "No!"

Her eyes widened. So gold. And her lips were so red and wet and—

He picked her up, took five steps into the dining room and spread her out on the table.

*Fucking beautiful.* He'd wanted to make a meal of her all night.

Her lips curved in a slow smile as she kicked off her shoes.

*I'd die for her.* The realization hit him as he watched her beautiful smile. Lie. Kill. Die. Anything she wanted. He was lost. And so desperate for her. A taste. Liam had to have a taste. It had been too long.

He caught the waist of her pants. Jerked the soft cotton down, and snagged the scrap of lace that shielded her secrets at the same time.

Sadie tossed her shirt away and unhooked her bra, showing those perfect lick-me breasts.

He caught her nipple with his mouth. Sucked and licked and tasted the sweet flavor of her flesh. The scent of her arousal filled the air around him. Rich. Tempting.

Her hands were on his back. Stroking and pulling him closer.

Liam freed her breast, only to immediately turn his attention to the other pink nipple. She tasted *good*.

And he was going to taste more.

So much more.

He licked his lips when he rose. "Spread your legs."

The table was a dark cherry beneath her, making her skin seem to shine in stark contrast.

Unbelievable—

Her legs parted, showing him the plump, pink folds of her aroused flesh. Pink and wet and perfect.

Liam's mouth captured her. Pressed tight to that sweet center and *took*.

Tongue and lips teased her. Pushed against the button of her desire. Tasted the silky flesh open to him.

Liam took from her like a man starving, because he was. The more he tasted, the more he hungered. His tongue drove into her body, the need for her essence burning down to his very soul.

He heard her shout of release, felt the ripples of her climax.

Still he took.

The taste he'd longed for in his dreams.

"Liam!" Sadie, demanding as she pulled his hair. "Th-this time . . . you . . . inside."

His cock was about to explode so that sounded like a damn fine idea to him. One final swipe of his tongue, then—

He shoved his jeans down. Caught his cock in one hand and pushed the broad head between her thighs.

Creamy flesh.

Liam sank into her.

Their eyes met.

He withdrew. Thrust deep.

Her breath choked out. He could see the edge of her teeth.

Her muscles clamped around him.

So. Damn. Tight.

They climaxed together, the release slamming through them. Liam held her tight, drinking the cries from her lips and knowing that he'd found—

*Everything.*

All, with his Sadie.

Dammit . . . why, *why* couldn't a monster have a chance at love?

Someone was pounding at the door. Sadie blinked, forcing the sleep from her eyes so that she could glare at the bedside clock. Ten fifteen.

Not exactly the crack of dawn, but then, she hadn't gotten to sleep until after six that morning.

An arm rested over her stomach. A strong thigh caged her legs.

She smiled, catching sight of Liam's tousled hair. He liked to hold her when he slept. She rather liked that. Made her feel . . . wanted. Ah, that was—

"James! Dammit, James, I know you hear me! Freakin' cat ears—you probably heard me drive up!" The pounding of a fist against her door, then Miller shouted, "Get your clothes on and open this door! We've got a situation—"

"That man needs an ass kicking," she muttered.

"Yeah, he does," Liam growled.

Sadie smiled at that and kissed his bare shoulder before she managed to slide free of his grasp. She grabbed her robe and belted it quickly. "Remind me to give him one."

Liam didn't get out of the bed. Not that she blamed him. Daylight and vampires really didn't mix well. His kind were too weak when the sun rose, often suffering headaches and nausea—no wonder they preferred the nightlife.

She hurried across the room and took the stairs three at a time, adrenaline beginning to kick in her blood. When Sadie jerked open her front door, Miller was still shouting.

His eyes widened when he saw her, his stare sweeping from her hair—and, oh, yeah, she knew it had to look wild, courtesy of Liam's fingers—to her bare thighs. Her silky black robe was short, she hated having her legs trapped by too much fabric. Leopards sometimes had confinement issues.

But she didn't mind it when Liam held her tight in bed. No, she didn't mind that confinement at all.

Miller drew in a hard breath. "What? Do you spend all your free time screwing vampires?"

*Ass kicking.* Her hands dropped to her sides. One more minute, and she'd let her claws out. She hadn't gotten enough sleep for this shit. "Do you spend all your time being a prick?"

Miller blinked. "Yeah, pretty much."

What?

His gaze drifted over her shoulder as he frowned. "Tell Sleeping Beauty to wake his butt up, I need him."

"Daytime's not exactly his peak performance time." *A fact Miller knew.*

"I don't need his strength." Miller looked back at her. "I need his contacts."

Her brow furrowed. Behind her, she heard the creak of the stairs. "What's happening?" She stepped back, knowing that she had to let Miller inside.

The door closed with a soft click. "Kent's awake and, unfortunately, her memory of the attack is crystal clear."

Sadie winced. Uh-oh. "Has she . . . started telling the hospital staff about what happened?" If she had, she'd either be headlining the news soon or she'd find herself shipped off to the psych ward for the foreseeable future.

"She told Micco. He was in the room when she opened her eyes and started screaming about men with claws and fangs."

A soft footfall behind her. A moment later, Liam's hand pressed against her back. "What do you want me to do? I can't make her forget. You know I can't work Thrall yet."

*Thrall.* The old vamp term for the ability to control a victim's mind. To get the unwilling to surrender, to bare a throat and beg to be Taken.

Born Masters had the ability with their first kill. For others, age brought the power, and, in terms of a vamp's age, Liam was still a newborn.

Though not quite as defenseless.

"You know the demons in this city, better than anyone. Even Moody."

Yeah, well, Sadie knew Moody wasn't exactly popular among his kind. Demons didn't tend to think too highly of anybody who looked or acted like a cop.

And Moody had been a cop for ten years before joining the Bureau.

"Do any of them still owe you favors?" Miller pushed.

Sadie glanced back at Liam. Dealing in favors—the way of the human world and the *Other*.

A nod. "A few."

"Good, 'cause you're gonna have to call in markers today."

Liam lifted his hand and pressed his fingers against his forehead. "What do you need?" What, not who.

He knew the game.

Miller flashed his shark's smile. "A level eight or nine demon, the stronger the better."

Level eight or nine. Sadie exhaled slowly. Demon power was on a scale from one to ten. The low level demons, the ones to threes, were barely any threat to the human population. It was the high level demons that the people feared. Those above a level seven distinction, or L7, were trouble.

Powerful. Deadly.

Level tens—they were the hell-on-earth guys with their supernatural powers. But a level nine—well, he or she sure wouldn't be someone to take lightly. Especially considering that one with that much power might be able to rip away the mind of a human.

"You sure about this?" she asked Miller.

"No choice, James. We need help. Someone has to make Ms. Kent forget all about her trip to hell."

A perfect job for a demon.

# Chapter Eight

The woman on the bed was covered in stark white bandages. Her straight black hair fell around her face and her almond-shaped eyes blazed with fear.

"I know you." Her voice was a broken rasp.

Liam hesitated just inside the doorway. "Do you now?" Yes, that was part of the problem.

A tear leaked from her left eye and she began to shake, then to scream, with a voice long gone hoarse. Horrible, gasping gurgles sprang from her throat.

"The bastard tortured her for hours," Miller said, shaking his head. He stood at the foot of Su Kent's bed, hands clenched behind his back. "Micco wants to send her to a psych ward—"

Where she'd probably stay for a long, long time.

Especially if she started talking about men who could become real monsters.

Su stopped screaming and fell back against the mattress. Liam noticed the straps that were tied to her wrists, anchoring her to the bed. He took a cautious step forward.

She flinched and turned her head away. "S-stop . . . M-make it all . . . st-stop . . ."

Her pain and fear filled the room.

*I'll find the bastard. And I'll stop him from hurting anyone else ever again.*

"Su." He said her name quietly.

Another man stepped into the room behind him and the door closed almost soundlessly.

The woman on the bed didn't move.

"*Su.*" He walked around the bed. Stopped beside her and saw that her dark eyes were open, but staring at nothing.

No, staring at a nightmare only *she* could see.

He reached for her hand. Damn. She was cold.

Her lips parted and Liam was afraid the woman was about to start screaming again.

"I never hurt you." He spoke to her as another tear rolled down her cheek. She stared right through him. "I hurt *him*. I stopped *him* before he could do anything else to you."

"Cl-claws . . . and t-teeth . . ." Dry heaves shook her chest.

Liam swallowed and wondered if she was talking about the shifter or him.

"I didn't hurt you," he repeated, trying to reach her. He wished Sadie were there. She always had a much softer touch than he did.

But Miller had sent her back out to that damn bloody building downtown. He'd wanted Sadie and her team to canvas the area to see if anyone knew anything about Michael Munroe—and to make certain the bastard hadn't left any telling tracks that would help them nail him.

Sadie was the best hunter they had. She hadn't been with the unit that swept the building the night before, and Miller was worried as hell they'd missed something without her.

*But she sure would have been handy right then.* With her soothing voice and understanding eyes, she would have been able to reach the shattered Su.

"Hurt . . . I-I hurt . . . s-so much. C-can't forget . . ."

"Do you want to?" He knew Miller's attention was locked on them. Her response was very, very important.

Her head moved in the briefest of nods.

Not good enough. Miller wanted him to help wipe out Su's memories. Before he gave the demon standing so still next to the door the all clear, he wanted to make absolutely certain Su understood what was happening.

She'd have a choice in this, no matter what Miller wanted.

"Tell me, Su. Tell me what you want."

"T-to for . . . get . . ." Her swollen lips trembled. "Go back . . . like before."

Wouldn't be exactly like before.

But it wouldn't be like surviving hell, either.

"I can do that. I can take all the bad memories away."

Her hand twisted, grabbed his with desperate strength and her eyes finally locked on his. No, finally *saw* him. "Do it." The clearest thing she'd said.

The choice was made.

The demon stepped forward.

The building reeked of the leopard. Sadie stood outside the old building on Burns and Montay, her nose wrinkling. That bastard had left his scent *everywhere*.

"Probably living here," she muttered to the two men at her back. Humans, but they knew the hunt wasn't for a normal killer. "His stench is too strong."

"Crime scene guys found traces of blood in two other rooms on the second floor." This came from Derek Martin, the blond agent who liked to keep one hand close to his gun at all times. Smart fellow. "Matched it to Donna Summers and Theresa Kite."

The first two victims. No, the two victims they *knew* about. Sadie was sure there'd been more.

Michael Munroe hadn't been a good little choirboy his whole life. There'd been other kills, but in Miami, he'd just stopped hiding the bodies.

Cocky asshole. Taunting the cops and scaring the humans.

"So this is where he brought his prey." The sun was starting to set, the red glow falling over the building like a shadow made of blood.

She'd already walked the streets for most of the day. Talked to every person she could find in the area, but no one remembered Michael Munroe.

It wasn't like the guy was easy to forget.

"We're going over this building," she said, pulling out her latex gloves. "Every single room." *Every single inch.* Six stories, twelve rooms per floor. Sure, the building had been searched three times already—

*But not by her.*

Her nostrils flared. That scent was driving her crazy. The jerk sure had marked his turf. "Let's get this done." Her stomach was in knots. "I want to find this bastard." She had to find him and stop him before he tortured and killed another woman.

The straps were gone from Su's wrists. She lay against the mattress, tears drying on her cheeks.

"That it?" Miller asked, frowning at the demon.

Charles LaMoyne gave a nod, then glanced at Liam. "You're in *my* debt now, Sullivan."

Just where he wanted to be, owing a demon. Liam inclined his head.

"I'll collect payment one of these days." A smile, not the friendly kind. "Count on it."

He would.

Charles turned away and headed for the door.

It had taken most of the day to find the demon. He wasn't one to advertise his presence in the city. Most of the strongest *Other* liked to keep to the shadows.

The better to watch the game mortals played.

LaMoyne hadn't helped the human out of the goodness of his heart. As far as Liam knew, there wasn't much goodness in there. But Liam had saved his hide a year ago, when he'd stopped a human under Thrall from taking the demon's head.

He'd hoped for an even debt exchange.

Should have known he'd have to pay a bit more for the help. Most demons didn't do favors for humans. LaMoyne had made a big exception for him.

Liam glanced back at the woman. Her eyes were closing and she looked almost . . . peaceful.

Maybe she'd stay that way.

LaMoyne's psychic talent was shading memories and twisting truth. When Su woke up again, she'd have the images from a car wreck in her mind, perfect memories to match her injuries.

She'd remember the squeal of tires and the crunch of metal—

But not the claws of monsters.

Liam turned away from her. He was bone tired, but, luckily, the sun would be down soon.

Maybe the headache pounding at the front of his skull would end then.

Hmmm . . . or maybe he should take a quick swing by phlebotomy for a little pick-me-up.

When Sadie stepped onto the second floor, every muscle in her body tightened.

Blood and death were in the air, so thick she nearly choked.

Liam had fought here.

Women had died.

And that sick freak had played.

His stench was so much stronger here. Her eyes narrowed. Stronger . . . and fresher.

Her claws cut through the latex.

Liam froze just outside of the elevator bank at Hudson Hospital.

For just an instant, he could have sworn that he'd caught a whiff of Sadie's scent.

But, no, that was crazy. She wasn't even close by. She was on the other side of town, searching that damn building.

A whisper of fear, a spike of anger.

Blood link.

*Hell.*

He attacked her first. Michael Munroe sprang from the room on the left, a fully formed leopard, and swiped his claws across her flesh.

Sadie fell onto the floor, hard, and heard gunshots blast around her. Her skin burned, blood soaked her shirt, and she knew that she was in serious trouble.

*Lying in wait.*

Leopards were patient hunters.

A man's scream.

Gritting her teeth, she tried to rise. She managed to get to her knees and she pulled out her gun.

She'd save the claws and teeth this time, a bullet would work.

The leopard was crouched over Derek, *his* claws less than an inch away from the man's throat.

The second agent, Collier Dulane, was on the floor, his eyes closed.

The leopard's ears twitched and those claws moved in for the kill.

"No!" Her scream was guttural. She could take the shot, but Derek would die. Those claws were too close.

Shit.

The leopard snarled at her.

Her fingers tightened around the gun. Without the weapon, *she* was a dead woman. There wouldn't be enough time to shift before he attacked.

*Liam.*

She needed him.

Her eyes dropped to Derek. His neck was twisted to the side and he stared at her, realization in his eyes.

*Do it.* He mouthed the words.

If she dropped her weapon, the leopard would attack her, she knew it.

And she knew that he'd kill Derek either way.

No. No, Derek was on her team, she couldn't let him—

The leopard roared.

So did she.

Then she fired.

The bullet hit the leopard dead center in his outstretched paw, exploding through muscle and bone, then slamming into the wall just beyond him.

Derek managed to roll to the side, pushing hard to his feet.

The leopard rammed into him. The agent's head hit the wall and he went down.

Sadie fired again. She hadn't been able to aim for head or heart with the first bullet, and he was moving too fast now to get a clear shot. Only the head or heart would stop him. She fired—again and again.

The leopard sprang at her and the beast within Sadie roared again for her freedom.

*Sadie.*

For a moment, her image swam before him. He felt a white-hot lance of pain across his chest. The cold splash of blood.

Then—nothing.

Terror had his heart nearly stopping. The blood link between them had grown so strong that he knew what was happening to her.

He was losing Sadie.

Hell, no.

Liam forgot about the elevator and ran for the stairs. Screw the damn sunlight that was still fighting the night. Sadie needed him.

*Hold on, a thaisce.* My treasure. And, dammit, she fucking was. The only thing of value in his world.

*Hold on.*

A red haze filled her vision. Blood. Hers. His. The leopard was in control of Sadie now, and she was fighting for her life—

And the lives of her two agents.

Pain was constant. The attack from him had been vicious. The guy outweighed her by a good forty pounds in animal form, and he had insanity on his side, always an advantage for a killer.

But she wasn't powerless. Sadie had rage and her desperate desire to stay alive.

So she fought him. Every slash of his claws led to an assault from hers. She wasn't letting him leave this room. He *wouldn't* kill again.

His teeth clamped on to her shoulder.

And another growl rumbled from the doorway.

Through the fury, she saw him, coming like an avenging angel—no, more like a pissed-off devil.

Another leopard. Golden fur lined with the dark rosettes of her kind. Mouth open in a snarl. Teeth glistening with saliva.

She recognized his scent immediately, even before she saw his glassy stare.

Kyle.

He launched across the room, his hind legs kicking back to send him soaring. His teeth locked on to Michael, ripped and tore, and the scent of blood deepened.

Sadie took a moment, panting, gathering her strength. This was it. She could feel the approaching kill in the air.

No escape. Michael Munroe was about to answer for his crimes.

And she didn't think the devil was gonna cut him any slack.

Her whiskers quivered as she leaned down in a crouch, waiting for the perfect moment to join the growling, biting blur that was the other leopards.

*Now.* She shot forward, teeth and claws ready.

Together, she and Kyle took the killer down, and his furious cries echoed around them until—

Silence.

Then the snap of bones.

Sadie and Kyle eased back. The battle was over. The leopard had shifted, an automatic survival instinct. Michael Munroe's wounds were deep. His choice was either shift or die.

When the transformation was over, Michael lay naked on the floor, breath choking out.

Sadie let the white-hot fire of the change sweep over her. The guy wasn't in any shape to attack now. She had to check on her men and get them an ambulance ASAP.

She didn't care about her nudity. Her clothes had shredded when she shifted into the cat. She'd been badly wounded, was still hurt—the shift hadn't healed her completely—but thanks to her rush of adrenaline, the injuries barely slowed her down. Kyle was snarling over his brother, so that situation seemed under control. Now her priority was her men. Men who looked like they were stepping too close to the cold door of death.

Derek groaned. He tried to raise his arm, but his hand dropped back to the floor. Sadie scrambled around him, searching desperately to find the cell phone she'd lost. *Ambulance.* Humans couldn't survive this kind of abuse without help. She had to get an ambulance—

The quiet *snick* of a gun's safety release whispered in her ears. She turned, too slowly, and saw that Michael had managed to get a gun. In a split second, she recognized it as Derek's weapon. She'd seen it fly across the room earlier, then forgotten about it in the snap of teeth and the swipe of claws.

Kyle, still in leopard form, snarled and swiped with his claws just as Michael fired at him.

The leopard fell.

Then, smiling, bleeding, Michael turned the gun on her—

And he fired again.

Liam froze just outside the building on Montay. All of the breath left his lungs in a rush and fire exploded in the middle of his chest.

The pain drove him to his knees.

A pain that wasn't his.

*No.*

He tried to rise, but fell onto the cement. "*Sadie.*"

She was slipping away from him. He knew it, and the pain seemed to rip his heart apart.

He'd reached her too late.

Tires squealed behind him. Doors slammed.

"Sullivan? *Sullivan!*" Miller grabbed Liam and jerked him to his feet.

The pain began to fade and an icy numbness took its place. He stared up at the building, now covered by the darkness of night.

"Is Sadie here? We can't get her team to answer us, there's no contact—"

Miller's voice was buzzing in his ear.

Yeah, she was there. He could feel her.

But for how long? She was hurt, bad, and he knew the cruel bitch that was fate was trying to steal his Sadie away.

Not going to fucking happen.

# Chapter Nine

He'd never forget his first sight of that room. The blood. The bodies.

Sadie lying like a broken doll, her lashes still against her too white cheeks.

He fell to his knees beside her. Touched her face. Slowly, so slowly, her lashes lifted. Her golden eyes didn't glow. They barely shined at all, and they were full of so much pain.

"Sh-shot her . . ."

His head jerked up at the hoarse whisper. Kyle Munroe was pushing himself off the floor. "M-missed my h-heart . . ." Liam saw the hole in his chest then. Damn, weren't shifters supposed to heal from—

"B-but he got h-hers . . ."

The room spun.

No, no that wasn't possible, he'd know, he'd—

*Hear the rush of her blood spilling out. The broken beat as her heart struggled. Bullet had clipped the side. Too damaged, can't work, weakening.*

"B-bastard's d-dead now."

Liam didn't even glance toward the body. He could smell the stench of death.

"B-but he-he got h-her."

"The hell he did!" His arms were tight around her. He wouldn't look at her chest. No, he didn't want to see the wound, but he could *feel* it, as if his own chest had been ripped open.

"You're not goin' anywhere, Sadie, you hear me?" He was rocking her, back and forth, faster and faster.

Her eyes were open, but her pupils were locked. Her breath barely seemed to whisper past her pale lips.

*How the hell is she even still alive?* The question blasted through his mind, terrifying him.

But he knew the answer. A shifter's strength. Right then, he thanked the God he'd forgotten two years ago, then whispered a prayer for his forgiveness.

Because Liam knew what he was going to do.

"Stay with me, *a thaisce*." His fingers brushed over her neck. His head lowered and his mouth hovered over her throat.

*Would she want this life?*

An insidious whisper from within that he ignored.

His teeth pressed against her flesh. The blood flowed faster from her now, but the scent didn't tempt him.

It scared the hell out of him.

"Sadie . . ." No more time to waste. She wouldn't have any blood left to take soon.

His teeth pierced her flesh. Blood trickled onto his tongue.

*Sadie. Don't leave me.*

"What the *hell* are you doing, Sullivan?" Miller grabbed him, trying to force Liam to release his hold on Sadie. "That's not what she wants—"

Liam raised his head, a rumble rolling in his throat. He wasn't about to let her go. "Fuck off!" A scream of fury that shook the room. "She's not dying. She's too strong. She's—"

*Needed too much.*

He'd just found her again.

How was he supposed to live for centuries without her?

No. No, he couldn't.

"She doesn't *want* this." Absolute certainty. "We can get her to a hospital. They can stitch her up, fix her like they did Munroe—"

"She's got less than a minute left." His voice broke. He lifted her, cradling her as gently as he could. He braced her, pushing her head toward his throat. Her cool lips skimmed over his skin. "I *feel* her leaving. If she were human, she'd have died when the bullet drove into her."

He knew Sadie. Pure shifter will had kept her alive. The beast inside fighting a battle to heal, a battle that couldn't be won.

Too much blood loss. Not enough strength.

"You can't do this!" Why was Miller getting a conscience? "She doesn't want—"

"I know what she fuckin' wants!"

He knew . . . and what he knew tore his guts apart.

Sadie wanted her beast. The leopard within that had been a part of her since birth. The leopard that would die if he turned her. He knew the stories. A shifter lost the power to transform when she was reborn as a vampire.

That life ended, and a new one began.

He caught the back of her head in his hand. "Sadie . . ."

Choices.

Piss. This damn life—always about choices.

He wouldn't take her choice away. His had been taken away. He wouldn't do the same thing to Sadie. But he couldn't just sit there and let her die.

*Fuckin' hell—don't leave me!* A cry that shook his soul.

"L-live . . ." Rasping.

His eyes widened. He tilted her chin back, stared into the eyes that *saw* him and held agony.

"Sadie?"

"L-live . . ."

Sadie James was the strongest woman he'd ever met—and she was a fighter, till death and beyond.

She was choosing—him and life, with seconds to spare.

He bared his throat to her, guided her head because she was too weak, and felt the sharp sting of her teeth.

*Live.*

Sadie took his blood . . . and died.

Very, very slowly, Sadie opened her eyes and she found herself lying on a soft bed—her bed. The lights were off and darkness cloaked the room.

But she could see perfectly.

Her nostrils flared and she caught the scent of flowers. The fabric softener she used on her sheets. The vanilla-scented candle she kept in the living room.

She raised her hand to her chest and found the skin healed.

She'd survived.

Part of her had, anyway.

Her fangs were out and the hunger, a great, gnawing hunger for food—no, *blood*—had her belly clenching.

The door squeaked open and her gaze shot across the room to zero in on Liam.

He stared at her, not speaking, and she could see the worry on his face.

Her hands clenched around the sheets.

"Sadie . . ." He shook his head. "Do you know what happened? Do you know—"

"That I'm a vampire?" Yeah, she knew. She remembered everything. Every horrifying moment. She could still feel the twisted thud of her heart. *Broken.*

She'd known death was coming for her, and while she didn't fear the other side or what waited, she hadn't wanted to leave.

It had been too soon.

In that moment, when the fog had cleared from her eyes and she'd seen Liam gazing down at her with such fear on his face, she'd known she would have traded anything, *everything* she had to stay with him.

Even her beast.

And she had.

"It's not as bad as you think. You don't have to kill to live. You can get blood from a hospital." He swallowed, then said, "You're not linked to any other vampires, just me. You have no Born Master who can control you. You'll be as strong as before— you just . . . have to take it easier during the daytime." He crossed to her side as the words poured out of him. "You're still the same, Sadie, you're—"

"I can't shift." Spoken quietly.

His jaw clenched. "No, no, you can't."

"But I'm alive." Some might disagree with that. Screw them. Sadie forced her fingers to ease their death grip and she reached for him. "I'm alive and I'm with you." She'd made the choice.

She'd made it long before Michael Munroe had taken aim on her in that room.

She'd decided last night when she spooned in bed with Liam, his arms around her. His scent had surrounded her, his whisper of *a thaisce* had filled her ears. She'd known that she never wanted to leave him. Didn't matter what he was, didn't matter what she was.

Being with him—that was her choice. And she'd been fully aware of the consequences all along.

"How long until you hate this? Me?"

Crazy vampire. "Liam, *my* choice." Being a vampire might not have been her lifelong dream, but she knew vamps weren't the heartless killers she'd thought. Like humans, like shifters, some were evil.

And some weren't.

The facts were simple to Sadie. She was still breathing. Liam was with her. As for that bastard Munroe . . . "Tell me you killed that murdering shifter."

Liam shook his head and her heart sank. No, no, he couldn't still be out there. He couldn't—

"Kyle finished him off before I could."

Her shoulders relaxed.

"Seems old Michael made a habit of torturing his brother. Kyle left home when he was sixteen and said he'd hoped to never run across his brother again, but then he caught his scent here one night."

*He'd killed his brother.* Talk about a hard choice.

But one that had saved lives. Sadie knew Michael Munroe had developed a taste for the kill. She'd seen his eyes, *she knew.*

"Michael took Su to send a message to Kyle, didn't he?" she asked.

He nodded. "Punishment for him, a lure for me."

But they didn't have to worry about him any longer. One more killer off the streets.

Pity there were always more out there.

"Can I—can I hold you, Sadie love?"

She blinked, her lips parting in surprise at the question. When had Liam ever asked? When had he needed to? "Yeah, yeah, you can—"

He was on the bed before she'd finished speaking. His arms hard around her, his lips on hers. Kissing her with a feverish passion and a stark intensity.

Her tongue met his. Her arms locked just as fiercely around him . . . and deep inside, she heard the purr of her leopard.

Sadie froze. *What? How?*

Liam stiffened against her. "Sadie, no." The words rumbled against her lips. "Don't turn away from me. Things can be the same between us. Give your new life a chance. Give me a chance to—"

Her fingers pushed between them. "I am." His eyes were black. Were hers? Hunger heated her blood, and her teeth had begun to ache.

She wanted to taste him.

To bite him.

But she could have sworn she'd heard her leopard. *Felt* her.

That was impossible. All the stories said the transformation killed the beast.

And made room for the vampire.

Her fingers caught the V of his shirt. Yanked and sent buttons flying. The white shirt hung loosely on him, now revealing the delicious lines of his muscled chest.

Her mouth was dry.

Need filled her. Desperate desire for his body and his blood.

Sadie rose onto her knees. Her mouth pressed against his flesh. Tasted the sweetness of his skin. She tongued his nipple, and the small nub stiffened with the strokes of her tongue.

His hands smoothed down her back, caught the curves of her bare ass and squeezed.

She bit him. Pierced the flesh right above his nipple with her teeth and tasted the nectar of his blood.

*The leopard purred.*

The sound was so familiar to her, but it wasn't a sound she heard with her ears. Only her heart.

As she drank from him, feeling his blood energize her body and send her sensual hunger soaring to a new height, Sadie realized that the stories hadn't been true, not completely anyway.

"Ah, damn . . . that feels so . . . good . . ." Liam grated and his mouth moved to her throat. His teeth scraped over her flesh. "My turn, love . . ." and he took her. Mouth. Tongue. Teeth.

Sadie moaned against him. Her nipples tightened and her sex clenched. Her tongue swiped over the small wound she'd made. No wonder vampires were all about blood and sex. It was a freaking great combination.

Liam tumbled her back onto the bed, keeping his teeth on her. *In* her.

Sadie shoved the sheets out of their way. She was naked and more than ready for him.

The bulge of his arousal shoved against the front of his jeans. She unsnapped the button, eased down the zipper with a hiss—and had the hot, heavy length of his arousal filling her hands.

She licked her lips and thought about having a taste.

Liam's head rose. His face was brutally hard. Etched into taut lines of need.

"You almost died on me."

No, correction, she *had* died. That's why she was a vampire now.

"Don't ever fuckin' do that to me again." Desperation, she knew it when she heard it.

"I won't." Dying wasn't on her agenda. Having mind-blowing sex, yeah, that was.

The bad guy was dead. She'd survived. And Liam was exactly where she wanted him. Well, *almost*.

He drove into her. A plunging, driving thrust that had her sucking in a sharp breath because he felt so *good*.

She still didn't like things easy, especially not her sex.

Her hips lifted high, drove right back at him. She needed this—the rush of pleasure, the spike of need.

*Needed this. Needed him.*

Because death hadn't held her—no, *he* had. Liam had fought for her and given her a chance to live again.

To spend her days and nights with him.

Her muscles tightened as she thundered toward her release. Her sex was so sensitive, every glide and drive of his cock had her twisting beneath him.

His fingers caught her breasts. Fondled her nipples.

His cock swelled within her, filling her so fully that she nearly screamed.

He withdrew, thrust deep—

And she did scream. Sadie climaxed on a driving wave of pleasure. Her sex clenched around him, squeezing that thick length tightly and she gasped as her body shivered with aftershocks of pulsing heat.

Liam was with her. She felt the hot tide of his release within her. Saw the wild flare of pleasure in his eyes.

Oh, yeah, he was with her. For every single moment.

He kissed her. She tasted his hunger, his pleasure, his need.

And knew that he tasted hers.

A rumble trembled in her throat.

Liam lifted his head. "Sadie?"

Not a rumble, really, more of a purr.

His lips curved into a smile. "I love you, Sadie James."

Her heartbeat had just begun to slow. The beat immediately kicked up.

"Spend forever with me?" he asked, eyes flickering from black to blue.

Beautiful blue eyes.

"Try to stop me," she whispered. "Because I sure as hell love you too, Liam Sullivan." She'd loved him for years.

Loved him.

Mourned him.

Missed him.

Hell, no, he wasn't about to get away from her again. She'd cheated death for her chance with him.

*Forever.*

She smiled and kissed him again.

And the leopard was content.

Forty-eight hours later, Sadie James stepped into the night with her vampire lover by her side. The stars shimmered so brightly that even the lights of the city couldn't lessen their glow. Music beat in a steady drumbeat, coming from the clubs downtown. Voices, whispers, filled her ears, and the scents from the city had her nose flaring.

Her senses were almost as advanced as before. Her strength was still ten times better than a human's.

Sure, the blood hunger would take a bit more adjusting, but all in all, Sadie thought she was doing damn well for an undead woman.

Of course, when her brother found out about her new, um, life choice *and* lover choice, Jacob probably wouldn't be thrilled.

Serious understatement, she knew.

But he was her brother, and unlike that twisted freak Michael Munroe, he'd be glad she wasn't lying in a morgue somewhere. Fangs and blood hunger—he'd learn to deal with them. She knew her brother. He'd rage and then he'd hug her until she felt like he was squeezing her to death.

Brothers. Sometimes they were great. Sometimes they were devils.

Liam's fingers closed around hers. She glanced at him, unable to stop the curve of her lips.

Being this happy should be illegal. She was with Liam. The night was beautiful, and, deep inside, her leopard stretched.

She couldn't shift anymore, but her leopard hadn't died. She was inside, safe, with a spirit ready to fight at a moment's notice.

Liam brought her hand to his lips and pressed a kiss against her palm. She felt the wet swipe of his tongue.

And the surge of her pulse.

That man could turn her on. But they had a job to do. As tempted as she was to go back inside and jump his sexy bones, Miller was waiting to brief them on another case. Always another case.

"Ready to go?" Liam's deep voice stroked over her.

"Yeah." No, but the sex would wait.

After all, they had plenty of time.

And, as vampires, plenty of stamina.

"Another night, another city full of killers," he murmured.

Story of their afterlife.

Her fingers tightened around his. "Let's go hunting." Her leopard wanted to play.

She saw the white flash of his teeth as he grinned. Those teeth would be in her neck by morning and she'd love it. *Love it.*

But for now, they had work to do. Miller waited.

And so did the night.

Such a beautiful night.

Her partner was by her side—a man who would always have her back. He'd fight to the death and beyond for her, she knew it. No more hunting alone, ever.

He'd have her back, and he'd be in her bed.

A perfect team.

The killers they tracked, the monsters gone bad, they wouldn't know what hit them.

Time for the games to begin.

# City of the Dead

SHERRILL QUINN

# Prologue

"You sure you don't want me, *cher*?" The hot, wet glide of a tongue on her lower lip had Dori Falcon clenching her thighs together. Still, she couldn't stem the tide of lust that crashed through her core.

Detective Jake Boudreau leaned against her, pressing her more firmly against the wall next to her hotel room. This close to him she could feel the heat of his big body and smell his tantalizing scent—a spicy mixture of cologne, coffee, and male.

She was sure she *did* want him. She was equally sure that the more she was around him, the harder it would be when things ended between them.

Why did he have to be so sexy, so hard to resist? He was human and she was a witch. She really shouldn't feel this attraction to him. It would only lead to heartache when he rejected her heritage.

In her experience, he *would* reject her. That's what men did to witches once they discovered their secret.

All in all, it was better than being burned at the stake, she supposed.

Boudreau was just so yummy. He tasted wonderful, like rich, dark mocha. Her favorite.

As her body tightened with need, Dori squirmed. Damn, but he was one fine looking man.

She had to pull herself together. She was in New Orleans to

find her brother, not continue an affair that realistically had no hope of going anywhere. She'd been told her entire life to stay with her own kind, the Magicks. To bond with a human was to court sorrow.

But Boudreau seemed different somehow. For one thing, his aura was bright with honesty and loyalty, and the ever-present humor. There was no hint of subterfuge or bigotry. In Dori's experience, auras didn't lie.

The other thing, the really *big* other thing was that she had never felt like this about a man. Not once in her thirty-three years had she had such an overpowering need to join with a man. Oh, she'd been attracted to men, had been aroused to the point of madness, but it had all been completely physical.

Never emotional.

With Jake, her emotions were definitely involved. All of them, it seemed. Tenderness, lust, fear, sadness, happiness . . . you name it, she felt it.

So, what now? Should she take a chance on him?

Could she?

*What if she didn't?*

With a broad palm curved around the base of her skull he tilted her head to the angle he wanted and slanted his mouth over hers. It was the kiss of a man staking his claim—a hungry, dominating kiss, one that spoke to his need and desire.

He ate at her mouth like a starving man, each kiss blending into another until it seemed like one endless caress. Finally he gentled, as if he'd been able to take the edge off his need. His tongue slipped into her mouth in a silken stroke that curled her toes.

A moan left her throat and was swallowed into his mouth. She pressed against him, feeling his thick cock pressing into her belly, his firm chest pushing against the hard tips of her breasts.

It was too much.

It wasn't enough.

She wanted him, *but she was so afraid.*

At last he pulled away and rested his forehead on hers. "You taste like whiskey an' honey, my favorite."

*He* tasted like coffee and spice. He tasted like . . . home.

"I've missed you, *cher.*" His deep voice was as raspy as the sexy stubble on his jaw. "This long distance thing is hell." He drew away and stared down at her with eyes dark with lust and something more. Something . . .

Deeper.

Dori had never thought of having anything other than a fling with him whenever she was in town. She couldn't let herself think of anything more.

She thought her heart would burst from her chest, it pounded so hard. She had to get away from this man before she made a mistake. In the mixed-up state she was in, sleeping with him tonight was out of the question. "I . . . I have to go, Jake. I'll talk to you tomorrow."

She ducked under his arm, avoiding the good night kiss she knew he meant to give her, and escaped into the safety of her hotel room. As much as her body wanted to, getting involved with this man on a level any deeper than the casual arrangement they had was a bad idea.

Of course, one more date wouldn't hurt, right? One more taste, that's all she wanted.

She pressed her cheek against the door, heard Boudreau's heavy sigh and the tread of his boots as he walked down the hall toward the exit.

Away from her.

The next day her brother Art showed up, and she left New Orleans without saying good-bye.

# Chapter One

*Six months later*

Dori sighed and stared at Jake Boudreau's implacable face. Dark brows were drawn down over eyes that held a look of concern sparked with a small amount of irritation.

Not just because of the way she'd left things between them six months ago, but also because here she was again, trying to encourage him to help her find her wayward younger brother.

Arthur Falcon had come to the Big Easy to meet a very dangerous and unpredictable witch named Alex Sabin. Art planned something that Dori had tried and tried to talk him out of. As much as she'd loved her father, trying to bring him back to life was not a good idea.

In fact, it was a very *bad* idea.

Now Art was missing. According to Sabin, her brother never showed up at their rendezvous point. At least, that's what he'd said. But Sabin was enigmatic. Why he'd agreed to let Art use the Eye of Bastet in the ritual resurrection was still a mystery to her. The Eye was dangerous, coveted by all those who served the cause of evil and wished to see witches destroyed.

Though if anyone could control the amulet's power and protect them, it was Sabin. His power was scary, even to someone like her. He had stronger magick than any witch she knew, than any she'd ever known of. No one knew why.

Others of her kind didn't trust him. But she knew from his clear, clean aura that he was good and decent, even if there was a shadow in his aura that she'd never seen before.

But now she couldn't find Sabin, either. He'd gone to ground after informing her of her brother's disappearance.

Which left her with Boudreau. The one man she should stay away from. The one man she hadn't been able to forget.

If she told him *why* Art had come back to New Orleans he'd never believe her. The reason wasn't important, anyway. She needed Boudreau's help.

"It's different this time. He was supposed to meet someone at the old St. Louis Cemetery. He never showed. I think something terrible has happened to him." Dori stared up at the handsome detective, trying to will him to do what she wanted. Damn, if only she could cast a spell, just a small one.

*Don't do it*, her conscience whispered.

*Unless it's a love spell*, her bad girl replied. Her clit thumped in response. Her nipples seemed happy with the idea, too, and tightened into little buds.

*Aargh*!

His scowl deepened. Dori matched him frown for frown, but, *damn*, it would be so much easier if he was butt-ugly. Even scowling he was beautiful.

His looks were damned distracting. Not to mention damaging to her brand new panties. It had been months since she'd last seen him, and he still affected her like no other man. With his handsome face, sexy drawl, and bad boy attitude, he turned her into nothing more than a pair of boobs and a pussy waiting for the train to pull into port. Or was that ship?

*Aargh*! *Focus, Dori.*

"... an' I understand your concern," Boudreau was saying. "But with his history, *cher*, until he has been missin' for twenty-four hours, there ain' anythin' we can do. You sure he's not gonna just pop up like he usually does? You got a store to run back in Chicago, Dori. Why don't you go home?"

His mouth said one thing, but the look heating in his eyes suggested he wanted her near.

Ignoring that for the moment, she waved off what she was

sure were surface concerns. "I have trustworthy people running the shop. I don't need to go home." She put all the pleading she could into her voice, hoping to sway him into action of some kind. Anything was preferable to sitting around and doing nothing. "Please. You have to do something."

"I can't do anythin' for another six hours. However," he raised his voice when she would have interrupted, "however, I will make some inquiries. Okay?"

Dori ground her teeth. *Inquiries.* Detective-speak for *sitting on my ass.*

"Fine," she gritted. "Fine. But don't expect me to just laze around my hotel room eating bonbons."

Boudreau leaned even closer. "You'd better not do much more than that, *ma petite*," he said, his words slow and relaxed, his eyes narrowed. "New Orleans is too dangerous for you to be alone at night."

His lazy drawl made the name of the city sound like "noo awlins" and it didn't fool her for a minute. He'd used that low, easy tone each time she'd come down here searching for her miscreant brother. The slower and lower Jake talked the more it meant his patience had worn thin.

Unsurprisingly, he inevitably talked in a raspy drawl when he was around her. Probably wouldn't help her case if she told him how sexy she found it.

"As you no doubt saw when you came into town, we're *still* cleanin' up after Katrina, even six years later. It didn't help when Gustav rolled through the area, either. Some of our . . . less than upright citizens and the out of town criminal element are takin' advantage of resources stretched too thin." He tapped her on the chin. "An' the cemeteries are dangerous enough in the daytime, let alone at night. You stay away from them, *hein*?"

This was the second—or was it the third?—time that she and the detective had butted heads over her brother. On her last trip, they'd shared dinner and a sizzling kiss that promised silken sheets against bodies twisting with passion.

Something she hadn't turned down before.

But when the discussion turned serious . . . well, it had scared her spitless, and she'd backed away. She'd gone home, pushing her loneliness to the back of her mind with the responsibility of being the sole proprietor of a combination herbal and aromatherapy store.

With Art as a brother a leave of absence wasn't that unusual, and she knew her three employees would manage the store well in her current absence. As they'd done before.

She looked at Boudreau and tried to remember why it was a bad idea to desire him. Right now, staring into his dark eyes, she desperately wanted to taste him again. She needed to feel his lips against hers like she needed water to drink, air to breathe.

*Oy. Get a grip, Dori.*

Boudreau cocked an arrogant eyebrow, waiting for a response. Just that fast she wanted to replace the kiss with a swift kick to his backside.

His big hands came out of his pockets to fist on his hips. Another sign his patience was about used up. She took her time giving him her answer, knowing it would aggravate the hell out of him. Knowing it would irritate him even more, she gave him a once over, starting from the top and working her way down.

He was tall, at least half a foot taller than her own five-foot-eight, with dark brown hair that fell over his forehead and grew long over his collar. Gray had started at his temples, either because of the stress of the job or because he was only a few years on the underside of forty. Maybe a bit of both. Eyes the color of dark chocolate framed by long, silky black lashes stared at her with flashes of irritation in their depths.

His bladed nose was mostly straight except for a bump in the middle that suggested at some time it had been broken. Given his vocation and his damned cocky arrogance, that was probable. Lean cheeks with a hint of dimples framed a sexy mouth that drew attention to a strong chin with a delicious cleft. All in all, it was a face that just begged to be kissed.

She'd only ever seen him in suits, and most of the time his tie hung loosely around his neck. His partially unbuttoned shirt revealed a hint of a tanned, muscled chest dusted with dark hair.

A long waist tapered to not-too-slim hips and long legs, down to big feet encased in worn black leather boots. Big feet, big hands. Hmm.

"Dori." His deep voice was flat, hard. He had finally lost patience with her.

With a raised eyebrow, she looked up from his feet and grinned. Color rode high on his cheekbones. Should she ignore it?

Nope, it was surely just too good to pass up. "Something wrong, Detective?" she asked with studied nonchalance and moved her gaze back to the hardened center of his body.

Boudreau flexed his shoulders as if they felt tight. "Please stay out of trouble." He sat in the chair behind his desk, apparently deciding to ignore the emotions that flared between them.

Forcing her to make the first move.

She briefly closed her eyes, realizing she was tired. Tired of chasing after Art, tired of always being the responsible one.

Tired of fighting Boudreau, of fighting her emotions.

Fighting the fear. With what Art was trying to do, she might not see tomorrow. Might as well enjoy today.

She'd wanted Jake Boudreau from the minute she'd laid eyes on him. He was a living, breathing advertisement for tall, dark, and handsome, and he was so sexy she could die a happy woman if she could have his cock just once more.

If she were going to die, she'd damned well make sure she was happy.

"Oh, I'll certainly try." Dori walked over and plopped down in his lap, enjoying his startled look. "But you know me . . ."

When she wriggled her bottom against his erection, his eyes narrowed. "You don't know what you're startin' here, *cher*," he rasped, eyes going nearly black with lust. "Don't be startin' somethin' you have no intention of finishin'."

*Like last time* hung unspoken between them.

"Who says I don't intend to finish it?" she whispered, leaning forward and taking a deep breath. *Oh, God.* Big, hard male and Drakkar Noir. She was in heaven.

Her weight shifted against his penis, and he drew in a sharp breath. With both hands on her hips, he lifted her and stood in one fluid motion. He hauled her out of the squad room and away from the other detectives who had started to watch their interaction with a good amount of interest.

Once he got her to the relative privacy of the bathroom area, he pushed her back against the wall and planted his palms on either side of her face. "You are confusin' the hell outta me, *ma petite*," he growled. "What game are you playin'?"

"It's not a game," she murmured, her eyes on his lips. She leaned forward, intent on planting one right on that sexy mouth. She wanted to kiss him, to see if he tasted as good as she remembered. She *needed* to kiss him again.

He jerked his head back. "Are you sure? It seems to me the last time I had you in my arms, you seared me down to my toes an' then you ran." He slid his fingers through her hair and tucked a stray strand behind her ear. His hand lingered as if he couldn't stop himself from touching her. "Without even a good-bye."

He made it sound like she'd hurt him. Her lips tightened at that thought. Feeling the warmth of his fingers against her cheek, she swallowed at his touch even as it gave her hope that he still wanted her. "It wasn't you, Jake," she whispered, looking into his eyes. "It was me. You . . . you scared me."

"*I* scared you, *cher*? Or you scared yourself?"

Dori wanted to scream. She needed him to kiss her, and he was *talking*. What kind of man talked when a woman was practically throwing herself at him?

"Does it matter?" She reached for him again and he straightened. Huffing a sigh, she tried a different tactic. "I've missed you."

"You have, hmm?" As if he needed the physical contact even while he tried to stay out of reach, he cupped her cheek in one broad palm. "Six months and not a phone call or e-mail from you, *cher*. You wouldn't just be sayin' that because you need my help now, would you?"

She saw red. How could he think she'd use feminine wiles on him? That wasn't her style, and he should know her enough by now to realize that. "Of course not, you buffoon."

Forget about kissing him, she was back to wanting to give him a boot in the ass. "Never mind," she muttered and ducked under his arm. If she had to put up with that arrogant mouth, she could do without his cock.

"Not so fast." He pushed her gently back against the wall. Crowding into her, his mouth covered hers and caught the breathy little moan that escaped.

Jake pushed his groin against Dori's soft belly, feeling her hands clutch convulsively at his shoulders. He slipped his tongue past her lips. When her tongue tangled with his, he groaned. She shuddered against him, and her hips swayed closer to his.

He slid his mouth to her neck, nibbling and licking her soft skin, feeling her shiver in his arms. "You taste so good," he growled, his mouth at the crook of her neck. Closing his eyes at her soft moan, he found an erogenous zone with the tip of his tongue.

He moved his mouth back to hers and thrust his tongue inside, hard and fast, in and out, mimicking the act of sex. Almost out of control, he took one of her slim hands in his. Pressing her fingers against his erection, he rocked into her palm. She gasped against his mouth, and his knees buckled when he felt her unzip his pants.

Her warm fingers slid through the opening of his boxers and touched his shaft. He growled and thrust his hips against her, shuttling through the circle of her fingers and gritting his teeth against the building need. Her hand felt so incredible, and when she moved her thumb . . . *Merde!*

"*Mon Dieu*, Boudreau," a gruff male voice muttered. "Get a room, why doncha?" Another cop stomped past them and into the men's room.

She gasped and withdrew her hand. He could feel the heat from her blush against his face.

Jake leaned his forehead against hers and sighed, clenching his jaw at the loss of her fingers. "What the hell are you doin' to me, *cher*?" he asked, his voice barely above a rasp. He was thirty-seven years old and ready to come in his pants like a randy teenager.

"I want you," she whispered.

The desire in her voice made his cock jerk. He groaned and pressed against her. "Let me come to you tonight, Dori. I need to be with you. I need . . . more than this. I want to slide my cock into your cunt so deep you'll feel empty without me."

Dori felt her womb clench at the graphic words he muttered against her cheek. She wanted the feel of him against her, she wanted to kiss her way around his body like it was a map to heaven. She felt close to tears at the desperate need for him that pulsed throughout her body.

Was she ready for this? It would be more than sex, she knew. She was already half in love with this man, and if she got another a taste of him, felt him in her body again, it would be all over.

Would he stay once he knew what she was? Could he love a witch?

She wasn't sure she'd survive it if she fell in love with him and he walked away. But she had to try. She refused to live a life of what ifs. The last six months had been lonely as hell, and she wasn't going to walk away from him this time without trying.

"I'm staying at the Monteleone," she said softly, and reached up to place a soft kiss on that sexy mouth while she carefully zipped his pants. "Room thirteen-thirteen." At his raised eyebrow she grinned. "It's my favorite number." Her smile faded as sensual anticipation began to build. "Come around nine."

Another kiss, and she moved away from him. As she walked away, she was very aware of his dark gaze following her movements.

Jake watched Dori leave the squad room, her shapely jeans-covered ass swaying with each step and kicking his arousal up another notch. He rubbed the back of his neck, wondering, and certainly not for the first time, why she blew so hot and cold. Her clear green eyes betrayed her desire every time they were together, but for whatever reason she kept pushing him away.

She was everything he'd ever wanted in a woman—spunky, independent, sexy. And irritating as hell. *Merde*, but she could get under his skin in the blink of an eye. Half the time he didn't know if he should lock her up or just kiss her until she couldn't sass him anymore.

Kissing her kept coming up the winner. Although the thought of putting her in his handcuffs and spanking her ass until it was pink was a close second. Either way, sex wouldn't be far behind. It wasn't a question of *if*, it was just a matter of *when*. If Lady Luck was on his side, *when* would be tonight.

He had a feeling that, when the two of them did finally get together, it would be magic.

# Chapter Two

"**D**amn it, Art, why in the hell were you here?" Dori tripped over a rock and banged her wrist against the corner of a crypt. She cursed under her breath, rubbing the injury against her hip to take the sting out of it. "I mean, I know you were supposed to meet Sabin here, but Jeez Louise! Couldn't you have said no and arranged another meeting place? Now you've got me talking to myself, damn it."

Dori tiptoed past another crypt and wished, not for the first time, that she could find her brother so she could wring his neck. Of all the places in the world where he had to come up missing, why did it have to be from the oldest cemetery in New Orleans?

She kept up her dialogue with her nonexistent brother. "Why can't I just cast a spell so I can find you easier? Because of Sabin, of course." She stopped and turned, gazing into the deep, dark night, listening, sure she had heard something from behind her. When she heard nothing more, she moved on. "Sabin the Wonder Witch," she muttered, "casting spells so that he can't be found and, therefore, making sure *you* can't be found."

She stopped again and turned the flashlight to the marker on the nearest crypt. It was old, crumbling, and covered in graffiti, mostly in the form of X marks. Dori flashed the light to the other crypts, then back to this one. It was the only one that had been defaced.

"The Voodoo Queen's final restin' place."

Dori shrieked at the sound of that deep, masculine voice. She whirled to face Boudreau, squealing again when he pulled the flashlight out of her hand.

"Don't shine that in my face, *cher*. What're you doin' here?"

"Jake?" She blew a breath from between pursed lips and willed her heart to settle back down into her chest from where it had lodged in her throat.

Boudreau's handsome face looked spooky in the beam of the flashlight. Almost demonic. "Yeah. Answer the question."

She fought back a shiver at the creepiness of this place. "I thought I might find something that would lead me to Art."

"Well, at least you're truthful." He gave a slight smile, which quickly faded. "I thought I told you to stay away from this place, *hein*? It's too dangerous after dark." He stepped forward, directing the beam of his flashlight downward. He handed her light back to her. With a shake of his head he muttered, "You never listen to me. You shouldn't have come here alone."

Even in the near blackness she could read the disapproval in his dark eyes.

"Yes, well, you weren't doing anything, so . . ."

"Who says I wasn't doin' anythin'?" He propped one fist on his hip and scowled.

She frowned right back at him. "Oh, come on, Detective. As soon as I told you Art was missing, you pretty much just patted me on the head and told me to go home, that he would turn up."

"You call what we did in the hallway a *pat on the head*?" His voice was so incredulous she found herself battling back a blush. "*Merde*. If my captain hadn't walked by, you would've gone down on me, wouldn't you? Your hot little mouth would've been wrapped around my dick, suckin' me 'til I came in your mouth. Yeah, that sure was some pat on the head, *cher*."

"You can be such an ass sometimes, Boudreau," she gritted. It didn't help that he was right. She was so desperate for a taste of him it wouldn't take much for her to get down on her knees and do her best to swallow his cock. Damn, she hated it when he was right.

"But you like my ass, don't you, *cher*?" he drawled, amusement creeping into his voice. "Besides," he went on without giving her a chance to respond, "this ain't the first time you've come down to New Orleans to file a missin' persons report on your brother, *ma petite*. This is the third time he's come down here, gotten involved with an unsavory element and disappeared. Each time he's popped back up with a grin, with little to no explanation. I still don't understand why you keep droppin' everythin' to come to his rescue." He ran his hand through his hair, making the silky strands fluff a little before they settled once more against his head. "Just what makes you think this time's any different?"

He could always make her feel so defensive. She knew he was a good man, under all that Cajun brashness. Right now she didn't care about whether or not he was good, because he was just plain irritating.

She wished her upbringing hadn't been so steeped in what a witch could and couldn't do. Since he was being such a jerk, she dearly wanted to turn him into a toad.

After she kissed him silly, of course. He was, after all, a very sexy jerk. *Here we go.* Raging libido, in a cemetery. Her timing— and choice of places—could've been better.

"He's my brother, Jake." She shook her head. "I'd have thought you of all people would understand what that means."

"Why? 'Cause I come from a big family?"

"Yes." Dori frowned. "You don't turn your back on family, especially when they need you."

He pursed his lips. "All right, I'll give you that. So, what makes this time different?" he asked again.

"That you *wouldn't* understand," she muttered.

"Try me."

There was just enough sarcasm in his rich voice to make her mad. Maybe he'd make a sexy toad. Who knew? But, fine. He wanted an explanation? She'd give him one. "Art came to meet a man who could help him . . . make our father well."

Okay, so it was a watered down explanation. Since her father was dead, she could truthfully say he wasn't well. But she couldn't tell Boudreau that Art had come to meet another witch for the legendary Eye of Bastet, rumored to have the power to revive the dead. He'd never go for that.

"Hmm. Try again, *cher*." He studied her. One lean hand reached out and tucked her hair behind her left ear. His hand lingered near her cheek, then dropped back to his side. "What if I told you I know your brother's here in town to meet a man named Sabin? And that this Sabin is very dangerous? Would you trust me then?"

Dori fought to breathe normally after feeling the touch of his fingers against her face. What was it about this man that drew her so? He was hard but compassionate, strong but gentle, brash and sexy.

Her body began to throb with need. She cleared her throat. "Art is in no danger from Sabin, Detective."

"Stop calling me that," he muttered, his deep voice raspy. He stared at her a moment, then asked, "How can you be sure he's safe from Sabin?"

She stifled a sigh. He was like a terrier after a rat. "Because Sabin and my father were . . . are friends. Sabin wouldn't hurt Art." She looked around at the darkness. The shadows cast by statues and ironwork were gathering, almost like living things reaching out with withered, skeletal fingers.

She sidled a little closer to Boudreau and cursed herself for her love of horror movies. She'd rather not be having thoughts about vampires, ghouls, and zombies right now.

Apparently Boudreau caught her nervous glance, because he stepped forward and took her elbow gently in his strong hand. "This can wait 'til morning, *ma petite*. Let's get outta here."

"No!" She pulled away from him and stumbled against the rough stone of the defaced crypt. With a small cry, she jerked away from the power emanating from within those cold walls.

"That's it." Boudreau grabbed her arm less gently this time. "We're leavin', *cher*. We can come back in the mornin'. No argument, or I swear to God I will handcuff and carry you out of here."

"Wait." She resisted his tug on her arm, ignoring the flash of heat at the thought of being handcuffed by him. "Whose . . . whose crypt did you say this was?"

"Marie Laveau, the Voodoo Queen of New Orleans. She was the most powerful of all the *voudouiennes*. Legend has it that if you knock three times on her crypt, or make three Xs, she'll grant your wish."

"Then Emile Bernier's crypt should be near." She couldn't leave now. That was where Art was supposed to meet Sabin. There might be a clue to his disappearance in that crypt. "Please,

Jake, just a few more minutes. Help me find Bernier's crypt. Please," she pleaded again when he hesitated.

"Oh, very well. Just a few more minutes, though. Then we leave it 'til mornin', *oui*?" He waited for her nod then preceded her to the next row of above ground resting sites.

City of the Dead. Dori shivered. That's what most cemeteries in New Orleans were called, because many of the family crypts looked like miniature houses, complete with iron fences. She wasn't sure why she was so frightened. It wasn't as if she had no defense. Her amulet and the protection spell Aunt Clara had said over her should shield her from most evil. But there was something out there . . . something she couldn't define, but it was heavy and dark, like an oily cloak of malice.

"Here it is."

She jumped at the sound of Boudreau's richly accented words. Jeez, she *had* to stop watching so many horror movies. With her amulet, blessed with a protection spell, there was nothing there that could harm her.

Maybe if she said it enough, like a mantra, she'd begin to really believe it.

She turned her flashlight to join the light from Boudreau's, and read the inscription. "Emile Bernier, 1797 to 1852. Dead to life, but alive to eternity."

Dori probed around the door with her fingers.

"What are you doin', *ma petite*? We shouldn't enter a crypt that isn't family." Boudreau grabbed her hand just as her fingers encountered a small latch at the inside molding of the door.

She heard his low exclamation and realized he was standing just behind her. His warm breath tickled her ear and his spicy cologne teased her nose. She wanted to do nothing more than turn around in his arms and give in to her desire to kiss him.

But not here, not now. She had to find Art.

"What now?" he asked.

"Now we go in."

To her surprise, he didn't argue, merely squeezed her hand and then let it go. He drew his gun out of its holster and thumbed off the safety. "You stay behind me."

Flashlight in one hand, gun hand balanced on his outstretched wrist, Boudreau walked slowly into the crypt. A cement stand that was thigh high was central to the small room, with its ornate coffin resting on top. Dori stayed away from the casket and kept behind him, flashing her own light around to look into the corners of the crypt.

After looking for a couple of minutes, she let out a sigh. "Nothing," she whispered. "There's nothing here."

"I don't know what you expected to find, *ma petite*. It's only an old grave." He holstered his gun and stepped up to her. Sliding the flashlight under his arm, he cradled her face in his hands. He pressed a kiss against her forehead. Her flashlight, still tilted upward, showed his face, so near to hers, covered with concern. "It's late, an' we're both tired. If you want, we'll come back again tomorrow an' look things over when we can see better. Okay?"

She nodded. Looking up into his shadowed face, she gave in to her longing and drew his face down to hers. His face was rough and scratchy under her palms. The touch of his mouth against her lips was all she remembered and more, and not nearly enough.

"*Mon Dieu*," he breathed when their lips parted. "You mus' be tired, to kiss me like that."

She rubbed her forehead against his shoulder. Resting her cheek against the warmth of his chest, she closed her eyes. "What has me so tired is fighting what I feel for you."

His chest rose against her and held for a moment, and then released. His breath puffed against the top of her head. "One thin' I will say for you, *mon amie*, is that you tell the truth." He chuckled and pressed a kiss to her hair. "*Mais oui*, you tell the truth."

She bit her lip at his words. She hadn't outright lied to him. She hadn't. But with his strict code of honor, he might not see the difference between not volunteering the truth and telling a lie. She hoped he would.

Dori sighed against his chest. There were so many things between them, so many differences. Were they destined to be driven apart before they were ever together?

He turned her in to the cradle of his arm and urged her toward the open door of the crypt. "So, we agree to stop fightin' this attraction, yes? And we'll go get some sleep—maybe—and come back tomorrow." He tightened his arm around her briefly. "I have to admit, I'm intrigued with the hidden latch on this door. I'd like to get a better look at it in daylight."

Dori started to agree just as the door slammed shut. She screamed and grabbed Boudreau.

He clamped one hand over his ear. "*Merde, cher.* You got a scream that'll wake the dead."

"Don't say that!" She smacked him on the arm and kept her flashlight focused on the door. "Well?" she asked as his lean fingers scrambled to find a handle or knob of some sort.

"Damn! There's nothin' here on this side." He glanced back at her, his face angles and planes in the light and shadows created by the flashlight.

"Most of the time those on the inside have no desire to leave."

Dori whirled toward the new voice and backed up against Boudreau, aware he'd once again drawn his gun. Into the light stepped a tall man, powerfully built, dressed in black turtleneck and slacks.

Sabin.

"It's okay, Jake," Dori whispered in relief. "It's Sabin."

Boudreau stopped her when she would have moved away from him. "Stay put, *ma petite.*"

"I told you, it's all right."

"*Non.* What is your business here tonight, Sabin?"

The other man shrugged and leaned one shoulder against the rough wall of the crypt. "The same as you, I imagine. I'm trying to find Arthur."

"B . . . but he was supposed to meet *you* here, two nights ago." Dori gripped her fingers together against the growing fear. Her instincts had been right—Art was in terrible trouble.

"As I've told you, he never showed. I've come back the last two nights, thinking that perhaps he was merely delayed." He frowned and waved a hand toward Boudreau, still holding the pistol pointed at him with a steady hand. "That will not protect you against me, *mon ami.* I am immune to your bullets."

Boudreau snorted. "You tellin' me you're some sort of Superman, *homme?*"

Sabin smiled, teeth glinting in the dim light of the wavering flashlights. "No."

Getting her first clear glimpse of the other witch, Dori felt cold, then hot. She stumbled back even as Sabin moved more fully into the beam of their combined flashlights. His canine teeth were long and pointed; his eyes glittered with a silver hue.

"I'm telling you that I am a vampire. The undead in this City of the Dead."

Boudreau offered a pithy but quite heartfelt response.

Jake sat in the backseat of Sabin's Mercedes and closely watched the route the vampire took to his house. If things turned bad, he wanted to make sure he could get Dori out. Glancing at the front seat, where she sat talking quietly with Sabin, he grimaced. If she wanted to leave.

He hadn't wanted her to go with Sabin. She'd been resolute. He'd stubbornly insisted that if she was going, he was going. And so here he sat in the backseat of a car being driven by a vampire. *Merde.*

Jake's main talent seemed to be getting in to more trouble than he could easily get out of. From the moment he'd seen Sabin's glowing eyes and sharp teeth, he'd known he'd done it again. Acted the Laurel to his own Hardy. *It's a fine mess you've gotten me in to this time.*

He would have preferred that Dori sit in the back with him, but she'd said she had things to talk over with Sabin. So he sat in the back with his hand under his jacket, on his gun, ready to pull it from the holster if he needed to.

This was his first time meeting a vampire, and he wasn't sure what to expect. All things considered, he thought he was handling himself rather well. The fact that Dori seemed so at ease with the creature . . . well, that was something he and Dori would have a little chat about.

The powerful car turned onto a narrow roadway that wound through large oak trees with ghostly shrouds of Spanish moss hanging from their branches. The sprawling main house came in view, and his eyebrows rose. The large structure looked to be at least ten thousand square feet, brick and glass with a three car garage on the east side.

Being a vampire obviously had some perks.

"Did you have hurricane damage?" he asked, his curiosity

roused by the pristine condition of the grounds and the main structure. Of course, with the house and car he assumed Sabin had money to burn and could have had any damage repaired early on.

"I have wards around the grounds to protect the house from harm. They keep unwelcome intruders out and protect against nature's fury as well." Sabin pushed a button above the rearview mirror and one of the garage doors slid open. He pulled the car neatly into the garage and parked next to a metallic black Porsche Boxster convertible.

"What the hell are wards?" Jake climbed out of the Mercedes and tried to keep from drooling over the sports car. Next to the Porsche sat a black on chrome Harley Fat Boy. Seduced by the big boy toys, he took his hand off his gun and ran it up and over the fender of the Boxster. A snort of laughter from Sabin drew his attention.

The vampire stared at him with amused speculation in his now normal-looking deep blue eyes. "Do you have adult-onset ADD, Detective?" he asked, very clearly poking fun at Jake's sudden lack of interest in finding out about wards in light of the expensive machinery sitting all around him. "Want to try her out?" Sabin added, nodding toward the Harley.

"You serious?" Jake walked over to the motorcycle and ran his hand over the leather seat. "She's a real beaut."

He heard Dori huff.

"What is it about men," she asked, her voice tart but still sensuous enough to tug at his loins, "that makes them lose focus whenever they see a motorcycle?"

"Testosterone," both men responded together. Jake saw Sabin's lips quirk and figured that was about as close to a smile as the vampire ever got. The surrealism of talking about motorcycles with a vampire wasn't lost on him.

"Well, we don't have time for you to try *her* out." Dori opened the door to the main house. "We have work to do." She paused, looking at Sabin. "Well? It's your house."

Sabin shrugged. "She's right, *mon ami*. Perhaps another time." He motioned toward the door and waited for Jake to precede him through the opening.

"I may hold you to it," Jake murmured.

"Any time. Just through there." Sabin pointed toward a large, elegant room. Dori walked in first and went directly to the tall window to the left, fingering the brocade curtain, staring out into the night.

At a glance, Jake took in his surroundings. The opulent room was dominated by leather and dark wood furniture. Scatterings of rich plum and gold velvet accented the more somber colors. It appeared as if the doorway through which he'd just come was the only entrance to—or exit from—the room.

He went over to Dori and put his arm around her. "Come on, *cher*, sit down. You're gonna worry a hole in that thing." He guided her to the sofa and sat beside her, studying her pale face. She'd never been this upset over Art's disappearing acts before. Something was very wrong this time.

Well, something was very wrong besides the fact that a vampire was somehow involved.

"I'll be right back," Sabin said. "I'll have Grady prepare something light for an evening snack." He looked at Jake. "Unless, of course, you need something more filling?"

Jake narrowed his eyes at the other man's tone. There seemed to be an underlying cynicism. Maybe the vampire just didn't like cops. But his stomach was empty; he wasn't going to turn down the offer of food. "Somethin' light is fine."

Sabin gave a slight nod and left the room. Jake waited until the vampire's footsteps faded, then he looked at Dori. It was time he got some answers. Starting with how she came to be linked to Sabin.

# Chapter Three

Dori glanced at him and then at the large set of windows that overlooked the front yard. She shrugged and offered, "Don't look at me. I have no idea who Grady is."

"That wasn't what I was gonna ask." Jake shifted his weight and faced her more fully. "How is it you know Sabin?"

She twined a strand of hair around her finger. "I told you. He and Art are friends." She looked down at her other hand, plucking at a small tear in her jeans.

He tilted his head. She wouldn't look at him, which was interesting. It told him one of two things: either she was lying, or she wasn't giving him the entire story. It didn't matter either way. He'd learn the truth.

"I think there's more to it than that, *cher*." Jake used his best cop face, staring her down.

She looked unimpressed. Raising one eyebrow, she crossed her arms. Her earlier nervousness seemed gone. But he noticed that her foot started swinging. She wasn't as calm as she wanted him to think she was.

What was she trying to hide?

He leaned forward and cupped her cheek in his palm, turning her face toward him. "Talk to me, Dori. Tell me what's really goin' on."

Just then Sabin came back into the room, an elderly man bearing a silver-covered tray behind him. The vampire stopped just inside the room while Jake lingered over Dori. It might be juvenile, but he wanted Sabin to see that Dori belonged with *him*. Sabin looked at him with a raised brow, telling him he'd got the message.

Jake gave him a slow smile and sat back, keeping his arm along the back of the couch behind Dori.

The gray-haired man placed the tray on the glass coffee table in front of Jake and Dori.

"Thank you, Grady," Sabin murmured. The older man inclined his head and left the room with a sedate, steady pace.

Jake leaned forward and removed the cover of the tray. There was a selection of sandwiches and some vegetables. He bypassed the celery and carrots and picked up half a sandwich. Ignoring the amused look the vampire shot his way, Jake lifted the upper slice of bread and checked out the ingredients.

Brown mustard, tomatoes, lettuce and thinly sliced roast beef. Taking a big bite, he settled back onto the sofa and watched Sabin pace in front of a fireplace that was tall enough for an adult to stand in.

Yep, definite perks to being a vampire. Had a lot of time to accumulate wealth, for one thing. He'd never been in a house before that had a fireplace that was over six feet tall and nearly as wide.

Dori picked up a few stalks of celery and crunched off a piece of one. Jake's lips quirked. Her munching was timed to Sabin's pacing, though he doubted she was aware of it. He took another bite of his sandwich, enjoying the way the flavor of the beef was brought out by the spicy brown mustard and sweet tomatoes.

The vampire's long strides took him to the window, where he paused for a moment and stared into the inky night. He turned and paced back toward the fireplace, and Jake saw that Sabin's teeth had lengthened again, protruding over his lower lip. That feeling of surrealism came over Jake again, wrapping around him like a thick woolen blanket, muffling his senses.

"If you're right and others think that Arthur has the Eye, then I fear that Ra'Ziel reached your brother before he could meet with me, Endora. If that is so, then there is only one reason." Sabin stopped and looked at Dori, his face strained, his dark blue eyes sparking with anger and distress.

"Endora?" Jake latched on to the one thing his poor brain had the power to interpret. "Your name's Endora?" He took another big bite of the sandwich.

"Nobody calls me that." She shot a hard look at Sabin. "My mother had a funky sense of humor." When Jake continued to stare at her, she fidgeted on the sofa and then shrugged. "What can I tell you? She liked *Bewitched*."

Jake bit his inner lip against a grin. "So why didn't she name you Samantha? Or Tabitha? Or even Serena?"

The muscles in her jaw twitched. "Because I'm the youngest of four girls."

Meaning, he guessed, that her older sisters were Samantha, Tabitha, and Serena. "Well, at least she didn't name you Clara." He put his arm around her shoulder and rubbed his hand up and down her arm. He popped the last of the sandwich into his mouth, appreciating that final burst of hot mustard on his tongue.

Sabin let out a laugh. "That's because there's already a Clara in the family. Endor . . . Dori's mother's sister."

Jake swallowed, hard. "So you have an Aunt Clara, too?" *Wonder if the family doctor is named Bombay.* He bit the inside of his mouth to fight a face-splitting grin. He had the distinct feeling that if he laughed, Dori would smash his face with the fists she had clenched in her lap. "Is your dad's name Darren?"

"No, his name was Edward. And before you ask, my mother didn't have a very exotic name, either. Her name was Mary. Which may explain why we got stuck with the names we did." She gave him a look that suggested he move off this very touchy subject.

Sabin must have had the same thought, for he said, "We digress. We must find Ra'Ziel and save Arthur."

Jake clamped down on the urge to offer a comment about her brother being named after yet another character on the witchy TV show, but managed to restrain himself. He knew Dori wouldn't appreciate it, and they had more important matters to deal with.

Jake felt out of his league, but he wasn't going to bail now. He'd known from the start that Dori was different from the other women he'd been with. Something they needed to talk about, for sure. How different he probably wasn't prepared for, but he had a feeling she was worth it . . .

If they survived the night. He still wasn't so sure about Sabin, the *vampire*. Dori and Art might be safe from him, but was this Cajun cop?

Later, at some point, he'd have to make sure she understood they wouldn't be naming any of their babies after characters on the damned television.

He stilled. Where the hell had that thought come from? He and Dori hadn't even made love yet this time around—and he had no assurances that they would, though she seemed willing—and he was thinking about babies?

God help him. He was in so much trouble.

He focused his attention on the current discussion. Dealing with bad guys was something he could handle. "And Ra'Ziel is . . . ?"

"Ra'Ziel is a half-breed demon who seeks to annihilate all witches. The Eye of Bastet that Art seeks in order to revive his father can also be used to destroy any who practice the Arts. So, it is not just Arthur and Dori in danger here, it is all witch folk."

A demon. The bad guy was a *demon*? Jake shook his head. Forget about being able to handle *this*. But . . . he frowned. What was that other part?

Dori was a witch, and her father was dead.

"Whoa, wait a minute there, *homme*. Revive his father?" He looked at Dori, suspicious when she ducked her head. *This* was what she'd been hiding. "*Ma petite*? I thought you said he wanted to *heal* your father. There's a big difference there, I think, hmm?" The little fact that she was a witch would be discussed later, for sure.

She looked at him with apology reflected in her green eyes. "I was pretty sure you wouldn't believe me if I'd told you, at the time, that Art wants to bring our father back to life." She looked at Sabin. "I told him this was a bad idea. But time was running out. If he's going to do this, it has to happen tomorrow night."

"The witch must be revived within seven nights of his parting, or his death remains," Sabin explained to Jake. The vampire looked back at Dori. "From what I understood, I thought you and Arthur were in agreement."

She shook her head. "Death is part of life, Sabin." She frowned.

"Well, for some people it is," she said with a pointed glance at the vampire. "I tried and tried to talk him out of it."

"Wait a minute." Jake did his best to understand. "Wouldn't her father be a warlock, since he's male?"

"You've watched too many television programs, Detective." Sabin heaved a sigh. "Warlock is a term for anyone who practices the dark magick."

He didn't tack on the word *imbecile* at the end of the sentence, but Jake saw the look in his eyes.

"Witches practice light magick," the vampire went on. "The seventh night is tomorrow night, which means that is the time Ra'Ziel will make his move to use Art to bargain for the Eye. We have only tomorrow to make our plans."

"But you jus' said they'll all die if Ra'Ziel gets his hands on the Eye." Jake stood. "No way can we let him have it."

"But Art!" Dori wiped at tears and shot a pleading look to both men. "We can't just let him have Art."

"There may be a way, little one." Sabin knelt in front of her and took her hands.

Jake stood back, clenching his hands at the familiarity with which the vampire touched her, the two dark heads—one a rich auburn, the other inky black—so close together. He'd never thought of himself as the jealous type, but just seeing the other man touching her had his blood boiling.

Didn't matter that the guy was one of the undead. Jake had a fleeting thought wondering whether that meant he was undead all over. He certainly hoped so, seeing how he was holding Dori's hands so tenderly.

Civility slipped from Jake like water sliding down a rock, and he fought the urge to slam his fist into Sabin's face.

"We must make the trade in the cemetery at midnight on All Hallow's Eve when the barriers between our world and the spirit world is at its weakest, thus allowing us to tap into the supernatural realm." Sabin gave a nod, his expression savagely satisfied.

In spite of his jealousy, Jake was glad they were on the same side.

Sabin tightened his grip on Dori's hands briefly and then re-leased them. "We will make the exchange by Madame Laveau's crypt. Her magick was the most powerful this city has ever seen.

We can tap into that and also use the power of the Between—the time between night and morning. Combine all of that with your power and mine, I'm confident we can defeat the demon." He twisted to look at Jake. "You must stay here, *mon ami*. We cannot save Arthur and worry about protecting you as well."

"I can protect myself, *merci beaucoup*." Jake scowled. He'd joined the Academy after eight years as an MP in the Marines. He'd never really been a believer in the supernatural, but he hadn't disbelieved, either. But demon or no, if he could see it, touch it, he could fight it. "You don't have to worry none 'bout me, *homme*."

"No?"

One moment Sabin was crouched at Dori's feet, the next he had Jake by the throat, holding him off the floor. "I am something of a paradox, Detective. A vampire who is also a witch—something most witches will tell you cannot exist. Power cancels power, or some such nonsense. But I do exist, with all my powers very much intact. Do you doubt, even for an instant, that I could end *your* existence right now?"

"Sabin, stop it!"

Jake heard Dori pleading with Sabin, but he could do nothing more than dangle from the vampire's fingers. He felt his eyes bulging and had the quizzical thought that he must look like something from a cartoon, with eyes ready to pop out of his head.

He felt a rushing wind blow past him just before he was flung to the floor. He lifted his head to see Sabin picking himself up from across the room.

Dori knelt beside Jake and caressed his bruised throat. "Are you all right?" Even under the circumstances, her soft hand against his skin had his randy cock lengthening in his pants.

"You should be more worried about yourself, Endora." Sabin stopped a few feet away. His eyes blazed with silver fury, his hands curled into big fists at his side. "You have so little concern for your own safety that you would dare attack me with your power?"

She stood and faced the vampire with more courage than Jake had at the moment. He was too busy trying to get air without coughing.

"You leave him alone, Sabin. We need each other, you and I, to defeat Ra'Ziel. But believe this. I. Need. Jake."

"If he comes along and is injured, or worse, how will you feel then?" The vampire crossed his arms and relaxed. The silver slowly bled from his eyes until they were once more a deep, dark blue.

She swallowed. "Then I'll deal with it. But somehow I feel he's supposed to be there. I can't explain it, Sabin, but Jake is key. We need him."

Jake climbed to his feet. *Merde*! That creature had a grip of iron. He rubbed his throat and tried to unobtrusively adjust his erection to a more comfortable position.

Sabin heaved a sigh. "Very well. Bring your policeman lover along." The vampire looked at Jake, his sharp gaze flicking to the bulge between his thighs. "Do not distract us, mortal, or you will wish Ra'Ziel had killed you."

"You—" Jake stopped on a cough then swallowed, trying to work the soreness out of his throat. "You don't worry 'bout me none, *homme*. You make sure Dori is safe or you'll wish Ra'Ziel had killed *you*."

The other man stilled, and for a moment Jake was sure he had gone too far. But Sabin gave a bark of laughter and clapped a hand on Jake's shoulder.

It nearly knocked him off his feet again.

"I think I like you, Detective," Sabin said. "You have brass." He chuckled again. "You two may stay the night here. I have plenty of guest rooms. Dori, why don't you take Boudreau to the Blue Room—top of the stairs to the left—and get some sleep. Or," he paused, his gaze skating over the two of them, "not. We won't need to leave until early evening, so long as we reach the cemetery before dusk. You have plenty of time to fuck each other senseless and get some of this sexual tension released."

Jake raised his eyebrow at the other man's frank speech and glanced at Dori. She was such a frank little thing herself, he was surprised to see her cheeks redden with a blush.

Sabin had an excellent idea. Jake's enthusiastic cock certainly thought so, anyway. "Yeah, let's go to the bedroom, *cher*," he drawled, taking Dori's slender hand in his. They needed to talk, for sure, but later. Right now, he had to get her naked. "We need to finish what we started at the station."

Barely giving her a chance to say good night, he hustled her out of the room.

Dori felt her cheeks flare hotter at the look Boudreau shot her. His lust was almost palpable, his eyes were dark with passion, his face tight. Her body softened and moistened in response.

They started up the stairs. Halfway up he got tired of the easy pace, picked her up, threw her over one shoulder, and then loped up the stairs two at a time. He pushed open the door of their room. "Get the light," he muttered and kicked the door shut behind him. She fumbled along the wall and found the switch, flipping it on.

Boudreau dropped her on the bed and stood there, looking at her, his eyes heavy lidded as he shrugged out of his suit jacket and laid it on a chair next to the bed. His chest rose and fell with his labored breathing. Long fingers unbuttoned his shirt, and pulled the tails from his pants. His shirt, too, went over the back of the chair.

"You still got your clothes on, *bébé*," he said, his eyes glittering. He unbuckled his belt and slid down the zipper on his trousers. She was mesmerized at the sight of those long, tanned fingers easing the metal over his obvious erection.

His voice rasped over her eardrums and sent a shiver through her. "If you want those clothes to stay in one piece, you'd better get 'em off."

Dori felt her clit swell with need, flooding her pussy with cream. She'd never been so turned on so fast by any man in her life. She scrambled off the bed and took off her clothes with abandon.

With her fingers hooked around the elastic of her skimpy red panties, she looked at him standing there naked, his hands on his hips. Dark hair swirled over his chest and down the hard contours of his abdomen to end in a thick nest surrounding his genitals. His cock was huge, smooth except for the bulging veins that ran its length. The head was darker than the rest, and pointing straight at her. As she stared, his cock twitched and lurched upward, the throbbing head straining toward his navel.

"God, your breasts are pretty." Boudreau stalked forward, a

lean, loose-hipped stride that nearly made her go cross-eyed with need. "You'd better hurry, *cher*, if you wanna wear those little panties again," he drawled. A foil packet was gripped between the fingers of one big hand.

She was entranced by his male beauty, his muscles rolling and bunching beneath hair-roughened, tanned skin. His handsome face wore a days' worth of stubble, making him look a little dangerous, and a whole lot sexy. She remained still, her fingers hooked at the top of her underwear.

His eyes narrowed.

Before he could say anything more, she did what she'd wanted to do for a very long time. She dropped to her knees and closed her lips over the engorged head of his cock. His low groan encouraged her to flick her tongue around and over, tasting his salty essence as a drop of pre-cum seeped from the tip.

"Oh, God, *cher*." His hands came up to clasp her head. "Yeah, suck it, just like that."

She gripped his shaft with one hand and stroked it as she took as much of him as she could into her mouth. With her other hand she took his heavy sac in her fingers and massaged the twin globes within.

His breathing turned harsh and loud, gasping with pleasure. "Yeah. Take it. *More.* Take all of it."

She flushed with heated arousal, her pussy swelling and pulsing with need. He didn't hold back, telling her how it felt, what she was doing to him. It increased her own arousal. She wanted him inside her, but she wanted to give him this pleasure, too. She loved the feel of him, so smooth, so strong. Life pulsing under her tongue.

She moved her mouth and licked her way around the head to the sensitive underside. She nibbled gently along the heavy shaft until she reached the base, where she promptly drew one of his tight balls into the warmth of her mouth.

He shouted and arched against her, nearly throwing her back onto her butt. She wrapped her hands around his thighs and held on, swirling her tongue around the hair-roughened skin while she gently suckled.

Dori moved to the other testicle and gave it the same tender treatment, moaning around him as his hips pumped against her mouth. His skin tasted of salt and vinegar, and she whimpered with her own skyrocketing need.

"God. Take it in your mouth again, *bébé*. Suck my cock. Please." He groaned again, muttering her name. She could feel the muscles in his abdomen and thighs trembling. It gave her an incredible rush that she could bring this strong man to the brink of sexual insanity. She took his cock in her mouth again, opening as wide as she could.

His hands tightened in her hair, and he began shuttling in and out of her mouth, his buttocks clenching and releasing. She looked up at him through her lashes, exulted at seeing his face tighten with the extreme pleasure she gave him. Tentatively she swallowed, tightening her throat around his cock head.

Jake felt his gut turn over at the sight of his cock thrusting into her mouth. Her green eyes were half closed and dark with passion. The thick stalk of his sex spread her lips wide, stretching them, reddening them with the pressure.

And the feel of it . . . God, he thought his head would explode.

Both of them.

"Dori, you . . . ah," he groaned, pumping into her mouth with steady strokes, his breathing harsh and labored, his fingers tightening in her hair.

Her mouth was wet and hot, her lips so tight around his shaft he knew he wouldn't last long. She scraped her nails lightly across his balls. He growled and plunged faster, still coherent enough to not force too much of his length into her mouth.

She moaned and swallowed, and Jake surged against her helplessly. She gagged.

He pulled away, instantly contrite. "*Merde*. Honey, I'm sorry." He started to bend over but she waved him off and went after his cock again. She rubbed the tip of her tongue against the slit at the tip. She licked a pearly drop of pre-cum onto her tongue, and his eye narrowed at the sight.

She was so sexy she was about to kill him.

Her tongue lapped around the crown, then tapped on the sensitive underside. She pulled the head back into the heat of her mouth and trapped it there, sucking lightly. Little by little she pulled more of his hard flesh between her lips.

She peeked up at him through her lashes again and went down on him in earnest. He watched as long as he could, loving the way her breasts jiggled with her movements. Her nipples were hard, the tips a deep red, surrounded by pretty pink areolas.

When she scraped her nails lightly across his balls again, he closed his eyes. His head fell back. He pumped into her mouth, hands gripping her head. She swallowed again. He groaned as her throat tightened around the head of his cock. "God, *bébé*, swallow it," he growled when she repeated the motion. "Yeah, swallow my cock."

He fucked her mouth harder, leaving her lips feeling tight, but Dori loved the feeling, loved that she could bring him such pleasure. She loved watching the lust that darkened his face every time her throat caressed the head of his cock.

His hips bucked against her, pushing his hard flesh as deep as it would go. She felt his balls tighten, drawing up against the base of his shaft.

He tried to pull away from her. "I'm gonna come," he warned, his voice a deep rasp, his eyes black with lust.

She sucked harder and faster, moaning with her own arousal as he helplessly thrust into her mouth. Slipping one hand under the lace of her panties, she gathered some of her own cream on her fingers. She brought her fingers back to his body, slipping them from the soft skin behind his balls to the puckered rim of his anus.

"Dori . . ." he panted, eyes closing as she teased the skin between his cock and anus. "I'm gonna come. God, take it, *cher*. Take my cum."

She cupped her other hand around his balls and tugged. Hot, liquid bursts of semen accompanied his shout of release. The sweet and sour taste of his cum hit the back of her tongue. His cock stroked over it, sliding through the viscous liquid.

He pumped his hips against her a few more times, thick, hard pulses of cum spurting down her throat while she continued to lave him with her tongue.

Finally, his hips stilled and he pulled his semi-hard shaft out of her mouth with a sigh. "You've about killed me," he muttered, reaching down and drawing her to her feet. "Let's see if I can return the favor."

Sweeping her up in his arms, he took two steps and dumped her on the bed, laughing when she let out a small squeak. He quickly followed and, wasting no time, swept her panties off. Pulling her legs over his shoulders, he put that sexy mouth of his to work.

Dori closed her eyes against the sensations building in her body. His hair-stubbled cheeks and chin rubbed against the bare flesh of her pussy, stinging her, adding to her building arousal. He was relentless, sucking on her clit, sweeping his tongue down her slit, seemingly desperate for her to find her own release. Heat flowed through her sex with each fiery caress.

He lightly tongued his way through her silky folds until he could suck her clit back into his mouth. He suckled it strongly, moaning against her flesh as she couldn't restrain the helpless movement of her hips.

She needed a deeper connection, she needed to be filled.

As if he could sense her thoughts, he thrust his tongue into her passage, and she cried out. Her hands came to grasp his head, fingers threading through the thick strands. Boudreau pumped his tongue in and out of her cunt, flicking the hard tip against the sensitive walls.

Her orgasm crashed through her. She screamed and bucked against him. Her hands fell away and gripped the bedcover and her entire body tightened as if drawn by a wire. Even as she came down from the high, she realized Boudreau continued to lick through her folds.

"You taste so goddamned good." He swiped from her snug opening up to her clit, then back down again. "Like honey. And cinnamon." He groaned. "And woman."

He slid a long, thick finger inside her. She gasped and clamped down around it. He pumped it gently and added a second finger.

Just as the unbearable tension was about to crest, he drew away from her, gentling her with soft kisses against her inner thighs. "Not yet, *bébé*," he whispered, his breath hot against her swollen labia. "When you come again, I want your sweet pussy wrapped around my cock."

Rearing back, he grabbed the condom packet from where he'd thrown it on the bed when he'd tossed her down. Ripping open the packet, he quickly rolled the condom over his cock, once again thick and hard.

He positioned the tip at the entrance to her body, slowly forcing his way past the swollen, clenching, slippery muscles of her cunt. "You make me feel like a teenager, *cher. Mon Dieu!*" he gasped as he worked his cock in an inch or so. "You are so goddamned tight an' wet."

He pulled away and thrust in again, one long, slow glide until his cock slid in to the hilt and his balls slapped against her rear. He slid his cock out until only the tip remained in her pussy. He moved one hand to her clit and gripped it lightly between thumb and forefinger, pulling on it, twisting it. He slammed his shaft back into her and they both moaned at the sensation.

He started rubbing her clit in hard little circles, first slowly, then faster. His cock pistoned in and out of her channel, stretching her, filling her. She felt the first ripples of her climax and fought it.

"Come with me, Dori," he muttered, his teeth clenched. "Don't fight it. I wanna feel your cunt squeezin' my dick."

His darkly whispered words sent her over the edge. With a heavy groan, he followed her, his cock jerking inside her as he found his own release.

He moved her legs gently down to the bed. He disposed of the condom in a bedside trash can and collapsed beside her, his arm a heavy weight across her stomach before he gathered her in his arms. "*Mon Dieu, petite.*" He sighed, moving his head to her breast and resting it there. Pressing a kiss to her nipple, he murmured, "I knew it would be magic."

They rested in each other's arms for long moments. Then Boudreau stirred against her, propping up on one elbow, his chin resting on his fist. Dark eyes searched hers. "Now, *cher,* about this whole witch business . . ."

Dori chewed on her lower lip. When he reached out and rubbed his thumb over her lip, freeing it from the punishment of her teeth, her breath hitched. "I just wasn't sure you'd believe me." She pulled her lip between her teeth again, then added softly, brokenly, "Or accept me."

He brought his left hand up and combed his fingers through her hair, then cupped the back of her head. "I grew up on the bayou, Dori. I've seen a lot of things that are strange and wonderful." Leaning down, he kissed her, lips moving over hers gently. "My Mamau dabbled a bit here and there. It's no big deal." He pulled back and gave her a stern look. "That's not to say I'm happy you didn't trust me."

"It's just . . ." She sighed and sifted her fingers through his chest hair. Keeping her eyes focused on her hand, she said, "I haven't had the best track record, Jake. Other men haven't been as . . . understanding as you."

His big hand came under her chin and tilted her head. "Look at me." When she stubbornly refused, he gently shook her chin. "Dori, look at me."

When she raised her gaze to his, she felt tears well at the look of tenderness in his eyes. "I understand about lovin' people who want to change you. I do." He kissed her, a light meeting of lips, a deeper meeting of souls. "But I love you for who you are, *cher*. For what you are. I wouldn't change a thing."

He swiped at two fat tears that rolled down her cheeks. "That doesn't mean that you get to keep lyin' to me."

"I never—"

"Withholdin' the truth is the same as lyin'." He pressed her back onto the bed and loomed over her. "Promise me, Dori. I can't help you, can't protect you, if I don't know the full truth. No more secrets."

She cupped his face in her hands, breath catching as he pressed kisses into both of her palms. "I promise, Jake. No more secrets."

With that vow, she knew she had to tell him one last thing. "I love you, too."

# Chapter Four

Jake came awake slowly and savored the feel of warm, womanly curves pressed against him. Dori lay on her side, her shapely buttocks snuggled against his groin, her head resting on his right arm. Early morning sun painted light and shadow across her soft skin and highlighted the fire in her hair.

Easing carefully away from her, he got off the bed and padded into the adjoining bathroom to take care of his full bladder. After washing his hands, he splashed water on his face and scrubbed his teeth. On his way back to rejoin Dori, he stopped to grab another condom from his pants' pocket.

As the mattress dipped beneath his weight she murmured in her sleep. He lifted the sheet up and off and moved his eyes down the slender line of her back and legs.

He stared at her, amazed—not for the first time—at what the sight of her did to him. Her slender beauty drew him, gave him a nonstop hard-on and had his emotions closer to the surface than they'd been in years. He'd taken her several times since that first wild coupling, and still his cock thickened and lengthened at the sight of her.

If he had a hundred years, he'd never get enough of her.

Her heart-shaped ass drew his gaze . . . and his hands. He rubbed his palms over her silken buttocks and smiled when she made a faint sound. He hadn't really wanted this now, this emotional entanglement with another person. But, here he was.

Entangled. Ensnared. Entranced.

Bewitched.

He smoothed his hands over her ass cheeks again, finally grasping them to pull them apart. Leaning forward, he licked a path to the soft folds of her cunt.

"Jake?" Her voice was raspy with sleep as she wriggled against his face.

He let her turn onto her back. "I didn't spend enough time down here earlier, *cher*," he murmured against her slit. He groaned as her pussy juices hit his tongue. "You taste . . . spicy an' sweet, just the way I like it."

Grabbing his pillow, he folded it in half. Lifting her hips, he placed the pillow under her buttocks so she was at a more accessible level. He pushed her legs apart and moved his tongue across the lips of her smooth pussy, delving between them to swipe over the swollen petals of her flesh with the flat of his tongue.

He pushed his tongue inside her, moving just the pointed tip around her opening. He felt her legs tremble, and he smiled against her, loving the feel of her rising passion. Moving his head slightly, he drew her clit into his mouth and suckled hungrily.

Her cries sounded in his ears, echoed in his burgeoning shaft. He was so hot, so ready to fuck. He wanted to slam his cock into her hard and deep, to take her with all the brutal lust inside him so that she'd feel empty without him there to fill her, so that she'd never want any other man but him.

Dori was his. He'd known it for a while, and once he'd gotten his cock in her pussy, there was no way he was letting her go. She was *his*. Before this day was through, before they went to face possible death, she'd know it, too.

She had told him she loved him; now she'd admit she was his as surely as he belonged to her.

He lapped at her soft folds, gentle strokes that had her grinding against his mouth, demanding more. She was sheened with sweat, panting as he tongued her. She tasted so damn good, he couldn't help himself from stabbing his tongue into her channel as far as he could so he could draw her taste into the back of his throat.

His cock was so hard he felt as if it could drill through wood. He was on fire for her, and if he didn't get inside her soon . . . but, first, he wanted to drive her crazy again. He plunged two fingers into her wet channel and sucked her clit back into his mouth.

"Jake!" She wailed his name, ending on a gasp when he scissored his fingers in her slick sheath. He flicked his tongue across her clit, tiny, quick taps that tightened her vagina around his plunging fingers.

"Ohmygodohmygodohmygod." Dori pushed against his face. "More!"

Jake would have laughed if he could have, but his gut was so twisted with the taste and sight of her he could only groan as he complied with her demand. He added a third finger, pumping them into her grasping pussy fast and hard.

Her groan of arousal went straight to his straining cock, making it harder yet. He sucked on one of her outer labia, rasping his tongue over the sensitive flesh, then repeated the action on its twin. Dori gasped and curled her fingers into the bed sheets.

"Jake . . ."

He lifted his head and smiled slowly at the sight of her. Auburn hair spilled wildly around her face, which was pink with arousal. Her mouth was swollen and even as he watched she bit down on her lower lip.

"Tell me what you want, *cher.*" He blew softly on her clit. "Tell me, an' I'll give it to you." He wiggled his fingers in her pussy for incentive.

"Oh, God," she wailed, squirming against him. "God, Jake, please . . ."

"Tell me." *Merde,* she had him so hot he felt like he was going to explode. He could barely talk through the constriction in his throat, a constriction that matched the death grip his cock had on the rest of his body.

Another wiggle of his fingers, and she shuddered around him.

"Suck my clit. Please, Jake, suck my clit." Her voice ended on a shriek when he sucked her pleasure bud back into his mouth and drew on it with hard suction, knowing it would throw her over the edge.

She went over with a yell, bucking her hips so hard she nearly broke his neck. Her cunt clamped down on his fingers and she convulsed, crying out with pleasure.

Dori came down from the peak, feeling her pussy still gripping his fingers with small, soft spasms. She realized that Boudreau had moved up her body and now sucked hungrily on one of her nipples.

"You doin' okay there, *cher?*" He switched to the other nipple, taking it gently between white teeth before drawing the nub into his mouth. His wicked fingers kept stroking into her slick passage, curling into her G-spot.

"Mmm. Oh, God, Jake—" She broke off on a gasp when he started sucking at her nipple, hard. She was so turned on she was ready to come again.

He moved his hand steadily, pushing his fingers in, pulling them out. In. Out. In. Out.

"Jake!" Dori wailed, thrashing her head against the pillows, canting her hips upward to give him better access.

"Am I hurtin' you, *cher?*" he asked, his voice deep and dark, raspy with need.

"No, oh, God, no. It feels so good."

"Help me here." Withdrawing his hand from her pussy, he handed her a foil packet. She ripped it open with shaking fingers, nearly dropping it when his fingers once again started up their rhythm inside her. She fumbled, rolling the condom over his erection. Immediately, he pulled his fingers out and his cock burrowed into her pussy, the length thick and hard and hot. He pushed until he was in to the hilt, and she moaned at the fullness of his cock in her slick channel.

"Fuck me," she whispered, feeling her cheeks heat from the word she'd only used before as an expletive. Never as a verb.

"Fuck you how, *cher?*" he asked, his voice a growl. "Soft an' slow? Or hard an' fast?"

"Hard and fast. Oh, God, I want you to fuck me hard." Dori lifted against him, gasping when his cock slipped another inch inside her.

He gave a short, hard thrust, then pulled back slightly, only to push in deeper.

Boudreau flexed his hips and rammed into her, thrusting hard and fast, and, *oh, God,* so deep. He pounded into her so hard her breasts bounced and the headboard of the bed thumped against the wall. The sound of flesh smacking flesh filled the room, the smell of their arousal permeated the air.

She stared at him with eyes she knew were wide with arousal and excitement. His own eyes were narrowed and gleaming with lust, his irises almost swallowed up by the black of his pupils. Sweat glistened on his bronzed shoulders and chest. Leaning forward, she swiped her tongue and licked up a bead of sweat rolling between his pectorals.

The action tightened her around his thick shaft and they both gasped. "Fuck me, Jake," she whispered and leaned up until she could slide her hands around and grab his butt cheeks. She squeezed the hard flesh and rubbed her fingers over the sensitive skin between his buttocks.

Muttering a thick curse, he slowly pulled out and pushed his way back in.

Dori cried out at the easy thrusts of his thick cock, at the incredible building, spiraling need. He pulled his cock free by several inches before surging back inside her snug sheath.

"More," she cried. "Harder. Fuck me harder."

"Rub your clit, *bébé*." His voice was deep, guttural. "Rub it. Show me how you like it."

Dori moaned and rubbed her fingers against her clit in short, hard circles. He growled her name and picked up the pace, fucking into her with hard, deep thrusts.

"You're mine, Dori." He plowed into her and held himself still. "Say it."

"Jake." Dori tried to push her hips against him, tried to get him to move. She could feel his balls pressing against her ass and it was driving her crazy.

"Say it, *cher*. Admit you belong to me, an' I'll give us both what we want."

She stared into his eyes and saw the burning need there. Not just physical need, although she knew he felt that. The emotional need in his gaze was so strong it brought tears to her eyes. As much as she was his, he was hers. If he thought differently, she'd make sure he knew the truth before the day was done.

"I belong to you." She moved both hands around to cup his neck. Drawing his face down to hers, she kissed him, pushing her tongue inside the heated depths of his mouth. She pulled back enough to whisper, "And you belong to me."

With a growl, he tunneled into her so fast and deep that she tumbled into an orgasm so intense she could barely breathe. Vaguely she heard Boudreau's shout as he climaxed, and she felt the pulsing of his cock as his release jetted with hot spurts into the condom.

When he made to move off her, she murmured, "Stay." She clasped her ankles around his thighs to hold him in place. "I want to stay just like this."

"Like this?" he asked, and pumped his hips against her, pushing his cock deeper into the hot clasp of her body.

"Mmm . . . ahh." She ran her fingers down the smooth skin of his back, drawing circles over his damp flesh. She loved his back—long, lean muscles she could curve her hands around.

"I'm too heavy for you, *cher*. You won't be able to breathe." He gently suckled one nipple, then the other.

She sighed and pressed his head down to rest against her chest. "I'll breathe later."

Dori roused, unsure of what woke her. She stretched against Boudreau, realizing that at some point he had pulled his cock free from her pussy and had taken care of the condom. His brawny arm lay heavily across her stomach. One hairy leg anchored hers to the bed. She stretched again, smiling at the pleasant ache in her muscles.

"It's about time you woke up."

She gasped and grabbed the covers, pulling them over her breasts. "Sabin! What . . ." She glanced at Boudreau, whose eyes were still closed. His chest rose and fell steadily. "What are you doing in here?" she whispered, glaring at the vampire.

"It *is* my house," he whispered back. His face was somber, but his deep blue eyes held a mischievous twinkle. It was disconcerting, seeing that lightness of emotion in his intense eyes. As usual, he was clothed completely in black.

"Yes, well, we're not exactly dressed for visitors." She tried to glare harder. It was irritating when it seemed to have no effect. Damned vampire. Always acting so superior. It didn't help that, with his level of magick, Sabin *was* superior.

"Give it up, *cher*," Boudreau murmured. He propped up on one elbow. "What is it?" he asked the vampire. His voice was husky from sleep, but had a hard note that made Dori look at him. A muscle twitched in his tightly held jaw.

Sabin spoke before she could ask what the problem was. "It is nearly nine a.m." Sabin looked pointedly at his watch. "I have given you all the time I can. We must make our plans and gather our supplies." Without waiting for either of them to respond, he turned and walked to the door. "Get dressed and come downstairs. Grady is preparing breakfast."

He closed the door behind him.

"He's a man of few words, eh?" Boudreau leaned down and pressed a kiss against her shoulder, then one in the sensitive crook of her neck. His voice was once again that of her sexy lover.

She sighed and tilted her head, giving him easier access. "Mmm." His stubbled jaw rasped across her skin, sending hot/cold shivers through her body. "What—"

"As much as I'd like to follow this to its logical conclusion, *cher*, we don't have time." Deep regret colored his tone.

She knew he was right, but it still sucked. Big time. She heaved a sigh and gave him a lingering kiss, then threw off the covers. Getting out of bed, she stretched.

From behind her came a low groan that was part growl. She looked over her shoulder to see Boudreau crawling across the bed toward her. Hard muscles bunched and released, dark eyes glittered with feral, lustful intent.

She held up her hand. "Jake, we don't have time. Remember?"

He stopped, holding her gaze for a moment before dropping his head. "Damn." He flexed his shoulders. "Go take a shower, *cher*. I'll wait." He flopped down, head and arms hanging over the edge of the bed.

Walking into the bathroom, Dori gave him a lingering look. Long legs, tight ass, strong back and shoulders. Her fingers curled with the need to dig into his hard flesh. With a sigh, she went into the bathroom and closed the door behind her.

They didn't have time. Maybe tomorrow. But if they weren't successful tonight, there would be no tomorrows.

For either of them.

# Chapter Five

Half an hour later, Jake sat at the table watching Dori pick at her breakfast. Experience had taught him not to allow circumstances to affect his appetite. To eat was to stay healthy and strong. His plate was clean. "Come on, *cher*." He picked up her fork and brought a bite of egg to her lips. "You need to eat."

"Boudreau is right, Dori." Sabin leaned back in his chair and sipped from a cup. At Jake's raised eyebrow, he shrugged and offered, "Coffee. It doesn't do anything for me, but I enjoy the flavor."

Dori took the fork from Jake and ate a few more bites. She pushed the plate away. "I'm done. I can't eat any more."

Jake could see a spark of defiance in her gaze and knew that to push her on this would get him nowhere. Another thing he'd learned as a cop: fight the battles you can win, or the battles you have no choice but to fight. This particular skirmish didn't fit either of those scenarios.

Sabin must have agreed, for he motioned to Grady, who came forward and cleared the table. As soon as the older man left the room, Sabin leaned forward and placed his elbows on the table. "First, we need to gather supplies. I have a sufficient amount of juniper berries, but we'll need more Dragon's Blood than I have available."

Jake's eyebrows climbed his forehead. "Dragon's Blood?"

Sabin sighed. No doubt impatient with his lack of knowledge. Again.

"It's resin from a plant, Jake," Dori said, with a hard look at the vampire. "I have some at the hotel. Never leave home without it," she quipped in response to Jake's questioning look. She glanced back at Sabin. "My supply is from the *Dracaena Draco* tree."

"Hmm. Mine is *Sangre del Drago*, from Mexico." Sabin paused, tapping his chin. "It should not matter. You will go and retrieve your supply and, while you're doing so, I will craft a spell of protection and ready the incense for power amplification. Then we'll finish this, once and for all."

"Bossy, ain't he?" Jake sat back in his chair and looped one arm over the back. When the vampire looked at him, Jake quirked an eyebrow. He knew his entire demeanor was almost guaranteed to provoke Sabin, but he didn't care. He'd had enough of the other man's arrogance.

The fact that Sabin had seen Dori's breasts still rankled, although Jake was doing his best not to act on it. It wasn't just that he was certain he'd come out with the short stick in a match up between him and Sabin. He wasn't sure how Dori would react to such a primitive display of possession. Never mind that she'd agreed she belonged to him; it was said during the heat of sex. In the cold light of day, he wasn't sure she'd be so agreeable.

Independent, take-charge women could surely try a man's patience.

Remembering this particular woman's take-charge attitude from the night before made a certain unruly part of his anatomy rear up and take notice. *Dieu*, she could try his patience to next week and back if she'd always go down on him as enthusiastically as she had last night.

Sabin inclined his head. "You're right, Boudreau. It was thoughtless of me to enter your room uninvited. It will not happen again."

*Merde*. The man could read minds, too?

Sabin's lips tilted on one side. "Your face is very expressive, Detective. Especially to one who has been around as long as I have." He stood and pushed his chair against the table. "But, don't worry. I don't read minds. I merely put myself in your place and asked how I would feel if I'd awoken to find another man had seen my woman's nudity."

He walked to a long-doored cupboard and opened it. From around the door came his voice. "I would have been most displeased."

"Displeased, nothin'," Jake muttered. "I was pissed."

Dori sent him a look, making him realize she had just figured out why he'd seemed angry upon finding Sabin in their room. Her eyes widened slightly, then she dropped her gaze to his lap. Seeing his erection, her face flushed, and she looked away, biting her lip.

"Would you two get your libidos under control!" Sabin plunked two jars on the table.

Jake leaned forward, ignoring Sabin's comment and trying to ignore his hard-on. One of the jars contained small berries. "They look like blueberries."

"Yes, when dried they take on this darker color. But, believe me, if you tasted one you would know immediately you weren't eating a blueberry." Sabin screwed off the lid and picked up one of the small, round berries. "They are quite bitter."

The vampire pointed to the other jar. "That is Dragon's Blood resin."

Jake picked up the jar and shook it. The contents clanked against the glass. "Look like li'l red rocks."

"They act as a power enhancer." Dori pushed her chair away from the table and stood. "We should go, Jake."

"Yes, yes, go." Sabin took the jar of resin nuggets from Jake. "I will get everything prepared." He walked to the back door, where he plucked a set of keys from a hook on the wall. "Here, take the Boxster." He glanced at Dori. "Unless you'd rather take the Harley?"

"No way." Dori crossed her arms. "I'm not even sure I want him driving the Boxster. Can't we take the Mercedes?" The look on her face suggested that she thought they'd be safer in the bigger car.

"Aw, come on, *cher*." Jake pulled her into his arms and kissed the corner of her mouth. Pitching his voice deep and giving it a deliberate rasp, he promised, "I'll give you the best ride of your life."

She pinched him in the side, hard.

He tried not to flinch. *Merde*, but she had strong fingers. "Now, *cher*, don't be so mean." He pressed a kiss to her full bottom lip. This was one battle he was willing to fight. It wasn't every day he was offered a chance to drive such a powerful sports car. "I'm only tellin' you true."

She sighed and shook her head. "Fine. I'll be sure to say 'I told you so' after you wrap us around a tree."

"You wound me, *cher*. I've had the best driver's training the State of Louisiana has to offer." Jake gave her a quick kiss on her mouth then reached around for the keys.

Sabin placed them in his hand, a small smile playing about his mouth. With a stern look belied by the humor gleaming in his eyes, the vampire said, "If you wrap my car around a tree, I'll do more than say 'I told you so.'"

Jake gave a derisive snort. "We'll be fine. Come on, *ma petite*."

Dori led the way to the garage. She walked around to the passenger side, aware that Boudreau was right behind her.

"Let me get that for you, *cher*." He reached around her to open the door and she inhaled his scent, a lingering odor of soap and musky male that made her bones loosen. She would've thought she had her desire under control, as many times as they'd made love during the night. He'd reached for her more than once, and that last time . . .

With his cock buried deep in her pussy and his demand that she admit she belonged to him, she'd never felt so dominated . . . And liberated at the same time. Somehow, defying logic, giving up control had set her free.

She pressed a kiss to his hard jaw and then got into the car. He carefully closed the door and walked around to the driver's side. Once inside, he buckled his seatbelt, pressed the automatic door opener, waited until the garage door was fully open, and turned the key in the ignition.

The powerful engine hummed to life. When he pressed the accelerator a few times, gunning the engine, she grinned. "Just can't resist, can you?"

"It's a beautiful thing, *cher*. A work of art."

She'd never understand the male fascination for automated vehicles. It didn't seem to matter if they were sports cars, diesel pickups, motorcycles, or luxury automobiles. If it had an engine, men were in love.

He adjusted the mirrors then ran his fingers around the black leather steering wheel. Touched the dashboard. Curled his hand around the gearshift. His expression was enraptured, like a child seeing Santa Claus for the first time.

It was irritatingly endearing. But when he rubbed his thumb across the knob of the gearshift, she decided enough was enough. "Oh, for crying out loud, Boudreau. Put the damned car in reverse and let's go."

He grinned at her like a little boy, but obligingly shifted the lever into reverse before he backed the car out. Pushing the gearshift into first gear, he looked at her expectantly. "Ready?"

"As I'll ever be," she muttered and grabbed at the door, not really finding anything to latch on to.

"We're not even movin' yet, *cher.*"

"I'm just getting ready." When the car didn't move, she looked at him.

He stared at her with one arrogant brow cocked over twinkling brown eyes.

"Well?" She tried to lift just one of her eyebrows and failed. Damn, she'd never been able to pull off that look as well as Boudreau could.

He merely grinned and pressed the accelerator. The car surged forward. She watched his square-tipped fingers skillfully handle the steering wheel, coming down periodically to smoothly shift gears. Remembering those long fingers on her body, she squirmed in her seat.

*Focus, Dori. We have work to do, and you lusting after his body isn't going to help.*

But he was too alluring to not touch at all. She reached out with her left hand and twined her fingers in the silky hair at the nape of his neck. His eyes immediately went half-mast with pleasure. That fast, and he went from boyishly charming to a self-assured, aroused man.

"Damn, *petite.* You put your hands on me, an' I'll follow you anywhere."

With a pleased smile, she settled back into her seat and kept her hand on his nape. Too soon they'd turned onto Royal Street and were pulling up in front of the Monteleone. She gave his skin a lingering caress then removed her hand. The doorman opened the car door and helped her out of the low-slung car. "Thank you, Charlie," she murmured.

A wide smile brightened the doorman's dark face. He tipped his hat. "It's good to see you again, Miss Falcon." Looking at Boudreau as he walked around the car and joined them, he asked, "Shall I have the valet move your car, sir?"

"No, thanks. Charlie, is it?" Boudreau waited for the man's nod. "We won't be long. The car will be all right here, then?"

"Yessir, it'll be jus' fine here. Don' worry."

She and Boudreau walked through the opulent lobby. When she smiled and waved at the concierge, Boudreau commented, "You don' meet any strangers, do you, *cher*?"

"Not many." While they waited for the elevator, she looped her arm through his. He briefly squeezed her arm against his side and pressed a kiss against her temple.

As soon as the elevator doors closed behind them, Boudreau pushed her against the wall and slanted his mouth hungrily over hers. When she opened her lips under his sensual assault, his tongue slipped into her mouth like wet, hot silk. The sensation rocketed straight to her pussy, and she gave a moan. Her eyes fluttered shut. Opening her mouth wider, she rose up on her toes and twined her arms around his neck.

She needed more of him. She wanted to drink him down.

He didn't waste the opportunity. One broad hand flattened against her back, pulling her groin against him. The other hand clamped around the back of her neck, holding her head immobile. He controlled the kiss, and at that moment she didn't want it any other way.

His head lifted, and she opened her eyes to find him staring down at her. His breath came hard and fast. Moving his hands to cup her rear, he lifted her. Reflexively, she wrapped her legs around his hips, clasping her ankles under his buttocks.

The action fit the notch of her pussy against his erection. They groaned in unison.

He kept one hand under her ass. The other one wrapped in her hair and tilted her head, and he pounced once again on her mouth.

She closed her eyes and groaned again. Boudreau was the only man who could turn her on so fast, so hard. Even with the slight sting in her scalp where his hand gripped her hair, the bruising of her lips from the force of his mouth grinding onto hers—or maybe because of it. Her panties were so wet she was sure her arousal would seep through her jeans.

He took the kiss deeper, fucking into her mouth with his tongue. Pressure gathered in her pelvis, making her pussy clench and weep in response. She rubbed her mound against him, feeling an orgasm hovering just out of her grasp. She whimpered into his mouth and strained against him. Her nipples tightened painfully. Mindlessly, she dragged her breasts back and forth against his chest.

He tilted his pelvis just a fraction and that was all it took. Her womb clenched, her nipples stabbed into his chest. She exploded with one long wail that was swallowed by his mouth.

Strong teeth nipped her bottom lip, and the slight sting sent another round of shudders through her body. Dori hung suspended in his arms, fighting to breathe while he drew her orgasm out with purposeful expertise. Once the last spasm had faded, she rested her head on his shoulder and let her feet slide to the floor.

His big hand released her hair and rubbed up and down her back. He pressed his face against the top of her head. "You okay, there, *cher*?" The deep rumble of his voice sent another convulsive shudder through her.

"Hmm." She rubbed her face against his shoulder then rested her ear against his chest. His heart raced, thumping loudly in her ear. "I feel great. How 'bout you?"

His chuckle reverberated against her face. Taking one hand in his, he drew it down his waist, past his belt, to the hard ridge of his cock. "What you think, *cher*? How do I feel to you?" His voice was raspy with lust.

Dori felt the thick pike of his cock and curled her fingers over him. Her tongue swiped over swollen lips that felt too dry even as smoldering desire flickered to life low in her belly. Flattening her palm, she caressed the length of his shaft with one firm stroke and watched his eyes narrow in response.

With a muttered oath, he reached to the side and hit a button, and the elevator—which she hadn't even realized he'd brought to a stop—lurched on its way.

It came to a smooth stop on the thirteenth floor and the doors pinged open. With a blush, Dori pulled her hand away from Boudreau and stepped in front of him. They exited the elevator, nodding politely to the elderly couple waiting to get on.

"What was the holdup?" the woman muttered to the man, with a glare directed at Dori and Boudreau.

"Never mind, dear." As he was passing Dori, the older man grinned and winked at her.

Dori gasped, then laughed and dragged Boudreau away from the elevator.

"What?" Boudreau pulled her into his arms, clasping his hands behind her back.

"They knew exactly what we were doing. At least *he* did."

"And that embarrasses you?"

His voice was devoid of emotion. She recognized the tone. He was trying very hard to hide what he was feeling. She pulled back from him and searched his face. The dark depths of his eyes gave her what she was searching for. He cared. Deeply. And was afraid that, even though she'd admitted her love to him, she didn't share the depth of his feelings.

She loved this man; she would tell him as often as she needed to. Especially since, if things didn't go as planned with the demon, she wouldn't have many more chances. Reaching up, she clasped his face between her palms. Holding his gaze with hers, she said in a tone as firm as she could manage, considering she wanted to cry with joy, "I'm not embarrassed. I love you, Jake Boudreau."

His eyes closed. When they opened again, they blazed with such love that she did weep. His thumbs reached up and brushed the moisture from her face. "Ah, don' cry, *cher*." He rubbed the moisture from her eyes. "I love you, too."

"I know."

When he raised an eyebrow at her cockiness, she grinned through her tears.

"Hmm." He kissed her, a lingering meeting of lips and souls. When he pulled back, his eyes had gone black with desire. "Don' think that this gets you outta trouble, *cher*. I'm still mad at you for not tellin' me the whole truth."

Dori did her best to look guilty, but she was so happy she knew she didn't pull it off. She took his hand and pulled him down the hallway toward her room. "If I promise to behave from now on, Detective, will you let me off for good behavior?"

"Nope." He ran a hand over her ass, then pinched, making her jump.

"Hey!"

His grin had a definite feral edge to it. "When this is over, you an' me, we're gonna have a serious talk. After I paddle your cute little butt."

She narrowed her eyes at him. Never mind that her heart thumped faster at the image of her facedown over his lap, his big hand turning her ass cheeks red. She clenched her thighs against the renewed pulsing in her pussy.

"Never mind, *cher*. We can talk about it later."

She fished the door card out of her purse and opened the door to her room. Morning light filtered through the gauzy curtains, throwing wispy shadows onto the mint green carpet. As soon as the door shut behind them, Boudreau swept her up into his arms and strode to the bed. He plopped her down on the edge and went down on one knee in front of her. Big hands drew off her shoes and socks.

"Um, Jake?" Dori watched his big hands curl around her feet, felt his thumbs stroke across her insteps. "What do you think you're doing?"

She knew, of course. She wasn't dense. But he was just so much fun to tease.

He stared up at her with glittering dark eyes. "I'm thinkin' I'm gonna do some lovin' here."

She pressed her lips together to hold back a grin. "But . . ." She sighed and looked down at her hands, clasped in her lap. "We don't have time."

"There's time enough for this." He got to his feet and shrugged out of his jacket. Lean fingers went to his shirt buttons and started to slide them out of their holes.

She cleared her throat and stood, easing around him. Bending, she scooped up her socks and shoes. She tucked her socks into the shoes and turned, thinking she'd sit on the chair at the small table tucked into the corner.

"I don't think so, *cher*." Boudreau emptied her hands, dropping the shoes onto the floor. Before she could do much more than blink, he had her flat on the bed, both arms raised above her head. He grabbed his handcuffs off his belt loop and clasped one around her right wrist, threaded the handcuff chain through the slats of the headboard, and then fastened the other cuff around her left wrist.

Her gut tightened and heat spread to her core. Finally, he was putting his handcuffs to good use. But she couldn't let go of the game, not just yet. "Boudreau," she said, giving the cuffs a jiggle, "this is unauthorized use of city property, isn't it?"

He grinned, humor sparkling in his eyes, though there was enough hot passion in his gaze to spark an answering excitement in her. "No, *cher*. The use of cuffs to subdue an uncooperative suspect is entirely acceptable."

He leaned over her, left hand braced by her hip. His partially unbutton shirt gaped open, and her gaze centered on his broad, muscular chest with its light covering of dark hair. Her fingers curled with the need to touch him there.

"I'll behave," Dori promised. "Take these off me."

"Uh-uh." He shook his head. Bending, he took her mouth with his, demand and dominance in his touch. His tongue swept between her lips, tangled with hers. When he withdrew, she followed, claiming him as surely as he'd claimed her.

With a groan, Boudreau lifted his head and took a deep breath. "God, I could spend a lifetime on your mouth." His whiskey voice rasped against her eardrums and set her clit thumping.

He straightened and brought his hands to her blouse. Long fingers unbuttoned it and pushed it to her sides. "Pretty," he commented upon seeing her lavender bra. "But it's in the way." Reaching behind her, he unclasped her bra and eased the cups up to rest above her breasts.

Her nipples peaked, and not just from the cool air hitting them. The look in his dark eyes, the way his fingers held a slight tremble when he lightly touched one hard nub, did just as much to tighten her nipples as anything else.

He rubbed his finger back and forth. Her clit thumped, her pussy clenched, empty and wanting. He flicked his short nail lightly against her taut nipple, and she shuddered as his touch sparked an answering flare deep in her creaming pussy.

"Jake . . ." Her voice ended on a gasp as he pinched her nipple between his forefinger and thumb. Dori jerked her wrists in the cuffs, needing to touch him in return.

Boudreau tugged on her nipple, twisting and pulling. With graceful speed, he bent once again and latched on to her nipple with his mouth, suckling strongly at her.

Tugging uselessly at her bonds, she arched into the heat of his mouth with a small cry.

# Chapter Six

Jake drew back and studied her. One nipple glistened from his mouth, the nub taut and red. Damned if it didn't make his cock sit up and take notice. His gaze drifted to her other nipple. It looked forlorn.

Rubbing his thumb back and forth over the nipple he'd just sucked, he bent and took the other nub into his mouth, sucking and licking and nibbling, his need building at her breathless moans of desire.

"Jake, take off these damned cuffs."

He lifted his mouth long enough to shake his head and say, "I like you just like this."

"But I can't touch you."

He rose up, bringing his mouth so close to hers he could feel her warm breath puffing against his skin. He smiled, a slow, feral smile that came from deep in his soul. "Oh, but I can touch you." He brushed his mouth against hers, ever so slightly, before he pulled away.

Reaching out, he traced across the upper slopes of her breasts with his index finger, forcing himself to go slowly, to build her arousal, when all he wanted to do was slide her under him and rut on her like some wild animal.

Her nipples puckered, the tips red and hard. Tempting.

In cases like this, his motto was always to give in to temptation.

With a groan, he bent over her and licked across one taut nub. She shivered and moaned. He rubbed his face against her, feeling her nipple tighten further against the stubbled skin of his cheek.

Turning his head, he captured the peak of her breast between his lips. He suckled her, gently at first, then with more force. He cupped her, pushing her ample breasts together, and kneaded them roughly.

Her hips arched, and she gave a keening wail. He nipped sharply at the tight bud, then moved to her other breast. Pulling her nipple into his mouth, he trapped it against the roof of his mouth. She was so soft, her breasts perfect under his hands.

"Jake, let me loose!" Dori bucked against him, more in frustrated arousal than any real anger. She wanted to run her hands over his taut biceps, his hard chest. She wanted to rip his pants off and wrap her hands—her body—around his big cock.

He ignored her demand. His hands went to the waistband of her pants. He thumbed open the button, then took hold of the zipper tab. The rasp of the zipper sliding down sounded loud in the room.

"Lift your hips." His voice was low and rasped along her nerve endings like rough velvet. She braced herself with her feet and arched, lifting her hips off the bed. He slid both jeans and panties down and off her legs.

He stared at her pussy, his face hard with need. When he lifted his gaze to hers, she gasped at the heat blazing in his golden eyes. One broad hand cupped her, fingers sliding through her slick folds.

"You're already so wet," he growled. His fingers probed, scissored around her clit and tugged lightly.

She moaned and lifted her hips. "I'm always like this," she gasped, "with you." Her pussy clenched at his touch and the dark look in his eyes. When he pushed one long finger into her channel, her muscles clamped down. She felt her cunt begin to flood in earnest.

His eyes sharpened, his nostrils flared, and she knew he could smell her arousal. She tugged at her bonds restlessly.

Moving his focus from her sex, he looked up, frowning. "Are your arms all right?"

"That's what I keep telling you." She matched his frown. "Get these off me."

"Answer the question."

She huffed a sigh. Looking into his eyes, she thought about lying, but when one eyebrow rose, she knew, somehow, he'd know she was fibbing. "They're fine," she grudgingly admitted.

A smile quirked a corner of his mouth. "Then let's get down to business, shall we?"

He wedged his brawny shoulders under her thighs and separated her labia with his fingers. One thumb grazed her swollen clit and she jerked.

Craning her head, she looked down at him, perched between her legs, his gaze focused hungrily on her sex.

"God, you're so pretty here." His voice was low and filled with wicked sensuality. The first long swipe of his tongue over her sensitive flesh made her moan. When his pointed tongue stabbed between her labia, she arched in ecstasy.

"Jake!" Her head fell back onto the pillows. Her eyes closed as she focused completely on what he was doing to her.

Flicking his tongue over and around her opening, he licked a wide path, making sure each pass caught her clit. He lapped at her, licking the cream that spilled from her sheath. At the same time, his fingers molded and fondled her outer lips, pinching and pressing the swollen flesh.

When he pulled her clit into his mouth, she groaned and ground her pussy against his face. One long finger slid inside her sheath, moving in and out in a steady rhythm, setting up corresponding pulses in her sex.

Sharp need spiked through her, dragging the breath from her in ragged gasps. He licked her slit, plunged his finger in and out, added another finger.

In. Out. In. Out.

Dori clenched her fingers, her nails digging into her palms. Her hips pumped against his mouth, onto his fingers, without any conscious direction from her. Removing his fingers from her sheath, Boudreau dipped his tongue inside and flicked the tip against the sensitive walls of her passage. His tongue fucked inside her with hard, blistering strokes, and her body answered by spilling more heated liquid into his greedy mouth.

Fire gathered inside her, turning her core molten. The flat of his tongue swiped a wide path through her folds. His mouth opened over her clit, and he began to suck. Hard.

Dori bucked against him, dislodging him for a moment. With a soft snarl, he placed a large hand on her belly, pushing her back down, and began to suckle again.

His tongue pulled with steady rhythmic pulses on her clit. Long fingers speared inside her and thrust deep and hard. She felt her face flush and the world spiraled down to one focal point at the juncture of her thighs. She pushed against him, trying to bring him deeper.

He gave a hoarse, satisfied groan and kept sucking. Adding a third finger, he plunged into her faster. Her entire body stiffened, and she keened as her orgasm rushed through her.

It wasn't enough. She shuddered, staring up at him as he straightened from between her thighs. "Jake, please," she gasped. "I need you inside me."

His lips and chin were shiny with her juices, his eyes almost black, hot with lust. With a low growl, Boudreau swiped his hand across his face, then finished unbuttoning his shirt, pulling it off and dropping it on the floor.

He bent and took off his shoes and socks. Straightening, he set his big hands on the zipper tab of his jeans. She licked her lips and watched as he slowly drew the tab down. Then, with economy of movement, he pushed his pants and boxers off and kicked them away. His erection bounced against his belly, the slitted tip already streaming pre-cum.

Dori licked her lips again, imagining the tangy, salty taste of him against her tongue. "Let me loose," she pleaded, pulling against the restraints. "I want to touch you."

Jake wanted to feel her hands against him. Needed to feel her fingers wrapped around his cock, but not yet. If she touched him, his control would be shot. He needed to get inside her and fuck them both senseless. Only then would he be able to bear her touch without going completely primal on her. "Not yet." He groaned at the sight of her, nipples still hard, pussy slick with cream. "Not just yet."

He stared down at Dori, watching her as she writhed impatiently against the mattress. Her fingers curled around the slats of the headboard so tightly her knuckles shone white.

He rubbed one hand over her breasts, feeling her nipples tight and hard under his palm. God, he had to get inside her. Now. He started to reach for his pants to retrieve his wallet.

"I'm on the Pill," she said, her voice low and raspy. Her tongue slid out and wet her lips, and his eyes followed the movement. "And I haven't . . ." she broke off with a slight blush.

"You haven't what?"

"I haven't been with anyone for a long time. So I'm clean."

Settling on top of her, he took her mouth in a ravenous kiss. "I'm good to go, too," he muttered as he curved his hands under her ass and lifted her, driving his cock inch by inch into the heated clasp of her body, gritting his teeth against the pleasure.

Skin on skin. He shuddered at the feel of her surrounding him without the usual latex barrier.

She was hot. Wet. And so goddamned tight she was about to kill him.

Jake braced himself on his elbows, flexing his hips, thrusting deeper, feeling her legs wrap around him, her heels digging into his ass. The muscles in her slick channel fluttered around him, gripping him like tiny little fingers as he began shuttling in and out.

Lowering his head, he speared his tongue between her lips, mimicking the action of his lower body. She moved beneath him, hips arching against his, his mouth swallowing the strangled mewls that came from her.

Slow, long thrusts became fast, hard lunges as he fucked her with the desperation and strength of the hungry lust that surged through him. Dori's cunt rippled around him with the beginnings of another orgasm and he fought his way through the contractions that sought to hold him in one place.

His orgasm tightened his balls, and he shoved against her, holding himself firmly in place. Shudders racked her, clamping her inner muscles tight around his cock.

He threw back his head and shouted his release, flooding her with hot, thick spurts of semen. When the last spasm abated, he lowered his head and nuzzled her, keeping himself still inside her.

"Wow," she breathed. "That was . . . that was . . ."

"Hmm?" Bracing himself on his elbows, Jake stared down into her face. Her green eyes were slumberous, her face flushed. He leaned down and licked a bead of sweat trickling down her neck. "That was what, *cher*?"

"Good."

He lifted his head and stared down at her, pretty sure she'd just insulted him. "Good? Just . . . good?"

"Really good." She pressed her lips together, and he could see she was fighting back a grin. The little witch. When he didn't respond, the grin broke through and she said, "Really, really, *really* good."

"Well, that's okay then. 'Cause I was goin' for really, really, *really* good." He grinned and kissed her, a quick, hard caress of affection.

Reality intruded. He lifted his head and slowly eased out of her.

"Jake," she protested, wrapping her legs around his hips.

"We don't have time for more, *cher*, remember?"

She grumbled but loosened her hold. He unlocked the handcuffs and helped her off the bed. "I'll be right back." She headed toward the bathroom.

He watched her go, and grinned again at the exaggerated sway of her ass. As she reached the bathroom door she looked over her shoulder, and a wide smile spread over her face. She glanced down at his cock, stirring at his groin, and the smile widened.

"Yeah, you can smile all you want, *cher*." Jake started pulling on his clothing. "Jus' wait 'til I get you alone when we have all the time in the world."

"Promises, promises." She winked and closed the door behind her.

That evening, Jake watched Dori and Sabin put the final touches on their preparations. Most of what they did was fascinating to him and far beyond his comprehension.

Both witch and vampire put juniper berries into small pouches. Dori tied one at her waist, then did the same for Jake. "For protection," she said. She kissed him lightly on one cheek and went back to Sabin's side.

Jake touched his cheek, feeling again the wonder that this incredible woman loved him. Him. The boy from the bayou. The hard-nosed cop. It made him believe that, with her love, he could accomplish anything.

Even defeat a demon.

Sabin lit small charcoals of incense and added granules of Dragon's Blood. He motioned Jake closer. When he reached the vampire's side, Sabin took his right hand. Dori held his left, and joined her left hand with Sabin's right.

Jake watched the Dragon's Blood boiling on the charcoals. It resembled the substance it was named after, roiling and bubbling in a dark red sheen on the hot coals.

Sabin started to speak, drawing Jake's attention. He saw that the vampire stared into the flames of the three white candles burning beside the incense burner.

"Crafted in fire, crafted well, crafted higher. Woven of shining flame, none shall hurt or maim. None shall pass this fiery wall. None shall pass; no, none at all." Sabin repeated the chant. Releasing Jake's hand, he drew an object out of his pocket and placed it in the resin.

"The Eye of Bastet." Dori reached out and took it out of the resin, handling it carefully so as not to get burned.

The amulet was copper in color, with a large chunk of ivory in the middle. It had four points, like a compass, each point filed to the sharpness of a dagger.

Sabin retrieved the amulet and put it back in his pants' pocket. "We must go," he said. He looked at Jake solemnly, his eyes glittering. "Dori," he said. "One thing we can do for this mortal is offer a protection spell. Otherwise, I'm not sure he'll be able to withstand Ra'Ziel."

"Yes!" Dori took Jake's hands in hers and closed her eyes. Sabin stood behind her, hands on her shoulders. "Hail and welcome, Ruler of the East, spirit of air and daybreak. Hail and welcome, Ruler of the South, spirit of fire and midday. Hail and welcome, Ruler of the West, spirit of water and twilight. Hail and welcome, Ruler of the North, spirit of earth and midnight. With the force of your wind, the flame of your power, the tide of your love, and the richness of your spirit, protect and guard Jake Boudreau from all manner of harm. So mote it be."

"So mote it be," Sabin repeated.

Dori made the sign of the cross on Jake's face, touching his forehead, his chin, left cheek, then right cheek.

"Witches are practicin' Catholics?" Jake asked, trying to lighten the mood of the moment.

Sabin scowled at him. "It is the sign of the four points on a compass. North, South, East, West. She asks for the Mother Goddess to protect you with Fire, Air, Water, and Earth." He shook his head. "Half-wit."

So much for being liked. Jake stopped Dori when she started to put her necklace around his neck. "What's this?"

"It's a protection amulet, very powerful."

"It's *your* protection amulet, *cher*. I will not wear it."

"Listen, Jake. If everything goes right, and I'm hurt, Sabin can heal me with the Eye of Bastet. If things go wrong, well, then it won't matter." She stared at him, pleading in her dark gaze.

He knew she was right. If he was protected against the demon, he could help protect her as well.

He acquiesced, struck once again by her courage, and she placed the chain around his neck. She kissed the amulet and laid it against his chest.

"Let's go." Sabin strode out of the room, not waiting to see if they followed.

Jake grabbed Dori just inside the front door and gave her a hard kiss. "We get through this, *cher*. You an' me, we got some talkin' to do, remember? About all this, and us."

She nodded. "I know, Jake. I love you. The rest of it . . . we can work it out. I know we can."

They went out the door together, climbed into Sabin's Mercedes, headed toward the City of the Dead.

# Chapter Seven

"**Y**ou must be ready to make the three marks, Detective. The magick will not be strong enough until you do." Sabin stood directly in front of Marie Laveau's crypt. His cool eyes stared at Dori. "I'll keep the Eye so that Ra'Ziel focuses first on me, then I will transfer it to you, Dori." He studied her intently. "Are you ready, little witch?"

The hint of condescension in the vampire's voice stiffened Dori's spine, as she was sure he meant it to. Which was doubly annoying. "Yes, I'm ready." She moved into position beside Sabin.

Sabin stood on the east side of the crypt. Going clockwise, he drew a circle around the crypt with salt. Once he'd closed the circle, he turned to face the East, palms facing forward at his sides. "I conjure thee, O circle of power, as thou encircle every tower. Mighty Aegis of the Lady and Lord, rampart of thought, action and word. In peace and power, work thou free; those who walk between two worlds, I conjure thee."

"A boundary to protect, concentrate, and contain; that power raised here be not in vain." Dori took up the chant, putting all her belief into the spell. "The Sacred Circle is now around us. We are here of our own free will, in peace and in love. We now invite thee, Lord and Lady, Father and Mother of all life, to attend our spell, to guard us within this circle and without it, from all manner of evil and harm. So mote it be."

"So mote it be." Sabin turned and looked at Boudreau. "Ra'Ziel will be here soon. You must be prepared."

"I got it, Sabin. You don' need to worry 'bout me."

Out of the corner of her eye Dori saw Boudreau duck behind the crypt. Timing was critical. She only hoped she hadn't led him to his death.

"Here comes the demon," Sabin murmured. "Prepare yourself. His like you have never seen before."

Ra'Ziel walked into view, his massive size dwarfing Arthur, who limped at his side. Dori bit her lip at the sight of her bruised and obviously shaken brother then gasped as she got a better look at Ra'Ziel.

The demon was monstrous in appearance, with a head the size of an eighty pound pumpkin and just as misshapen. A big, bulbous nose sat squarely on his face just below eyes that glowed red. A set of horns protruded from his forehead.

As he came closer, she saw his mouth—complete with two hideous rows of razor sharp teeth that were dingy and a sickening shade of green. A forked tongue flickered briefly as he tasted the wind. One massive hand grasped Arthur by the shoulder.

"Let us not waste time, vampire." The demon's voice boomed through the stillness of night.

Dori shivered, even though the light wind died down. Nothing stirred here except the players in this most dangerous game.

"Thou hast what I desire, I have something that thou desires. An uncomplicated exchange."

"Uncomplicated?" Sabin moved two steps in front of Dori. "I think not. For me to give you the Eye of Bastet would mean the destruction of tens of thousands. Including myself and my friend here." He motioned to Dori with one hand. Keeping that hand behind his back, when she reached forward he transferred the Eye of Bastet to her. "What assurances do I have that you won't simply make us disappear once the Eye is in your possession?"

"No assurances, thou cursed abomination. That I must speak to thee at all is galling to the extreme." The demon scowled, showing off his nasty pointed teeth. "Thou hast thy vampire magick to protect thee. Why doest thou worry about these pitiful witchfolk who give thee no respect?" He pushed Arthur to his knees. "Give me what I want, or this one dies. Now."

Dori stepped back until her heel touched the bottom step of the crypt. "Now, Jake," she whispered and handed him the Eye.

Boudreau moved around to the front of the crypt and took the jewel. He reached up and made three quick marks, then said, "I wish to defeat the demon Ra'Ziel."

At the sound of his voice, the demon reared back and blasted Boudreau with a wave of heat that threw him violently against the side of the neighboring crypt. Dori reached for him but he waved her away. "I'm okay," he wheezed. "You do what you gotta do, *cher*."

Dori and Sabin linked hands, and she quickly chanted a spell of protection for Arthur. She sensed Boudreau moving away from her, but maintained her concentration on Arthur and the demon.

Too late Ra'Ziel realized what was happening and, with a roar, he reached for the witch at his feet. His hands grasped at air, though Arthur remained solid. Ra'Ziel directed his fury toward the other two.

Dori and Sabin staggered under the onslaught, but remained on their feet. "Now would be a good time for your lover to make his move," Sabin muttered, his grip tightening on Dori's hand. "This is getting a bit uncomfortable."

"You're telling me." Dori tried to ignore the beads of sweat rolling into her stinging eyes, tried to block out the one drop that clung stubbornly to the tip of her nose. "Come on, Jake," she urged quietly. "Come on."

A surge of pain flowed through her, and she bent over, nearly losing her connection with Sabin.

"Don't let go," he said through teeth clenched against the agony assaulting them. "Boudreau is almost there."

As she peered through pain-misted eyes, she saw Boudreau take a flying leap at the demon. Ra'Ziel's upper lip curled in a snarl, and he reached out and swatted Boudreau aside as if he were nothing more than a pesky gnat.

Boudreau gave a grunt and flew through the air nearly twenty feet, landing with a painful-sounding thud and rolling several yards before coming to an alarmingly still stop.

"Jake!" Dori tightened her fingers around Sabin's hand.

Boudreau didn't move.

Heart in her throat, Dori took a step forward.

"Don't." Sabin's fingers squeezed hers. "If we lose our focus now, all will be lost."

"But he's hurt." She didn't want to voice the thought that followed. *Or worse.* He wasn't moving.

"And if you let go of me, let go of our combined power, we will all die." He paused, tilting his head to one side. "He's still alive." As the demon increased the force of his onslaught, Sabin gave a little grunt and hunched his shoulders.

Dori gasped against the building pain. Her joints ached as if she had the flu, and agony knifed through her head. "How do you know?" She looked at Boudreau again. "I can't even tell from here if he's breathing."

"I can hear his heartbeat." Sabin's voice was gruff, filled with pain. "We must hold on, Dori. There is no other choice."

She forced her attention away from Boudreau and back onto Ra'Ziel. The demon's face was scrunched with concentration, though she thought she saw a flicker of pain crease his brow.

At least he was feeling some of what she and Sabin were.

From the corner of her eye she caught movement and forced herself to stay focused on Ra'Ziel. If Boudreau was back in the game, the last thing she wanted to do was draw the demon's attention to him.

"Thou hast no hope of defeating me." The demon narrowed his eyes, his attention directed toward Sabin.

Dori frowned, then gave herself a mental kick for caring that the demon had yet to even look at her. She should count her blessings.

"If thou gives me the Eye now, perhaps I will find a way to spare thee."

Sabin lifted his chin. "You really want it, don't you?"

"To rid the world of witchfolk is my calling. My duty." He turned that red-tinged gaze onto Dori.

*Damn. See what you get for being miffed he'd ignored you?*

"Starting with this one." His lip curled. "And her brother."

Boudreau ran in to her field of vision, the Eye held tight in his right hand. She caught her breath as, with a shrill cry of battle, he leaped through the air and thrust the Eye of Bastet right between the demon's horns.

Blood spurted around the wound and, with a thunderous cry, Ra'Ziel clawed at the amulet protruding from his forehead. One powerful fist backhanded Boudreau, once again catapulting him several feet through the air. He thudded against the unforgiving stone of a crypt wall.

Ra'Ziel teetered and began to fall forward. Sabin stretched out his hand and made a quick motion, using his magick to move Arthur out of harm's way.

Before the demon could reach the ground, his body was already ashes.

"Thank you, Madame Laveau," Dori whispered, then ran to her brother. "Are you all right, Art?"

He nodded, and rubbed a shaking hand down his bruised cheek. "A little worse for wear, but I'm okay." He motioned toward the unmoving body of Boudreau. "Go check out your friend."

"Jake!" She knelt at his side and pulled his head onto her lap. "Jake, please wake up."

He moved his head restlessly. His lashes flickered, but his eyes didn't open.

She brushed silky strands of hair away from his face. Leaning over, she gave him a gentle kiss on his dry mouth. "Please wake up," she whispered.

"Ah, *cher*. Do that again, an' maybe I'll wake up." He grinned and popped open one eye, then the other. "'Course, you do that again and sleep will be the last thin' on my mind."

Resting her hand on his chest, she felt the strong beat of his heart. Sending a silent expression of gratitude to the Mother Goddess, she leaned over and kissed him again.

"Let's get out of here, shall we?" Sabin reached down and hauled Dori to her feet, then did the same for Boudreau, keeping a steadying hand under his arm. "There will be restless spirits here tonight with all the power we have stirred up."

"What about the Eye?" Art swayed unsteadily at Sabin's side.

Sabin looked back to where the ashes of the demon still smoldered. "I fear the Eye of Bastet is lost forever. I am sorry," he said to Art.

The other man shrugged and looked at Dori, who held onto the man who had saved his life. "Some things aren't meant to be,

I know that now. In my blind quest to bring Dad back to life, I nearly got myself and three other people killed." He shook his head and added quietly, "Nearly got all witches killed."

She reached out and squeezed his hand. "Dad was a believer in following the natural order, Art. He wouldn't have wanted this."

Her brother nodded. "I know. You tried to tell me, but . . ." He sighed and looked at her with eyes shining with tears. "He was our patriarch in every sense of the word, Dori. What are we supposed to do without him?"

Of all of them, Art had depended the most upon their father. The youngest of five children—and the only boy—she knew he'd be lost without the elder Falcon.

"We'll muddle along just like every other person who's ever lost a parent." She tightened her grip on his hand and fought back her own tears. "You're not alone, honey."

"I know." He left the support Sabin provided and took two limping steps forward, sliding one arm around her shoulders in an awkward one-armed hug.

When Boudreau eased away from her, she wrapped both arms around Art and held him. Tears suppressed since the night her father took his last breath broke free, and she held on to her brother. She'd almost lost him, too, tonight.

But she hadn't. If she was lucky, Art had learned a lesson and would stay out of trouble from now on. Faint hope, but there it was.

And the goddess had given her a brave and honorable man who loved her for who—and what—she was. Truly, she was blessed.

Art made to draw away from her, and Dori let him go, swiping at her wet cheeks with her fingertips. He blinked and cleared his throat, knuckling away his own tears, looking embarrassed by his display of emotion.

Sabin walked over to Art and slipped one arm around his waist, encouraging Art to lean on him. "I am sorry for your loss," he murmured, his voice deep and husky. "Edward Falcon was a man greatly admired among witchfolk." He looked at Dori. "Are you ready to leave, little witch?"

She nodded and moved her shoulder under Boudreau's arm,

giving him the support he needed, though from the look on his face he didn't like having to depend on someone else.

He'd just have to get used to it. He needed her, and she needed him, especially in the coming months to help her through the grief over her father's death.

The four moved slowly out of the cemetery. Every few steps she'd hear Boudreau's breath catch, and knew he was more injured than he let on. At the very least, from the way he'd smashed up against those crypts, he probably had a few cracked—if not broken—ribs.

At the car, Boudreau stopped and looked back at the rows of white and gray crypts. "*Mon Dieu*," he said softly. "I would never have believed this had I not been here." He looked at Dori. "I'm glad I ran in to you last night, *ma petite*. Had I continued the investigation on my own, well, I'm sure I'd be joining my ancestors here." He leaned down and kissed her softly at first, then with growing need.

"We'll talk about that, too," Dori told him when the kiss ended. Her body felt alive and vibrant, as if her skin was the only thing keeping her from bursting into a million pieces. He wasn't afraid of her and her magick.

She helped Boudreau into the car and, just as she started to climb in, she looked to the front where Sabin was getting behind the wheel. He placed his clenched fist in the pocket of his jeans, then withdrew it.

She pursed her lips, but said nothing. The Eye of Bastet was not lost, literally. But, knowing Sabin, no one on this earth would ever see it again.

Which was as it should be. She and Boudreau had a conversation waiting and the rest of their lives together, she hoped. The last thing she wanted to worry about was an amulet that could put an end to her existence.

Sabin put the car in gear and drove away from the City of the Dead. "These two need medical attention, I think," he said, and turned the car toward the local hospital.

"*Adieu*," Dori murmured, staring through the back window at the cemetery.

"Good riddance, I say," Boudreau muttered, shifting against the seat and wincing.

She smiled and pressed a kiss against his neck before resting her head against his shoulder.

He might be brash at times, but he was a good man. And he was hers.

And they would be magick together.

If you liked this book, try Jami Alden's UNLEASHED, out this month from Brava . . .

He did a double, then a triple take.

*No fucking way.*

His breath caught and his nostrils flared as he took her in. He knew the thick black waves spilling to her waist, the mouthwatering curves elegantly draped in black wool. Her dress went from neck to wrist to knee and should have been modest, but only served to highlight the lush swell of her breasts, the deep curve of her waist, the sexy flare of her hips. The heels of her black pumps tap-tapped their way down the concrete steps and headed in his direction.

He dragged his gaze up to her face. Her luscious mouth was painted red and set in determined lines. Even though the sun was hidden behind a thick layer of clouds, like him she wore sunglasses, her oversize frames hiding half her face. As though, like him, she didn't want to chance anyone getting a peek into her soul.

Caroline fucking Palomares.

No, he reminded himself. Caroline fucking Medford.

Raw emotion spun up inside him, threatening to take him down. Lust. Anger. And a bunch of other crap he wouldn't touch with a ten foot pole.

As she strode toward him, shoulders back, hips swinging like she had every right to be walking back into his life, today of all days, he struggled to put the lid back on the swirl of emotion struggling to break free. He reminded himself savagely of who she was. Caroline *Medford*.

Wife of James Medford, rich attorney twenty years her senior. The same James Medford who could give her the affluent lifestyle he hadn't realized she coveted until it was too late.

The same James Medford she may very well have killed to keep herself in fast cars and high fashion.

She was not the seventeen year old who'd promised she'd never leave him when she gave him her virginity. She was not the twenty year old who'd sobbed when he'd announced his plans to join the Special Forces after he graduated from West Point. She wasn't even the twenty-two-year-old who'd told him to fuck off one final time before walking out on him without another word.

As she drew closer he focused on those differences. She was thinner, for one, he noticed as she got closer. And older, her mouth bracketed by fine lines that came from stress and age. Not to mention the wardrobe. He bet her outfit topped out at over a grand, even more if you counted the purse. A far cry from the wardrobe of a girl from a working class neighborhood who shopped at discount stores and went to private school on scholarship.

She was nothing like the girl he'd known, and he was nothing like the dumb kid who'd entertained romantic illusions like true love and happily ever after.

He took of his glasses, feeling a smile curl his lips for the first time in several days as she stumbled a little.

She was off center. Just the way he liked it. And he was in perfect control. Because Caroline Medford meant nothing to him.

If you're HOLDING OUT FOR A HERO, check out HelenKay Dimon's latest, out next month from Brava . . .

"You know something." Josh cocked his head to the side as the corner of his mouth tugged upward. "I just figured out what it is about you that doesn't fit."

"Pardon me?"

He pointed at her forehead. "The way you talk. It's what throws off this whole picture."

A wave of confused dizziness hit her. "I have no idea-"

"There's emotion in your voice, well, sort of, but your body never moves." He nodded his head as if warming to the subject. "Makes me wonder if there's any feeling inside there anywhere. I'm betting no."

The shaking moving through her turned to fury. Ten more seconds of his garbage and he'd be feeling her hand smack across his face. "You don't need to worry about my body."

His eyebrows rose. "If you say so."

"I need your detective skills."

The lazy grin vanished as his back snapped straight again. "No way."

"What kind of response is that for a grown man?"

"The only one you're going to get."

"Could you at least try to be civil?"

"You killed that possibility a long time ago, lady."

Okay, she deserved that. He refused to understand her position, but she couldn't exactly blame him for the anger. "I'm not asking for me. I'm asking for Ryan."

"You pay a whole team of professionals to poke around in other people's private lives for you. Get some of them to do your work. You don't need me."

*Lot of good all that money did her so far.* "I actually do."

"Well, that's a damn shame since I already have a job."

Time for a reality check. "Word is that might not be true soon."

"Visiting my office again, Ms. Armstrong?"

As she watched, he turned into a serious, uncompromising professional. He talked to her with a tone part soothing and part condescending. She sensed he would handle an interrogation the same way.

His disdain lapped against her. He didn't say the exact words, but he didn't have to. His actions spoke for him. He hated her.

Gone was the laid-back surfer dude laziness that hovered around him making the business suit seem all the more out of place. Blond, blue-eyed, with a scruff around his mouth and chin, he could play the lead role in any woman's bad boy fantasies. But behind those rough good looks lurked a man serious and in charge, tense and ready for battle.

Well, he wasn't the only one in the room fighting off a deep case of dislike. He needed to know she was not one of his frequent empty-headed bedmates. She could match his intellect and anger anytime, anywhere.

"Most of the information I need about you and your current predicament is in the newspaper," she said.

"Most?"

She shrugged, letting him know he wasn't the only one who could tweak a temper.

"More snooping, Ms. Armstrong?"

"I call it investigating."

"Well, just so you know." His back came off the wall, slow and in command. "Sneaking around in my personnel file isn't the way to make me listen to you."

"Then let's try this." She reached into her purse and grabbed her checkbook. "I want to hire you."

"Don't."

She clicked the end of her pen. "Some money should get us started."

His hand shot out and grabbed her wrist before she could start writing. "Trying to buy me off isn't going to get you where you want to be."

When she dropped her hand, he let go as if touching her one more second repulsed him.

"That's not what I was doing." It was, but she figured pointing that out would only make him less receptive to her plan to help Ryan.

"Sure felt like it."

She skipped the crap and went right to her point. "Ryan didn't do it."

"Look, Ms. Armstrong. I get that this is a family issue."

She refused to blubber or beg. She'd cried enough for ten lifetimes since the whole mess started. "Call me Deana."

"We're not friends or colleagues, so Ms. Armstrong is fine." Josh took his pen out of his pocket and tapped it against his open palm. "And you may as well know I don't really care what happens to Ryan from here on."

She refused to believe Josh would be satisfied to let an innocent kid rot in prison. "You can't really mean that."

"I do. Trust me on this."

"You think it's okay to lock him away?"

"He had a trial."

"Well, I don't have the luxury of forgetting Ryan since I'm all he has at the moment."

"I'm sorry about your brother and his wife." Josh's voice softened along with his bright aqua eyes.

She could not let her mind go there. Not now. She had to keep her focus directly on Ryan. It was either that or lose her control, and that was the one thing she could not afford to do in front of Josh. "Then help me."

"I can't."

"You mean won't." Despite her attempts to stay calm her voice increased in volume as his decreased.

"We can use whichever word you prefer."

"Why not?"

"Simple."

"I have to tell you that I've found nothing simple in dealing with you so far."

"Then try this: I'm out of the rescuing business."

"That's ridiculous."

"It's a fact."

This was one brick wall she might not be able to work around. "I hardly believe you can turn it on and off like that."

"I didn't think so either."

"And now?"

"I know I can."

"What is that supposed to mean?"

"Basically? Find another hero because I'm done playing the role."